Also by Mercedes Ron

My Fault

Your Fault

Our Fault

OUR FAULT

MERCEDES RON

Bloom books

Cover design by Emily Wittig
Image credits © Shifaaz shamoon/Unsplash, CDustin/Unsplash, Jordan McQueen/Unsplash, Aron Visuals/Unsplash, Alexander Grey/Unsplash

Originally published as *Culpables: Culpa nuestra*, © Mercedes Ron, 2018. Translated from Spanish by Adrian Nathan West.

Published by Bloom Books, an imprint of Sourcebooks
P.O. Box 4410, Naperville, Illinois 60567-4410
(630) 961-3900
sourcebooks.com

Originally published as *Culpables: Culpa nuestra* in 2018 in Spain by Montena, an imprint of Penguin Random House Grupo Editorial S. A. U., an imprint of Penguin Random House Grupo Editorial.

Cataloging-in-Publication data is on file with the Library of Congress.

Printed and bound in the United States of America.
LSC 10 9 8 7 6 5 4 3

To my cousin Bar. Thanks for being with me along the way. This book is as much yours as it is mine.

PROLOGUE

If Nick and I had broken up more than a year ago, why was I crying as if it had only really happened now? At one point, I had to pull off the road, cut the motor, and hug the wheel so I could sob without worrying about crashing into anyone.

I cried for what we had been; I cried for what we could have been; I cried for his sick mother and his baby sister… I cried for him, for disappointing him, for breaking his heart, for getting him to love me and then showing him love didn't exist, at least not without pain, and that pain had now scarred him for life.

I cried for Noah, the Noah I had been when I was with him. That Noah full of life, the Noah who, despite her inner demons, had known how to love with all her heart. I had loved him more than anybody, and that was something to grieve, too. When you meet the person you want to spend the rest of your life with, there's no going back. Lots of people never learn what that feels like. I knew that Nick was the love of my life, the man I wanted to be the father of my children, the man I wanted by my side through good and bad, in sickness and in health, till death did us part.

Nick was *the one*; he was my other half, and now I'd have to learn to live without him.

Part One

WE MEET AGAIN

1

Noah

The noise at the airport was deafening. People were coming and going frantically, dragging their suitcases, their carts, their children. I looked at the screen overhead, trying to find my destination and the exact time of my departure. I didn't like traveling on my own—I'd never cared much for flying at all—but there weren't many options. I was alone now; it was just me and no one else.

I looked at my watch and back at the screen. I had time to spare. I could drink a coffee in the terminal and read a while. That would probably calm me down. I walked through the metal detectors. I hated that, hated getting patted down, and it always happened because I always had something that set off the alarm. Maybe it was that heart of iron I'd been told I carried in my chest.

I dropped my backpack on the conveyor belt, took off my watch and bracelets, took off the necklace with the pendant that I always wore—even if I should have taken it off a long time ago—and set it all down next to my cell phone and the spare change I had in my pocket.

"Your shoes, too, miss," the young TSA worker said in a weary tone. I got it—the job was the very definition of dull; it probably gave you brain damage, doing and saying the same things over and over, all day, every day. I put my white Chucks on the tray and was glad I'd chosen plain socks instead of little kiddy ones with some embarrassing design. As my things moved forward on the belt, I passed through the scanner, and of course, it started beeping.

"Step to the side, please, hold out your arms and spread your legs," the person ordered, and I sighed. Did I have something metal on me, a sharp object, some kind of...?

"I don't have anything on me," I said, letting the officer pat me down. "This always happens. I don't know why. Maybe it's a filling."

The guy grinned, but that only made me wish he'd take his hands off me sooner.

When he finally let me go, I grabbed my things and went straight to the duty-free shop. Hello? Giant Toblerones? Sign me up. That was the one pleasant thing about going to the airport. I bought two, stored them both in my hand luggage, and went to find my departure gate. LAX was huge, but luckily, I didn't have to go far. Walking over arrows meant to point me in the right direction, I passed by signs that said *goodbye* in dozens of languages before I reached where I was going. The gate was empty, so I grabbed a chair near the window, took out my book, and started in on my Toblerone.

Things went fine until the letter I'd stuffed between the pages fell into my lap, reviving memories I'd sworn were dead and buried. I felt something hollow in the pit of my stomach as a stream of images rose in my mind, and what had been a relaxing day took a nosedive.

NINE MONTHS EARLIER...

The news that Nicholas was leaving reached me through unexpected channels. No one had wanted to talk to me about him, and it was clear he'd told everyone not to in no uncertain terms. Even Jenna was mum on the subject, and I knew they'd seen each other more than once. The worry I saw on her face sometimes must have reflected things she'd seen when she and Lion had gone to Nick's apartment. Her back was against the wall. Once again, that was my fault.

I hadn't seen Nick again, and I couldn't have predicted how he'd act. Just two weeks after we broke up, boxes with my things in them appeared at my apartment. When I saw N in an animal crate, I had an anxiety attack and cried my eyes out until I was exhausted. Our poor little kitty; now he was all mine... I had to leave him with my mother because my roommate was allergic. It was hard to say goodbye, but I didn't have another option.

That period in my life when I just cried and cried, I referred to as my dark ages, because that was how it was: I was in a black tunnel with no lights, sunken in shadows, unable to come out even when the sun shone, even when I had a light on by my bed. I'd had almost daily panic attacks until I finally went to the doctor, and she sent me straight to a psychiatrist.

At first, I wasn't remotely interested in therapy, but I guessed it did help me because at last I started getting up in the morning and doing the basic things a human being did...until that night. The night I realized Nick was leaving, that everything was over, and that this time it was forever.

I found out through an everyday conversation at the cafeteria on campus. Even the college girls knew more about Nick than I did at that time.

This girl was gossiping about my boyfriend—sorry, ex-boyfriend—and without realizing it, informed me that he was headed to New York in just a few days.

Something took hold of my body and forced me to get into my car and drive to his apartment. I had tried not to think about that place, about all that had happened, but I couldn't let him leave, not without seeing him, not without at least talking. It was our first time seeing each other since the night we'd broken up.

With my hands trembling, my legs on the verge of buckling over the asphalt, I made it to his building, got in the elevator, and stood in front of his door.

What was I going to tell him? What could I do to make him forgive me, to keep him from going, to get him to love me again?

I nearly fainted as I rang the doorbell. I was scared, sad, yearning, as he pulled the door open.

We didn't say anything at first; we just looked. He hadn't expected me. I'd almost guarantee his plan had been to go without looking back, to forget me, to pretend I'd never existed. He didn't realize I wouldn't make it that easy for him.

The tension was almost palpable. He looked incredible: dark jeans, white shirt, hair messy. Incredible, but there was something more; he always looked good, but that look, that light that appeared in his eyes whenever he saw me arrive, was gone, and with it, the magic that had entranced us whenever we'd stood across from each other.

He was so handsome, so tall, and he used to be mine... I felt like I was being punished, like someone was rubbing my nose in all that I'd lost.

"What are you doing here?" His voice was cold as ice, and hard, and made me emerge from my stupor.

"I, uh..." My voice failed me. What could I tell him? What could I do to get him to look at me as if I were the apple of his eyes, his hope, his life?

He didn't even seem to want to listen and tried to shut the door in my face, but I made a decision: if I had to fight, I'd fight. I wouldn't let him go. I couldn't lose him because without him, there was no way I could survive. My soul hurt when I saw him there and couldn't even ask him to embrace me, to calm that pain that consumed me from one day to the next. I stopped him, pushed my way through, invaded his apartment—that apartment that had once been my refuge.

"What do you think you're doing?" he asked, following me into the living room. It was unrecognizable: there were boxes everywhere, white sheets on the sofa and coffee table, and memories, endless memories of breakfasts together, kisses stolen on the sofa, cuddles while watching movies, him cooking, me sighing with pleasure on the cushions as he took my breath away...

All that was gone. There was nothing left.

Then the tears started welling in my eyes, and unable to contain myself, I said, stuttering, "You can't leave."

"Go away, Noah. I'm not doing this," he replied, his jaw clenched.

His tone surprised me, and I sobbed harder. No. No, dammit, I wasn't going. Not without him, at least.

"Nick, please. I can't lose you." My words weren't eloquent, but they were sincere, totally sincere. I couldn't survive a life without him.

Nicholas seemed to be breathing harder. I was scared I was pressuring him too much. But I was there; I might as well give it my all.

"Leave."

His command was clear and concise, but I was an expert at disobeying him. I always had been. I wasn't going to change now.

"You don't miss me at all?" I asked. My voice cracked halfway through the sentence. I looked around, then back at him. "I mean,

I can barely breathe without you… I can barely get up in the morning. I go to bed thinking about you. I get up thinking about you. I cry over you…"

I wiped away my tears impatiently. Nicholas stepped forward—not to calm me down, but the opposite: He grabbed my arms tight. Too tight.

"What the hell do you think I do?" he asked, enraged. "You destroyed me, goddammit!"

Feeling his hands on my skin, even if the gesture was an ugly one, gave me strength. I had missed the contact with him so badly, it felt like a shot of adrenaline right into the middle of my soul.

"I'm sorry," I said, lowering my head. It was one thing to feel him, another to look into those gorgeous eyes and see them seethe with hatred. "I made a mistake. A huge one, unforgivable, but you can't let that ruin what we have." I looked up. This time, I needed him to believe me, to see that I was speaking from the heart. "I'll never love anyone the way I love you."

Those words seemed to burn, because he pulled away, turned, ran his hands through his hair in desperation, and then looked back. He seemed almost deranged, caught in the worst struggle of his life.

"How could you?" he asked, and my heart broke again as I heard how hard it was for him to speak.

I took a hesitant step forward. He was hurt, it was my fault, and all I wanted was for him to hold me in his arms, embrace me again, tell me there was a solution to it all.

"I don't even remember…" I said in anguish. And that was true—I didn't. My mind had blocked it out; that was how destroyed I had been on that fateful night when I thought he had done the same thing as I; the notion that I couldn't stop him had made my mind, my soul, pull away from my body. "I don't remember anything but you, Nick. I need you to forgive me. I need you to look at me the way you used to." I lost my train of thought; my heart was aching. Even though I saw him there, he felt so far away. "Tell me what I can do to make you forgive me..."

He looked at me incredulously, as if I were asking for the impossible, as if my words were ridiculous, incoherent even.

And that was how I felt, too. Could I have forgiven someone for cheating on me? Would I have forgiven Nick?

I felt an immense ache in my chest. That was enough for me to know the answer... No, of course I wouldn't have. The mere thought of it made me want to pull out my hair and forget the image—Nick and another woman—that question conjured up. I wiped my tears away with my forearm, realizing there was no point. We remained in silence for a few moments, and I knew I needed to go. I couldn't bear the feeling of loss, and I *had* lost him, and no amount of begging would bring him back.

My tears continued streaming down silently. So that was our goodbye. Goodbye... My God, I was telling Nick goodbye! What was the script for that? How did you say goodbye to the person you loved most, the one you needed in your life?

I walked toward the door, but Nick moved past me, planted his lips on mine, grabbed my shoulders, pulled me close, immobilizing me as I received a kiss I'd never have expected.

I took his face in my hands. I didn't have time to analyze what was going on. My back struck the wall, and he held me there, searching for my mouth as if it were his lifeline. I brought him close as his tongue explored my mouth and his hands slid down my body. But then something changed; his attitude became more insistent, his kiss harder, colder. He pulled back, pressing me away from him with force.

"You shouldn't be here," he said. I opened my eyes and saw the tears streaking down his cheeks. I'd never seen him cry like that. Never.

I felt suffocated; I needed to go. What we were doing wasn't right, not at all. I wanted to stroke his cheek, wipe away those tears, hug him, say I was sorry a thousand times over. I didn't know what he saw in my face just then, but his eyes seemed to light up with rage and pain, a pain I knew all too well.

"I loved you," he said, burying his head in my neck.

I felt him trembling, and I grabbed hold of him as though I never wanted to let him go.

"I loved you, dammit!" he repeated, shouting this time, pulling away from me.

He stepped back to look at me, as though he'd never seen me before; then he looked down; then he looked me in the eyes. "Get out of this apartment, and don't ever think about coming back."

I knew then that everything was lost. Tears were continuing to fall from his eyes, but there wasn't a trace of love in them anymore, just pain—pain and hatred—and there was nothing I could do about it. I'd thought I could get him back, had thought my love for him would be enough, but I was oh, so wrong. Hate was just one step away from love…and I was watching him take that step.

I hadn't seen him since.

"Miss," I heard a voice next to me say, bringing me back to reality.

I looked up from the letter and saw a flight attendant looking at me impatiently.

"Yes?" I said, sitting up, and the book and the Toblerone in my lap fell to the ground.

I looked around. Shit! I was the last one left at the gate. The airline employees were staring at me from the Jetway that led to the plane. I stood up. Dammit!

"I'm sorry," I said, digging around inside my backpack for my ID and ticket. The girl took them and walked to the doorway.

I followed her, looking around beforehand to make sure I wasn't leaving anything behind.

"Your seat is in the back to the right... Have a good flight."

I nodded and walked down the passageway, a nervous feeling in the pit of my stomach.

A six-hour flight to New York. That was what I had ahead of me.

The trip seemed eternal. I didn't want to even think of how muggy New York would be in mid-July, and I was happy I wouldn't be there long. I only had one thing I needed to do.

I walked straight from the plane to the AirTrain, which I rode to the Jamaica station. From there, I'd catch the train to East Hampton. I couldn't believe I was going somewhere so snooty, somewhere I'd never once cared about visiting, but Jenna—Jenna!—had wanted to pull out all the stops for her wedding and had spent months organizing every last detail. Her mother had owned a mansion there forever, and they almost always summered there. Jenna loved it, it harbored all her childhood memories, and of course, it was *the* place to get married for a rich girl like her. I'd looked around online to see how many millions the houses there cost. It was insane.

Jenna had told me she wanted me to spend a week with her before the wedding. It was Tuesday, and she wouldn't be giving up the single life forever until that Sunday. Lots of people said it was crazy to get married at nineteen, but who was I to judge another couple? If they loved each other and were ready and were certain of their love, then to hell with convention.

So there I was, in Jamaica station, with another two and a half hours on the train ahead of me to accept the fact that I wouldn't just be seeing my best friend get married, I'd be seeing Nicholas Leister again after ten months of knowing nothing of him apart from what little I'd found out on the web.

Nick was the best man, and I was one of the bridesmaids... Just imagine. Maybe the time had come for our wounds to heal. Maybe it was time to forgive. I didn't know, but one thing was clear: we were going to be face-to-face, and it might lead to World War III.

2

Noah

I ARRIVED AT MY FINAL STOP AROUND SEVEN IN THE EVENING. The sun was still hovering on the horizon; it wouldn't go down until nine, and it felt good to get out, stretch my legs, smell the warm scent of the sea, and feel the cool air coming from the coast. I hadn't seen the beach in a while, and I missed it. School was a decent drive from the ocean, and I avoided my mother's house as much as I could. Our relationship was no longer what it had been, and even if many months had passed, we hadn't solved anything. We talked now and again, but when the conversation touched on matters I wasn't interested in getting into, I just hung up.

Jenna was waiting for me in her white convertible in front of the station. When she saw me, she got out and ran over to me. I took off running, too, and we met in the middle of the road, hugging and jumping up and down.

"You're here!"

"I'm here!"

"I'm going to get married!"

"You're going to get married!"

We cracked up until the passing cars started honking at us to get out of their way.

When we got in the car, she immediately told me how stressed she was about everything and what we still had to do before the big day came. We would have only a couple of days together because soon the other guests would arrive. Her closest friends would stay at her family's house, and everyone else either had their own house in the Hamptons—and by *house* I mean *mansion*—or would stay with friends in the area.

Jenna hadn't wanted people to have to fly out on her account, so she'd chosen the vacation season, since half the people she knew would already be there, if not in the Hamptons, then in the Finger Lakes or Maine.

"I've made an itinerary, Noah; we're talking a hundred percent chill: we're going to lie on the beach, go to the spa, drink margaritas, and that's it. I don't want some dumb bachelorette party, I want to relax, and I'm going to do it."

I nodded as my eyes wandered over the surroundings. My God, that place was gorgeous! I felt I'd been transported back to colonial times. The homes in town were white brick with beautiful sloping roofs and front porches with swings on them. I was so used to LA, with its ranchers and Spanish Mission Revival, that I'd forgotten how picturesque a place like this could be. As we drove on, I started to see grand estates sitting on enormous lots. Jenna veered off on a secondary road toward the ocean, and farther off, I saw the towering roof of a white-and-earth-tone mansion.

"Tell me that isn't yours..."

Jenna laughed and took a remote out of the glove box. She hit a button, and the immense outer gate opened soundlessly. There it was, her summer home, stately and impressive.

It was done in the neoclassical style, old-fashioned but exquisite, on a property that overlooked the sea. Even from the car,

I could hear the waves. Soft lights lined the road to the garage, which had room for at least ten cars.

It was a structure of white brick with a porch surrounded by immense columns. The surrounding gardens were of a green I hadn't seen in ages, and there were two-hundred-year-old oaks that seemed to be bowing to greet us.

"You're getting married here? Jesus, Jenna, this is amazing," I said, unable to take my eyes off her home...and it wasn't like I wasn't used to luxury. I'd lived at the Leister residence, but this was something totally different... It was magical.

"Actually, I'm not getting married here. That was the plan at first, but when I talked to my father, I realized how much he wanted me to do it somewhere we'd always talked about, a vineyard about an hour away, that he used to always take me to when I was little. We'd ride on horseback there, and I remember one time, he told me he wanted to see me there in my wedding dress. It's a place that's almost enchanted in a way I can't really describe. I was barely ten, but I remember dreaming of being a princess getting married there. Dad still remembers it, too."

"If it's prettier than this, I can't even imagine."

"It is. You're going to love it. Lots of people get married there."

We walked over to the stairway and climbed the ten steps to the porch. The wood creaked softly under my feet. It was music to my ears.

You can't envision what it was like inside: You hardly noticed the walls in that immense space with its wood floors. In the center, several sofas surrounded a modern fireplace. To one side stood ornate bookshelves and armchairs next to a stairway leading to the second floor, where a banister allowed a view of the space below.

"How many people are staying here, Jenn?"

Jenna slung her blazer over one sofa and guided me into the kitchen. It, too, was huge, with a sitting area with plush yellow chairs and a breakfast nook. The broad windows opened onto the backyard. Beyond it was the beach with its immaculate white sand and, no less tempting, a large swimming pool.

"Let's see...in total, I think ten, counting you, me, Lion, and Nick. The others, the ones who don't have a house nearby, are staying at a hotel right on the water."

When I heard Nick's name, I looked out the window and nodded, trying to look unflustered to keep her from seeing how much her mention of him affected me.

But she did notice and locked eyes with me after taking two bottles of ginger ale from the refrigerator.

"Noah, it's been ten months... I know it still hurts, and I waited this long in part for you guys, because I wasn't about to get married without my two best friends, but...are you going to be okay? I mean, it's been..."

"I know, Jenna. And I'm not going to lie to you and say I'm over it and I don't care, because that's not true. But we both knew this had to happen at some point. We're basically family... It was just a matter of time till we'd have to see each other's faces again."

Jenna nodded, and I had to look away. I didn't like what my eyes revealed: When people talked about Nick, it was like stepping into a quagmire. I could manage my pain; I had done it, and I would go on doing it day after day. I didn't need anyone's pity. I had ruined our relationship, and being alone with a broken heart was my punishment.

Jenna showed me to my room. I was happy to be there: I was exhausted. She hugged me and showed me how the shower worked, and as she walked off, she shouted that I'd better rest, because the next day, there was no stopping. I smiled, and when she left, I turned the tap, ready for a relaxing hot bath.

I knew the next few days would be hard. I'd have to keep my composure for Jenna so she wouldn't see what a wreck I was.

That upcoming week would require an Oscar-worthy performance on my part… Not just for Jenna, but for Nick, too, because he would see my vulnerability and would take any opportunity to wound me in my heart and soul… Anyway, I guessed that was what he wanted.

I woke up early, roused by the sun shining through the open curtains. As I looked out, the ocean's waves seemed to tell me good morning. We were so close to the sea, I could almost feel the sand between my toes.

I threw on a bikini and went to the kitchen, where I found Jenna awake and talking to a woman who was sitting in front of her, drinking coffee. They both smiled when they saw me.

"Noah, come here and let me introduce you," Jenna said, standing up and taking my arm. The woman was very pretty: Asian with immaculately styled brown hair. She was…neat. That was the best word to describe her. "This is Amy, my wedding planner."

I shook her hand and smiled. "It's a pleasure."

Amy gave me an approving look and took a booklet out of her purse, flipping the pages quickly and confidently. "Jenna told me you were pretty, but seeing you now… The bridesmaid's dress is going to look amazing on you."

I smiled, blushing, while Jenna sat next to me, taking a bite from a piece of toast.

"Now listen, I need to be the best looking one at my wedding." With her mouth full, I could hardly understand her, but I knew she was joking. She was pretty enough to stand out in any crowd.

"Look, Noah, here's your dress," Amy said, showing me a photo. It was Vera Wang, gorgeous, red, with a V cut and two thin straps crossing sexily in the back. "You like?"

How could I not? When Jenna had asked me to be her

bridesmaid, I almost burst into tears, but we made an agreement: if I said yes, she had to find me a dress that didn't make me look cheesy. And she'd taken my request seriously. It was out of this world.

"Who are the other bridesmaids?" I asked, unable to take my eyes from the picture.

Jenna grinned. "I decided just to have one," she confessed, and I froze.

"Wait, what...?" I exclaimed. "What about your cousin Janina or Janora or whatever her name is?"

Jenna turned around and walked to the fridge while Amy ignored us, walking to a corner of the kitchen to listen better as she took a call.

Jenna grabbed strawberries and milk and set them on the counter. She shrugged as she turned to take the pitcher from the blender and make herself a shake. "Janina is unbearable. My mother almost forced me to make her my maid of honor, but I wouldn't budge, and when I said, 'Fine, she can be bridesmaid number two,' she realized two would look even weirder than one, so she gave in. 'We need to keep it proportional.' Those were her words."

I rolled my eyes. Great. Now I was going to have to do it all by myself, stand there in front of hundreds of guests, with no one to share in my misfortune.

"Anyway, you know...Lion's only going to have one friend up there, so I don't have to worry about it being weird. It'll look like that's the way we planned it."

Before I could take in what my friend had just said, the sound of the blender filled the room, drowning out my contrary thoughts.

Wait... She'd only have one friend up there, and if the same went for Lion...

"Jenna!" I shouted, standing up and crossing the kitchen. She was busy staring at the blender. I turned it off, and she turned to look at me. "Am I the maid of honor?"

A guilty look crossed her face. "I'm sorry, Noah, but Lion doesn't have a dad, and obviously you knew Nick would be his best man. I wasn't gonna have my mom at the altar if Lion's dad couldn't be there, it didn't seem right, so we decided to have our best friends stand up with us."

I closed my eyes. "Do you realize what you're asking of me?"

Not only was I going to have to walk into the church with Nicholas, but we'd also have to collaborate to make sure everything went according to plan. That meant seeing each other at the rehearsal as well as the ceremony.

I hadn't thought about all that because I'd taken it for granted that Jenna had chosen a maid of honor, and I figured I'd just see Nick in the distance... I'd be in the same room, but we wouldn't have to interact with each other. But now I realized I'd be stuck with him throughout the whole ceremony, even during the dinner afterward.

Jenna grabbed my hands and looked me in the eyes. "It's just a few days, Noah," she said, trying to transmit a calm that I wouldn't have been able to feel in a million years. "You've turned the page, months have passed... Everything will go smoothly, you'll see."

"You've turned the page..."

She must have meant him. Because I was constantly struggling to catch a breath so I could rise, however briefly, to the surface.

3

Nick

I LOOKED AT THE CLOCK ON MY DESK. IT WAS FOUR IN THE morning, and I couldn't sleep a wink. My mind was spinning thinking about what was going to happen in a few days. Jesus Christ...I'd have to see her again.

I narrowed my eyes, glancing at the wedding invitation. There was nothing in this world I hated more just then than a stupid ceremony with two people pledging eternal love. What bullshit.

I'd agreed to be Lion's best man because I wasn't enough of an asshole to say no, realizing that Lion's dad was gone and that he probably wouldn't want his brother, Luca, an ex-con to be part of the ceremony. But the closer the day came, the more irritable and nervous I grew.

I didn't want to see her... I'd even talked to Jenna, had even tried to force her to choose, had said it was Noah or me, but Lion got so mad, he nearly whooped my ass.

I had a million reasons not to go, but none of them was enough to justify leaving my two best friends in the lurch.

I got up from my chair and walked over to the floor-to-ceiling window with its stunning views of New York. There, on the sixty-second floor, I felt so far from everyone and everything... A glacial cold overtook me. That's what I was: ice, a block of ice.

Those ten months had been a nightmare. I'd gone to hell, all on my own, had been burned alive, and had emerged from the ashes a completely different person.

No more smiles, no more dreams, no more feeling anything for another person beyond carnal desire. Standing up there, far from the world, I was in a prison, and there was no room for anyone else.

I heard someone walk up behind me. Then a pair of arms wrapped around me. I didn't flinch. I didn't feel anything anymore. I just existed.

"Why don't you come back to bed?" I heard the girl say. I'd just met her a few hours before in one of the best restaurants in the city.

My life was one thing now. Work. Work, work more, make money, make more, rinse and repeat.

Just two months had passed since my grandfather's body decided he'd had enough of this world and wanted to leave it. It was at that moment, when I received the call telling me he was gone, that I finally let myself break down. Another person I loved had been taken from me. And at that moment, I realized life was shit: you give someone your heart, you let them hold it for you, and then you find out that not only did they not take care of it the way you hoped, they actually crushed it until all the blood drained out. And the people who really did love you just up and left this world one day without even warning you; they didn't leave a trace behind, and there you were, unable to understand what happened, asking yourself why they had to go...

Well, he didn't leave without any trace at all. There was a document that had changed my life and turned everything upside down.

My grandfather left me absolutely everything. Not just his house in Montana and his properties—he even left me Leister Enterprises in its totality. My father didn't inherit a thing. Not that he needed it—he oversaw one of the most important law firms in the country. But the empire, all the Leister corporations, even the financial arm, which my father had used to dominate the banking industry, was mine. I'd always wanted to work in finance with my grandfather. What I'd never imagined was that it would just fall in my lap like this.

All at once, I'd had to step into that post I had yearned for, and I was officially the owner of a vast array of businesses, all at the age of twenty-three.

I'd given so much of myself to my work, to show I could get through all the obstacles, to show I could be the best, that no one doubted my abilities anymore. I'd reached the top...and yet I couldn't ignore how terrible I felt.

I turned and looked at the brunette chick who'd been trying to turn me on a few hours before. She was tall and thin, with blue eyes and perfect tits, but she was a warm body, nothing more. I didn't even remember her name. She should have left a long time ago. I'd told her I just wanted to fuck, and when we were done, I'd book a car to take her home. But after dealing with a situation that made me angrier than I could admit, I felt the urge to get rid of all that tension that had built up inside me, and that meant keeping her around.

She rubbed my chest and tried to meet my eyes. "I've got to admit, the rumors were true," she said, pressing against me.

I grabbed her wrists and stopped her. "I don't care what anyone says about me," I replied cuttingly. "It's four a.m. I've got a car coming for you in half an hour, so you better make good use of the time."

Those were ugly words, but she smiled.

"You've got it, Mr. Leister."

I clenched my teeth and let her keep going. I closed my eyes, letting momentary pleasure and basic sensual satisfaction keep me from feeling the void inside. Sex was no longer what it had been, and for me...it was better that way.

4

Noah

The calm of the past few days vanished as soon as the doorbell rang early that morning.

We'd been chilling at the spa in Sag Harbor, eating fresh shellfish in fancy restaurants, toasting ourselves in the sun to get the perfect tan, even if it would probably give us wrinkles for the rest of our lives. Amy, the wedding planner, had let us run free, and we needed that friend time, but as the wedding got closer, and with it the dates of the guests' arrival, it was impossible to keep going with that dolce far niente lifestyle. Jenna was getting more and more nervous. I could tell because she wouldn't stop talking. When the anxiety attacks hit, she'd call Lion. After months preparing for an aptitude test as administrator for one of the branches of Jenna's father's company, the wild one of our group finally seemed to be on the straight and narrow. The two of them had forgiven each other for everything in the past and were more in love than ever.

That morning, I finally saw the wedding dress. The tailor had come with Amy to let Jenna try it on one last time and make any adjustments if needed. It was incredible: white lace with a snug waist and a bell skirt. It reminded me of something from a movie or a fashion magazine, the kind of thing you could drool over. Jenna's mother had designed it in tandem with one of the costliest designers in LA, and it fit her like a glove.

A group of workers arrived not long afterward to arrange flowers around the doorway. Others set out tables throughout the house for the canapes and snacks that would greet friends and family on arrival. Of course, it was a smorgasbord. The yard was full of bustling people preparing a welcome for the ages.

The wedding dinner itself would take place in two days near the beach. I was nervous. I wasn't ready to see Nick again, let alone spend two days with him in the same house.

The place was soon packed with people: family and friends kept pouring in, asking Jenna about the ceremony, chatting about her dress and everything under the sun.

She'd invited her closest friends and younger members of her family to stay in the mansion. The adults preferred to book a hotel where their peace of mind wouldn't be interrupted by drunk twentysomethings.

Jenna's cousins surrounded her as the caterers started pouring in through the front door. I took off for the guest house, hoping to get a bit of relaxation in my room, but just then, a car parked at the top of the drive. I lifted my hand to shield my eyes from the sun and saw Lion's brother get out with his eternal sinister smile.

He spun his car keys around his finger and stared into my eyes once he spotted me.

"Look who we have here," he said, climbing the steps. "The little fugitive princess."

I rolled my eyes. I'd never really cared for Luca. He'd spent years behind bars, and from what Jenna told me, he was still getting into trouble—trouble Lion had to get him out of. I had to admit, Luca had changed a lot since I'd last seen him months back, at those terrifying races where Jenna had split up with Lion. Nick and I had fought terribly that night, too, and as always, the fight ended in sex, sex that solved nothing, sex that just helped us forget the inevitable: that bit by bit, we were destroying each other.

"How you doing, gorgeous?" he said, coming up to me. Lion was big, but Luca was no slouch. His tattooed arms would have terrified your average yuppie, but he was proud to show them off, and I couldn't care less.

"Great, Luca. Happy to see you," I responded, taking a step back. He was a little too close for comfort. "Jenna's inside. Go say hi to her."

Luca looked past my shoulder, not especially interested. He had his brother's green eyes. They looked down now, following the curves of my dress. Then he looked me in the face again, and crinkles appeared as he smiled.

"I've got plenty of time to talk to the bride... Speaking of...is it true you're single now?"

His question threw me off, since I had no interest whatsoever in talking about my emotional life, especially with the gangster brother of my ex's best friend, who already must have known what was up. I wanted to run off and shut myself up in my room even worse than before.

"I'm sure you know the answer to that question," I replied coldly. Remembering it made me feel a pain in my chest.

Just then, Jenna appeared. She smiled at Luca and opened her arms to pull him into her chest.

"Hey there, future sister-in-law," he said, giving her a pinch. "You thickening up? Be careful; we don't want you to come busting out of that dress."

He smiled, and Jenna wriggled away, glaring at him.

"You're an idiot," she snapped, slapping his arm.

Looking back at me, Luca said, "I was just asking Noah where my room was... You know, it's not every day I get to stay in a castle on the beach. Plus, I'm tired from the trip."

"You're the only person in the world who would cross the country in a car. Have you never heard of airplanes before?"

I opened my eyes wide with surprise. "You drove here from California?"

He nodded, adjusting his backpack. "I love me a good roadside diner," he said, moving past us into the house. "Where to?"

Jenna shook her head and smiled. Just then, someone called to her from the kitchen.

"Noah, take him upstairs and tell him it's the room on the right next to the balcony."

"But—"

Jenna disappeared before she could hear my objections, walking down the hall and leaving me alone with Luca.

"Come on, princess, I don't have all day."

After showing him the room, I turned to leave, wanting to get him out of my sight and climb into my own bed. I was only two doors away. But Luca intercepted me.

"Let's go to the beach," he said, determined.

"No thanks," I said, reaching past him, trying to grab the doorknob.

"I don't want to stay here... Come on, don't be a pain. I'll buy you a hot dog."

I eyed him up, trying to guess what he was getting at. Luca was the nervous type, hard to control, and I was sure having to stay there with all those guests was stressing him out worse than he'd admit. "I don't want a hot dog. I want to go to my room and read a nice book, so please, step aside."

"Read?" He pronounced the word like it was an insult. "You can read when you're dead. Let's go walk on the...grounds, isn't that what rich people call it?"

"Luca, I can't just up and go. Jenna needs help. Plus, we don't know our way around here, and honestly, getting lost in the Hamptons isn't high on my list of things to do."

Luca turned his cap backward. "Getting lost with me is the best thing that could ever happen to you, babe, but I'm not interested in all that right now. I just want to have a bite with some good company, and you'll do, even if you act like a stuck-up little princess."

I could have slapped him. But instead, I crossed my arms, and he burst into laughter before I could answer.

"It's a joke! Come on, don't be boring. I promise I'll bring you home safe and sound. God forbid Jenna not have her bridesmaid."

Just then, we heard a group of people from Jenna's family making their way upstairs, and soon the hall was busy, with people talking loudly. Suddenly, the idea of going out with Luca didn't sound so awful.

"I'll do it, on one condition," I said sternly.

Luca smiled his bad-boy smile. "You name it."

"I drive."

Contrary to my expectations, Luca couldn't have cared less about me getting behind the wheel of his shiny black Mustang. Actually, he seemed happy not to have to bother with the road and to be able to enjoy the views of the coast. The sun would go down soon, and the breeze was pleasant.

A comfortable silence enveloped us. I enjoyed driving on those empty roads with no real purpose beyond getting out. I knew Lucas was holding back with me: he wasn't the typical guy who just hangs out with a girl, but his intentions didn't matter to me. After driving aimlessly for a while and seeing the sun go down, I stopped at a hot dog stand by the ocean. It was surrounded by tables occupied by two couples and a family with two little kids.

"I'm starving," I said, turning the car off.

Luca smiled and got out.

"I didn't know you could drive a stick," he said when I reached him, taking off his hat, wiping the sweat from his nearly shaved head, and putting it back on.

"Of course you didn't. It's not like you and I go on a lot of drives together."

I hurried over to the stand. It may have been unhealthy, but it smelled delightful. I ordered a hot dog with everything, some fries, and a Coke. Luca ordered the same, but with a beer. When it was ready, we sat at one of the tables. It was weird, being there with the brother of my best friend's boyfriend, an ex-con with a bad rep. But he'd been nice so far.

"I guess you're not the dieting type," he said, pointing to my greasy meal.

"I exercise," I said, taking a bite. It was delicious.

Luca nodded, took a sip of his beer, and stared at me. "You said earlier we didn't know each other. Why don't we play twenty questions?"

I put down my hot dog and looked away.

A small part of my brain realized he was basically flirting with me, but the other was taken immediately to the memory of a long time ago when Nick and I had gotten close, playing that stupid game and trying to get to know each other better.

The memory of that time when we barely knew each other, the memory of being with him, not knowing about any of his problems and him not knowing about mine, the memory of that moment our relationship should have stayed in, all that overwhelmed me, but I did what I had to do, given the circumstances: I closed my eyes, took a deep breath, and concentrated on something else.

I had an attractive guy in front of me, a guy who wasn't right for me at all, one who would only make my complicated situation even more complicated, but what he didn't know was that it didn't matter what he did or said. Nothing he could do would move me the way a mere glance from Nicholas Leister could. That was what I missed sometimes, just his look, his eyes focused on mine in that unique, unforgettable way.

Luca waved his hand in front of my face to get me to react, and I looked again at his tattoos and his green eyes full of curiosity.

"I'll give you one question," I said, to keep from being nasty.

He smiled, stroked his chin, and leaned across the table. "If you'll only let me have one, I'll get straight to the point."

I shifted uneasily in my seat. I think that was the first time in months I'd been alone with a guy, and I didn't like that guilty feeling in my stomach.

"Would you go out with me tomorrow night?"

His question was blunt, my answer even more so. "No."

Clear and concise—that was me. I got up—I'd lost my appetite—and he grabbed me by the wrist, turning around to face me and keeping me from walking off.

"Why not?"

"Because I can't."

Surprised, he asked, "Why not? What kind of answer is that?"

I tried to wriggle out of his grasp. "I don't want to," I said, focusing on his shoulder to keep from looking him in the eye.

After a few seconds, he understood. "I get it... You're still in love with him." It was an affirmation, not a question.

I finally jerked away from him. "That doesn't concern you, got it?"

Luca raised his hands in resignation and chuckled. "Noah, I was just going to say you could go for a run with me. It's not such a big deal. I mean, damn, everyone told me you had a lot of personality, but…" I glared at him as if to say he'd better not go down that road. "When the sun goes down and it's not so hot. That way we can escape from all the craziness, with all the guests who still haven't shown up yet. I'm just looking for an excuse to get away, that's all, so don't keep scowling at me like that. You can be in love with whoever you want. I couldn't care less."

His response made me rethink his request. This was Luca, after all, a guy who didn't give a fuck about anything. He didn't care about my personal life; he'd just opened his mouth and said the first thing that popped into his head.

Run…that was something I *could* do… It was boring. Boring and impersonal. Anyway, who had ever invited someone to go running with bad intentions? I'd be sweaty and gross, so there wasn't any danger…was there?

"Just a run?" I asked, cursing myself for that insecure voice I didn't recognize as my own.

Luca furrowed his brow and nodded, forcing a smile. "Just a run."

I sighed and sat back down, waiting for him to finish eating.

We spent the next half hour talking about the wedding and other nonsense, but still, I couldn't escape the feeling that I'd laid myself bare before him, letting him glimpse the self-doubt that had dogged me for months and that I didn't like at all.

It was just a day and a half till the wedding, and Luca wouldn't leave my side. We'd gone running as he'd asked, and to my surprise, he didn't bother me: he put on his headphones, I put on mine, and we ran next to each other to the marina and then back on the beach. We had needed the getaway. I could barely move with all the guests in the house, and the arrival of Jenna's parents meant I finally didn't have to be by her side at all times.

Her mother was a born hostess, and she and Jenna's dad, Greg, seemed happy surrounded by friends and family, celebrating the wedding of their child.

Just when I felt I couldn't run anymore, Luca insisted we go a bit farther, but my legs were trembling, and I thought I'd have to walk back.

"Come on!" he shouted, turning around and running backward, watching me and making fun of me at the same time. I flipped him the bird and tried to ignore him, but soon I had to stop for a drink of water. It would be nighttime in a few hours, and we'd need to be showered and dressed for dinner. The catering company Jenna's father had hired would be taking care of it: it was a constant celebration at that house, with a tent set up outside with refreshments at all hours. The Tavish home was now a five-star hotel, and everyone loved it.

"Don't wimp out on me!"

I exhaled slowly and poured water over my head. My pink sports bra was soaked, but at least I could wipe the sweat off my stomach, chest, and face. That was it, I was walking back; I'd pushed my body enough that day. "Keep running yourself, dickhead!"

He shook his head, stopped, and came back over. "I thought you had more in you, princess. I'm disappointed."

"Shut up."

We walked over to the sidewalk and headed toward Jenna's place. We had a big hill in front of us, and in the distance, the sun was falling, and the colors in the sky were amazing.

"The big day's almost here. You nervous?" Luca asked. Now he was the one dumping a bottle of water over his head. He shook and splashed me all over. I shoved him, and he smiled like an idiot.

"I'm not the one getting married, Luca," I said, pretending I didn't know what he was getting at.

We hadn't spoken much over those two days, but it was still enough for him to know that this subject was off-limits. But I understood that with the wedding about to happen, he was getting curious.

"You're the maid of honor... You've got an important job," he said.

I didn't respond, but my suppressed anxiety came back all at once, and my stomach turned. I hadn't wanted to ask Jenna when Nick was arriving; I wasn't even sure whether he'd show before the day itself... Maybe he would just appear right before the ceremony started. For me, that would be better. Just the thought of seeing him again made me tremble.

Right then, a car passed by us so fast that Luca pushed me aside for safety.

"Dickhead!" he shouted, but the black Lexus had already nearly vanished up the road.

I had a strange feeling, and I wanted to get back to the house as soon as possible.

5

Nick

It was six in the afternoon, and I was still in New York. My secretary had screwed up and had scheduled me a meeting with two pompous assholes who'd done nothing but waste my time.

It had taken two hours to answer all their stupid questions, and when it was finally over, I closed and locked the door to my office. Looking at my watch, I realized I'd be arriving later than I'd intended. Taking off for the Hamptons just after rush hour was crazy, but I couldn't put it off anymore.

Steve was waiting for me outside once I was ready to go.

"Nicholas," he said, bowing slightly and grabbing the briefcase I handed him.

"How's traffic, Steve?" I asked him as my phone started vibrating.

I ignored it and got into the passenger seat of my car. I needed to close my eyes and still the whirlwind of thoughts passing through my mind.

"Same as always," he said, sitting behind the wheel and heading east. If it thinned out, we could make it in two and a half hours. Maybe.

Steve was now my right-hand man, my driver, my bodyguard, my fixer. He'd been working for the family since I was seven, so he knew me better than almost anyone. More importantly, he knew when to talk and when to keep silent. He knew perfectly what I had to face in the coming days, and I was grateful when he put on some relaxing music, neither too fast nor too slow. It was the ideal rhythm to help me try to convince myself I wouldn't lose it at the wedding. I'd need to control myself, my mood, keep an eye out for anything that could break the fort I'd built around myself, high up and far away from anyone...anyone and everyone, especially *her*.

We stopped an hour and a half later at a roadside gas station. I'd let myself doze off a little, and now I was feeling edgy, so I told Steve to step aside and let me take the wheel. He didn't care. I suddenly wanted to chat and take my mind off things.

Going just over the speed limit, we talked about the Knicks and Lakers game so excitedly, we barely knew it before we were in the Hamptons.

Mixed emotions overtook me as we entered that part of the state that brought back so many memories. My father and mother used to have a house close to the beach; it had been a wedding present for them. It was a small place, nothing like the stereotypical mansions there, and I could still remember a little of the summers we'd spent there.

We didn't get the chance to go too many times, unfortunately, but unless memory deceives me, I do think that was one of the few places where we'd been a real family. My father had taught me to surf on the beaches of Montauk, and I tried hard to improve so he'd be proud of me.

I thought about that, and a few bitterer things, as I turned onto the road that led to Jenna's parents' house. When my mother had left, my father started bringing me to the Hamptons for a week every summer to stay with the Tavishes. I had my first kiss during one of those visits... Christ, I'd been so nervous, and Jenna had been so calm. For her, it was just an experiment. Me...I almost took off running.

We did it under one of the big trees in the backyard. We were playing hide-and-go-seek, and when I found her, she grabbed my shirt and pulled me back there with her.

"You've got to do it now, Nick. Otherwise, it'll be too late."

I didn't know what the hell she was talking about just then, but years later I'd learn that under the same tree, shaded by the leaves, Jenna's father had asked her mother to marry him. Jenna had just found out, and the dreamy, romantic girl she kept hidden inside her had decided to emerge. She said our kiss was gross...but for me, it'd been a new beginning, and I never looked back.

Those thoughts made me stomp on the accelerator. I was so out of it that it took me a few seconds to hit the brakes when I saw what looked like a couple walking along the road. They were dressed in workout clothes, and when I flew by them and saw their blurry image, my stomach suddenly ached. Then I looked in the rearview mirror, and that ache turned into a cold sweat.

6

Noah

I GOT OUT OF THE SHOWER, LEAVING BEHIND A HUGE CLOUD OF steam. I'd been in there longer than I was supposed to, but it was that or let my muscles stay as tense as the strings of a violin.

I wrapped myself in a towel and looked out the window at the backyard full of people. Everyone was dressed in white. That was Jenna's dad's idea, and everyone had liked it, and now the dinner in honor of the future newlyweds looked like a party in the Mediterranean.

When we'd gotten home, sweaty and stinking, I'd found Lion giving Jenna a bear hug by the steps. He'd just gotten there, I guessed. Jenna finally looked whole.

Lion had never said anything about my breakup with Nicholas. Not just that, he'd refused to take sides or get involved. After we split, I'd pestered him constantly in an attempt to get Nick's new number. But it had been impossible, and Jenna decided to be impartial, too. Neither of them ever spoke of Nick in front of me unless it was to give me support during moments when I truly needed it. And since then, I never saw Lion except when Jenna was around.

I stepped back and started hurriedly getting ready. I didn't have a white dress except for one I liked to wear to the beach, so I opted for a pale skirt that fell just above my knees and a tight white spaghetti-strap top. I squeezed my hair with the towel, not bothering to dry it, since I knew the sea breeze would take care of it in minutes.

As I was walking downstairs on my way to the backyard, I heard the doorbell ring, and I stopped by the banister. Jenna was outside with all her guests, and the house was empty apart from waiters and waitresses coming and going from the kitchen with plates of seafood.

I walked to the door and forced the same welcoming smile I'd been pasting on ever since the first guests had started to show.

That smile froze when I saw Steve staring at me. He looked as surprised as I was, but he greeted me cordially right afterward. I nearly panicked seeing him there with a suitcase in each hand.

My heart was racing as I looked past him to see a guy in a suit getting out of a black Lexus, his sunglasses still on, a phone pressed to his left ear. Nick took the sunglasses off as he uttered something curt. Then he looked me in the eye, and I thought I'd faint.

He was so different... He'd cut his hair. It used to be long and unkempt, that was how I remembered it, especially when he first got up in the morning. Now it was short and neat and made him look serious, even intimidating. And his suit put the finishing touch on his new businessman look. He'd taken off his jacket and slung it over his elbow; his top two buttons were unbuttoned, his sleeves rolled up over his forearms. He was tan and far more muscular than the last time I'd seen him.

I saw all this in just a few seconds; then the ferocity in his eyes made me look at the floor to try to recover from the impact.

When I looked up again, he'd said goodbye to whoever was

on the phone and was putting it in his pocket as he walked toward the door.

I held my breath, uncertain what to do or say as he approached me. In the brief time he needed to walk past me, not even slowing down, I thought I would die. I hadn't felt that way in months; it was as though I'd been lost in a desert and had found an oasis in front of me...but actually it was a mirage, playing tricks on the little sanity I had left.

Thank God Jenna showed up to rescue me. I couldn't force myself to go back inside until I heard Nicholas and Steve walking upstairs. I hurried off to the back door and out to the yard, trying to disappear amid the rest of the guests, when what I really wanted was to disappear completely, vanish inside the earth forever.

I'd made a huge mistake coming there. I knew that now. Jenna was my best friend, but this was too much. Months had passed, months, and one simple look from him had turned my world upside down.

Ten minutes later, there he was, walking down the steps and chatting with the bride- and groom-to-be. Nick was the one person there who hadn't bothered changing into all white. He looked the same as when he'd arrived, pants dark, shirt sky blue, no tie. It made my heart ache to see how handsome he was, even from a distance.

Soon he was mingling. People walked over to say hi to him. He talked to everyone, his manners elegant, but kept his distance.

When I saw Luca and Lion walk up beside him, I knew I was completely alone. This wasn't my place. These weren't my friends. The only person here I could be certain cared about me was Jenna... I got so sad that I could have cried. But I kept a hold of myself. Since there was nothing I could do—or rather, nothing

I could undo—I decided to make the best of a bad situation and tamp down all the feelings I still had for him. Maybe time had cured his wounds; maybe time had made him stop hating me; maybe we could act like adults, treat each other with cordiality and respect, be friends, someday.

I know it sounds ridiculous, but it was that or throw myself off a balcony, and however tempting the second option was, it obviously wasn't the right one. So I started talking to people and forced myself to relax. As long as I stayed far away from him, there was no reason for anything bad to happen, and I could spare my heart the unbearable torture.

Jenna's parents introduced me to a family friend and one of Greg's associates, Lincoln Baxwell. He was a nice guy. He chatted me up about my studies and what I wanted to do in the future. You could tell from a mile away that he was someone important, so I was grateful when he handed me his card. I had no idea what to do with my future, so the more options, the better.

What I didn't suspect was that Lincoln Baxwell was friends with Nicholas Leister. We were chatting pleasantly, and then he suddenly waved at someone behind me. I turned around, and there was Nicholas right in front of me.

They shook hands, Baxwell introduced us, and I could see a vein twitching in Nick's neck. I'd rarely seen him so stiff. To save the situation, I started talking.

"We've actually already met, Mr. Baxwell," I said, hating the tremble in my voice that revealed in a split second how insecure and uncomfortable I was.

Baxwell smiled and looked back and forth between us. Nick's eyes were pinned to mine momentarily, and it hurt me to hear him say, "Really? We've met?" A shiver went up my spine when I heard that same deep voice that haunted my dreams, that voice that had told me *I love you*, that had whispered so many times into my ear.

I was hypnotized; I could hardly open my mouth.

"You do remind me of someone I *used to* know..." he continued, coolly and impersonally.

Then he nodded to his friend and walked off to mingle further.

I thought I heard a sound just afterward: my heart sinking to the ground.

The next morning, I got up at dawn. I'd barely slept. I just couldn't... That day when I ruined everything, that day when I did something I still couldn't understand, replayed itself in my head.

There's no going back now.

I can't even look you in the eye.

We're done.

I still remembered Nicholas's face when he realized what I'd done with Michael. I couldn't even recall that name without feeling guilty.

I got out of bed and threw on some clothes, hoping I could leave the house before anyone else woke and saw me. I didn't even bother telling Luca I was going for a run. I needed to be alone to think and clear my head. Above all, I needed to be alone to come to grips with the fact that I'd have to keep seeing Nicholas in the days to come. Even more: I'd have to walk with him up to the altar.

Running did me a world of good, and the rest of the morning flew by mercifully because there were a million things to do. As the guests went on enjoying themselves, midday passed, then the afternoon, and before I knew it, they were setting up for the rehearsal dinner that night.

The goddamned rehearsal dinner.

I'd skipped lunch, and I hadn't seen Nicholas or Steve again. At some point, I ran into Jenna's parents, who were waiting for her and Lion to finally go to the vineyard where the wedding would be celebrated. Everyone who would be part of the ceremony had to practice their entrance, and we needed to get a move on before nightfall.

Just as Jenna and Lion were coming down, the front door opened, and there was Nicholas in a white shirt and jeans. No one knew where he'd been that morning or afternoon, but it was obvious his main goal had been to avoid me.

"Nick, you're finally here. I was starting to ask myself where you'd run off to," Jenna's mother said, walking over and kissing him on the cheek. Nick smiled briefly, kissed her on the cheek as well, and started nervously spinning his keys around in his hand.

His and Jenna's eyes met. There was something strange in their expressions. I felt sick to my stomach. The rest of the day was going to be hell.

Outside, we realized there were too many of us to fit in one car. Along with Jenna's parents and Lion's mother—a woman with an innocent smile who'd made a wonderful impression on me, especially when she gave me her recipe for apple pie—there were Lion, Jenna, and Jenna's five-year-old cousin, a little boy who would be the ring bearer. Plus me and Nick, obviously.

That made eight in all, and I just prayed no one would make me ride with Nick, but in vain: Jenna's parents and Lion's mother went straight for the Mercedes parked near the other cars. Jenna's face told me she was sorry as she grabbed her cousin's little hand.

"Jenna, don't even..." I said, getting angry. Nicholas had made it clear he didn't want to be around me, so there was no way I was getting in a car with him. No fucking way.

I could see the guilt in her face as she said, "Nick's got a car seat is the thing...you know...because of Maddie...and I have to go with my parents."

Nicholas interrupted us, ignoring me, picking up little Jeremy, throwing him high in the air, and catching him.

"Ready to be my copilot, little buddy?"

Jeremy laughed. Nick rested him on his hip and walked toward the car. I looked back at Jenna, who was biting her lip.

I shook my head and walked past her and over to the Lexus. I had no idea what had happened to his SUV. I also wasn't about to ask. I got comfortable in the passenger seat while Nick put the boy in the car seat and pulled up a game on his phone. I tried to ignore how nervous I felt, being basically alone with him. His comment the night before had felt like a kick in the gut, and I wondered, even as I feared, what would happen over the next hour.

Nicholas got in, started fooling with the controls, and adjusted the rearview mirror. It only took a second, and then we were on the road.

Almost instantly, I could smell his aftershave and his cologne filling the car, and that same attraction I always felt when he was around started pulling me toward him again. My God, there he was, next to me, the man I'd longed for as I'd never longed for anyone... I was dying to reach over to him, to give him a kiss; I needed his touch more than the very air I breathed. My whole body was getting hot; even his hand resting on the gearshift made me nervous... His arms were so thick, his other hand so relaxed, leaning on the wheel... What was it that was so damn sexy about watching a man drive?

I couldn't stand it; I had to roll down the window, let the cool air in to get rid of his fragrance. But right away, he rolled it back up. I turned.

"I'm hot," I said. It was the first time I'd spoken to him in nearly a year. I pressed the button again, but he had locked it, and the window stayed up.

Without a word, he put on the AC. The cold air blasted me in the face. Well, that would take care of my temperature, but it wouldn't do anything about the scent that permeated the car and made me woozy. I wriggled in the leather seat and saw from the corner of my eye how his eyes shifted from the road to my bare legs.

I hadn't thought much about what to wear, but those short shorts must have done the trick. I couldn't ignore how he gripped the wheel and stared intently ahead after catching sight of my naked flesh.

Jeremy's game beeped and buzzed the whole way, and I realized that gave me an opportunity to talk to Nick without worrying about him leaving me stranded on the side of the road. He'd have to control his attitude, and his words, with a kid in the back.

"Nicholas, I wanted to tell you—"

"I don't care," he cut me off, turning at an intersection that led to a huge lake.

I took a deep breath. I was going to talk to him, dammit. "You can't go on ignoring me."

"I'm not."

I looked at him, conscious of how cruel his tone was. After all this time, I needed him to say something to me. I needed to talk. "You can't go on hating me like this."

A bitter smile crossed his lips. "If I hated you, that would mean I still felt something for you, Noah. So don't worry, I don't feel hatred—what I feel is indifference."

I tried to find a sign that what he was saying was a lie...but I couldn't. "You're saying that to hurt me."

"If I'd wanted to hurt you, I'd have cheated on you. But wait... you're the one who did that."

That was a low blow, but I had to admit I deserved it. "If we want to survive the next few days, we need to come to some kind of truce... I won't be able to deal with it if we can't even be in the same room."

I couldn't read his thoughts; I'd never been able to. He was complicated, and at best I'd managed to do it for a few seconds when we were alone, in moments when we were close in a way I'd only ever known with him.

"So what do you propose, Noah?" he said, turning so I could see the fury on his face. "We pretend nothing happened? I grab your hand and fake that I love you?"

I couldn't respond. *Fake that I love you?* I could feel my broken heart bleeding.

Behind us, I heard a sudden silence and turned to find Jeremy observing us, his eyes wide.

"How much longer is it?" he asked with a frown.

Shit! Don't let him start crying now!

"Just a little bit, Jeremy. You want me to put on some music?" Nicholas asked, turning a knob. A rap song started playing at full blast.

The boy smiled, and I looked ahead again. I knew who Nick had really wanted to shut up.

7

Nick

For me, Noah had always been a drug, a drug that knocked me out with her mere presence. Everything about her made me want to get closer to her; she turned me into a junkie, a weakling.

It had been hard for me to get away from her. It had hurt knowing I'd never touch her again, never kiss her, that I wouldn't be there to take care of her, that she wasn't the love of my life... Pain turned to hatred so fast, it even scared *me*. I had opened up to her, had given her my heart and soul, and she had done the very thing I was most afraid of: she'd betrayed me. In all those times thinking of everything that could go wrong, it had never passed through my head that she'd let another guy touch her. That fucking psychologist. I couldn't even think of him. His mere name made me see red, and I could barely hold on to my sanity.

That guy had touched my girlfriend, had taken off her clothes... The image of it, which was impossible to erase, must have been the thing that had truly broken me. Never in my life had I felt so horrible, so utterly miserable... A wall rose around me. I became someone else. I no longer had room for anything but the barest feelings of a man without a soul. What little capacity for love I held on to was there for my little sister. And that was it.

I'd worked so hard to make absolutely sure I'd never cross her path, and now seeing her again had thrown me off completely. I was furious...enraged... Just one look at her had made me feel something again, made my heart speed up, my breaths turn to panting, and I hated it. I hated that feeling, any feeling. I didn't have feelings anymore; I had gotten used to not feeling, and now she was here torturing me, and it made me want to drag her off with me to my private hell.

She was every bit as irresistible as ever, every bit as tempting, and she was right fucking there...and something about my presence made her shrink. She no longer had that glimmer, that air of superiority that had always been behind her every word. This Noah had changed, too; she wasn't the same, and I hated...the pain, I hated seeing what had become of us, I hated blaming her.

When I stopped, she hurried out of the car, unfastened Jeremy's seat belt, took him out, and jogged off to the vineyard without waiting for me. Her shorts and her plain yellow blouse had penetrated my defenses and thrown me off guard.

I could smell her fragrance, that aroma she and she alone possessed, the same one I still dreamed of on certain nights and that woke me up with a huge erection and the desire to strangle someone... That damned scent had now seeped into every inch of my car, and worst, most irritating of all, was that a part of me had enjoyed it, like an alcoholic taking a sip of brandy after years of abstinence. I hadn't even opened the windows; I hadn't managed to avoid all those images from the past coming back to haunt me, reminding me of the things I could do to sate that need I still had for her and always would.

I looked up to where my best friends were going to marry. I

couldn't believe it was happening. I found out Lion had asked for Jenna's hand a month after Noah and I had broken up. My friend had kept it secret like a pro. A part of me was thankful for that. I was happy for them, but it also rubbed salt in the wound.

Corey Creek Vineyards was a lovely place to get married. I had gone there more than once to walk between the vines and buy a bottle of their surprisingly good merlot. Jenna and her father had taken me with them. I remembered riding horses there and sometimes catching sight of newlywed couples. One of the owners was friends with my father and Greg, so they'd often given us the run of the place.

Jenna told us where to go: first a tasteful reception in the winery itself, with its high wooden beams and animal-skin carpets, probably trophies from the owners' hunts. There were oil lamps and big crystal chandeliers hanging almost menacingly over our heads. Jenna was standing close to a stressed-looking Asian woman. A few minutes later, they introduced her to me as Amy, the wedding planner.

We went out back, where the vineyards started, and I knew for a fact the wedding was going to be magnificent, just like the ones I had seen there before, or maybe even better.

They'd put the altar with the flowers overlooking the vineyards, which seemed to extend forever below the July sun. There were benches and bouquets that had yet to be arranged, but I had an idea of how everything would look when it was done.

"The best man and the maid of honor?" Amy asked, looking back and forth.

Noah stepped forward, looked back at me furtively, and listened closely to Amy's words. Then Amy took me by the arm a minute later and told me where we had to stand. We were arranged in pairs: first Lion and his mother, then Jenna's mother and Jeremy, who seemed interested in anything except what the wedding planner was telling him, and finally, Jenna and her father.

Standing next to Noah, I did everything I could to try and cover up my irritation.

When Amy came over to us, noticing we were the only two who barely touched each other, she scowled and asked us, "What the heck is up with you guys?"

No idea, babe. No fucking idea.

I could feel Noah staring at me, and I had to count to ten not to say to hell with it all and run away.

8

Noah

Like a leper—that's how Nicholas was treating me. When Amy stared at us like a couple of idiots, I swear I nearly died of embarrassment.

"Noah, come on, take his arm," she said, motioning energetically.

I turned to him, afraid of his reaction. He just stared straight ahead and motioned for me to do as the woman had said.

His arm was hard beneath mine, and an electric current seemed to run through us. I looked up and watched him briefly close his eyes. After that, there wasn't much time to analyze our feelings because Amy made us go back and forth ten times, change formation, start off on our right foot, not go too slow or too fast... Jeremy was the one who had the hardest time with it. On the third go-round, he decided he'd had enough and wanted to go play.

It was terrible. Nicholas wouldn't even look at me. He acted like I didn't exist, and I got so tense, my arm fell asleep. Everyone else was laughing and chatting and acting silly whenever Amy turned away.

Night soon fell, and we couldn't rehearse anymore. Amy

wasn't convinced by our performance, but at least Jenna and Lion had a good idea of the order of operations and who had to do what when.

Jeremy had fallen asleep by then, and he didn't wake up when we packed him in the back of the car. This time, he wouldn't notice what Nicholas and I were saying.

At first, the silence was deafening. Nick didn't even turn on the radio. The road was straight, and the sky, as dark as my thoughts Being there alone, in such a small space, with so many thoughts throbbing just below the surface, I felt myself drowning; I couldn't bear his indifference. I needed him to know what I still felt for him. It didn't matter if he couldn't see me anymore, if his love for me had become something ugly. I just needed to do something.

"Nick..." I said, looking straight ahead.

I knew he'd heard me, even if my voice was just a whisper.

"I'm still in love with you."

"Shut up, Noah," he ordered between clenched teeth.

I turned to face him, my heart in my throat. He was looking ahead, his jaw so tense, I was afraid of what was coming next. But I didn't let him intimidate me, I needed him to know.

"I'm still in love with you, Nicholas..."

"I told you to shut up," he said, turning to me and glowering. "You think I care what you feel about me? Your words don't mean shit, so you can save your breath. We're going to do this stupid wedding tomorrow, and then we never have to see each other again."

How could I be so stupid? What did I think was going to happen? That he was going to tell me he felt the same?

A tear rolled down my cheek. I wiped it off, but another came, then another, then another.

He didn't love me anymore. Nicholas didn't love me anymore. Worse, he didn't even want me in his life. All that we'd been through together didn't matter; it didn't matter how many times he'd sworn he loved me more than anything—he had just told me it was over. Forever.

I know we'd been apart for ten months, but all that time, we hadn't seen each other, hadn't talked, and a part of me had refused to believe that it was over. I'd hoped somehow I'd see him again and find out he was just as much in love with me as I was in love with him.

How wrong I'd been.

During the rehearsal dinner, I didn't speak a word to anyone. I sat next to Luca. He did the talking for both of us. When I had the chance, I escaped to my room and cried into my pillow until I fell asleep, my mind playing tricks on me, forcing me to remember every moment, every caress, every word spoken, every mistake.

The distance between us hurt so much, it was as if every tear I cried were a drop of blood drained from my heart.

The next morning, I was exhausted, and worst of all, it was the day of the wedding, and I had to look good, keep smiling, be the best maid of honor in history. I couldn't drop the act till the night was over. Tired as I was, it seemed impossible.

I washed my face with cold water and looked at myself in the mirror, realizing how much I had changed in those months. Something was different: the look in my eyes, it was sad now. All I wanted was to get out of there. For hours, my psychologist—my new psychologist—had talked to me about how what had happened with Nicholas didn't need to define my future: there were millions of men in the world; I was young and pretty, and any of them would fall in love with me in an instant. But just thinking about getting close to someone, the mere possibility of it, made me sick. I would remember how things had ended the last time I was with another man, and that reminded me of the dangers of being with anyone who wasn't Nicholas. I looked at myself in the mirror and tried to pull myself together. I couldn't go on like that. It was just one more day. One day, and then I wouldn't see him again… When I felt the pain overtake me again, I stared at my reflection and forced myself to calm down.

It's over, Noah. Forget him, forget him, the sooner the better… Do it now, or you'll never get over it.

That little voice in my head had been pursuing me all morning. Luckily, Nicholas was at the vineyard with Lion, where they'd be getting dressed. I was staying home with Jenna. We'd be the last to leave; not even her parents would be riding with us. When Jenna was ready—she was stunning; she took my breath away—I got misty-eyed. Good thing the makeup we were wearing was tear-proof.

My tailored red dress fit like a glove. They'd chosen that color because the room would be full of red roses, and Jenna's bouquet would be red roses, too. It was silk and lace, hung to the floor, and had a slit up the side to show off one leg, with a V neck and thin lace covering my bust and arms—like Jenna's wedding dress, but hers was white. Against her dark complexion, with her perfect figure, it looked amazing. Lion would lose his mind, I knew, and I told her so.

Jenna was so excited, I'd worked extra-hard to keep her from noticing how sad I was those days. I devoted all my energy to taking care of her, supporting her, calming her down. We'd laughed, drunk champagne, and I'd listened attentively to her every worry, trying to help as much as I could.

Amy came into Jenna's room and told us it was time to go.

I was nervous, but I kept it in. Hundreds of people were going to be there, some of them very important. If it had been my wedding, I wouldn't have been able to take all those people watching me walk to the altar. I'd never really thought about what I wanted my wedding day to be like, but all that craziness...that wasn't for me.

A white limousine was waiting for us by the door. I helped Jenna down the stairs so she wouldn't trip. When we were in the back seat, sitting in a puff of tulle and lace, I couldn't help but laugh.

"Who'd have thought we'd be here after that night when you slapped the shit out of Lion?" I said.

Jenna laughed along with me, and I tried to take a mental snapshot of that moment, which was so beautiful. Us slightly buzzed off champagne, cracking up in a limo, our nerves frazzled, was something I'd never forget. My friend was the very image of love and happiness.

When we reached the vineyard, the organizer told us to go straight through the winery to the back door and out to where the altar was set up and the guests were waiting. We could hear the murmurs of people surely as nervous as we were, but when Jenna's father started walking over, we both breathed a little easier. As much as we wanted to feel like we were adults, the presence of a real adult, a responsible one, was calming in that moment.

Mr. Tavish's smile lit up the room. My heart ached when I saw the tenderness in his eyes as he looked at his daughter. She gave him a kiss on the cheek, hugged him, and grabbed his arm to follow him to the doors leading outside. But, of course, Nicholas and I would have to go out first.

I looked around for him, but he wasn't there. When I opened the door to peek out, I almost bumped into him. I looked up from his chest to his eyes and saw him looking down at me. I was hurt, the way I'd been every time I'd seen him, but I was angry, too, and bitter at what he'd said to me the night before. I held on to that bitterness. It would get me through the night. At least, that's what I was telling myself.

He stared me up and down, and when his gaze rested on my face, I think he was surprised to see me scowling.

"We go out in two," I said, then turned around. I knew he was behind me. I could feel his eyes on my back and neck. My hair was pulled back into a high ponytail with a few curls, and it reached the middle of my back. Knowing his tastes, I was certain that lace back was making him hot, even if he hated me with all his might.

Despite all that had happened, we'd never stop wanting each other. One look at his blue suit, his gray tie, his white shirt, his incredible body, his presence, had thrown me off course completely... Why in God's name did he have to be so good-looking?

Couldn't he have lost fifteen pounds the way I had? Couldn't he have dropped his standoffish air? Why weren't his eyes swollen from crying like mine, instead of retaining that gorgeous celestial blue that seemed tailor made to make any woman melt?

In a side room, I found the wedding planner helping Jenna with her dress while her assistant gave orders to people. The music started on the other side of the door, and a big hand touched my lower back—a little too low for comfort.

Amy motioned for us to stand at the head of the line before I could say anything, and Nicholas guided me softly forward until we were standing in front of the closed door.

I took a deep breath, trying to calm down.

"Take my arm, Noah," Nicholas said, and I swear his voice, just his whisper, made me tremble. It had been so long since I'd heard him sound like that...

I did what I was supposed to do, wrapping my arm around his, feeling his tense muscles. We waited for our cue. When it came, we walked to the altar in what I assumed would be our last act as a couple.

The ceremony was perfect. Lion nearly cried when he saw Jenna. I did cry. Damn it, why did I have to be so sensitive?

They read the vows, repeated the words *I do*, and that was it: they were bound for life. When they leaned in for a kiss that made more than one guest blush, I looked at Nicholas, and to my surprise, he was looking at me. It was one of those magic instants when everything around you seems to disappear and all that matters is the person in front of you. Would that be the last night we'd ever see each other? After a while, I looked away because the intensity in his eyes was about to make me faint.

We walked out behind the bride and groom. I touched his arm—for the last time? We were holding each other, but at someone else's behest, and it was almost like it wasn't real. That hurt so much that when we crossed the threshold, I turned around and walked away. I needed to get a hold of myself, and fast.

9

Nick

I FELT NAUSEATED AS I WATCHED HER WALK OFF. THROUGHOUT the ceremony, I couldn't take my eyes off her. I didn't even realize Jenna and Lion had said *I do* until the applause pulled me out of my trance.

Dammit...why did Noah have to be so gorgeous; why did she have to make me lose my mind like that? My hands were twitching, I wanted to touch her so badly, and knowing I couldn't, I wouldn't, had put me in an awful mood. Seeing her stop before going outside to ready herself for her performance, in that dress that gripped her body, each and every curve of it, I had reached out to touch her against my will, and that contact with her lower back had made me feel alive again for the first time in ten hellish months.

I couldn't wait for the whole affair to be over. I needed to leave, get back to my life, where everything was under control. Noah had always brought me chaos, and by the end, I was completely at her mercy. That wouldn't happen again. When she walked away from me once we were back inside, I was secretly thankful. I couldn't handle having her so close.

Soon, the reception started. On the other side of the vineyard was a huge white tent with tables set with white tablecloths and red roses. It was obvious what Jenna's favorite flower was. Seeing her with Lion talking to all the guests, I couldn't help but feel a little envious. There were couples gathered inside and waiters walking among the guests handing out canapés and glasses of rosé champagne.

Soon we'd be sitting down for dinner, but fool that I was, I spent the whole time looking for Noah. She was nowhere to be found.

She's not your problem anymore. Let it go.

Trying to follow my inner voice's advice, I ran into a girl with big green eyes who did everything in her power to seduce me. I hardly paid her any mind, but when she said we already knew each other, I stopped and looked at her, not wanting to be rude.

"Sorry...I don't remember," I said, not making much of an effort to do so.

She came even closer, invading my personal space with her expensive perfume, which was too strong for my taste. "Come on, don't be a dummy... It was one of the best nights of my life," she said. I cursed myself. I'd slept with her a month or so ago.

I didn't know her name, and I was about to turn on my heel. I didn't care if she didn't like it. Then, on the other side of the room, I saw Noah hanging off Luca's arm and smiling as only she could.

My jealousy, dormant for so long, awakened with the strength of a hungry lion, and I had to take a deep breath and let it out slowly so I didn't lose control.

That wasn't the first time that had happened since I'd gotten to the Hamptons. When I'd realized Noah had been the one jogging with that guy on the roadside, I'd taken off for a gym and hit the bag for two hours before going to Jenna's.

Steve chewed me out, told me I couldn't make a scene, couldn't start fights, had to act like a saint. Now that I was the owner of the company, I couldn't go around starting scandals, especially not because I was jealous. For that reason, I'd stayed on the sidelines, working with my economists, bankers, and investors, and taking some girl home once in a while, doing my best to keep my problems under wraps. And those problems could be summed up in exactly one word: Noah.

"You really don't remember me?" the girl went on, getting my attention again.

Noah was still with Luca. Now he had his hand on her back.

I needed a distraction, now.

"Of course I remember," I said, grabbing her arm and moving her strategically so I could talk to her and watch Noah at the same time.

As if she could sense what I was doing, Noah looked up then and saw me.

I smiled like the asshole I was and looked back at the brunette.

"You feel like dancing?" I asked. Now Noah was concentrated on Luca, who had taken her to a corner. She was laughing, but I knew her well enough to realize it was just to keep up appearances.

I wrapped my arms around the girl's waist. It was hard to concentrate on her with Noah wandering around. I remembered now where I'd seen the girl: at a downtown club. We'd smashed in the VIP section. Quick and cold.

My hand climbed her back and came to rest on the back of her neck.

"You want to go upstairs?" she whispered.

Upstairs. The offer was tempting. The problem was, I felt absolutely nothing for her. Nothing compared to what I felt for Noah. She'd barely touched me a few hours before, and it had given me an erection I could hardly hide. This girl...this girl was everything but. She was the opposite of Noah in every way.

"Not now. Maybe later," I said, stopping as the song ended.

Just then, they told us we could sit down for dinner.

I was glad not to have to sit at the brunette's table. I was with the bride and groom, Jenna's parents, Lion's mom, Noah, and Luca. She barely looked over when we were all seated and the first dish was set out. She spent the whole dinner talking and laughing with Luca and everyone else, pretending not to know me. Pretending I didn't exist.

Since I'd arrived two days before, every time I'd turned, I'd seen her looking at me. Whenever we were together, it felt like she wanted me to herself. And she had talked to me, she'd opened her heart, and I'd almost fallen to pieces when she'd told me she was still in love with me.

Love? Bullshit!

I slammed my glass down too hard on the table, and almost everyone turned and looked. I apologized and got up to go to the bathroom.

Why was I suddenly bothered that Noah wasn't paying attention to me? I'd hated feeling her staring at me all the time; I'd hated seeing the regret in her eyes, the pain... I'd hated feeling guilty when I wasn't the guilty one, and now I was pissed because she seemed to be testing me to find out how I'd react.

One thing was for certain: I needed to be careful.

10

Noah

I TRIED TO STAY AWAY FROM HIM. I USED ALL MY STRENGTH TO try to stop myself from glancing over at him. Luca helped a lot: when I'd escaped everyone after the ceremony, when I'd broken down and needed a few minutes to recover, he had given me his hand, had helped me up, and had made a funny comment that had brought a smile to my lips.

Who could have ever imagined that Lion's gangster brother would turn out to be so fun? He had promised me he wouldn't leave me on my own that night; he'd laughed at me, saying I was like Nicholas's lapdog, looking at him all the time with that cow-eyed stare. If Luca had noticed that, then Nicholas definitely had, too.

I didn't want to make him uncomfortable. I didn't want him to feel sorry for me. I didn't want anyone to feel sorry for me, really. So we made a deal: Luca would be my life raft that night. As long as we were together, I could avoid the temptation to look, let alone break down and ask Nicholas to forgive me, even though it had passed through my head countless times since we'd seen each other again.

When I saw him dance with that girl, flirt with her, I felt my heart shrivel. If a mere dance made me feel that way, how must he have felt when he'd found out I'd slept with another guy?

I wasn't an idiot; I knew Nicholas hadn't taken a vow of celibacy after breaking up with me. The list of girls he'd been with was probably endless.

Luca saw me watching him and pinched me on the hip and reprimanded me. After that, I turned away, concentrating on the people in front of me. Of course, that was harder when we were all sitting at the same table. My eyes turned in Nick's direction a few times, but whenever they did, Luca pinched me under the table. The last time he did it, it tickled, and I laughed out loud. That was when Nicholas almost shattered his glass slamming it down on the table. He got up and disappeared toward the bathroom.

"He's jealous," Luca said, scowling after him.

Jealous?

"No... He just can't stand having me here in front of him," I replied, depressed, and took a sip of my champagne.

Nicholas came back with a girl on his arm. People were standing up now; the band was playing, and the time to dance had come. The bride and groom took to the floor first, and the whole ambience changed: the lights shifted, the floor filled with people shaking their limbs, and people switched from champagne and wine to high-octane cocktails.

Luca pulled me out onto the dance floor. I was glad to be rid of Nick and not have to watch him feeling the brunette up under the table. It was gross, gross, and I was so, so jealous. Luca and I danced the way friends do. He was behaving. Not for one second did he try to make a move on me or even suggest he might. We found Lion and Jenna, and the four of us danced together, laughing and having a ball. It was the best moment of the night. Nicholas wasn't there; God knew what he and the girl were up to, which made my blood boil, but the drinks in me helped make everything easier.

What happened afterward...I have to admit, it was my fault.

A moment came when I turned around and saw him... I saw him kissing her, and she was sitting on his lap, but that wasn't the worst of it: he was staring at me while he did it, his lips pressed into the brunette's neck and his eyes looking straight into mine. He smiled. I stopped dancing. And what I did next...damn it! Was I never going to learn?

Luca knew what I was looking at, and he came over to say something. He bent over to whisper in my ear over the thundering of the music, and then...then the old Noah took over, and everything I'd learned during those months, all those sessions with the psychologist, all my regrets, all of it went to hell just then, and I grabbed Luca by the neck, pulled him downward, and pressed my lips into his.

The weird thing was he didn't pull away. I felt his tongue in my mouth, his hand on my back pulling me into him.

What was I doing?

I didn't have much time to think about it because someone pulled him backward right away, and the next thing I knew, Luca was on the ground, his lip busted open and bleeding. I looked up and saw Nicholas completely out of his mind. Shaking his injured hand, he looked at Luca and then at me. His wounded gaze made me tremble...but I was also seething. He clenched his teeth and turned around. Luca got up—or rather, the people around him helped him up—while Nick walked off to the other side of the room.

I didn't know what the hell was going on with me. Maybe the champagne had clouded my judgment. But I went after him, and not to ask for his forgiveness.

He had gone out back to where the wedding had been held,

where the chairs were still perfectly arranged, as were the flowers. It was deserted there, but still, the noise from the party was deafening.

"Where are you going, Nicholas?" I yelled.

I almost stumbled down the stairs. He turned, red-faced, angry I had followed him.

"You had no right to do that!" I roared.

I was out of my mind, half-drunk, pissed off. A bad combination.

I walked toward him. He looked serious, trying to decide what he was going to do. He was scary, even. But I didn't bow down. The opposite, actually. His attack of jealousy showed something; there was no denying it... He hadn't forgotten me. I refused to believe that now, and if I had to face his fury to get him to confess it, then so be it.

I shoved him. "You liar!" I shouted. I cocked back my fists, ready to strike him in the chest as hard as I could. "You're a fucking liar, Nicholas!"

For a second, he barely moved, but then I saw his chest rising and falling. He let me keep hitting him, but just two more times before his hands came up and stopped mine. That contact angered me more than anything else.

"You say you forgot me? Well, your actions don't show it! You said nothing could come between us!"

He looked at me incredulously. "You're the one who broke every single fucking promise, Noah, the one who decided to ruin everything, goddammit! You're worthless, Noah—to me you're completely worthless."

His words made me stop short. I froze, on the verge of vomiting.

I swallowed, cleared my throat, tried to look into his eyes, but I couldn't see him well, could hardly see at all. My vision was blurry... It took me a little time to realize it was because my eyes were full of tears.

"How can you say that?" I asked, my voice cracking.

Standing there, looking as upset, as sorrowful as I felt, Nicholas observed me... How could he have said that? To me?

"Because it's the fucking truth."

He turned around and took a few steps.

"I made a mistake, Nicholas! One fucking mistake!" My shouts didn't stop him. "Your crazy ex-girlfriend made me think you were cheating on me! You kissed Sophie right in front of me, but *I'm* the one who screwed it all up?! You did that! You forced me into making the worst mistake of my life! You allowed me to be used, to be used as if...as if I..."

I couldn't keep talking through the sobs. I was bitter, burned, torn apart inside...and yet what I was saying was what I felt: if it hadn't been for his lies, there was no way I'd ever have wound up in a position where someone else could take advantage of my weakness, using things I'd told him in confidence... I looked up, and there Nick was in front of me. He'd come back. The rage in his face was so pure, so terrifying, that I almost wanted to step backward, but then he did the last thing I would have expected: he wrapped an arm around my waist, and his lips touched mine. I thought it was a nightmare at first, one of the many I'd had recently, when sleep overwhelmed me and I thought I was with the Nicholas from before—we were happy, we were kissing, and suddenly, he'd leave, and there was nothing I could do to stop it. I'd run, run behind him, but my legs could never move fast enough.

This was no dream, though. Not in the least. He picked me up off the ground; my breasts squeezed into his hard chest; his tongue wove its way hungrily into my mouth. For a moment, I wasn't sure what was happening, but my body lit up from the contact. I wrapped my arms around his neck and pulled him tighter. God, I had needed that contact! It was as if he had returned all the energy to my body after months of depletion.

I felt his arms tight around me and the hunger, the voracity in his kiss. I grabbed his hair, but it wasn't like before; it was too short for me to pull it the way I used to. As he panted, his hand climbed my back to my neck, gripping me as he pulled away and stared… His pupils were dilated, dilated with excitement, desire, a pure carnal desire I thought I'd never see again.

As we looked at each other, I wanted to say so much…but something changed…a thought flickered behind his pupils, tormented him, and I knew I'd lost him again. Desperate, I pulled him back in and kissed him, but the response wasn't the same. His arms slackened, and he set me down. Panic crept in, panic that he'd leave, panic that I'd lose him again.

I cried, my lips separated from his, and buried my face in his neck. But I refused to let him go. I refused to let him just leave.

"I can't do this, Noah," he said very clearly, but his voice was choked with feeling.

"No." I refused him; I held him tight. My tears were leaving streaks on his shirt, but I didn't care. I couldn't let him go. I needed him; he needed me. We needed to be together.

His hands moved from my waist to my wrists. He pushed until I had to let go. He brought my hands close to his face and looked straight at me.

"Don't leave me," I pleaded. I was begging, I know, but he was leaving the next day, and I wouldn't see him again, and that feeling was killing me.

"When I close my eyes, I see you with him," he confessed. He blinked, and I was yearning for him to stay, to love me, to protect me once more.

"I don't even remember it, Nicholas," I told him, refusing to let him let me go. And it was true: I couldn't remember what had happened that night. I knew we had slept together, but I hadn't really been a part of it; I had let him do it to me because I didn't have the strength to say no... Nothing had mattered to me then because my life was hell.

His eyes misted over, and I felt myself dying.

"I can't do it... I'm sorry."

He turned around and walked off, leaving me there...

Jenna found me two hours later sitting in one of the chairs from the wedding, hugging my knees and trying to pull myself together. That kiss, those words...they hadn't helped. She hugged me, and I felt even worse, knowing I had screwed up her special day.

"I'm sorry, Jenna," I said, trying to stop crying.

"I'm the one who's sorry, Noah. All this is my fault," she said, and I looked at her, not understanding. "This whole situation, you guys being the maid of honor and the best man, putting you in the same car, in adjoining rooms... I wanted to give you guys a chance. I thought...I thought if I pushed a little..."

"We kissed," I admitted, knowing that despite that kiss, a last kiss, things wouldn't get better regardless of what Jenna did.

She looked surprised, confused, then glanced around, as if trying to understand what had happened and why Nick was gone.

"It's over, Jen," I said, bringing a hand to my mouth to stifle my sobs. Christ, I was pathetic...but it hurt, damn it... It hurt so badly, losing him!

She hugged me again. I let her console me. Some pair we were: her on the happiest day of her life, and me in a black hole of misery.

Resolutely, she said, "I shouldn't tell you this, Noah, I really shouldn't, but I know Nick, and when you were with him, he was completely happy. Even if you had problems, I've never seen him so centered, so... How should I say it? So normal. He had a hard life; I saw how he cried for months when his mother left, and then he turned tough, and he put on that suit of armor he wears, trying to pretend he's untouchable... You managed to break through that. I'm not saying it's going to be easy for you, Noah, but dammit, he's the love of your life! I want my best friends to be as happy as I am. I need that; I'm asking you for it, Noah. I'm asking you not to let him go, no matter what he says, no matter how many times he tells you he doesn't love you or can't forgive you... There's got to be a way."

I got up and looked at her with a sad smile. "I know you want to believe what you're telling me, Jen... I do, too," I said, looking back to where he had been standing. "But I broke his heart... I thought he had cheated on me, and I was dying inside, I really was, so I know what he's feeling... He won't forgive me. He just never will."

She was about to say something, but then she closed her mouth. I think it was the only time I'd ever seen her speechless. I came close and kissed the top of her head.

"Go enjoy your day."

After that, I tried my hardest to go back to being the girl I had been all week. I wasn't going to let Lion and Jenna spend that time without their two best friends, so I stayed at the party for as long as I had to. I forced myself to dance and enjoy the people around me. At one point, I bumped into Luca. There was wariness in his green eyes but not an ounce of rancor at the fact that I'd used him to make Nicholas jealous.

"I'm sorry," I said, and I meant it. I hoped my words were enough to make him forgive me. I'd acted like a fool, like the immature little girl I'd sworn I'd stop being, and I felt terrible for giving Lion's brother false hope.

"I'm not," he replied, taking my hand and pulling me in close. "Relax," he said as I panicked, wanting to get away before something else happened between us. "I don't mind you using me to make that dumbass jealous, and honestly, you're helping me out, too." He turned me around, my back pressed into his chest, moving to the rhythm of the music as he bent down and whispered clearly. "See that chick over there?" he asked, pointing subtly at a group of girls next to the bar. I nodded, amused, realizing what he meant. "That blond has been watching us and trying to act like she doesn't care about what we're up to." He spun me back, put his hands on my spine, almost touching my butt, and I glowered at him. "She and I slept together like a month ago. I mean, to tell the truth, we've been sleeping together ever since I could crawl. Or ever since I could...you know." I rolled my eyes. "We lost touch when I was locked up. Then we ran into each other at a party in my hood. She's the oldest daughter of one of my mom's friends, and I bet she'll lose it when I feel you up like I'm about to do."

I cracked up and pushed him. He put his hand to his heart as if I'd hurt his feelings. Then he pulled me in slowly and whispered in my ear, in a very different tone, "Don't give in, Noah. What you did was wrong, but we all make mistakes."

What he said wasn't exactly a revelation, but it did make me realize that everyone could see what was going on between me and Nicholas.

But what was I to do? I hadn't made just any mistake. Cheating—that was the hardest thing to forgive. And the lies, our past, the intensity of our relationship, that had brought us to a point of no return.

I danced more with Luca, and with other people, too, until the time came for Jenna and Lion to leave. They'd done all the formalities: cutting the cake, which I barely tried, throwing the bouquet, all that. I mean, she pretended to throw it. Actually, after a moment's hesitation, she turned and smiled at me, handing it to me with a smile on her lips before I could realize what was happening.

"This is so you'll know I still believe your day will come, Noah, and you and I both know who it will be with."

I didn't know what to say. I admired her determination, her hope, but it only made me more sorrowful. I couldn't take it anymore, being around all those people, and when Jenna kissed me on the cheek and ran off with Lion to the limousine that would take them for a night in a luxury hotel before their honeymoon, I got into one of the chauffeured cars waiting for the guests and told the driver to please take me home.

I needed that night to be over with.

11

Nick

I KNEW I'D FUCKED UP KISSING HER THE NIGHT BEFORE, BUT I couldn't help myself—she'd been there shouting at me, blaming me. Me! She'd called me a liar. A liar? I didn't even know what the hell she was talking about, but it didn't matter: either I kissed her, or I lost control completely.

Seeing Luca's disgusting hands on her body, his lips on hers… Noah destroyed what little self-control I thought I had left. The sight of her with another guy made me relive all those images I'd managed to wipe from my mind. Now that I'd seen her again, it was obvious I was back at square one, just like the day I'd found out she'd cheated on me.

Feeling her slender body, beautiful but much thinner than I remembered, I'd lost my mind for a few moments. My senses were in a whirl; I was suddenly the same guy I used to be, completely in love, completely lost, thanks to one girl. When I stepped back to look at her, to fill myself with the light that always emanated from her, I saw it in her eyes, that same longing, that same barely suppressed desire, the very thing that brought us together, but there was something else, too: penitence, desperation, nostalgia...and it was as if a knife was stuck into my heart and twisted, and I suffered just as I had when I'd found out the truth months before.

Those images...those goddamned images my imagination used to torture me flashed once again on the screen of my mind. Noah naked in bed, sighing with pleasure, so sensual, so innocent, so full; those sounds that came from her lips, those sounds that drove me wild, that brought me to my knees. But I wasn't the one provoking those sensual sounds; it was another: another man's hands on her body, stroking her, not slowly, trying to please her, but roughly, squeezing her, without the love that invaded me every time I touched her. And Noah liked it, she enjoyed it, and she wasn't shouting my name...

When I thought of that, it was like someone had drenched me with a pitcher of ice water, and I had to push her away even if she refused, holding on to me with all her might. Maybe she thought I wasn't strong enough to do without her, but I had been, and I hadn't regretted it.

And now, after a sleepless night, I was having another moment of weakness when I wanted to say to hell with everything, go to her room, beg her to finish what we'd started.

It was time to go.

I packed my bags, left my room in silence, but stopped in front of Noah's door like the complete idiot I was. I closed my eyes, furious at the thought that she was there just a few feet away and had probably cried all night because she'd held me again, but there was nothing she could do to fix things. As soon as I was strong enough, I left.

I put my bags in the trunk—I hadn't brought much—and splashed my face with water from the bottle I found in the console to try and wake up. I hadn't slept a wink. After the reception, I'd rented a surfboard at Georgica Beach and surfed for a few hours, trying to calm down, trying to figure out the reason why I was staying away from Noah, because when I'd kissed her, all justification had seemed to vanish. I surfed there till the sun peeked over the horizon. Then I'd decided to go back, shower, and get away.

12

Noah

I DIDN'T HEAR HIM GO, BUT I FELT HIS ABSENCE. THAT WAS IT; IT over. Now all that was left for me was to go back to the same old routine.

I said goodbye to all the guests still there. Some of them would stick around for a few more days. Jenna's mother gave me a hug, and her dad said he'd take me to the station where I'd catch the train back to New York City. Along the way, he asked me what my plans were for the summer, and I told him that after spending a few days in the city, I'd get back to work. I didn't want to say much about what I was doing. He was an oil magnate; how could he understand that the stepdaughter of his millionaire best friend was working as a waitress? He didn't pry, though, and I was grateful.

"Where are you going to stay in the city, Noah?" he asked, turning through the pretty streets. It was early, but there were already people out walking their dogs, carrying their oversize designer bags...almost everyone had on sunglasses. I was sad to leave without getting to know the town. But the chaos of the wedding had made it impossible.

I told Jenna's dad the name of the motel I'd booked in New York. It was a dump, but I didn't care. I would barely set foot in there; I just needed a place to shower and sleep. The rest of the time, I'd be wandering around, discovering the big city.

Jenna's father gave me a strange look. He didn't recognize the name. I guess it wasn't close to the two properties he had in town.

Things got uncomfortable when he told me he wanted to book me a room at the Times Square Hilton. I thanked him, but I didn't want anyone's charity. People like him, people who had money and just assumed everyone who didn't was suffering, well...they were wrong. I didn't mind staying in a motel. It wasn't such a big deal!

"Noah, I'm not trying to get in your business, but it's your first time in town. You don't know your way around here the way you do in LA. I'd feel better if I could help you out."

He went on like that until we reached the train station.

"Mr. Tavish, there's just no need. I know how to take care of myself. I'll be fine, really... Plus, I've got a friend I'm meeting. There's honestly nothing to worry about." That was a white lie, but there was no harm in it. Mr. Tavish didn't seem convinced: he was preoccupied, angry even, but whatever—he wasn't my dad.

"Fine. Well, you've got my number if you need anything. I'll be in the Hamptons this week, but I've got many friends in New York, friends who would be happy to meet you if need be."

Friends...yeah, sure. I knew what he meant when he said *friends*. I thought of Steve and his role in the Leister family. I didn't need a bodyguard.

I said goodbye to him and hurried into the station, worried he might call my mom or something. At this point, nothing would surprise me.

I got on, handed my ticket to a nice employee, and settled in, looking out the window and waiting for the capital of the world to appear. I tried to forget that time Nick had offered to take me there, telling me he wanted to be the guy to show me its wonders. That was a whole lifetime ago now. Or at least, that was how it seemed.

When we arrived, I immediately caught a taxi to my motel. As we drove around, I was stunned by everything I saw through the windows—the endless skyscrapers, the people milling about like ants; it made me feel as small as a grain of sand... It was spectacular, but at the same time overwhelming.

It was around four in the afternoon when the taxi driver turned down a desolate street, and I was worried, but he wasn't up to anything bad. That was just where my motel was. It could have been worse, but it looked nothing like the photos online.

The driver grabbed my suitcase, I gave him a sorry tip, and he drove off, leaving me God knew where in the Big Apple. I took a deep breath and went inside. The place looked more like a homeless shelter than a motel.

The girl behind the counter barely looked up from her magazine when I dragged in my suitcase.

"Name?" she said, smacking her gum. It was gross. I'd always hated chewing gum.

"Noah Morgan. I've got a reservation," I said, looking around. This was no motel: this was just a dump with a few rooms for rent.

She sighed, opened a drawer, and took out a key from among a pile of them. "Here. Don't lose it. It's the only one. If you want breakfast, there are machines. No restaurant, no room service."

I nodded, trying to keep my first hours in New York from depressing me. Whatever. I just needed a bed. At least the machine had Oreos in it. What else could a person want?

I left my suitcase in my minuscule room and went out for a walk, leaving behind the grim street the motel was on and checking out the city. A few blocks away, I found Central Park, just as the website had said I would.

I wouldn't know how to say what it was like. Just that after ten minutes, I wanted to live there. It was warm, people were lying around sunning themselves, kids were playing ball, people were walking dogs...there were runners and all types of other people working out. Just the feel of it was incredible, all that nature in the middle of a city full of smog and traffic.

I walked over to the lake and saw people feeding the ducks that cut furrows across the water. I looked up into the blue July sky and let the feeling of being alone carry me away. Alone, yes, but also happy, in the middle of a place where no one knew me, where no one knew my story, where no one could judge me for that breakup—not Nicholas, not William, not my mother. No one would scowl at me or pity me. God, it had been terrible. Nick was a legend on campus, and the rumors spread like wildfire. We had been the couple everyone admired, stared at, and screwing it up so bad... I don't want to go into it, but let's just say people can be cruel.

I spent the whole afternoon in the park. I read, ate a hot dog, strolled. I must have looked crazy. There were so many places to see, but I just stayed there. I didn't want to act like a tourist. Sometimes it's good to just be, just be there among others; that was what I wanted then—I wanted peace...peace and tranquility.

But it didn't last long.

I almost had a heart attack when I turned the corner on the way to my motel and saw a tall man in a suit emerge from the shadows. I nearly took off running, but then I recognized who it was, and I brought my hand to my heart, trying to recover from the fright.

"Dammit, Steve!" I didn't even feel bad for cursing. What the hell was he doing there?

"Noah," he said with a grimace. He grabbed my biceps and

walked me forcefully toward the door to my room. "Get your things, please."

I let him guide me, angry, and we passed the lobby and receptionist, who must have thought the whole thing was strange as I did. I got over the stupor and jerked away to face him.

"What the hell, Steve?" Only then did I realize how pissed off I was. "What are you doing here?"

"Nicholas told me to pick you up. This place is dangerous." Steve's response was par for the course. He was practical, a man of few words. Lord Leister commanded, and his lackeys obeyed. Thank God I wasn't one of them!

"I'm not going anywhere," I said, walking past him and opening my door.

What was I thinking? That I'd just leave Steve there, shut the door in his face? It wasn't his fault his boss was an idiot.

"Noah, forget Nicholas. This is about you. You shouldn't be walking around New York alone, especially not here. This is a rough area. Just let me take you somewhere safe."

This was ridiculous.

"How did you even find me?" I shouted, turning around and bringing my hands to my head.

The window by the bed opened onto a back street lined with fire escapes. You could see the trash cans and people smoking on the corner. I admit it: it was no Shangri-la; I'd already considered blowing the rest of the money I had saved on a somewhat-nicer room elsewhere; but someone forcing me to leave, especially Nicholas, really pissed me off. He had no right to play my protector anymore, so what was this about?

"What exactly did Nicholas tell you?" I asked, turning back around.

"He told me to get you out of this dump and take you to a decent hotel."

Take me… So he was giving orders to Steve but didn't have the balls to look at me. Well, to hell with that.

"I want to talk to him," I said, crossing my arms.

Steve's expression was doubtful. "He's got plans after work today, he has a dinner reservation…"

My rational self wanted to punish me for being so silly. *What did you think, stupid, that he had sworn off sex?*

"What time?" I asked, trying to control the tremors in my voice.

"In half an hour."

"Then call his cell. He won't answer me."

Steve held my stare for a moment and nodded. But before doing so, he picked up my suitcase and took it outside, to where he'd parked his car. He opened the passenger door to let me in, got in on the driver's side, and called Nick.

"Nicholas, Noah wants to talk to you," he said when Nick responded.

"I don't want to talk to her," he said after a second.

I turned off the Bluetooth and grabbed Steve's phone, putting it to my ear.

"You can't say my name anymore?" I scolded him, unable to hold back.

"I don't do it unless it's strictly necessary," he replied.

I knew he could hang up at any moment, so I tried to calm down. It didn't work. "You can't utter my name, but you send Steve to put me up in some fancy hotel… Explain that to me, Nicholas, because honestly, it's all very confusing."

My words must have affected him, because he sighed into the phone.

"Greg called me; he told me he was worried about the place you'd decided to stay for the next few days," he said reluctantly.

Fucking Greg Tavish! Couldn't he mind his own business? He wasn't my father.

"So you did it for Greg, then?" I asked. The disappointment in my voice was obvious.

"Noah, drop it," he said, and his voice changed, as if he were suddenly on the edge of fury. "I've made a reservation for you at the Arlo. You want it? Great! If not, I really don't fucking care."

I didn't have time to speak again before he hung up.

Steve looked at me expectantly, wanting to know my decision. But there was no way I was just doing as Nick said. He'd kissed me, and then he'd run off without saying a word. And all of a sudden, he wanted to buy me off with a hotel room...and there was nothing I could do about it? He could fake it as much as he wanted, he could tell me he didn't care what I did...but I knew him. This was Nick, and that was all bluster.

Just then, I made a risky decision.

"Take me to his place."

Steve didn't seem to care for the idea, but I told him it was that or I wouldn't get out of the car. I felt bad for putting him in an uncomfortable spot, but I didn't give in one bit. If he wanted me out of that hotel, this was his only option.

I looked out the window on the way. I didn't like to admit it, but Steve gave me a sense of security. Being alone in New York without anyone to share the experience with was depressing and a little scary.

"We're almost there," Steve said.

I was getting nervous, and the feeling worsened when we reached an impressive building, soaring, that overlooked the Upper East Side. The river was to the right, to the left the trees of Central Park. We'd driven long enough that I assumed we were on the other end of the park from my motel.

I started toying with my hair. What was I going to say to him? I wasn't nervous about talking, really; I was nervous to know what his life was like now, in that environment, what it meant for Nicholas Leister to be living alone in an apartment in the heart of New York: a lawyer, a businessman through and through… I didn't know that side of him; the Nick I knew had been the party guy, the Nick who liked to hold me, the one who felt me up in the dark, who risked his neck in drag races and made money in underground fights…the Nick who was in love with me, adored me, would die if more than twenty-four hours passed without him hearing from me, talking to me, seeing me.

Where was that Nick now?

Steve parked in the underground lot of that tower, and I started to break down.

"Is he home?" I asked, getting out and following him to the elevator.

"No."

I took a deep breath and watched Steve punch in a code. Good God. The building had sixty-two floors. And we were going to the very top.

The elevator felt supersonic, and I jumped when the door dinged, breaking the silence between us.

The doors opened directly into a large vestibule with a huge mirror where I could see my reflection. I barely recognized myself: I looked terrified, and I tried to change my expression to a more self-assured one.

I wished I had on something different from that jean skirt, those pink Converse, and that plain white T-shirt. I looked like a fifteen-year-old child.

Before following Steve, I pulled out my hair band and let my hair fall loose over my back. That would help, right?

I followed Steve inside. Man… This was nothing like his apartment in Los Angeles. This was…a whole different league. I knew he'd inherited a fortune from his grandfather, and I knew money had never been a problem for him, but still… I could never have imagined all this.

It was open concept, with scattered columns to mark off the spaces. The kitchen was to the right, and the sofas in the center were turned toward the floor-to-ceiling windows that showed the city in all its splendor. The floor was gleaming wood, with the odd beige rug that looked soft enough to sleep on. In one corner was a glass bar next to a dark marble staircase.

So this was where Nicholas lived now? This was his? All his?

Steve grunted and looked at me. "Are you sure you want to do this, Noah? He's not going to like it one bit."

"Please, Steve," I said, almost begging him. "Let me do it my way… I just…I just need the chance to talk to him."

Steve looked at me the way you'd look at a child who'd just found out Santa Claus doesn't exist: with pity.

He nodded and told me to let him know if I needed anything. Then he left. I climbed the stairs. I felt tired. I opened the first door I found: it was a bedroom. Maybe Nick's, maybe the guest bedroom. Either way, I lay down in bed and looked at the ceiling.

I'd wait for him… I'd wait for him until he came back, and when he did, I'd do absolutely everything to make him believe in me again, in us, in forgiveness, in love.

13

Nick

I GOT INTO MY CAR AND DROVE OUT OF THE OFFICE PARKING deck, stepping on the accelerator until it almost hit the floor. I should have canceled dinner; I should have left; I should have said all those things I was dying to say, all the things I still had inside that I knew would have to come out one day.

I squeezed the bridge of my nose, trying to calm down. I couldn't show up at dinner like this. It wouldn't be right... It wouldn't be fair.

I needed to get Noah out of my head. She wouldn't turn down the offer of a hotel; she wasn't an idiot, she knew better than to stay in a bad neighborhood, and if she refused to pay attention to me, then it wasn't my problem. A voice inside shouted, *Liar!* loud and clear, but I ignored it, crossing the city and reaching the *it* restaurant that month, hoping the night would go by pleasantly.

When I tossed the keys to the valet, I saw Sophia by the door. Her dress was fancy and attractive, her high heels made her look tall, and her dark hair shined in a cascade that fell down her back.

"Hey," I said, forcing a warm smile.

Her white teeth glimmered when I wrapped an arm around

her waist and bent down to kiss her on the cheek. She smelled like raspberry and lemon...she always chose fruity scents. I liked that.

"I didn't think you'd come," she confessed as I guided her into the restaurant, my hand on the small of her back. I tried to be discreet. It was a bad time, and the last thing I needed was some journalist trying to snap a photo of us.

"Something came up, sorry," I said, then gave the host my name. He hurried to take us to the table I'd reserved a month before.

The place was pleasant, warm. The soft lighting helped. A pianist was playing in the corner. That relaxed me, for some weird reason... I took a deep breath and tried to enjoy just sitting across from the woman who had supported me ever since the breakup with Noah, staying by my side, becoming a true friend.

"You look nice," I said, knowing that would make her smile. One of the things that made her different was that with her, everything was clear-cut. At least for me.

Sophia smiled timidly and picked up the menu. The server came over. We each chose different wines. She went for white wine; I was a red man, concretely a fan of good Bordeaux from '82. I remembered Noah for a moment. She didn't know a thing about wine or food or, really, anything. Her simplicity had captivated me; I'd imagined I would be the one to teach her everything, to give the world to her...

I cleared my throat and came back to reality.

Was she at the hotel already? In the shower? Crying? Sleeping? Eating? Missing me?

Stop! I told myself, focusing on my beautiful companion.

I hadn't even intended for things with Sophia to go anywhere. After Noah, I became incapable of even carrying on a coherent conversation. Everything bothered me; I was irate, pissed at the world, wounded, and I didn't want to be around anyone.

I'd shut myself up in my apartment, wallowing in self-pity. The phone would ring, and I'd ignore it. My emails piled up, and I didn't even read them. I turned self-destructive. I'd drink till I passed out on the bed, break furniture, hit things...twice I wounded my hand. I got into a bar fight. Fortunately, word didn't get out. My mind would wander; I'd imagine things. I was trapped in a loop of hatred, sorrow, and disappointment. No one, not even Lion, could help me get a grip. My father came, yelled at me, tried to talk to me calmly, yelled at me again, and then disappeared. I didn't want to listen to anyone. I didn't care... In those moments, I felt an unbearable pain in my chest. I felt betrayed. Then, one day, Sophia showed up at my apartment.

She'd always been a sensible girl. Her head was screwed on straight. She reamed me out—no point in lying about it—not because I mattered to her or she was worried about me, but because her job depended on mine, and I barely showed my face around the office. If I was so fucked up, she told me, I should take off to New York. She threw one thing in my face after another, told me my attitude was immature and irrational, and in the end, I could only think of one way to shut her up.

I grabbed her around the waist and rammed her into the wall. We stared at each other. I was destroyed, she was confused, and I just did what I wanted with her, what my body needed, what my sick mind wanted to do to get revenge on Noah.

We fucked all night, without stopping, without resting, without remorse, and best of all, when we were done, Sophia got up, dressed, and left like nothing had happened.

The next day, I went to work. She talked with me normally, as if we were the same old coworkers who tolerated each other while they shared the same office. I acted like her, like nothing had changed, but then one day, she got up, shut the office door, came over, sat in my lap, and convinced me to do it all again.

Let's get one thing straight: We both knew this was going nowhere. Sophia was well aware that I was a wreck after Noah, and all she needed was a warm body now and again. Whenever we talked, she accepted my conditions without putting up a fight: sex was sex, and we were both free to do as we pleased.

She saw me with other girls. She was free to go with other guys if she wanted. But we never talked about it. She knew what I was like and what I did, and I didn't care who she went out with, slept with, or met for coffee. But…I treated her with the respect she deserved. She was my friend, the one friend who'd managed to help me, to get me to pull myself out of bed and focus on the job.

Soon after all that, I took the job in New York. Then my grandfather had died, and the rest was history.

Now we were having dinner in a nice restaurant—she was in town for business at the office I no longer worked at, but she was leaving the next day. She had told me she needed to talk to me, but all I could think about was the fact that Noah was in town, and I was dying to find her and make love with her the way only I could, to remind her of who she'd betrayed and what she'd lost.

I ran my hand across my forehead and focused on Sophia.

"I need to ask you a favor," she said after a bit of small talk, most of it work gossip. Sophia seemed to never rest. Her ambition was limitless, and her father was about to run for governor of California. Everyone was after her; everyone wanted to get to know her. It didn't matter to me, but when she started talking, I forced myself to pay attention. "I need us to formalize things," she said.

I didn't understand what she was saying.

"I mean publicly," she explained, bringing her glass to her lips. "My father wants us to look stable, like a united front. He keeps introducing me to guys, his friends' sons, and all they want is to be with me because I'm Senator Riston Aiken's daughter. It's gross, and I can't stand it."

"Wait, wait, wait," I said, trying to grasp her words. "Are you telling me you want the press to get wind that we're together? Like an official, regular couple?"

She nodded and speared a ravioli with her fork. "Obviously you can keep doing whatever you're doing...as long as it's discreet. But in public, I need a proper boyfriend. Can you do that for me?"

At any other time, I would have laughed in her face, but that day, after talking to Noah, after kissing her at Jenna's wedding, feeling the past smack me across the face again...well, what Sophia was offering didn't sound like such a bad idea.

I heard a little voice in my head telling me what the consequences would be. If I did it, if I admitted I was *going out* with her, if the press declared us boyfriend and girlfriend, Noah would suffer... Agreeing meant I was an asshole, a big one. But if I did it, maybe she'd finally understand that we needed to move on.

I got home at one in the morning. Sophia asked me if I wanted to sleep at her hotel, but I said no thanks: I wasn't in the mood.

A little later, I was standing in my apartment. The soft light made it feel cozy. I dropped the keys on the kitchen table and went to pour myself a drink.

The apartment had been the property of a friend of my dad. When he heard I was moving to New York, he offered it to me at a price I couldn't refuse. I had wanted to start from zero, in a place I could call my own, and not accept my father's offer of his apartment in Brooklyn (he had office space in Manhattan, too). I didn't want to remember what I'd experienced in that city when I was a boy.

The discovery that my father had been cheating on my mother throughout almost their entire marriage made my hatred for her transform into something different. I started to understand why everything had gone to hell, and I was angry at him for making me feel bad for her. I still hated her, that hadn't changed, but the way things had turned out with Noah made me ask myself whether that hatred was justified.

Cheating… Could I blame my mother for losing her mind when I'd lost mine for the exact same reason?

I'd never forgive her for abandoning me, there just was no justification for that, but who was I to judge what happened between a husband and wife after such a deception? I thought of Noah again… It was so hard to watch the future you'd created with someone, all those images of the things you thought you'd do together, go up in smoke in front of your nose.

I'd imagined us leading a full life together. I knew it wouldn't be easy; I wasn't so stupid that I couldn't see there were things in our relationship that weren't ideal, but the problems had always come from outside… I would have put my hand on the Bible and sworn Noah would never go behind my back with anyone; the very idea of it was crazy…

But now, here we were.

I finished my drink and went to my room.

I didn't bother to turn on the lights. I just took off my shirt and tossed it on the floor. The maid would pick it up tomorrow.

Facing the bed, about to turn on a light, I froze when I saw someone in my sheets.

My heart was pounding so hard, it almost hurt, and I could hear a ringing in my ears. I started wheezing; my whole body reacted to the sight of Noah sleeping there. It was as though the past had come back: there she was, waiting for me, the soft skin of her legs wrapped around a pillow, her arms on top of the sheets, her hair spread around the mattress.

I closed my eyes and waited. I could almost feel myself lying next to her, pushing the white sheets off her body, letting my fingers stroke her skin... Slowly, she'd turn toward me, open her eyes, half asleep, smiling, happy to see me, glowing the way she always did when I touched her. *I was waiting for you*, she'd say, and I'd swell with all that love I never thought I'd feel. I'd get on top of her, push her blond hair carefully aside, press my lips to hers, so soft, a little swollen in sleep, longing to touch mine. My arm would descend her back, slide into the hollow at the base of her spine, lifting her and squeezing her against me. I'd kiss her neck, her ear, breathe in the scent of her skin, which smelled not of fruit or honey or any costly perfume, but of Noah...of her and nothing else.

I opened my eyes, forcing myself to return to reality. I almost wanted it to be a mirage, her lying in my bed, between my sheets. I couldn't let myself go, even if my hands were twitching with the desire to touch her. I wouldn't give in. I had no idea what she was doing there, but rage stifled any other sensation, and I stomped out of the room.

14

Noah

I HEARD A NOISE, AND MY EYES OPENED. I DIDN'T KNOW WHERE I was at first, but the scent that enveloped me was calming. I was home. I was with Nick.

But that didn't make any sense, I soon realized...not anymore. I sat up in that unfamiliar bed, and the faint light coming through the cracked door was enough for me to get a sense of my surroundings. Stomach quaking, I got out of bed and walked down to the living room. The lights were off apart from the dim glow on the stairs, to keep you from falling if you got up in the middle of the night for a glass of water. I kept walking till I found him. He was sitting on the sofa in front of a glass table with a half-empty bottle, his elbows on his knees, his head in his hands. It must have been hard to find me in his bed, as if it were my apartment and I had a right to sleep there while I was waiting for him to come home. I felt like an intruder.

I guess I made a sound, or maybe he just sensed me, because he turned his head slowly toward me. His eyes were glassy, his jaw tense, and I wanted to take off in the opposite direction. I knew him; I knew him well enough to recognize beneath all that hatred that was consuming him was the love he felt for me or had felt before. It was still there in his heart, just as it was in mine, waiting for the right moment for us to love each other again.

"What are you doing here, Noah?" he asked, and I almost collapsed when I heard the pain in his voice.

"I'm here for you," I responded, shrugging slightly. My voice was like an echo of his. He leaned back, closed his eyes, and sighed.

"You need to go… You need to get out of my life." He still hadn't looked at me.

He bent over to serve himself another glass, but I didn't want him like that, drunk; I needed him lucid, lucid for me. I needed him to understand what I had to say to him.

I closed the space between us, grabbed the bottle, grazing his fingers slightly, and put it back down on the table, but too far for him to reach.

He looked up and saw me standing between his legs. His eyes were red, but it wasn't just the liquor.

I reached out to stroke his hair. God! I needed to wipe that pained expression off his face, that pain that was my fault. But his hand caught my wrist before I could. I didn't care because at least I was touching him, and for me, that was enough. The spark, that spark that always flared up between us, that feeling of fire, of pure, carnal desire, the same desire we had felt from the first moment I set foot into the kitchen of his old home and saw him looking through the refrigerator…it was back. Right from that moment, I knew there was a part of myself that was no longer mine.

He hesitated for a few eternal seconds, then pulled me close. I struck his chest, and he reached around me and sat me down until I was straddling his lap, both my knees on the sofa, hugging his thighs. I wrapped my hands around his neck; he gripped me around the waist. Our eyes met in the shadows. I was scared to keep going. I stopped; so did he. It was as if we were both about to plunge over a precipice. Maybe we'd get lucky and land in the water, or maybe we'd hit the rocky shore. And we'd only know if we jumped.

He looked at me and kissed me. It was rough. I didn't know how to take it. My lips opened to let in his tongue, which filled my mouth and made me tremble. We were kissing as if our lives depended on it. While I desperately held on to the back of his head, he caressed my thighs, my knees, my butt, then squeezed, and our bodies ground against each other, bringing us pleasure. It had been too long…too long feeling nothing, nothing at all. I had started to think my body was dead, my libido gone after our breakup. How wrong I was! One touch, light as a feather, from his hands was enough to make me lose all composure.

I pulled away to breathe, but he kept kissing my face. His chest was exposed; my hands attacked it. The touch of my fingernails made his abdominals flex.

He grunted and pushed me away so he could look at me. "What do you want from me, Noah?"

Sweat pearled on his torso. We were tense, thinking of how our worlds were about to change, again, because of what we were doing…

"Just…make me forget…" I asked him, on the verge of tears. "For a few minutes…just pretend you've forgiven me."

His chest was rising and falling, his breathing accelerated. But the tension in his hands vanished. I ran my fingers through his hair, forcing him to look at me and not past me. I came in to kiss him. The taste of him…it was like nothing else. Kissing him was what I had missed most; I was addicted to his kisses, I needed more, I needed to feel those lips all over, I needed him so badly, it hurt.

"I will…" he said, sitting up into me. Our noses touched. "For a few minutes, I'll forget what you did… But tomorrow, you're leaving; you'll get out of my life and leave me in peace."

My heart stopped, but I ignored the end of his sentence. He was going to forget, right…? He'd said that. That was enough. The rest I'd deal with tomorrow.

I nodded, knowing I wasn't being honest, but I couldn't turn down the chance to be with him; after just half an hour, he'd made me feel alive again, and there was no way I would give that up.

He grabbed me around the thighs, picked me up off the sofa, and started carrying me. I hugged him and kissed him again. He smelled and tasted so good. Like himself, like my Nick, the person I loved madly, desperately.

He took me to his room and dropped me almost reverently on the mattress, as if he were afraid I would disappear. Then he stood there, observing me. I propped myself on my elbows to look back at him. How could he be so perfect? His hair was disordered, his lips swollen from kissing me, his stubble sexy. It had scratched me; I didn't care; I wanted to feel it all over my body. I was trembling, trembling from desire, pure, carnal, for him.

"We're not fucking," he said, taking off his belt and dropping it on the floor. The surprise on my face must have been obvious, the disappointment, too, because he smiled, not warmly, the way he usually did with me, not with lust or love, but as though teaching a lesson to a little girl whose naivety he found amusing. "We can do other stuff, though."

He took his place between my legs, pushing my stomach until I lay flat. He bent over me, pulled my skirt down, and tossed it aside. His knee separated my legs while he pulled my shirt over my head.

He stopped to look at me, to contemplate my breasts in their pink lace bra, nothing fancy, but it was comfortable, or at least that was what I'd thought when I threw it on to go out and see the city. He reached around my ribs, pulling me up softly and kissing my belly button.

"You've lost weight," he whispered, but I could barely even hear him.

His lips were now on the seam of my panties while his hands were stroking my legs. He was burning with desire. He got out of bed, kneeled, and pulled off my underwear.

I was nervous. Not shy, exactly, but it had been so long since Nick had touched me. I turned, edgy, and he must have noticed because even if his breathing revealed that he was dying to go on, he gave me a gentle look, as though to ease my mind. For a second, he was Nick...the Nick from before, the one who was truly present when we looked at each other. I closed my eyes to keep from forgetting that, and I held on to that vision until I was more relaxed.

"Nick..."

"Shhh."

His lips traveled up my thighs, first kissing, then biting, then licking. I twisted and turned, but his hand on my stomach immobilized me.

"Please..." I almost begged him, no longer ashamed.

He ignored me, kissing me all over, everywhere except for the place I needed him most. "What do you want, Noah? Tell me, I want to hear you say it."

I shook my head. Why should I have to?

Now his mouth was hovering over my body, not even touching me. I was flustered.

"Say it, Noah. Say what you want, and you can have it."

But I couldn't. Not aloud, at least. And he knew that. Was this his way of punishing me? I opened my eyes and saw him there waiting.

"Kiss me," I whispered.

He climbed on top of me. His lips touched mine. He kissed me briefly, and I moaned with frustration. Then I felt his hips pressing into mine, and for a few seconds, I was relieved. But just for a few seconds. Then he rose up on his hands.

"This isn't like it was before, Noah." He took hold of my chin. "You're not the inexperienced, sweet little girl who needs to be carefully taught what to do."

I could sense in him the contained rage begging to break out. I didn't like it, and I sat up until I could bring our lips together again. I pulled him close. I wanted to feel him as a part of me. I wrapped my legs around his waist and heard him slowly expelling air. Then, suddenly, I wanted it fast. I didn't want there to be time for reproaches.

When I slid my hand down to his pants, I knew he'd lost the battle. I'd forgotten what it meant to have him in my arms, what it was to feel him lose control. I wanted to feel that connection again, feel his halting breath, feel us moving together, giving each other pleasure—no games, just togetherness, letting everything flow.

We rolled over, and I got on top of him. I felt insecure that way, but I wasn't going to let him know that. Hands trembling, I tried to pull down his jeans and finally accomplished it with his help. Seconds later, he was naked, and all I had on was my bra. He trapped me again in his arms.

"I told you, we're not going to fuck," he said, trapping my hands behind my head.

"Jesus, Nicholas..." I said, frustrated. I needed to be touched. I needed that contact more than anything in the world.

Without warning, one of his fingers slipped inside me. I grimaced. To my surprise, and his, he was hurting me.

"You haven't...?"

I blushed with embarrassment... What was I going to say? That after what had happened, I hadn't let anyone even look at me more than once? That my sexual appetite had vanished like water in the desert? That the last time we'd done it in his apartment, when I'd drawn on his skin, had been the last time I'd felt anything?

No way. I wasn't that pathetic. But my body gave me away.

Something in his expression changed. Relief, maybe, I don't know, but he stopped delaying, got on his knees, brought his face into my crotch, and started tracing out circles with his tongue. I moaned. That was all he needed to keep going.

He seemed as hungry as I was. His finger went inside me again, this time more carefully, and instead of pain, I felt relief. The pressure became stronger, his mouth went on working, and his other hand crept under my bra and squeezed my breast.

It was all too much, too much time without him, too many emotions repressed, too much stimulation. I arched my back and shouted. I couldn't control myself. My orgasm was like an explosion that wiped away everything. I was in heaven, but I was burning with the fires of hell.

Nicholas didn't stop until it hurt. Then he pulled away to let me recover. I did, but slowly. I needed more; he did, too; I could tell when I saw him start touching himself with his right hand, staring at me with a hard expression, as if he wanted to give in but couldn't.

We weren't going to do it that night, but that didn't mean I was ready to stop. I sat up and pulled him down until he was sitting. He couldn't control his breathing. That was fine. I would be taking the reins this time.

I came around and kneeled between his legs, pinning him with my stare.

"What are you doing?" he asked hoarsely. There was no going back. We were both playing the game of passion, love and hate at the same time, and we couldn't just step away.

Instead of answering, I did the thing I had never done before.

I had no idea what I was doing, but he seemed to like it. And when I looked up at him without stopping, it drove him wild. Soon his hand was in my hair, and he was moving rhythmically.

"Fuck..."

He didn't let me finish. He pushed me away, and I lay beside him in bed. He rubbed himself against me, then masturbated, and I did the same. His eyes were burning, and as a second orgasm came on strong, I started to see stars.

We came at the same time, staring into each other's eyes. We'd barely touched each other. All we'd needed was to stare and ask each other, ask ourselves, how we'd gotten here.

I fell asleep in his bed, hugging a pillow instead of him. When we'd finished, he had gone into the bathroom, showered, and walked out.

I guessed my grace period was over. Either way, I didn't have the energy to deal with it. My feelings were raw, and I just wanted to close my eyes and not think about what had happened, because if I did, I'd realize there was a kind of cold veil over everything we had done. It wasn't love; it was relief, something carnal while our feelings and emotions were hidden in a corner our souls couldn't reach. We had touched, but it had only been the most primitive parts of ourselves.

I wished Nicholas would hold me, squeeze me in his arms, and tell me everything would be okay. Instead, he left, and I didn't have the strength to follow.

I let sleep and exhaustion take me away. I closed my eyes, and everything disappeared.

15

Nick

As soon as I walked out of the room, I regretted it. I had given in, had succumbed to temptation, had eaten the forbidden fruit again, and I was sure the consequences would be terrible.

I don't know if it's possible for your heart to physically hurt, but I think mine did, so badly that I had to get away from her. I shut myself up in my home office, pretending with all my might that Noah wasn't in my bed just then, trying to forget her naked body, her hands caressing me, her mouth giving me pleasure...she had done it so well, for a moment I was even angry.

Had she done it with someone else?

Just the thought of it drove me insane. In bed, she'd seemed the same as always. But it didn't matter. The same pure Noah I used to know had screwed another guy. Who was to say she hadn't kept going once we were apart?

The thought of another guy's arms around Noah made me need to leave...forget the feeling of her there under me, how soft her skin was, how sweet her kisses were.

Her fragrance was still pursuing me, even after my shower. My apartment suddenly felt small, and my body was drawn to go back to that room and finish what I'd left undone.

I put on a pair of shorts, a white Nike T-shirt, and my running shoes and headed off for Central Park. It was only five a.m., but there were already people out jogging and working out. I didn't dawdle; I didn't even warm up. I just ran and ran, wishing with all my heart that I'd get home and find Noah already gone. That she'd keep her promise and disappear from my life.

Did I really want that, though? Yes. That was one thing I knew for sure. Being with her hurt too much, and I couldn't imagine ever having the strength to forgive her. I just wasn't capable of it.

I got home two hours later, and everything was exactly the same as when I left. I went to my room, and she was still there between my sheets.

She was sleeping facedown, the sheet covering her lower body, and her bare back was shouting at me to rub it until she woke. I'd kiss her, make slow love to her, and then we'd go to a fancy café for breakfast. I'd buy her chocolate, show her all my favorite secret corners, and then, when she was tired of being a tourist, we'd come back, and I'd sink once more between her legs and make her shout my name until she was breathless.

I slapped my face to bring myself back to reality: None of that was going to happen. All that was over; it had ended the night I'd found out she'd been with another man.

I went to the bathroom and took a cold shower. When I came out, dressed in a pair of gray pajama pants, I found her sitting there, leaning back against the headboard, holding the sheet tight in her hands, trying to cover up every inch of her nakedness. She looked at me hesitantly, probably with no idea what she should do. I bent down to pick up her shirt off the floor and tossed it to her.

"Get dressed," I ordered her, trying to control myself, trying to stay calm.

She wasn't sure whether to obey. When I looked at her, with her hair still uncombed and those lips I wanted to nibble, I had to force myself to turn around and walk out. In the kitchen, I grabbed my phone and called Steve. He'd moved to the city; his place wasn't too far from mine. My father had said he now worked for me and me alone, and I was grateful to have someone I could trust watching my back.

"I need you to get her out of here," I said. I sounded desperate, but I couldn't help it.

Steve sighed, but I knew he'd do as I said. He owed it to me. He should never have brought her to my apartment.

I hung up and made coffee. A minute later, she was standing there in my kitchen. She wasn't dressed. Not in her clothes, at least. She was wearing my white button-down, which hung to her knees. I guessed she'd showered because her hair was slicked down and her face looked clean and fresh, without a trace of our kisses from the night before.

"I called Steve to come pick you up," I told her, pouring my coffee. I was trying to stay calm, as if what I was doing were predictable, as if throwing out the person I had been in love with were the most normal thing in the world.

"I don't want to go," she whispered. I looked at her, saw the way our breakup had changed her. She was so thin... She'd lost so much weight, I was afraid I'd break her the night before. She wasn't the Noah I remembered, that brave girl always ready to face off with me, the one who'd made my life so interesting.

Our fights had always been brutal, but now...she was like a frightened doe. And that only made me angrier.

"What are you after, Noah?" I asked, my voice ice-cold. I didn't want to lose it and unleash all the fury I knew was still buried inside me. But I needed her to understand that nothing was going to change how I felt. "There's nothing you can say or do that can erase what happened. Last night was nice, but I can get the same thing from anyone, and I'm not interested in playing games with you."

"You're still in love with me," she said and stepped forward. She was going to try to touch me, and I jerked away, feeling disgusted at myself, disgusted because I'd let things go so far the night before. I didn't want to give her false hope. That hadn't been my intention.

"I was in love with you," I corrected her. "I *was*, Noah, in the past. You cheated on me, and I know there may be people who can forgive that, but you know me perfectly, and I'm not one of them."

"And I am?" she replied, wrapping her arms around herself. "You can't pretend that what happened a few hours ago didn't affect you as much as me... I can see it in your eyes, Nicholas. I saw it last night, and I saw it on the day of Jenna's wedding. You still have feelings for me, you still—"

"What do you want me to say, Noah?" I shouted. But in reality, I wasn't furious at her, I was furious at myself, furious because I hadn't managed to control myself, furious because I'd fallen not once but twice, furious because, however hard I tried, I couldn't hide what I felt for her. "You obviously know how to play this game way better than I do."

Noah blinked without comprehending. "I'm not playing, I just want..."

She didn't finish the phrase. She didn't need to. I knew perfectly what it was she wanted.

"You should go," I said a few seconds later. I picked up my cup and turned around to drop it in the sink. It gave me an excuse not to look her in the eye.

"How can you do this?" she asked, and then I had to face her. A flash of anger crossed her honey-colored eyes. "Tell me how you can just go on with your life! Because I can't!"

That was ridiculous. I didn't have a life anymore; it was just work, endless work, and there was no room for love. I was happy like that, without any sentimental burdens. Love was bullshit. I'd given everything for love, and look where it'd got me.

I knew if I wanted to get rid of her, I had to make her realize nothing was going to change. If I wanted to walk out that door and not get hurt again, I had to be hard, I had to stick my fingers straight into the wound.

I looked at her again, and something I hadn't noticed before captured my attention: she was wearing the silver necklace I'd given her for her eighteenth birthday.

I walked over, reached around her neck, and found the clasp. Noah was too lost to understand what I'd done until I stepped back with her pendant, stuffing it into my back pocket.

"Give it back," she said, incredulous, not really sure what had happened.

"You have to stop clinging to something that doesn't exist, dammit."

"Give me my necklace, Nicholas," she said through clenched teeth.

"Why?" I asked, loud enough that she flinched. "Why the hell are you still wearing it? Are you trying to make me remember something? You think you're going to make my sensitivity get the best of me? Well, you can forget that!"

She blinked, surprised by my words, then shoved me, hard. "You want to know why I wear it?!" she screamed. "It reminds me of you. That's it. You don't like to hear that?! Well, it's the fucking truth, you hear me?! I miss you!"

No, I didn't want to hear the truth. Not that truth, anyway. I didn't want to feel guilty. I didn't want to admit that I missed her, too… Damn it, I didn't want to admit that it hurt me as much as it did her to take something away from her that I'd given her so

I'd always be with her. I'd done that because I wanted her to know how much I loved her.

I needed to end this. Now.

"I'm with someone," I said, staring her down.

Noah froze, the ire drained from her face, and slowly, she absorbed what I'd said. She seemed lost, but finally she found the words. "What...what do you mean?"

I closed my eyes and wiped my face with my hand, fed up. Did I have to do this? Was it necessary? Was it necessary for us to hurt each other even more?

Yes, it was.

"I'm in a relationship, Noah. With Sophia."

Those words seemed to strike her in the chest with the force of a bullet. Her eyes opened wide when she heard that name, as if she felt betrayed, and now, dejection again gave way to wrath.

I wanted to pull her close just then, to tell her it had been a lie, but I couldn't; I had to finish this, and faster was better, without leaving room for doubt.

She looked at the ground between us. Outside, the sun was coming up, the first rays of sunlight were flooding through the windows, taking away the darkness of our lies, the shadows of what we'd done a few hours before. I'd said it. There was no turning back. When she finally looked up again, I knew I had destroyed her.

"It was her all along, wasn't it?" Her voice cracked. My heart, too. I couldn't believe how quickly she'd just accepted that lie. Had I done such a bad job of showing her how much I loved her? Was it so easy to believe that, so hard to accept that she was the only one who was ever real for me, her and her alone?

I clenched my fists.

"Yes," I said, loud and clear. "I fell in love with Sophie as soon as I met her, the very first time I laid eyes on her. She's pretty, smart, we like the same things, we have the same ambitions. And I'm sorry to say this, Noah, but with her, everything's easy. There's no drama, no problems. Sophia's a woman, not a little girl."

The sarcasm in my voice couldn't have been clearer. No one could have missed it. Except, I guess, for Noah. She blinked, wiped her eyes, tried to hold back the tears.

"All this time..." she responded, stepping forward to shove me again. She missed. It was a weak attempt. Looking back now, I think it was at that moment that we were finally finished: we were both broken, devastated...and the one way of putting ourselves together again was off the table.

"It's best if you go," I said with the little strength I had remaining.

She didn't even look at me. She just walked past me and disappeared into my room.

Later, I'd find out Steve had dropped her at a hotel.

Part Two

GETTING OVER IT... OR SOMETHING

16

Noah

You could say I'd been stupid, a fool...or that what little self-esteem I still had wasn't enough for me to keep going. Either way, Nick's words cut me deep. I believed them. Let's leave it at that.

After my stay in New York, where I didn't budge from my room until it was time to go to the airport, I went back to my apartment, feeling like the most miserable idiot on the face of the earth.

Nick and Sophia... Sophia and Nick... God, it fucking hurt so badly just thinking about it, especially knowing they'd lied to me for so long. But I wasn't an idiot. Nicholas had loved me; there was no doubting that. The best actor in the world couldn't have faked the way he felt. Still, it was easy to imagine him falling for her.

I was a wreck when I reached Los Angeles, but I was no longer scared. I'd gone almost a year without seeing Nick. Then the wedding came, and I'd learned to hope, had made myself believe that if we saw each other again, he wouldn't be able to keep on ignoring what he felt for me. I'd tried to grab hold of him, had gotten burned, and now realized there was nothing left to hold on to.

Back in my apartment, I noticed I had a missed call from Mom. She probably wanted to know if I'd made it home all right, and even though I knew she wouldn't ask, I imagined she wanted to make sure I wasn't a disaster after seeing Nick again.

It hadn't been easy to repair my relationship with my mother. In the months after the breakup, I didn't only have to admit Nick was gone and had left me, I also had to deal with a bad family situation. That night, the night of the anniversary of Leister Enterprises, I learned things that changed my perspective, especially as far as my mom went—things that made me hate everything about her.

Talking to her again was the hardest thing. At first, I didn't want to look at her; I refused to even let her into my apartment. If it weren't for Jenna's support, I don't know how I'd have emerged from the bottomless pit I'd fallen into. A few months after Nick left for New York, I decided to pick up the phone, and after lots and lots of talking, my mom told me her side of the story. She said she hadn't meant to start a relationship with William. She was working in a hotel at the time. I was six, and things with Dad were falling apart. One day they asked her to take room service up to a guest. It wasn't her job, but one of the waitresses was sick, and she had to fill in. The guest turned out to be William—William Leister, but thirteen years younger than now, rich, handsome, attractive, with the whole world in his hands. I'd seen Nick, so I could imagine what my mother must have seen in William back then. She had been just twenty-four at the time, and she'd never been with a man apart from my dad. She'd gotten pregnant when she was young, hadn't been able to enjoy her youth, and had become responsible as soon as she'd found out she was going to have a child. When William started flirting with her, her world turned upside down. No one had ever treated her like that, telling her all those sweet nothings, giving her flowers… My father was an asshole; he always had been, even before he started losing his shit.

So they had an affair, and William didn't even learn of my father's existence until six years later. William had thought he'd been the only one who was cheating. They didn't see each other often, just when he went to Canada, and when they met, it was basically… Well, you can imagine.

When she got the call telling her I was in the hospital, almost bleeding to death, William discovered all that my mother had hidden. The bruises, she'd covered up with makeup; plus my father never hit her in the face, or at least tried not to, because he didn't want anyone to know what was happening in our home. For the rest, my mother always told William they should do it with the lights off.

William was shocked. Even in his worst nightmares, he'd never imagined the woman who drove him wild, who had changed everything for him, the woman he'd leave everything for, was married, with a kid and an abusive husband…

At that point, everything got complicated. My mother lost custody of me, briefly, and the guilt consumed her. Worse than the abuse she'd suffered was the fact that she wasn't allowed to care for me… She ended things with William, turned her back on the world, started drinking so much, she had to go to rehab, which William paid for. After months in treatment, months when I was in an orphanage, they let her have me again.

My mother didn't want to see Will anymore. Never, she told herself, would she make that same mistake again. She swore from that moment on, she'd live for me and me alone.

"I've never forgiven myself for what happened that night, Noah," she confessed, choking on tears. "Your father had never laid a hand on you, and I…I was stupid, I was blinded by my love for Will. In those days, you and he were the only ones who could make me happy. We barely ever saw each other, and when we did, I was so happy. I felt so special…so alive. William was only going to be in town that night, and I needed to see him… I needed him like the air I breathed."

That day, I held the phone to my ear, thinking about how what my mother was saying was exactly like what I felt for Nick. I understood her, I understood the need to escape at least, and I was aware that I couldn't just condemn her forever. She had been there for me always, had made sacrifices so I could study, so I could have a better life.

I forgave her in the end. I had to. She was my mother. Our relationship wasn't the way it was before, but I went home, at least, we ate together, and I cried… I cried a lot, she hugged me, she told me she was sorry, and that she was sorry for what had happened with Nick. I told myself what I'd had with Nicholas had been real. Life might have caused problems, a lack of trust that separated us, but it had been real.

I dropped my bags on my bed and tried to touch the pendant that had been my anchor all that time, and when I remembered it wasn't there anymore, I let my hand fall with sorrow.

I had to keep going. After all, he had.

The months after that were better than I had expected. School and work distracted me. I didn't hear from Nicholas again. Not firsthand, anyway. Of course, the news that Nicholas Leister was going out with Senator Aiken's daughter made it into the papers.

Seeing them together holding hands wounded me. How could it not? But it also helped me transform my sorrow into anger, distance, coldness. I told myself that was better and that I didn't care… I was lying to myself, obviously, but it helped me get through the days and weeks. It was easier that way.

Before I knew it, Thanksgiving break had come, and after thinking it over and leaving my mother hanging the year before,

I told her I'd go to William's house, which was more than an hour away. I'd spend the time listening to music and thinking about my bills and trying to figure out how I'd pay for the book I needed for my law class. Luckily my lodging was paid for, and a new roommate soon took Briar's place, but still, I was struggling to get to the end of the month. I was working in a café on campus, but my boss had told me two days before that he would have to let me go. Someone had opened a bar two streets away, and we'd lost a lot of clientele. As the last one in, I was the first one out.

I needed to make a move, and fast.

I was planning on spending the weekend with my mother and Will, so I took a small suitcase out of the closet and stuffed it with random clothes. I wasn't planning on getting dressed up, and if I needed to, there was always my closet there. I did pack my law books. I'd have exams right after Thanksgiving, and hate it as I might, I had to study. I hated the subject; I didn't know if it was because it reminded me of Nick or if it was just that I wasn't good at memorizing laws, but it put me in the worst mood! I'd picked it because it was about copyright and intellectual property and other things I thought a writer might need, but I couldn't wait for the day I could put it all out of my head; all that information was probably on Google anyway.

I hadn't used the suitcase since I'd gone to the Hamptons, so, unsurprisingly, there were still things inside: a toothbrush I thought I had lost, some black lace panties, my waterproof eyeliner, and, to my surprise, a business card with the name *Lincoln Baxwell*. The card read: *Lawyer, Publicist, and Property Manager*.

I remembered him. He was a friend of Jenna's dad. He had been there at the wedding. Nice guy. If I remembered right, he'd given me his card in case I was ever looking for work in the field. I couldn't believe it! I'd totally forgotten he'd said that, probably because Nicholas had come over and said something nasty, forcing me to walk away.

I didn't have any idea what sort of work a nineteen-year-old student could do for him, but there was no harm in asking. I looked at my watch and saw it was too late to call, so I decided I'd do it tomorrow on my way to Will's, and if the world didn't hate me as much as it seemed, maybe I'd have a new job before I knew it.

The next morning, it was chilly, and I was glad to have the Audi with me. For a long time, I had avoided using it, much to my mother's dismay. It was a gift, she kept telling me, it was mine, and it was ridiculous to just let it sit there. And she'd been right. My old car was on its last legs, and there was no way I could buy a new one on my own. So eventually I gave in. I mean, the car was mine, and it *was* an Audi, after all.

When I was on the road and it was late enough, I decided to call Lincoln Baxwell. I was nervous. The phone rang several times, and I only heard a "hello" right before I was about to hang up.

"Hi, I was hoping to talk to Lincoln Baxwell. My name is Noah Morgan. I'm William Leister's stepdaughter," I said meekly. I didn't like using Will's name to open doors for me, but I wasn't in a position to be finicky.

"Just a second."

Baxwell picked up a few minutes later.

"Sorry about the delay. It's Noah, right?" Baxwell asked politely. He sounded friendly, just as he had at the party. I was embarrassed to say why I'd called, but I mean, he had given me his card, right?

"Hello, Mr. Baxwell. Yeah, this is Noah Morgan, we met—"

"At Jenna Tavish's wedding, I remember. You're Nicholas Leister's stepsister, right?"

"Yeah, that's me," I said with slight sarcasm.

Come on, Noah, relax.

It was time to beg, alas.

"I was calling because when we met at the wedding, I was interested in that project you had in mind, LN..." I hesitated.

"LRB," he clarified.

Shit! I could have at least gotten the name right. He must have thought I was an idiot.

"Yeah, sorry, LRB. So, basically, I'd love to take you up on that offer to work in a major company that's just about to open. I honestly haven't had any real intern experience off campus, and I'd like to try out different fields before settling on something..."

He knew what I wanted, right?

Baxter pleasantly agreed, saying, "No problem, Noah. I'll pull some strings and have my secretary call you. I have to tell you, I'm surprised you got in touch. It doesn't matter, though. I'd be happy to have you on my team; I'm sure you're a good worker. Send your transcripts to my secretary along with your class schedule and any references you might have. We're very busy, and what I need is people who will make my life easier, so if you're good with paperwork, we could have you in for a couple of hours a day without messing up your schoolwork. Sound good?"

I almost shouted with joy. It had been so easy! I couldn't believe it! I mean, I could have asked Will for a favor, but it was better this way. Especially since Baxwell was the one who had tried to recruit me, right?

I said thanks and goodbye, and almost rear-ended the car in front of me, which was stopped at a red light. My sense of relief had distracted me from the road.

I was no longer jobless!

17

Nick

There I was, looking at my computer screen, not really sure how I should feel. Everything seemed completely off-kilter.

I had an email from Anne, Maddie's social worker, telling me that they'd done all the tests and there was no further doubt about who Maddie's real father was. That fact, combined with my father's lawsuit against my mother for covering up her knowledge of his paternity for years, had resulted in the court granting him partial custody. That meant the visits that had previously gone through Anne would now be agreed upon by my parents.

I was happy when I found all this out—of course I was fucking happy. My sister was finally mine, and she was my sister, period, not my half sister, as I'd always believed. I'd always hated thinking of her father, how his presence meant she wasn't entirely mine, somehow. I'd hated having our visits cut down into a few hours; I'd hated seeing the nasty expressions on the Grasons' faces whenever I took her with me. Things would be much easier now. Or so I believed.

I sighed. Now, when it came to Maddie, I'd have to deal mainly with my father, a man who seemed to have lost any notion of how to act around kids. Not that he'd ever been known for his patience with them—just look at the way he'd treated me. Still, I was surprised by how determined he was to win her affection and how hard he tried.

As soon as he was able, my father tried to get shared custody and change her name from Madison Grason to Madison Leister. There were still details to work out there. Throughout the process, the one who had suffered most was Maddie, and that made me angry.

Her father—the guy who was supposed to be her father for more than five years—had washed his hands both of my mother and of the girl he had watched grow. The bastard didn't even want to help explain things to her. It was a delicate issue, telling her the man she thought was her father wasn't and that she had a new dad and he loved her very much. Often, in cases like this, the person who's raised the child will fight with the biological father for custody or at least for the right to continue being a part of her life. You'd think he'd have wanted to be there if she needed him. But none of that had happened, and all my sister could do was keep saying, *But I love Daddy, my real daddy*, and she couldn't understand why he didn't love her anymore and had just given her to a new father she barely knew.

She was irritable. Where she'd once been precious, with a smile constantly on her face, she was now hurt and angry at the world.

My mother left Vegas and got an apartment in downtown LA. Maddie couldn't adapt to all those changes. I was the only person she ever wanted to see, and she'd call me late at night so she could fall asleep. She was scared, she didn't like her new home, all her old toys were gone, she said, and her friends were far away, and her new school was ugly. She wanted to come live with me. That was what she said every time we talked on the phone.

"When are you coming to see me, Nick?" she'd ask with a

frown. "When can we go to the Ferris wheel? When is Daddy coming back? When will Mama start acting normal again?"

Those questions hurt, and they drove me crazy because they meant my mother wasn't taking care of her. She didn't want for anything, she was eating, she was healthy, but what about everything else?

In Anne's email, she said my father had asked for Maddie to spend Thanksgiving with him. The judge had ordered him and my mother to split the holidays, and my mother hadn't put up a fight. Before she signed off, Anne reminded me that I no longer had to consult with her about any visits, and that if I had legal questions, I should talk to my father. He had written to me, too, asking me to spend the holiday with him. Maddie would adapt better having me around, he said, and we needed to do everything we could for her.

To tell the truth, going home for the holidays—for Thanksgiving or any other day—hadn't even crossed my mind. There was no point in family gatherings or shared meals or anything like that. Was I really supposed to sit at the same table with a man who had lied to me for years and the woman who'd caused my parents to divorce and my mother to abandon me?

To hell with that. Going there could only hurt me. Because of the childhood memories. Because of the even more painful memories of things that had happened afterward.

For me, that house was Noah; I saw her in every corner; I imagined her coming downstairs in pajamas or in a pretty sundress and low-heeled sandals, throwing herself into my arms and kissing me passionately... Noah in the kitchen eating breakfast. Noah in her bedroom asleep, when I finally realized my heart sped up every time I saw her... Noah in my bed, naked, the first time we made love—I say *we* because for me it was a first time, too, the first time I ever truly loved someone.

I didn't know much about what was going on with her. Now and again Lion told me something about her. The same couldn't be said for me. With the way the press was hounding me nonstop, there was no way she didn't know every detail of my life.

I'd been in the magazines because of my relationship with Sophia, but also because of all the downsizing at Leister Enterprises. The papers were calling me ruthless, heartless. The whole thing had me stressed.

I always knew it wouldn't be easy to get that company back in shape. Nothing as big as my grandfather's company could be easy to run. But with everyone able to access information all the time, you couldn't keep things under wraps. That was the thing I struggled most with, the lack of privacy, not being able to run my business the way I wanted to. So I'd had to fire a lot of people, I'd had to shut down two subsidiaries, but I'd also opened a new one, and I'd be able to transfer many of the people I otherwise would've had to let go. It had just been a month, but I knew the new branch would create lots of jobs in the future, with better pay than what the employees had received at their previous firm, which had been badly managed and had little room in the budget.

Try telling that to people who just want a good headline, though.

I looked away from the computer. I was going to call my father the next day and tell him I'd be there for Thanksgiving. What other option did I have? My sister was the most important person in my life now, the only one I owed it to to never be angry, the person I needed to take care of, to teach that there were still adults in the world she could trust.

Maddie was seven and a half now; she was getting older, and she understood more and more of what was going on. She was sharp—you couldn't just buy her an ice cream or a toy and distract her. What she'd suffered in those months had marked her; she was growing up, and the lessons she'd learned made it hard for her to trust others.

I walked out of my office to get a glass of water. It was late, but I was still wide awake. I needed to do something. I walked to my bedroom and looked at Sophia's nude back. She should have left already. That was rule number one—we never slept together—but we were coming closer and closer to breaking it. I sat on the loveseat in front of the bed and observed her: her dark hair on the pillow, her curves under the white silk sheets... She was stunning, she couldn't be more self-assured, and I liked it. She wasn't like an earthquake that knocked down everything in her path; she was smart, seductive, and could get whatever she wanted with words.

I liked her. Of course I did. I wasn't an idiot. She was pleasant; she came from a good family; she was intelligent, had a backbone, and was nothing to sneeze at in the sack. We were good together in that way. Sometimes she took the lead; sometimes I did.

She would have made a good girlfriend, a perfect life companion. She was the kind of woman who would always be there, supporting you, giving you advice, hugging you when you needed it, kissing you till you were breathless. She'd be a good mother, too, a working mother, obviously, the kind who would put her kids in the best school, make sure they were always well cared for, well-dressed, and healthy. The kind of mother who knew everything. I imagined her coming home late to tuck the kids in when they were already asleep, giving them a kiss, then sitting down and resting.

Sophia was that and everything...but she was no Noah.

18

Noah

I GOT TO WILL'S PLACE AT ELEVEN IN THE MORNING, JUST IN TIME to have a nice hot breakfast. My mother came out to receive me in a crocheted shawl that I imagined was way more expensive than it looked. Her blond hair was shorter than the last time I saw her, coming roughly to her shoulders. Her blue eyes looked at me with love and joy as she saw me getting out and waving to her. When I reached the top of the steps, I let her hug me.

It had been an eternity since I'd gone home.. My mother and I had seen each other, but it was always at my apartment or at some fancy restaurant. The memories of Nick wouldn't leave me alone, and that was the reason I'd stayed away.

Now I was going to be there for two days with her and her husband. But at least I didn't need to worry about Nick showing up for the holiday. He hated being there; he had hated it even when we were together, and there had always been fights about it. So, Thanksgiving without Nicholas: all the better for me.

I walked to the kitchen, where Will was having a pleasant chat with Prett. She hugged me and he smiled. When he gave me an embrace in turn, it was much more comforting than I'd expected.

I couldn't help but remember what my mother had told me about him. But even if he was the man she'd cheated on my father with, he had taken care of her and made her happy during a very dark period in her life. I didn't even want to think about what might have happened if Will hadn't checked my mother into that rehab facility, but if I had to guess, she'd probably be treading water somewhere, still damaged from years of abuse and the loss of her daughter after her supposed negligence. I'd have grown up in orphanages; they'd never have let me live with her again.

We spent the morning catching up. I didn't want to say anything about losing my job. I didn't want to face my mother's disdain or hear Will say I should just focus on my studies and it would be an honor for him to help me out financially.

We talked about other things, and when the formalities were done, he said something that caught my attention.

"I had to really fight for my daughter to be able to spend Thanksgiving with us, and now I've got it, and I have no idea what to do to win her over."

His daughter... Oh, Maddie, damn, of course... Is that still a delicate subject or not? I looked at my mother. She seemed relaxed, much more so than on that accursed night when all the hidden truths had come to light at once.

"Maddie's going to be here for Thanksgiving?" I asked with slight reluctance.

I'd heard from Mom that Will was splitting custody and that they were trying to figure out how to explain to the girl what was going on.

"We need to make up for lost time," Will said, getting up from the table and smiling. After kissing my mother on the cheek, he walked out, and I used the opportunity to find out more.

"Did you want to add something, Mom?" I asked, taking a sip of coffee.

She took a seat in front of me and sighed. "William feels guilty for everything that happened. He wants to finally get his life in order... Everything's insane right now. I don't think anyone would be happy to find out from one day to the next that they've got a seven-year-old daughter with their crazy ex-wife."

I opened my eyes a little wider. My mother had never used that tone, at least not in front of me. It had been a tough blow for her. In the years after my father hurt me, things with William weren't exactly easy. There were numerous arguments and breakups; things were unstable. But none of that could compare to learning after the fact that he'd gotten his wife pregnant during all that. Mom would probably never get over that.

"How are you?" I asked, feeling a little sorry for her.

"When there are kids in the middle, it always fucks things up," she replied. If she was talking like that, it had to be bad. "The little girl doesn't understand a thing. Will's killed himself trying to get her to like him every time he's gone to see her, but she's just not having it."

Poor Mad... so little, so sweet, so precious. I remembered the times I'd gone with Nick to Vegas to pick her up. He'd always been like a father to her. He adored her: she was his little sister, the only person who never tried his patience. It must have been horrible for her to find out her father wasn't her father. How do you tell a child that? How do you explain it? Even for me, it wasn't easy to understand. Suddenly, something came to my mind, something logical but that threw me into a terror.

"Mom, Nick's not..."

I felt a knot in my stomach when I saw my mother look up from the table to me. Could she see the slow, painful panic that was taking hold of me?

"Relax. Nick hates staying here. William invited him to come, he does it every year, but I doubt Nick will say yes."

That response wasn't convincing, especially now that I knew his little sister was involved.

"How many days is Maddie staying here?" I asked, trying to calm my galloping heart.

"Just the weekend."

Nick was going to come. And he'd be staying there. I knew it... Dammit. I'd have to see him again.

Thanksgiving started with a cool, rainy morning. The sky was gray, and I felt sad when I thought of the sun hidden behind it on what was supposed to be such a special day. I woke up early, too early, and put on a warm lavender-blue robe and house shoes.

My mother had said we were having guests for lunch, among them a married couple Will was friends with, who were bringing their little kids. *At least Maddie will have someone to play with*, I thought.

She hadn't confirmed that Nick would stay there, so I tried to convince myself he would come, drop his sister off, and leave again to take his new girlfriend out to eat or keep working on one of his megaprojects in his new role as a big-time businessman.

I went down to the kitchen. Prett was frantic. I took a look at the turkey in the oven. It had probably already been there for several hours. On the counter were potatoes, peas, spices, and all sorts of other treats waiting to be prepared.

"Hey, Prett," I said with a smile, sitting down and savoring the aromas.

She wiped her hands on the front of her apron and smiled. She liked me, I knew that, even if she had always taken Nicholas's side in our arguments. I'd turned to her many times to complain about him, especially in the early months, when we were first dating. Prett had been cooking for the Leisters for years, ever since Nick was a kid, and she knew him well. She spoiled him, too. That drove me crazy sometimes.

"Can I help you?" I didn't mind cooking. I even liked it, especially on an occasion like today. She said there was no need, but I kept pressing, and two hours later, we were both working away, peeling potatoes, boiling water, kneading dough for pumpkin and apple pies, and all kinds of other things.

The morning flew by, and when everything was ready, Prett poured two glasses of cider, and we toasted to a job well done. She also laid out delicious cheese pastries. We deserved them; we'd been cooking like master chefs.

When I saw the time, I almost jumped out of my seat. If I wanted to look good for all invited, I'd need to get a move on. I said goodbye to Prett but promised I'd lend her a hand with the turkey when she was ready.

I smelled like food and spices, so I decided to opt for a bath, pouring in the lemon and mango salts I liked so much. Then I walked into the closet to pick my outfit. I found a burgundy skirt, a little fluffy, with a closure of two black strips. It was pretty, and I matched it with a snug light-colored blouse that buttoned up the back.

In the entryway, I found my mother greeting the new arrivals, a couple with kids, eight-year-old twins with blond hair combed back, in matching shorts, shirts, and blue ties. I thought I'd seen their parents before. I assumed they were Will's friends, judging by my mother's enthusiastic reaction. They came over and said a cordial hello, and I forced a smile until they walked off toward the living room where the guests who'd shown up earlier had congregated. The bell rang again, and to avoid socializing, I opened the door, not thinking.

A pair of icy eyes stared straight through me when I did. I was paralyzed, speechless, staring like a stupid little girl. Contradictory emotions overwhelmed me: longing, lust, rancor, love...

It had been more than three months since I'd last seen him, but they felt like nothing. Vividly, I remembered everything we'd done that last night. Warmth suffused me, and I tried to suppress all the images in my mind unsuited to an audience under eighteen.

Damn it.

He was incredible… He was dressed in dark jeans and a white shirt with the top two buttons unbuttoned. On his feet were gray Converse. His expression was surprised. Clearly, he'd had no idea he'd see me there.

Next to him was his sister, who barely reached his waist. Her tiny hand was hidden completely inside Nick's, and she was wearing a gray, red, and white plaid dress. Her shoes were black patent leather, and in her hair was a red ribbon that matched her dress.

I saw all that in a matter of seconds. Then Maddie recognized me, let Nick's hand go, and took off.

"Noah!" she shouted, pressing against my legs and wrapping her arms around my waist.

My eyes met Nick's briefly, and his initial astonishment had been replaced by a cold, impassive mask. I touched Maddie's impeccably styled hair and tried as hard as I could not to look at him.

"Hey, precious!" I greeted her, amazed at how much bigger she'd gotten since I'd last seen her. She was going to be a stunner when she was older, and there was now no denying she was Will's daughter. The traits she shared with Nick, which I'd mistakenly attributed to her mother, were clearly from the Leister genes. Those big eyes, those long lashes…they were natural to both Will and Nick, whereas considering Anabel's long blond hair, his mother's dark lashes were probably stick-ons.

Maddie stepped back, looked at Nick, looked at me, and then back at Nick. She seemed to be expecting something.

Nick stepped forward, and I stiffened as he put his hands on my waist and kissed my cheek. It was brief, barely a kiss at all, but it made every hair on my body stand on end.

"Happy Thanksgiving, Noah," he said, pulling back.

"Happy Thanksgiving, Noah!" Maddie shouted, jumping up and down and grabbing my hand.

I understood what was going on. Nick didn't want his little sister to know what had happened between us or that he could barely look at me without grimacing in disgust. Maddie had seen us together lots of times, had seen the way Nick hugged and kissed me, the way we laughed...Nick had told her thousands of times that we were his girls, his favorite girls, and he loved us like mad.

You could have cut the tension with a knife. The atmosphere was icy. The kiss he'd given me couldn't have been faker or more forced. I had no idea if Maddie had noticed, but if she thought she'd see the same Nick and Noah as before, she was wrong. I wasn't going to pretend in front of her. I couldn't bear it. Nicholas had hurt me, I'd hurt him, too, but I'd always been honest about how I felt.

I'm sorry to say this, Noah, but with her, everything's easy. There's no drama, no problems. Sophia's a woman, not a little girl.

I pursed my lips and glared at him, then forced a smile and brought Maddie inside.

Nicholas followed me, taking off his coat and hanging it on the rack. Maddie didn't seem so happy once she was inside, and soon, she was frowning. She looked scared, then irritated. I kneeled and took off her red coat. I reached up to pass it to Nicholas, who hung it next to his.

Will and my mother appeared in the vestibule. Nick walked up beside Maddie, and she stood there between us, hiding her head behind my body. Suddenly, she was nervous and timid.

"Hey, Maddie!" my mother greeted her nervously. "I'm Noah's mom. Can I see that beautiful dress you've got on?"

Maddie looked up at me once she realized it was my mother. I smiled, as though encouraging her to come out from her hiding place.

"You're Noah's mom?" she asked, looking her up and down, now curious.

"Yes, I'm Noah's mom, and I'm also married to your daddy, Will," she answered, coming a little closer. Will's anxiety was palpable. I'd never seen him like that, and it made me realize how important the weekend was for him.

Maddie's blue eyes turned to her father, and she grimaced. "He's not my dad."

That was cutting. Seven years old, and she could already bring four adults to their knees with her words! That was when Nick decided to intervene. He bent over, picked Maddie up, and started tickling her. She got distracted and laughed.

Once Will was over the shock, he managed a less-than-convincing smile.

"Let's go eat!" he proposed. "There's enough food for an army, so I hope you're ready to get stuffed!"

We went to the dining room where the other guests were gathered. Maddie looked happy to see two other kids she could play with and took off toward the remote-control train Will had set up to keep them entertained. As she sat down to watch, I noticed Will couldn't stop looking at her, and I wondered what he could do to finally win the girl's affections.

I was about to walk over and sit down when Nick grabbed my elbow and took me toward the vestibule again, away from the group.

"Are you staying for the weekend?" he asked, and by his expression, I could tell he was no happier than I was that we'd be back under the same roof again.

"I'm staying till Monday, I have a law exam on Tuesday," I

said, as if he cared. I couldn't stop thinking about the last words we'd exchanged and the photos I'd seen of him and Sophia. All the rage I'd tried to tamp down rose back up and was making me lose control.

"They should have told me," he said, more for himself than for me.

His words angered me. He wasn't the only one made uncomfortable by the situation.

I turned to go, wanting to get out of his sight, but he grabbed me again. I hated him touching me like that, and I jerked away. When I faced off with him, I saw something strange in his expression, at once exasperated and embarrassed.

"Before you go back..." he said, "you should know...my sister doesn't know about our breakup."

Just as I'd predicted.

"You didn't tell your sister we're not together?" I said, holding on to my rage.

"She's a little girl. She won't understand."

I looked up at the ceiling, huffing. "So what's your plan, then, Nicholas? Pretend nothing happened? I think we tried that, and the results weren't great..."

Damn it, I shouldn't have mentioned our fight in New York, but that wasn't all I meant. Nicholas looked at my body, then my face and seemed to get suddenly flustered, running his hand through his hair.

When he turned to me, he looked nervous and worried. "I know I shouldn't ask for this, but I just don't want to tell her, at least not right now, not when her parents have separated and she has to get used to a new family..." It calmed me down to see him so stressed; his eyes revealed anguish, and I knew why. That adorable little girl, his sister, was suffering. "Maddie's crazy about you, she can't stop asking about you, and I..."

"You hid the truth." I finished the sentence for him.

He smiled. I couldn't remember the last time he'd done it, and for a moment, he had me entranced. "Look, I'm not asking you to fake anything. Let's just get along this weekend, for Maddie, for us. I promise you I won't act like an asshole."

I bit my lip. *Get along*. Was that possible?

I didn't know if I'd be able to do what he was asking. Not when just the sight of him made me ache, and it got worse when I thought about how he had lied to me and was in love with another woman. I stepped back and looked toward the dining room. Maddie was alone, ignoring the family she barely knew. It reminded me of when I had come here for the first time.

"Okay," I said. "We'll get along. For Maddie."

He tried to say something, but I'd already turned around and was walking off.

In the dining room, it was clear Will and my mother had been aware of our absence and were observing us, hoping to see what mood we were in. I ignored their inquisitive gazes and sat down at the table, where Prett was serving the food. Nick did the same, turning to his sister, who had started to cry in our absence.

"Don't leave me here alone, Nick," she said as he picked her up and set her on his lap.

"Sweetheart, I just had to tell Noah something, but I'm here. You want some potatoes?" he asked warmly.

Nick waited patiently while the girl ate after giving her two soft kisses on the cheeks and wiping away her tears. That reminded me of the times he had kissed my tears away before kissing me on the lips. *Your lips are so soft when you cry*, he used to tell me… As if he were reading my thoughts, he looked up, and I stared down at my plate, uncomfortable. I played with my food, and when dessert came, I only managed a few bites each of pumpkin pie and apple pie, even if they were delicious.

After lunch, we returned to the living room, and Maddie started playing with the remote-control train. Nick sat on the sofa, and his dog, Thor, came over and sat at his feet, waiting for a scratch behind the ears.

Without warning, our cat, N, which had grown into a giant fur ball and which I'd had to bring home because my new roommate was allergic to cats, jumped into Nick's lap, making Thor growl. They'd never gotten along well, but this kind of dust-up was rare. Nick was surprised to see N, and I'd swear he gave me a guilty look after seeing him. I mean, he was our cat, and Nick had just left him behind.

"Good lord... What the hell's up with N?" he asked as the cat settled in, rubbing against him and purring, as if he'd forgotten Nick was our common enemy.

Traitor!

Maddie left the train and started playing with the cat. Since she was going to be around more, I was glad she had pets to entertain her. Nick looked over, but before he could say anything, I walked off toward the kitchen.

I put on an apron before talking with Prett and helping her dry the silverware. In spite of myself, I laughed at a story she told me about Nicholas when he'd been a little boy.

"One time he got the crazy idea to fill his pockets with grasshoppers, dozens of them, teeny tiny ones. I took off his clothes to give him a bath, and the nasty little things hopped all over the bathroom; they even got in the tub. It took three hours for me and Steve to get them all out of the house. Fortunately, when Mr. Leister got home, the boy was already in bed, fast asleep. I remember Mr. Leister even congratulated me for doing a good job keeping his little monster in line. If only he knew..."

I was amused to think of Nick as a boy with big blue eyes and unkempt hair, in shorts, hunting grasshoppers with God knew what scheme in mind. When I saw him, I stopped laughing, but Prett was still smiling and shaking her head.

"Tattling about my bad behavior, Prett? No one told you to bring out the dirty laundry. You should be ashamed."

"Dirty laundry, that's what you had for me and Steve every time you came back in from outside, yes, sirree," she said, getting back to her washing.

I had soap on my hands, I'd splashed water on my clothes, my hair was pulled back in a bun, and there he was looking at me pensively. And I couldn't ignore him.

"You coming back? People are asking where you've gotten off to."

People, or you, Nicholas? I wanted to ask, but I bit my tongue and pulled off my apron.

"God forbid I miss out on all the fun," I replied sarcastically.

Just then, I heard a sharp scream that echoed through the whole house. Nicholas stepped around me and ran toward the living room. I stayed close on his heels.

"We're older than you, so we get to play first!" one of the twins said to Maddie, whose little fists were clenched by her sides.

I looked at Nick, then at Will, wanting to see if they were listening to this.

"It's my dad's train, so I get to play first. Isn't that right, Will?"

William seemed unable to believe the words that had just come out of her mouth. Nicholas and I looked at her with surprise, and my mother smiled from where she was sitting by the fireplace. Will had to do something, and with characteristic elegance, he walked over, kneeled, and smiled at his daughter.

"This train used to be mine when I was a little boy, and then Nick used to play with it. You've never had the chance, and I think it's time for a new owner. Will you take care of it, Maddie? It's a family heirloom. No one who's not a Leister can have it."

She seemed absorbed by his words. She listened attentively and nodded when he asked that question.

"So, boys, the train belongs to my daughter, and if she wants to play with it first, you'll have to wait. But I know Maddie's a good little girl, and she likes to share, isn't that right?"

Will stood up while Mad watched him. She nodded and turned to the twins, who were pouting.

"I'll let you watch, but no touching!" she said with determination.

Everyone in the living room cracked up.

There were no more incidents that afternoon. The kids played without further problems, Nick and his father went to the office to talk about business matters, and I stayed there talking to my mother and her friend. We were in the middle of an intense conversation when we heard a door slam and shouting at the other end of the hall.

"I don't have to give you any more fucking explanations than I gave to the board!" Nick yelled. "Do you think I wanted to do this? I didn't have an option! The problem is no one had what it took to make that decision, and now you're angry that the Leister name is associated with it."

In the living room, we fell silent, and Nick and his father walked in.

"You should have at least consulted with me. It's very risky! No, Nicholas, listen to me!" Will shouted when his son opened his mouth to interrupt him. "If this doesn't turn out the way you plan, the company could go bankrupt!"

Father and son looked at each other furiously. The noise of the train the children were playing with punctured the silence. Nicholas was about to explode, I could tell; I knew him... The way he was balling up his fists, the way he looked at his father as if he were about to pounce on him and eat him alive... When he realized I was watching him, he shot me a cold glance that made me tremble, and not in a good way.

"It's time you started trusting me," Nicholas said, then turned around and walked out, slamming the door. In the corner, I saw Maddie staring at us, her eyes big as saucers.

I had no idea what had caused that argument, and I didn't want to see more of it, especially if it meant getting nasty looks I'd done nothing to deserve. I walked to the corner and scooped up Maddie.

"You want me to show you my room, Mad?"

She nodded, still starting at the doorway through which her brother had just disappeared. I smiled at the guests still there and climbed the stairs with Maddie resting on my hip.

"Do you live here, Noah?"

"I used to, sweetheart... I used to."

19

Nick

I LEFT MY FATHER'S HOUSE AND WENT TO ONE OF THE BARS ON the pier. In that weather, I was sure they'd be empty, and that was good; I needed to be alone right then.

I hadn't expected my father's approval when I told him what I was planning to do with the company, but I also hadn't expected him to give me shit about it. Since I'd been in charge of the company, I'd attended lots of meetings, seen lots of graphs, done lots of calculations, and I'd realized there were numerous small companies under the corporate umbrella that should have been liquidated long ago. They weren't making money, and they were causing problems. At first, no one agreed with my idea of selling them and using the money to open a new firm with a different focus and a more modern vision. Most of the Leister companies were fine; we had some of the best managers in the country working for us, which I knew because I'd had to visit them to make sure they were operating according to our standards. After months of work and trying to persuade the board, we had decided to off-load our dead weight. That meant downsizing, but it also freed me to open a new marketing and telecommunications company that would bring Leister enterprises into previously unexplored sectors.

It was a hard choice, but it was the right one, and I couldn't believe my father didn't trust me on this. He'd even warned me I'd drag the firm into bankruptcy. I could handle the board, but that was easy; I was the boss. My father was a whole different story. And the fact that Noah had been there watching had just made matters worse.

I ordered a whiskey and drank it in one gulp. That stupid Thanksgiving lunch had been the worst idea ever.

I paid and decided to go back. I shouldn't have left in the first place; I shouldn't have left Mad there, but even if I hated to admit it, I knew Noah would take care of her, and my sister would be fine. Of all the people in my life, including my father, the one person I trusted her with was Noah.

Noah... I didn't know if our truce had been a mistake. It was much easier to ignore my feelings for her when I was angry. Talking with her the way we had today, like adults, was dangerous.

Sometimes...more often than I wanted to admit aloud...I imagined myself forgiving her, forgetting everything that had happened, everything we had done to each other, and I tried to visualize what our life would be like now. But when I did, the reason why we'd broken up returned to torment me, and everything vanished except for the hate I'd gotten so used to feeling in that past year.

Fucking Noah... Damn her for ruining everything!

When I got back to my father's house, I saw it was much later than I had guessed. The lights were low, and the whole house was silent. From the vestibule, I could see a soft glow coming from the living room.

I took off my jacket, dropped my keys in the entryway, and walked in. Sitting on the ground, leaning back against the sofa, was Noah. She had changed into a snug sweatshirt, had pulled back her hair, and had put on her glasses. She was immersed in her reading and had several open books scattered all around her. I saw the fire in the fireplace was reduced to embers.

"What are you doing?" I asked quietly.

She twitched but waited to respond until I had come up beside her and picked up the book she had between her legs.

Intellectual Property Law, vol. I.

"Studying," she responded coolly.

I tried to analyze her expression. I didn't want her to feel uncomfortable in my presence. I knew she had put up with me earlier for Maddie's sake, and the best thing would probably be for us to spend as little time as possible together, but right then, for some reason, I needed Noah to be Noah.

"Is it giving you a hard time?" I asked, turning around to lay some wood on the fire, then bending over, blowing in the center to bring up the flames. Noah had tried, but the logs weren't close enough together, and so the wood she'd put in there was charred on the edges but hadn't caught fire and warmed the room. Once the flames were crackling and we were cozy, I turned around, rubbed my hands together, and looked at her. She'd been watching me closely.

Her cheeks were flushed. It wasn't even cold enough for a fire, but Noah was always chilly. That winter we'd spent together, she would curl up next to me under the sheets and warm her frozen feet on my skin. I was the opposite; I was always hot, at least when she was around.

"You could say that," she said, looking around at her books. "By the way, Maddie fell asleep on my bed, in case you go upstairs and wonder where she is."

I nodded and sat on the sofa next to her, but not so close that we couldn't look at each other. "Thanks for taking care of her," I said, trying to sound formal.

Noah's attitude was that of a person confronted by a large dog that might be sweet or might bare its teeth and go for the throat.

"It's fine. Will's the one who got her into her pajamas and read her a story. They tried to get her to sleep in her new room, but she said no, she wanted to sleep with me. She's been asking about you. You really shouldn't have left."

Her lips had distracted me as she spoke, but I needed to excuse myself after this last remark. "I had to think," I said. Just then, I noticed something that had escaped my attention before: on her left cheek, near her eye, was a whitish scar, straight, like a cut. "What is that?" I asked, surprising her when I reached out and grabbed her chin to get a better look.

What the hell?

She quivered and pulled away. "Nothing," she said, turning back to her book.

"If it were nothing, it wouldn't be there. What the hell happened?"

"I fell," she said, shrugging.

"You fell? Where? You didn't have that scar the last time I saw you." *Or did she?* I wasn't sure; I hadn't been in my right mind the last time I'd seen her.

Noah closed her book and faced me, starting to get exasperated. "It's been there for six months, so yeah, I had it the last time I saw you. I fell riding a motorbike. It was no big deal, but they had to give me stitches."

"Since when do you have a motorcycle?!" I didn't know why I was suddenly so pissed. I'd been fine, even relaxed when I'd come in. I was happy to walk in and find her there, but now...now, dammit, I wanted to break something.

"It wasn't mine; it was a friend's. Why are you acting like that?"

I stood and turned around. I was so mad, I couldn't help yelling the first thing that came into my head. "Only a fool would go around on a bike. Most deadly accidents on the road happen because of someone on a goddamned motorcycle!"

Noah got up, her lips pursed, dropping her book on the sofa. "You have a motorcycle!"

"I'm not you; I don't get into accidents."

"So you mean to say I'm a fool?"

"Just stay off the motorcycles, that's all I'm asking," I replied, trying to calm down. Noah had had an accident, a fucking accident, and it had been months ago... Where had I been?

Far away... Very far away.

Noah grabbed her books. "Too bad you don't get to order me around anymore, huh, Nick?"

As she walked off, I had a bitter taste in my mouth.

20

Noah

The next day, I got up earlier than I was used to, but I had a good reason for it, and I was excited.

Trying not to make noise, I turned to the girl sleeping next to me. She was out like a light, and I watched her, amused. She was small, but she wriggled around like a frantic little animal, and that reminded me of a certain someone who was sleeping nearby. Her little body was splayed out, taking up almost all the bed. I barely had room to move.

I didn't want to wake Maddie while getting dressed. The sun wasn't up yet, so I'd need to turn on the lights. I got up carefully and picked her up, knowing she was so deeply asleep that at most she'd murmur before dropping off again.

She wrapped her little hands around my neck as I walked out of the bedroom cradling her like a little monkey. I wasn't sure taking her to what would now be her bedroom was a smart idea; I didn't want her to open her eyes and be scared when no one was there, and so I stopped next to Nick's room. I could leave her there, they could sleep in, and when she opened her eyes, she'd have her brother next to her, making her feel safe.

I opened the door slowly. I felt uncomfortable invading Nick's privacy. I'd gone in there dozens of times before so we could sleep together and wake up in each other's arms. But I wiped those thoughts from my mind. Nick was deep asleep, spread out on the bed, his room pitch-dark. I left the door open so I could see a bit and came close, setting the little girl down next to him. As soon as she touched the mattress, she curled up and started sucking her thumb, as tranquil as she'd been just moments before.

But then I felt nervous. I tugged on the blanket to cover her up. Nicholas was never cold; he had left the heat off, and the room was ice-cold.

The blanket was stuck between his legs, and no matter how softly I pulled on it, it was impossible not to wake Nick. He smiled, and I stopped cold.

He reached out, grabbed my arm, and pulled me until I was sitting on the bed.

"What are you doing, Freckles, spying on me?" he asked. The question made my heart pound. A year—it had been a year since he'd used that name to refer to me.

He sat up, and his mouth sought mine without further prelude. It was an innocent kiss, strange, and I jerked away as if burned by fire. That brought Nick back to reality. He opened his eyes, looked around, saw his sister, then me, and cursed.

"I just thought for a second—"

"I know," I cut him off.

I understood perfectly what had happened.

I got up, hoping to disappear.

"I just brought Mad; I didn't want her to wake up without someone next to her."

Nick nodded, looking at her and then me.

"Wait, why…? Where are you going?" he asked, throwing off the blanket and running a hand across his face.

"I've got stuff to do… Errands." I wasn't going to tell him where I was going. We'd already been through that. Nicholas nodded, then opened his eyes wide when he realized what I was hiding from him.

"No way!" he exclaimed, too loudly.

"Shhh," I hissed. "You're going to wake her up."

Nick stood, grabbed my arm, and guided me into his bathroom, shutting the door behind himself and looking at me condescendingly.

"You're out of your mind," he said, but I could tell he was amused.

"Drop it! Stop laughing at me. It's a tradition. I like it… You'll just have to accept it!"

Nick shook his head incredulously. "You hate shopping; you talk trash about your mom because she's always out buying stuff, then Black Friday comes, and all of a sudden, you're a compulsive shopper. You want to tell me why?"

"I already did before," I said, trying to get past him, but he stood in my way with that damned body of his. He was smiling… Nicholas was smiling as he looked at me. That caught me off guard enough that I let him keep me there.

"Black Friday, shop till you drop, the stores open at six, you can get hot chocolate…" he said, trying and failing to impersonate me.

I was surprised he remembered what I'd said about that day since it had been two years ago. "If you know, why are you asking?"

He shook his head. "I'd hoped you would have grown up by now and gotten over all that stupid Christmas shit."

He was joking, but I didn't like that *grown up* comment. I

remembered what he'd said to me at his apartment in New York, and I was livid. "Just leave me alone, okay?"

I walked out before he could say another word. Sometimes I forgot how stupid he could be.

A half hour later, I was in the kitchen in my black jeans and my ragged white sweatshirt. I wanted to be comfortable. Black Friday was a gauntlet, but I was an ace at finding the best sales.

It was early, but Nick and Maddie were up five minutes after I'd poured my coffee. Both were in pajamas, and their hair looked like they'd touched a live wire. Nick was holding Mad up on one shoulder, and she laughed when he pretended he might drop her. Seeing me sitting there, Madison struggled until her brother let her go and she could run up and sit beside me. I helped her into the chair while Nick poured a coffee for himself.

"I want the same thing as Noah!" she said, bouncing up and down and pointing at my chocolate doughnut.

Nick frowned. "Check your blood sugar first, midget," he said, handing her the monitor and a glass of warm milk.

She sighed, but she did as he asked. I watched her, unable to believe a seven-year-old girl could do that on her own. Nick was busy beating eggs. I felt like I should do something.

"Can I help you, kiddo?" I asked, even though I had no idea about insulin or blood sugar or anything else.

"I can do it," she said, taking out a strip and a little plastic lancet. She placed it over her finger and hit a button, and after a click, a drop of blood welled up. I was amazed by how calmly she did that, and she had to three times a day. That was how it had been ever since she'd been diagnosed. She squeezed the blood onto the strip and put it into the machine. A few moments later, she read the results out loud.

"We're out of doughnuts, Mad, but I have cookies and an apple," Nick said, bringing everything over, along with his cup of coffee, while Maddie sulked.

Of course there were more doughnuts. I cursed the moment I'd decided to eat one that morning. I didn't want to make the little thing jealous, so I picked mine up and dropped it in the trash.

"I don't like those cookies," she said, crossing her arms.

Nick expelled a breath of air. "They're the same ones as always, Madison, and you do like them."

"No!" she shouted, jumping up and trying to run off.

Nick caught her in midflight just as Will appeared in the doorway in his pajamas, his face showing little love for his son.

"What's all this racket?" he asked, looking around. When his eyes settled on me, he asked, "Why are you dressed?"

I rolled my eyes and walked past him to take Nick's eggs off the burner. I scooped them onto a plate and brought them over while Maddie gawked at her father.

"Eat your breakfast," her brother ordered her, putting her back in her seat.

Will poured himself a coffee and picked up his newspaper off the table. Only then did he realize the three of us were looking at him.

I motioned in Maddie's direction, and he realized he needed to address her.

He cleared his throat. "How'd you sleep, Maddie?"

She sank her cookie into her glass of milk, ate it, and replied, "I slept with Nick and Noah."

William almost choked on his coffee. "What in the name of...?!" He set his mug down.

After a quick glance at me, Nicholas tried to explain. His father eventually calmed down, but his mood didn't seem to improve. I needed to get out of there.

"I'm going," I said, grabbing my bag and depositing my cup in the sink.

William's eyebrows arched. "You're really going to do it?"

Nick tried to hide his grin behind his coffee. I wanted to throw my bag at his head.

"Yes, William, I'm going shopping. It may be like walking voluntarily into Hell, but I'm doing it because I'm a masochist, okay?" I replied with irritation just as my mother walked in.

Christ. I'd forgotten what it meant to live in that house.

"Watch out for avalanches, Noah," she told me as she walked past me.

I shook my head, digging in my purse for my keys.

"Where you going, Noah?" Maddie asked.

"I'm going shopping, Mad," I said before anyone else could say anything stupid. That excited the little girl, and she didn't try to hide it.

"I want to go shopping!" she screamed, surprising us all.

William looked over the edge of his newspaper. "Like mother, like daughter," he said, then resumed reading.

I smiled; Nick groaned.

"Did you hear that, Nick? Maddie wants to go shopping," I said. I couldn't have been more amused.

He scowled and looked at his sister. "No, Mad wants to go to the beach with me, isn't that right, midget?"

She filled her lungs with air before responding. "Noooooo!"

How sweet vengeance was!

"Come on, Madison. You told me you wanted to learn how to surf."

"I hate surfing! I want to go to Rodeo Drive!"

Everyone but Nick exploded into laughter. He looked at her as if she'd transformed into a monster.

"Okay, I'm going," I said, turning around.

"You don't think I'm going to do this alone?" he said.

"Do what?" I asked, trying not to laugh.

"If I have to spend the day shopping with a seven-year-old girl, you're going with me. Don't even try to get out of it."

"I'm not going to Rodeo Drive. I'm going to Beverly Center." I was wallowing in spiteful joy.

"I'll pick you up there at lunchtime, Noah, and you better be there when I call."

"Nicholas..."

"And get Steve to drive you. Parking today's going to be crazy. I'll bring you back home."

"I want to go in my car."

"And I wanted to go surfing and enjoy the beach in winter, but now, thanks to you, I have to go shopping," he said, impassive.

Ten minutes later, I was in the car with Steve on my way to one of the biggest malls in the city.

Beverly Center was located in Beverly Grove in the center of Los Angeles, ten minutes or so from Beverly Hills. I'd had to cross the city to get there, and I'd need to rush to be able to meet Nick and his sister by lunchtime, but Black Friday was worth it.

Everything was crazy as always: the people were packed in like sardines, the lines snaked out past the entryways, children were running back and forth, crying, eating candy and junk food, smearing themselves, their parents, and anyone nearby with caramel, chocolate, or ketchup. Men and women ran in and out of the different stores as if they were on the hunt.

I liked being there alone. No distractions. I was fast, too: I knew within five minutes of entering a store if I'd like anything there or not. I didn't waste my time digging through clothing. It called to me, and if I walked in and nothing caught my eye, then I was out and that was it.

At two in the afternoon, I had almost all my Christmas shopping done. My phone dinged, and I saw Nicholas had sent me a message.

I'll pick you up at Macys in 10.

Great… I had no desire to see him whatsoever.

21

Nick

I KNEW NOAH HATED SHOPPING WITH OTHER PEOPLE. THAT WAS why I'd spent the morning with Maddie. We'd gone to the bookstore, the toy store, and the playground. She'd asked me to buy her a costume. Other girls her age liked tiaras and princess outfits, but my little sister wanted to look like a Ninja Turtle. That's right: I was on my way to Beverly Grove with a miniature Ninja Turtle and bags full of stuff I hadn't intended to buy.

My father had been right: like mother, like daughter.

"Where's Noah?" Maddie kept asking ever since I said we'd be meeting her.

"I could ask you the same thing," I said, waiting outside the mall for Noah to come out. Traffic was wild; people were double-parked outside, so it was practically impossible to find a parking spot.

Right when I took my phone out to call her, I saw her emerge. She had tons of bags, her sweatshirt was now tied around her waist, and the sleeveless shirt she had on underneath it revealed a lot of her, even her belly button.

Mad took off toward Noah while I pushed my sunglasses up my forehead and gawked at her like an idiot.

"I love your costume, Mad!" she said with a smile. Her teeth were impeccable, as always. I hadn't seen that smile in so long that it stung.

"They've got them in your size. We could find you one if you want," my sister said, and Noah chuckled.

Noah in a Ninja Turtle outfit...that was just what I needed! The thought of it made the image of Noah dressed in other things pass through my mind, and I brought my sunglasses back down, trying to hide my lusty thoughts.

"Hey," I said when we were close.

"Hey," she said dryly.

"Let me help you," I offered, grabbing bags out of her hands. She resisted at first but eventually gave in. She looked at my sister.

"How long have you guys been here?"

"A while," I said, taking my phone out and looking back at our messages. "We should go."

Five minutes later, we'd left all that madness behind.

I took them to a restaurant far away from all the shops, and we ate steak and potatoes. My little sister hogged the conversation. I was struggling to pay attention to what she was saying; I thought she was trying to play some kind of game with us. Either way, I had the sudden, overwhelming urge to be alone with Noah. She had barely said a word to me, and even if things were tense, or beyond tense, I still had high hopes for our truce.

When we walked out, I saw that the building across the street had a play space with slides and little trampolines and multicolored monkey bars and tons of kids playing and shouting.

"Mad, you want to go over there?" I asked, pointing to what must have been a paradise for any child under ten.

She jumped around like mad while Noah gave me a suspicious look. Fine, so my tactics weren't as subtle as I thought. I gave Steve a ring; I'd asked him to stay in the neighborhood, in case Maddie and I were late getting into town; he was around the corner having a coffee and said he'd come watch Maddie if I needed. While we waited, we observed Maddie awkwardly and tried and failed to make small talk.

When we were able to leave, we turned onto a pedestrian-only street full of bars, shops, and ice cream parlors. "You seem quiet," I said. "Are you tired?"

Looking straight ahead, Noah said, "Yeah, I guess… I got up really early."

For a while, we didn't say anything else. This was stupid. We'd never been together for that long and spoken so little. Especially Noah. She couldn't keep quiet even if she was underwater; lots of times I'd had to kiss her or caress her so I could get a bit of silence. Now she seemed interested in nothing, me least of all.

"Look, that's enough, okay. What the hell is going on with you?"

She looked at me with surprise. "Nothing…" she said, but she seemed hesitant. I waited, trying not to fly into a rage. "It's just…this isn't what I expected. I thought we were going to hang out with your sister. Why would you leave her at some random playground? You know how many diseases she could catch? Lice or whatever? We're all probably going to get lice just because you had a change of plans… I thought the three of us would take a walk in the park before we went home. I had more shopping to do anyway… You didn't ask me if I was done when you texted; you're too used to giving orders: *I'll pick you up in 10…*" She imitated my voice. "What if I wasn't ready? Did you ever think about that? Don't look at me like that. It's weird… I'm uncomfortable."

I almost wanted to laugh. So she had been hiding things from me…

"You're uncomfortable with what?" I asked with feigned incredulity.

She stopped and looked at me.

"With this!" She pointed back and forth between us. "With you and me. You acted like we were still together!" I could tell she was struggling to get the words out. "I accepted the truce for Maddie's sake, but I'm not going to lie to myself, and I'd appreciate it if you didn't lie to me. Or do you not remember everything you said to me the last time I saw you?"

I took a deep breath. Deep down, I knew Noah was right. I'd told her I was in love with Sophia to try to turn the page, but it wasn't going to be that easy.

"I've treated you like a friend. That's it," I said.

It took Noah a few seconds to respond. In the meanwhile, she glanced around, lost.

"I prefer it when you're hostile," she said. That cut me to the core. "I'm serious. I'd rather fight with you. I'm used to that. Whereas what you're doing now..." She shook her head, her eyes focused on the ground. I wanted to lift her chin, make her look me in the eyes. "I know you're doing this for your sister, but it hurts. It's confusing to me. I don't want to hang out. I don't want to go for walks or go to lunch or have you ask me where I got my scar or why I was riding a motorcycle... That's my life, and it shouldn't matter to you anymore, and I know I'm the one who screwed things up, but you've made your decision, supposedly, so I'd just as soon you stick to it."

I looked up into the trees behind her. I felt like shit. It was true that I'd done this for Maddie, but I also wanted to spend time with Noah. I missed her, dammit...

"Fine," I growled. "Let's go get my sister."

I turned on my heel and walked down the street. Noah hurried up beside me, and that feeling...that feeling of having her close but at the same time miles away turned me into a statue of ice, the one that had started to melt the day before, even if I hadn't realized it then.

We passed a couple of shops, and when we turned the corner by the playground, my mother—yes, my mother—ran right into us. I stopped when I saw her. I had still refused to see her, and the babysitter was the one who had handed Maddie off to me the day before. Seeing her again, which I hadn't done since the night she'd decided to spill the family's dirty secrets at the anniversary of Leister Enterprises, was the least pleasant surprise I could have imagined.

She was well-dressed, as always, in a cashmere dress and high heels, her hair pulled back; but she had bags under her eyes. With her lavish makeup and skin-care regime, she should have been able to cover them up a little better.

"Nicholas!" she exclaimed.

I bit down and ground my teeth before responding. "Yes, Mother, what an unpleasant coincidence, finding you here."

She stiffened, trying to absorb the blow, I guessed. I didn't care; our relationship was just as bad as ever... What am I saying? It still didn't exist.

"Hello, Noah," she said, and I could tell Noah was tense, too.

Given the circumstances, and what had happened with our parents, I could imagine my mother was on the list of Noah's worst enemies. Probably at the top. Noah didn't respond.

"We're in a hurry. If you don't mind..." I tried to keep walking, but my mother stepped back and grabbed my arm.

"I'd like to talk to you, Nicholas."

"Yes, I figured that out after the thousand messages you left with my secretary, but I think her response was pretty clear: no interest."

As a reflex, I grabbed Noah's hand. I felt myself drowning, and I wanted to get out of there. The two of us stepped around her, obviously trying to escape.

"It's about Maddie, Nicholas," my mother called from behind me.

That made me stop. Reluctantly, I turned toward her.

"Anything that has to do with my sister can be communicated to my father. He's more than happy to keep me informed."

My mother crumpled, looking at me with pleading eyes, and finally, I couldn't keep giving her the cold shoulder. My mother, begging? This was something I'd never seen.

"Just give me a few minutes, Nick, please."

I looked over at Noah. She seemed as intrigued as I was. "Fine. What's up?"

At once surprised and relieved, my mother led us over to a nearby café. Noah sat beside me; my mother sat in front of us. It was all so weird; I just wanted it to be over as soon as possible.

"Okay, shoot, we don't have all day."

Despite the weakness she'd shown when she'd asked me to give her a moment, she now turned stiff and, it seemed to me, a little nasty. That was the Anabel Grason I remembered.

"Fine, since you can't even try to have the least bit of tact with me, I'll skip the formalities and niceties. You want me to be brief, I'll be brief." She set down her cup. "I'm sick, Nicholas."

For a moment, there was silence, interrupted by the clang of porcelain and glass.

"What do you mean, you're sick?" I said. I was immediately angry. This had to be a trick. I wasn't sure what her angle was, but it was pathetic.

"What do I mean?" she responded, and when she did, I could see her start to crumble. There was a fear and insecurity there that I'd never known her to have before. She took a deep breath and peered at me before uttering the next words. "I have leukemia."

"What the hell are you saying?" I replied, hearing my voice lower two octaves.

She joined her hands in her lap and pushed her seat back a bit. "I was diagnosed a year and a half ago… I wanted to tell you, but not over the phone. Not that it mattered, since you never bothered to pick up. Your father found out months ago, but he promised not to tell you. I wanted to do it myself. I know you hate me, but you're my son, and..."

Her voice trembled, and I felt myself falling, falling into a deep dark pit, wondering when I'd strike the bottom... The ground was approaching me, it was seconds away, and I didn't know what would happen afterward, but I was sure it would be nothing good. Then I felt someone squeeze my hand, a warm small hand that had approached mine under the table, promising never to let me go.

I looked at Noah, who was next to me, staring at my mother with...pity? My fingers clung to her as if she were suddenly my only reference point. I heard my mother's words. Surely they weren't true?

"I didn't want to tell you this so you'd feel bad for me. I just wanted to try to explain my behavior these past few months, everything I did: Maddie, Anabel, your father..."

"What are you talking about?" I asked, clearing my throat, trying to get my words past the knot that made it almost impossible to speak.

"I'm letting your father have full custody of Maddie."

"What?" I asked, roused from my lethargy.

"I'm going to need to deal with some very difficult things in the upcoming years, Nicholas. These are things I don't want a little girl to have to deal with. When I found out about this, I knew one thing for sure: I would not allow my daughter to stay in Anabel's care. He's selfish. He can't see past his own nose. I've made mistakes, God knows I've made mistakes in my life, lots of them, and I know I don't even deserve to have you here listening to me now, but Maddie does matter to me. She matters, Nick, and I want to know that if something happens to me, if things don't turn out as I wish, that my daughter will be with a family that will love and protect her."

"Wait, wait," I interrupted her. "You're saying my father knows about all this? And he's agreed to take custody of her? What...?"

"Everything that happened with Anabel, the divorce, the genetic test... Look, I knew there was a possibility that Maddie was your father's daughter. And I wasn't wrong, just as I wasn't wrong when I thought that if I told him, he would want Maddie to be a part of his life. And that's what I want, too."

I couldn't believe what she was saying. All that chaos...was because my mother wanted my father to take care of Maddie in case...in case she died?

"What are you going to do?" I asked, feeling my anger spread. "You're just going to dump Maddie at my dad's house? Give up your parental rights and pretend your daughter doesn't miss you? That's crazy!"

"Nicholas..." Noah said.

"No!" I stood up. "That's not how you do things, dammit! You want to do the same thing to her as you did to me?"

My mother took a deep breath and looked down. "Sit down, please," she said, struggling to remain calm.

I did, and my legs shook, my whole body was tense, my whole fucking brain was a whirl of senseless thoughts trying to grasp a world where my mother's actions might be justified.

"I'm not going to abandon her, Nicholas, I'm just giving your father custody while I try to get through this. I'm in contact with some of the best doctors in the country, and I'm starting chemo at MD Anderson in Houston. The doctors are optimistic, but this could be a long process. You don't want me to take her to Houston with me, do you? Who will care for her while I'm in treatment? All I'm thinking about is what's best for everyone."

I just sat there for seconds or maybe minutes. I don't know. This was fucked, absolutely, completely fucked.

Then I felt a hand grab mine, but it felt different. I opened my eyes and saw it was my mother's. Had she always been so bony? Now I noticed the bags under her eyes again and how skinny she looked, much more than the last time I'd seen her. My fingers didn't care about my ambivalence; they held her tight without asking my permission.

"I'm sorry about all this, Nick," she said, then let me go and wiped away a tear. "Your father can explain it better than I can. Thank you for listening."

She got up, and I felt a sudden emptiness in my mind, my heart.

"Wait," I said, feeling more lost than I ever had. "I want to give you...I want to give you my personal number so you can call me and tell me when you're going, or when..."

I stopped talking, because I didn't know what it was I wanted. I opened my wallet, took out one of my business cards, and scrawled my number on the back. She took it gratefully.

"Thank you, Son," she said, then looked at Noah. "And thank you, too."

Ten minutes later, we gathered my little sister from the park. My life suddenly felt like it wasn't mine anymore, as if I were playing a part that didn't belong to me... I was so angry, so pissed at life for playing another trick on me, putting another obstacle in my path, that I could feel a burning beneath my skin, a tension in my muscles, an energy that I had no idea how to discharge.

Maddie came running toward me, and I crouched and opened my arms. I needed to hold her tight; I wished I could enclose her completely and save her from all the pain she was going to have to face at such an early age. Not just the disappearance of the man she'd thought was her father, who had no intention of ever seeing her again, but her mother's illness, having to live with a father she didn't even know.

I wanted to get her on a plane, take her to New York, take care of her, but…I wasn't her father, however much I wished I were just then. I squeezed her and picked her up off the ground. She was pink from all the running and excitement and couldn't stop talking. Noah must have realized how overwhelmed I was because she interrupted the few words I could get out, in my seriousness, to make Maddie feel normal.

Time…time was crucial now. The time lost, the time left to live. How long would my mother live? Would she make it through this? Would I ever see her again after she left for Houston? Would my sister?

We headed home, and when we got out and were walking toward the front door, I stopped, unable to take another step. Noah had been watching me, and she turned around and asked me something, but I didn't hear her.

"I need…I need to be by myself right now. Could you…? Would you mind taking care of her…?"

She hesitated, as if wanting to say something but not daring to. Then she nodded. She looked confused. But I wasn't in the mood to explain anything.

I got in my car and vanished for a few hours.

It was close to midnight when I got back. I'd had time to think, and thinking when things are that fucked up can have consequences you may come to regret.

I walked up the stairs in the dark, not bothering to turn on the lights. Why would I? I passed Noah's door and felt a needle jab me in the heart. The love of my life was in there…the same person who had hurt me the way everyone I'd ever let get close to me had.

Did I hate Noah?

I had hated her, and it was very likely I even hated her in that instant. Or maybe now was when I hated her most because now was when I needed her most, when her absence felt most acute, when my mind was screaming at me to go after her and my heart was yearning for someone to give me some kind of inner peace, some kind of relief from the pain.

I opened her door, not bothering to knock. She was in bed, awake, surrounded by books, same as before. My sister was sleeping next to her, splayed out on the mattress and sucking her thumb, just as she'd done since she was ten months old. Noah closed her book carefully, took off her glasses, and looked at me.

"Where have you been?" she asked calmly. "You've been gone for like five hours… Are you okay?"

I took the book from her hands and laid it on the nightstand.

"I want to talk to you," I said. I glanced over at the door. She hesitated, and I felt suddenly frustrated. "You owe it to me," I added through clenched teeth.

Minutes may have passed before she got up wordlessly and followed me to my room. Our eyes met, and I couldn't stop myself. I put my hands on her cheeks and kissed her as hard as I could. Her back bumped against the door. I could breathe again. In the darkness, I barely noticed how tense she was, but after a few intense seconds, she turned away.

"Don't do this to me, Nicholas," she warned me in a hardly audible whisper.

I brushed away a lock of her hair and tucked it carefully behind her ear, trying to draw out our contact as long as possible. Her fragrance enveloped me, driving me crazy with desire, with love… That scent was so dense, so special, so hers. One whiff of it was enough to intoxicate me. And I needed that right now.

I stroked her cheek, and she closed her eyes, her breathing

labored. Was she suffering as I was? Did the distance make her ache the way it did me?

"Why can't I forget you?" I asked, pressing my forehead into hers. "Why are you the only thing that can help me in a moment like this?"

"Nicholas..." she said.

Our eyes met with an almost electric charge, too much for me to stand, and I buried my face in her neck. I had to.

I kissed the soft skin of her throat, first slowly, barely touching it. My nose traced a line from her hairline to her clavicle. Grabbing her waist, I pulled her into me. I needed more. Much more. Noah's hands were on my chest, caressing me at first, but then, as I only noticed later in my trance, pushing me away.

"You're not thinking clearly," she said. "You don't want to do this."

Her nightgown barely covered her thighs, and I put my hands beneath it, sliding upward to her buttocks, where I stopped, wondering whether I was crazy, wondering whether I would regret this later.

I kissed her cheeks, the corner of her lips, her eyelids...then plunged into her throat. I wasn't kissing her anymore... I was sucking, nibbling, drinking from her. I was lost in her, lost in a limbo where we as separate people no longer existed. Noah yelped, and that made me want to keep going. I lifted her, and her legs wrapped around my waist. She cupped my face, and now we were truly looking at each other, as if we'd met again after an eternity. There was no rancor in her eyes; there was nothing but love, the same love I felt for her, the love for me that I knew must still be alive in her heart. A love that needed to disappear, dammit, a love I kept trying to bury and that kept coming back to the surface at the worst moments, making me violate all my principles.

"I need you," I confessed. Her breath mingled with mine, and

I thought I'd faint from pleasure. Touching her—that was the only thing that could calm my pain.

I didn't hesitate. I felt her lips responding against mine, and I put aside all doubts. I pounced on her, pressed her into the door, and her lips opened to receive me as if we were kissing for the first time. I had to have her, had to relieve my body's torment.

"I'm going to make love to you, Noah," I said, as if it were something inevitable, something that just had to happen. "Since we broke up, everything's been shit. My life is falling apart, and it's getting worse by the day. I hate needing you the way I do. I hate knowing that even now, you're the only one who can make me forget, even if it's just for a few minutes, that my mother is dying." Tears welled in my eyes. I kissed her so she wouldn't see them.

She shook her head, and in the moonlight, I could see her weeping, too.

"You know this will only make things worse," she whispered. I could feel her heartbeat, almost at the same rhythm as mine.

"They can't get worse... Things couldn't be more fucked up than they are now," I said.

"This will just hurt us," she whispered again. "Tomorrow morning, things will be the same as before..."

I kissed her, felt a tear beneath my lips, licked it, savored it.

"That night in New York, you asked me to pretend I'd forgiven you. Now I need you to do that for me."

She trembled against me, we kissed again, and I carried her off to my bed.

22

Noah

We were standing at the foot of his bed. His lips were tender, kissing every inch of my body as he peeled off my clothes. He lifted my nightgown so slowly that it hurt, pulled it over my head, dropped it beside us. I was in a trance as I watched him take off his shirt and pants. When he was just in his underwear, I looked away.

Neither of us seemed able to believe what was happening. This was nothing like New York. Then, we'd both been hurt and bitter, and our encounter had been cold, just sex; now, after our truce, after several days with hardly an argument and after hearing such painful news, we couldn't ignore the weight of our feelings anymore.

Doubts and fear gathered in my mind. He knew it, and he pulled me close, whispering in my ear: "Noah, please." His hand was rubbing my back up and down, giving me gooseflesh. His mouth moved down to my breasts.

I closed my eyes, held my breath, wished he couldn't control me and my body with such ease. He turned me around, squeezed my back into his chest, kissed the nape of my neck, toyed with my hair, and his hand kept going down past my stomach and into my panties, touching me without hesitation or shame.

I moaned when he licked my earlobe and prayed that we really would make love. I wanted to forget our past, pretend we were together. I wanted to do it with Nick, in Nick's bed, the way I had the first time when he took my virginity and told me he loved me.

He took off my underwear, laid me back in the bed, and climbed on top of me. He kissed my breasts, took my nipples in his teeth, and my back arched with desire. He lifted my left leg by the ankle, set my foot down next to his hip, kissed my thigh, passed his tongue over me, as though my skin were as sweet as chocolate. This torture lasted for minutes. *One more caress*, I thought, *and I'll explode*. He asked me something, and I said yes, but I didn't even know what it was.

I could feel his weight on top of me. He kissed me; we looked at each other for what felt like forever; and at last, he grabbed my waist and plunged inside me.

It hurt, and I cried out involuntarily.

Confusion and worry crossed his face.

"How long has it been, Noah?" he asked me, grinding against me, giving me pain, giving me pleasure... I didn't even know where I was or what I was doing; all I could concentrate on was feeling, feeling, yes, because for so many months, I had felt nothing.

"Too long," I said, grabbing hold of him.

He stopped and leaned back to look at me. "You haven't done it since New York?" he asked with what seemed like incredulity but might have been relief.

"I haven't done anything since we broke up, Nicholas."

His eyes lit up, and he kissed me hard and started moving again. His strokes slowed down, his movements were more affectionate, and he nibbled and sucked my lower lip. I gripped his arms in ecstasy as we shared that moment of togetherness. Our cheeks touched.

"Tell me you love me," I asked him, my voice cracking. He stopped. "Please…"

"Don't ask me for that. Trying to forget you is the hardest thing I've ever done. I don't even know how I'll manage to go back to my old reality after this."

"Then stay with me," I asked him, knowing how vulnerable he was just then. I didn't know if it was wrong, but I needed him, as much as or more than he needed me.

I dug my fingers into his hair, and his eyes closed. I kissed him. I never wanted to let him go. "Nick, please, say it."

He silenced me with his lips. His movements turned more intense. He wanted to make me hush; he thought his body was enough to satisfy me… He was sweating, clinging to me, skin against skin, in the deepest intimacy possible. He was angry, aroused, sad, everything all at once.

"Give it to me, Noah… Give me what I want…what I need… please."

He thrusted harder, faster. I lost all connection to my surroundings, my feelings, my problems, everything. I was on the verge of orgasm, the kind of orgasm that washes everything away.

I shouted with pleasure, arched my back until I was barely touching the bed. He kept thrusting and came inside me, his roar muddled by my shoulder, and then he collapsed on top of me. It was perfect, yes.

But he hadn't said *I love you*.

When we had recovered, Nicholas walked to the bathroom. I thought it would be like that time in New York, that he'd shower, throw me a T-shirt, and tell me to get dressed. But I was wrong. When he came back, he lay down beside me and pulled me into him. I didn't understand... Did that mean something? I rested my cheek on his chest, feeling as if I'd been given a direct injection of happiness. I didn't want him to go. I didn't want to lose him again. I hugged him tight and closed my eyes. I was exhausted. Nicholas stroked my hair until I started feeling sleepy. I knew I'd have lovely dreams that night, about him and me, together again... No hatred and no mistakes would exist in my dreams, and the love we professed to each other would be all that mattered.

But morning brought with it truths and insecurities, and when I opened my eyes, very early, I realized what had happened in that room wouldn't happen again. Nicholas was with another woman, and not just any woman. He was with Sophia, with *her*, with one of the people who'd made the planets align on that horrible night that ended with me doing what I had done.

He was asleep, squeezing me against his chest as though he never wanted to let me go. I'd have given anything to freeze that instant, but I knew that when he opened his eyes again, I'd see bitterness and regret, and I didn't know if I was ready for that.

He had needed me. His mother was sick, and he had used me to salve his wounds... *You owe it to me*, he had said, and it was true, I did owe him a conversation, but then it became more. And now, I saw how wrong what we'd done was: This wasn't how you did things. It wasn't how you asked for what you needed. That moment would be one more in a long string of painful memories. And yet I would cherish it; I would hold on to that goodbye, if that was what it was, waiting to see how he'd reject me once more.

Careful not to wake him, I lifted Nicholas's arm off me. It was better to leave, get away from him, from his sister, from any and all painful memories. I would make up some excuse for my mother, or maybe I wouldn't need to. I couldn't go on like this. I had to live my own life. Nicholas had been a part of me; he would always have a place in my heart... What was I saying! He'd always have my heart, every part of it, but I needed to be myself again, love myself, learn to forgive myself.

I packed my suitcase as quickly and quietly as I could. Maddie was still there, curled up in the sheets, sleeping like a little angel. When I walked out, dressed and ready to go, what I felt wasn't relief. I wasn't happy that I'd finally put an end to all that—no, I felt like I was closing a book that had touched me to the core, a book I would always remember...a magical, incredible book that, even if I read it again, would never be as it had been the first time. That morning, I ended an important chapter of my life. A chapter...but don't forget, a chapter isn't the whole story.

The drive home was unbearable. My body was screaming at me to go back, to climb into bed with Nick and to sleep until the end of time, but my mind kept repeating to me what an idiot I'd been, how stupid it was to think anything might have changed. But if Nick and I had broken up more than a year ago, why was I crying as if it had only now really happened? At one point, I had to pull off the road, cut the motor, and grab the wheel so I could sob without worrying about crashing into anyone.

I cried for what we had been, I cried for what we could have been, I cried for his sick mother and his baby sister... I cried for him, for disappointing him, for breaking his heart, for getting him to love me and then showing him love didn't exist, at least not without pain, and that pain had now scarred him for life.

I cried for Noah, the Noah I had been when I was with him. That Noah full of life, the Noah who, despite her inner demons, had known how to love with all her heart. I had loved him more than anybody, and that was something to grieve, too. When you meet the person you want to spend the rest of your life with, there is no going back. Lots of people never learn what that feels like. I knew, I know, that Nick was the love of my life, the man I wanted to be the father of my children, the man I wanted by my side through good and bad, in sickness and in health, till death did us part.

Nick was *the one*, he was my other half, and now I'd have to learn to live without him.

23

Nick

Much as I loved my sister, she wasn't the one I was looking forward to seeing when I opened my eyes. I sat up, trying to focus, trying to figure out why the left side of my bed was empty, how I'd failed to realize that Noah had gotten up and walked out. But there was an easy answer: I'd slept—really, truly slept—for the first time in over a year.

"Where's Noah?" my sister kept asking, jumping up and down on the mattress. The question caught me off guard.

What did she mean, where was she?

"Isn't she in her room?" I asked, getting up and rubbing my eyes, trying to get the lead out. In the bathroom, I splashed water on my face and tried to focus on the new day, a day when I'd have to explain lots of things and figure out lots more.

The night before hadn't just been sex—not at all. It had been more; I had let my old feelings move me…and for the first time in ages, I had felt good.

"She's not here, Nick," Maddie replied.

I went to her room and opened the door, and it was true, no one was there. I looked around for her things. Her books, her suitcase…everything was gone.

"Fuck!" I hissed.

"You said a swear word!"

I looked down. This wasn't the best time to have to look after Madison.

"Midget, go to the kitchen and get Prett to make you some breakfast." When she was about to argue, I added, "Now!"

"Did Noah leave?" she asked, visibly upset.

That made two of us.

"I don't know. Now go downstairs—I'm not going to say it again."

Her beautiful blue eyes narrowed; I knew this was going to have consequences.

She turned around and ran downstairs.

I went back to my room and grabbed my phone. Without even thinking, I called Noah, not once but twice.

Dammit, Noah. Did you have to leave like this?

I was pissed. Very pissed. I was ready to hop in my car and go after her. Why had she gone? Had I mistreated her? No, fuck no, I hadn't; I'd been the same as always, the same as I was when we were together. Okay, she had wanted something else...had asked for something else...

Tell me you love me...

I couldn't. It hurt too bad.

I went to the kitchen. My mood was awful. My father was there with my sister; they were chatting away about something, or rather, Maddie was, and Raffaella was smiling as she watched them. When they looked up as I walked in, I mumbled a good morning, got a coffee, and walked to the front door.

I felt relieved when I saw Noah's old hunk of junk. So she hadn't left after all. But where was she, then? And where were her things? I went to the garage. The Audi was gone.

So she had left. I realized that not telling her what she wanted to hear had been an easier way to get rid of her than all my lies. I'd gotten what I wanted; she'd turned the page. But…why did I feel empty inside, then? And why hadn't I felt that when I'd seen her?

It didn't help my bad mood when my father called me to his office to talk. After our argument on Thanksgiving, we hadn't spoken, but something told me that this time, his summons had nothing to do with work.

"Your mother called me yesterday to tell me she'd seen you and told you she was sick."

I laughed sarcastically, walked to his bar, and poured myself a drink. It was ten in the morning, but what did I care?

"I see you all are best friends now; you tell each other everything. How's Raffaella feel about that, Dad? Or are you hiding this from her, too?"

My father didn't take the bait; he just waited, his hands crossed over his stomach, sitting in his big leather chair. I emptied my glass and served myself another drink. When I could finally face him, I was enraged, enraged and deeply sad, and that sorrow was something I'd never felt before.

"When were you going to tell me?!" I shouted.

"Your mother asked me not to," he replied calmly.

I laughed. "You know what, Dad? It's almost funny how whatever you decide to say or not to say depends entirely on how it affects you. You had no problem with hiding the fact that you were cheating on Mom for almost your entire marriage, and you certainly didn't bother telling me that was why she left… You let me think she'd just vanished, with no justification whatsoever!"

He stood and walked to the window. "Your mother was already gone, Nicholas. I know her…and when she decided to leave you, she was perfectly aware of what she was doing. I didn't tell you anything because I didn't want you to keep hoping you might see her again. I didn't want you to chase a lie."

"My whole life has been a fucking lie!" I needed to calm down, control the tremors overtaking my body and hands. I balled up my fists. "What's going to happen to Madison?"

He turned. "She'll stay here. That's what's best for her," he responded, and I shook my head. Best? Best for her, or for him? "Nicholas, your sister needs to be somewhere stable and welcoming. I don't want her always at the hospital, surrounded by doctors, having to see the effects of Anabel's chemo—she's too little."

"She needs her mother."

My father's eyes, so similar to mine, looked at me without flinching. It had been a long time, years maybe, since he'd looked at me that way, and I felt myself on the verge of tears. He walked over and rested a hand on my shoulder.

"This isn't the same as what happened to you, Nick. I won't let that happen again, I promise. Maddie will see her mother. She'll be in constant contact with her. I won't make the same mistake again."

I shook my head. The words snagged in my throat. I felt like I was twelve years old again, and my father was telling me Mom would never come back.

"I never told you I was sorry for that... I'm doing it now... I was wrong, Nicholas; I thought I was doing what was right for you, I thought I could be enough, I thought your mother would just hurt you, but I should have fought. I should have done whatever I could to make her stay a part of your life, somehow, even if it meant living a lie. That's what a parent does—they say and do whatever they can to make their children feel loved and protected. But I didn't know how."

I blinked several times as my eyes watered, trying to see clearly. This was the last thing I'd expected. Life was full of surprises, and it kept hitting me and expecting me to get back up, wounded, hurt, but still able to carry on down that road...

"Don't keep Maddie from having a mother," I said, and I didn't just mean my own mother having to leave. My father understood. He understood exactly what I meant.

"I will do everything in my power to be sure neither of you is left without a mother, Nicholas."

As he said this, he pulled me in for a hug. I hadn't expected that at all. I didn't remember the last time he'd done something like that, the last time anyone except Noah had shown me affection in that way. And when I felt the peace in my heart, I realized, despite what I might have thought, that I needed to let my guard down, allow other people in, at least sometimes, to protect me from the dark.

24

Noah

Two weeks after Thanksgiving, I got the call. I was about to start work! The secretary told me that Simon Roger, one of the partners in the firm, needed a young, energetic executive assistant to make his life easier. I would come in for a short meeting with him on Monday at seven a.m. It was an internship, but it still paid better than my old job, so I was happy.

When I arrived, I met a pretty woman with light hair and big brown eyes who showed me to Mr. Roger's office. I knocked and waited a moment until he said I could come in. I was expecting an older man, not the impeccably dressed and groomed tall one who greeted me. He had green eyes and blond hair a bit lighter than mine. His blue suit and gray tie were of the finest materials, and I knew I'd looked at him for too long when I saw him smile.

"Noah Morgan, right?" he asked, standing up from his chair and buttoning his suit jacket with one hand while stretching out the other.

I wasn't sure how hard to squeeze, and I worried I'd been too soft.

"Yeah, that's me," I said, feeling a little stupid.

Roger motioned for me to take a seat, then came around his desk to sit next to me. He turned his chair to face me. His office was simple: a wooden desk with an executive chair and two leather chairs in front of it, a gigantic Mac, and shelves full of file folders.

"When Lincoln told me Nicholas's sister was looking for work here, I was surprised, but when I saw your grades and your references, I was happy you decided to work for me and not for Leister."

I didn't like hearing Nicholas's name, but since they knew each other, I guessed it was inevitable that my family would come to light.

"Yeah, I mean, I guess no one wants to work for their stepfather," I said, trying to sound friendly.

Roger looked up from a file and grinned. "I didn't mean William, I meant Nicholas, but sure, I suppose you're right." He put the file aside, amused. "The job is simple. You take care of my errands, take notes at my meetings, help me with whatever I need..."

I nodded. So like a secretary, basically.

"I'm sure your brother could find you something better..."

"No, no, the last thing I want is to go begging to Nicholas. Anyway, I'd have to go to New York, right?" I said with a smile. I had a job! I was dying to get started!

Roger gave me a curious look. "Yes, I mean, it's true that Nicholas is in New York right now, but this company is as much his as it is Lincoln's and mine. But it's normal you'd want to start from the bottom. That shows you have character..."

My mind froze, and I felt chills all over.

"Sorry, what exactly do you mean...?" A cold sweat dripped down my spine. "This company belongs to Nicholas?"

Roger looked at me as if I were an idiot and pointed to the emblem behind him, engraved on the window. I nearly had a heart attack. It couldn't be.

LEISTER, ROGER & BAXWELL INC.

Shit!

It was Nicholas's company, too?!

"We started the project together, but he's the majority shareholder... I assumed you knew that," he said, surprised that I obviously didn't.

How could I be so stupid? *Who just takes a job without even looking into it beforehand?*

"My brother and I don't have the best relationship," I explained. "I called because Lincoln Baxwell offered me a job a few months ago. I didn't have any idea this was Nicholas's company. I..." I felt a flush coming into my cheeks. "I'm sorry. I shouldn't have wasted your time. I'll go now."

Roger stood and grabbed my arm before I could walk out. "Wait, Noah," he said gently. "There's no need for Nick to know you're working here, if that's what you're worried about. He's in New York, and as far as I know, he doesn't have any intention of leaving."

I took a deep breath. My thoughts were racing. I knew all too well Nicholas wasn't planning on returning to LA. Not now, certainly.

"I'll be your boss, not him," he added, trying to convince me.

Could I do it? Could I work for Simon Roger knowing that one of the heads of the company was my ex-boyfriend, the same ex-boyfriend I hoped to never see again? If I'd had any other offer, I would have marched out...but I doubted things could get any better than this.

"What do you say?" he asked.

I swallowed my fears and suppressed my bad intuitions and said yes. Roger smiled, showing me his handsome white teeth.

"Welcome to the team, then... I'm very excited to be working with you."

Forcing a smile, I said goodbye and walked out. *Fuck, Nicholas… Why the hell is it so hard to get away from you?*

As the days passed, and I got comfortable with the realization that I wasn't just going to bump into Nick, that he really had gone to New York and was managing LRB from there, I relaxed and was able to work calmly. I liked the job. It didn't leave me much time to think, much time to ruminate, and that was exactly what I needed. I worked all morning when I didn't have class, and when I did, I would go to the office after to help Simon with whatever he needed.

The weeks flew by, and soon it was time for Christmas. I spent it with my mother, Will, and Maddie. Nick had told us work would keep him away, but deep down, I knew he was staying away because of me.

I spent New Year's Eve with Jenna and Lion. She tried not to talk about Nick when we were together, but the subject came up without either of us wanting it to.

"He's not in love with her, Noah," she said over dinner, with a pointed look. "He's still with her, though."

She had been insisting that now that I was single and could do it, I should go out, meet more people, let my hair down… As we were counting down to New Year's Day, I thought maybe she was right and it was time to go out with other guys.

One morning at work, Simon entered my tiny office, which was connected to his by a dark wooden door. I looked up from the computer screen and watched him as he walked over. He rested his hands on the back of the chair in front of me and smiled.

"You're doing a great job, Noah," he said proudly. I had the feeling he had taken me under his wing and was teaching me and protecting me, almost as if he wanted me to be his disciple. I'd only been there a month, but I'd learned a ton, and I was very grateful.

"Thanks, Simon," I said. As always, I blushed in his presence. He was to die for. That day he had on gray suit pants and a spotless white shirt rolled up to his elbows. His blond hair was combed up in the front, his green eyes cheerful.

"I thought I'd invite you out." I furrowed my brows, but he kept talking. "The whole office is going; we want to celebrate our deal for the new Coca-Cola campaign. Come on, don't look at me like that. You're supposed to be young, remember?"

I smiled and felt a tingle in my stomach. It had been a long time since I'd gone out just to have fun. It was chilly out, so I wrapped a light blue scarf around my neck. The two of us walked out together.

"Where is everyone?" I asked.

"They must already be at the bar. Not everyone works as much as you do."

I ignored that dig or compliment, whatever it was, and followed behind him. We turned the corner of the tall building that housed our company and walked down a street packed with cars and people... It was a typical afternoon at rush hour. We talked along the way, and I was surprised at how easy it was to do so when we weren't at work and how at ease I felt by his side. I was still laughing at a joke he told when he stopped suddenly.

"Can I be sincere with you?" he asked, looking me in the eye.

The change of tone made me nervous, but still, I nodded cautiously. "Sincerity is always better than the opposite."

I smiled again, and he tucked a loose lock of hair behind my ear. That made me relive a forgotten feeling: butterflies flapping lightly in my stomach.

"I like you, Noah... I mean, I really like you, and I'd like to invite you to dinner," he said. There was no embarrassment in his voice. He was self-assured, the way a man should be when he's accomplished a lot in a short amount of time and is brilliant, funny, and a good boss to boot.

"You want to invite me to dinner now...or are we still supposed to be going out with our coworkers?" I was nervous, and I was pretty sure he knew it.

"To be honest...I made that up. I'd been wanting to ask you out, but I was afraid you'd say no, so I made up a little story."

"I get it," I said. I wasn't really sure whether I was happy about him lying to me.

"It's just to get to know you better... We'll talk, we'll have a nice dinner somewhere, we'll order the most expensive thing on the menu, and then we'll each go to our respective homes."

It sounded nice, but...was it a date?

The restaurant he took me to was nice, but not too nice... Not so nice that I felt uncomfortable, anyway. On the walls were records from the eighties, the vinyl different colors, and the tables were set with red-and-white-checked tablecloths with candles in the middle, to give it a homey, informal feel.

It was Italian, so I was sure I would like the food. I ordered ravioli with alfredo sauce; he got a vegetarian lasagna. I enjoyed it, I enjoyed our talk, I enjoyed playing twenty questions and getting to know each other better. I hadn't been on a date in a long time... I'd only ever gone out with Dan and Nick, and afterward, I'd barely had time to meet boys or even get to know anyone, really.

Simon told me he was the oldest child in his family, brother to four sisters who drove him crazy. He was from a well-off family:

his father was an architect, his mother a doctor. He was the weirdo who'd decided to go into marketing and communications.

Dinner passed by fast, and we walked back to the parking deck at work. My Audi was parked next to his. Some coincidence.

"Well, Noah," he said when there was clearly no more walking left to do, "I loved eating with you, and if we can do it again, the sooner, the better."

I laughed. I couldn't believe how well it all had gone. No drama, no games, just a guy and a girl sitting together and talking about their lives. I'd had fun, but it was weird when he stepped forward and tried to kiss me.

Instinctively, I turned aside, and his lips landed on my cheek.

"Hm," he said, amused but disappointed.

"Sorry… I loved dinner, but I need to go slower," I said, feeling like a stupid little girl, unable to even give a guy a kiss on the lips.

He patted me on the cheek. That I did like.

"Sure… You're making it hard for me, but that's fine. I like a challenge."

He got in his car and left.

I stood there for a few seconds more, and when I moved again, I realized my eyes were filling with tears.

25

Nick

I LOOKED AT THE SCHEDULE MY SECRETARY HAD JUST PASSED ME and sighed. I'd barely have time to catch my breath. Between the opening of LRB and the closure of the other two companies, I was completely booked. I didn't complain; I liked to work, especially on this new project I'd had to try so hard to get off the ground.

I saw the morning paper and cursed. Simon Roger had called me that same morning to tell me we couldn't deal with any bad press right now. Our image was critical just then, he said. I knew he was right, but I hadn't had time to mug for the cameras and explain every one of my decisions. Convincing the board had been hard enough—now I had to convince the entire world?

Things would get better—I knew that—but it would take time.

My phone rang, and I answered without thinking. It was Sophia.

"I'm busy," I said, a little nastier than I should have.

"You always are," she replied. "Your secretary told me you're going to Los Angeles next week."

"I'm going to drop in at the LRB offices and make sure everything is going smoothly."

"She also told me there's going to be a grand-opening celebration."

"I see Lisa's keeping you up to date," I responded angrily. "Yes, Roger insisted that we throw a party; supposedly it's the right thing for our image."

"Had you considered informing me that you were taking off for California? I should remind you, it's been a month since we last saw each other."

I got up and poured myself a cup of hot coffee. I'd been so busy with work, and so unsettled by my last encounter with Noah, that I hadn't thought about Sophia at all, to tell the truth. "Sure, I was going to tell you, but nothing was set in stone yet."

Even from miles away, I could hear Sophia's brain clicking.

"Shall we say your place, then?" I couldn't fail to notice the excitement in her voice. It made me smile, despite the circumstances.

"See you there," I said, sitting back down. "You've got your own key, right?"

I couldn't help comparing the way I spoke with her and the way I spoke with Noah. I'd given Sophie the key months ago because she had to stay in LA sometimes for work, and my apartment there was sitting empty. I hadn't had time to sell it. But the memories in those four walls burned hotter than the fire now crackling in the fireplace in my office...

My flight to Los Angeles was early, so I'd arrive in time for the personnel meeting scheduled there at midday. I wanted to be sure they weren't making the same mistakes as last time. Plus, I wanted to see Maddie. I hadn't been back since the new year. Noah had made herself scarce. I longed to see her, though. Her mother had told me she was busy on campus, studying, supposedly, but I knew she had stayed away because of me. The last night we'd spent together, almost two months before, was still engraved in my mind: each kiss, each word, each sound, each sensation... I didn't know what would have happened if she hadn't left. Could I have left her? Would I have had the strength to get up with her in my arms and tell her we were done?

Those questions didn't have answers and never would. Fate had wanted her to make the decision, freeing me from the bother and letting us go on with our lives.

Now I had Sophia. But she was an obligation, a way of fulfilling expectations. I wanted to have kids one day; I wanted a wife. I would never love anyone the way I had loved Noah, but I couldn't just leave everything on hold. There would always be painful memories, and I would always hold her in my heart, in my very cells, as if she were a part of me. But that didn't mean I couldn't keep trying to have the things I knew I wanted for my future.

Steve was waiting for me at the airport. He'd left to spend a few days with his older son, who was graduating from college soon. I smiled when I saw him, and we walked toward his car.

"How's Aaron?" I asked, buckling my seat belt and turning on my phone to scroll through my missed calls and messages.

"He's glad the whole thing's almost over."

I smiled, distracted, and checked the time. "You should speed up; I don't want to show up late to a meeting I set up myself."

Steve did as I asked, and in half an hour, we were parking next to a building I'd shelled out millions for.

I wasn't surprised by the hustling and bustling when I came in. This was something I'd gotten used to seeing.

"Good morning, Mr. Leister; they're waiting for you in the meeting room," a secretary I didn't know told me.

"Thanks. Could you bring me a coffee?" I crossed the lobby. I knew I was running behind. "No cream, no sugar, thanks."

She hurried off, and I walked toward the meeting room. When I opened the door, I was surprised to find everyone laughing and out of their seats, surrounding someone or something that was apparently very funny. I snuck over, knowing no one had heard me come in, and saw a girl with long blond hair sitting down, arm wrestling with none other than Simon Roger.

It took me two seconds, I believe, to realize the girl was Noah.

I didn't get it. There she was, laughing, hand in hand with that dumbass, who of course was letting her win, at least for now. When my eyes settled on their hands, I saw red.

"If the ten minutes between when the meeting was supposed to start and now have given you all enough time to start this circus, I don't even want to imagine what you get up to when I'm not around," I said, loud enough for everyone to hear, including the two people who were the center of attention. They all stopped and turned toward me.

Noah jumped up when she heard my voice. Rage had overtaken my five senses. Nothing mattered to me then: not the employees I'd hoped to make a good impression on, not even the fact that, if Noah hadn't been there, I would have laughed along and probably gotten in on the competition.

My whole world started to crumble at the sight of her.

"The meeting's canceled," I almost shouted. "I want everyone here at seven in the morning, and we'll see if you get to hold on to your jobs. This isn't a goddamned playground!"

I scowled at everyone there, especially Roger, who was way too cozy with my girlfriend—dammit, I meant with Noah.

I turned around to walk out, but first I shouted, "Morgan, my office!"

26

Noah

I STARED AT THE DOOR, SILENT, JUST LIKE EVERYONE ELSE THERE, for the moment.

Then someone said, "Fuck that boss," grabbed his things, and walked out.

"I guess what the papers say is true," said another, making me turn around to see who it had been. People were looking at me with pity, since I was the only one he'd actually called out.

Simon leaned in and whispered in my ear, "You want me to go with you?" Everything about the past few weeks stopped making sense.

"Don't worry, it's fine," I said. "I know how to deal with him."

We'd had a few more dinners since that first one. One night, I'd told him about me and Nick. Obviously, it'd surprised Simon to find out that relationship was very far from us just being stepbrother and stepsister.

I smiled and walked toward the office Nick kept there, which was empty most of the time. I knocked on the door before entering, while everyone around me stared.

"Come in!" he roared.

When I did, I found him pacing anxiously back and forth.

"What the hell are you doing here?"

I took a deep breath while he stripped off his jacket, slung it into his chair, and rolled up his sleeves.

"I work here," I responded. "I thought you knew that."

He was jerking down his tie, but he stopped, looked over, and narrowed his eyes. "What the hell are you talking about?"

"I lost my last job, and I remembered Lincoln Baxwell giving me his card at Jenna's wedding. I called him, and he told me he'd find me something here." I shrugged, as if the story were all too convenient, but that was how it actually had been.

Nick leaned on the desk and stared me down. "Why didn't you call me?" he asked, sounding almost disappointed. "I could have gotten you something much better."

"You don't even know what I do."

"That's true. Who do you work for?"

I had a hunch he wasn't going to like what he heard, but I couldn't lie; he would find out the truth almost instantly, and I didn't want to piss him off worse. "I work for Simon… I'm his assistant."

He took a deep breath and blew it out slowly. "His assistant?" he replied mockingly, his eyebrows raised. "What the fuck does that mean?"

I crossed my arms. "What's it supposed to mean, Nicholas? I help him with his agenda, I make him coffee…"

"Coffee?" He pronounced the word like an insult.

"Yeah, you know that black stuff people drink in the mornings—"

"Don't be funny with me," he cut me off, sitting down. "Aren't you meant to be studying? Are you still pretending you need to work for some reason?"

"You're the one who doesn't need to work, *Mister* Leister," I responded.

He looked at me the way a principal looks at a badly behaved student. "You're really on fire this morning... Does acting like an idiot at work put you in a good mood?"

Fine: arm wrestling at work wasn't the most professional thing ever, but Nick was the one who'd showed up late.

"What puts me in a good mood is seeing how jealous you are that I'm having a good time with your employees."

"With Roger, you mean."

"*Employees*," I said, emphasizing the plural.

"I'm not jealous—I'm pissed off to see you wasting people's time when they should be busting their balls to get this company off the ground."

"So now it's my fault that we were killing time waiting for you to show up at a meeting you called..."

"Look, let's not start talking about what is whose fault, Noah. That could take all day."

I'd forgotten how fucking annoying he could be.

"Can I go?" I asked, staring daggers at him.

"No."

His eyes gleamed, with rage, with fury, with lust...

"You look good," he said after a tense silence. The compliment caught me off guard. "You've put back on the pounds you lost. That's a good thing. I don't like you looking like a skeleton."

I hadn't expected that. "Are you calling me fat?"

He laughed in a way that nearly gave me a heart attack. "Do you think you look fat?"

No, of course I wasn't fat, I'd never been fat; I'd just put back on the weight I'd lost after our breakup. I looked healthy now, less gaunt. That was a good sign. It meant I was moving on.

"You don't look bad yourself," I said, avoiding the question. "I guess being apart from me is doing you some good."

My tone was cold, I knew that, and Nick didn't reply. As he

observed me, I imagined he was remembering the last time we'd been together. I know I was.

"You want anything else?" I asked, popping the bubble the two of us seemed to inhabit. "I ought to get back to work."

He shook his head, almost leering. What was that look trying to tell me? I turned around and walked to the door, but before I left, I looked over my shoulder.

"You should take it easy on your employees, Nick. They're good people, and they were all excited to meet you today."

He leaned his head back as if about to say something, but then he just nodded. I left him alone, with a lot to think about, I supposed.

The meeting the next day was much better. Nick was nice to everyone, charming, but he didn't apologize for his conduct the day before. He was the boss, after all, and I could see that finding his entire staff giggling and goofing off would have gotten under any boss's skin. He had everyone there eating out of his hand by the end—everyone but Simon, who observed him politely but coldly. I didn't like that, but there was nothing I could do about it. Nick treated me with the respect I deserved, and he kept his distance, which I appreciated. Now and again, I caught him looking at me. I couldn't deny I liked having him there, even if it hurt me at the same time. Despite everything, I tried to concentrate on my work. It's not like I had many chances to talk to him. Most of his meetings were private and didn't require my presence. After all, I was simply an intern.

But everything got worse the day I emerged from my office and found myself face-to-face with…Sophia. We stared at each other for a moment, and even though I was dying inside, I struggled with all my might to stay calm.

"It's nice to see you," I said in the calmest, most buoyant tone I could muster.

Sophia gave me a surprised look, and Nick, who had heard my words on his way to Simon's office, came to a stop next to her, looking at me warily, but not without interest in his blue eyes.

"If you'll excuse me..." I turned on my heel and went straight to the bathroom, where I took a minute to try to relax and not cry.

Take it easy, Noah... You're on your way to getting over him, remember? Breathe, breathe...don't give them the satisfaction of knowing this is affecting you.

Seeing the two of them together, one right next to the other, would never stop tormenting me. It was one thing to see a photo; it was another to see the two of them together, and the way Sophia's face lit up as soon as she felt him next to her, and Nicholas's hand coming to rest on her lower back...

Fuck, no, no, don't cry now, don't do it, don't be an idiot...

I stood up straight and splashed water on my face, careful not to let my makeup run. I touched up my lipstick. I needed to look strong, be the strong, mature Noah I had shown everyone up to that point.

When I walked out, Nick and Sophia had left. I walked to Simon's office, knocked, and when he told me to come in, I nearly ran into Nick, who had hurried over to open the door for me.

He stared at me, and I looked away, edging past him to speak with my boss.

"I'll get you all those numbers you asked for, Nick, no worries there," Simon said.

Nick nodded, still staring at me.

Why are you just staring at me, Nick? Go be with your girlfriend; let me suffer in peace!

Nick must have read my thoughts, because he nodded again, walked out, and shut the door.

Simon came over and grabbed my hands. "You okay?"

I nodded, and he guided me over to his desk, leaning back against it.

Simon and I had just kissed, nothing more, and even that we'd only done twice. I knew I couldn't keep pretending we were just fifteen. He was twenty-eight, and he'd made it evident that he liked me. A lot.

When he took my face in his hands and put his lips on mine, I did feel something, a kind of tickle, but it was nothing like the intoxication that overtook me whenever Nick looked me in the eyes.

Simon must have known I wasn't into it, that I was distracted. He was right. At that moment, I was thinking of everything but him.

"I wanted to ask you something," he announced, walking back to his chair. He opened a box and took out a white envelope. "In a few days, we're having the grand-opening party. Everyone's going. I'd like you to be my date."

I opened my mouth a bit, ready to say an abrupt no. Go with him? Like I was his girlfriend? That would mean shouting to the four winds that we had something going on. At the same time, wouldn't it help keep Nicholas in check? He would be going with Sophia for sure, so what was the problem?

"What do you say?" Simon asked hopefully.

"I mean, I'll need to go out and buy a dress...if my boss will give me the time off, you know."

He smiled with actual joy, and I left before I could regret it.

I was entering the belly of the beast.

The next night, I went out for a drink with Jenna. We hadn't seen each other for weeks, and we'd decided it was time for a girls' night out. I needed to feel like I was still nineteen, and Jenna needed to let out the *old her*, the Jenna who wasn't married and never used to spend more than three nights in a row at home.

I put on a red leather miniskirt, which I felt the occasion demanded. It was a gift from my mother, as were the knee-length high-heeled boots. I crimped my hair and left it hanging loose down my back, and I painted my lips the same blood red as my skirt. Jenna would be proud.

After fighting with my GPS, I reached the bar where we were supposed to meet. My friend was waiting for me at the door and smiled wide when she saw me.

"You've gone all out today. Are we going on the prowl or something?"

"Me looking good doesn't have a damned thing to do with men. I'm getting dressed up for me. Anyway, you're married."

Jenna didn't even seem to hear what I was saying.

"This bar's not bad. It's not some dance-club shit, the lights are low... What do you want to bet that in half an hour, we'll have every guy in here trying to get with us?"

"I thought we were just going to have a couple of drinks, talk, have fun, you know... I'm not interested in looking for a guy. If it'll make you chill, you should know I've already got a thing... with my boss."

Her jaw dropped. "Tell all!" she shouted. She liked gossip even better than she liked attention from guys.

I shrugged as if it were no big deal. "Buy me the first drink and I'll tell you, but I'm warning you...it's not a very long story."

She nodded, still excited despite what I'd said, and dragged me inside. It was a small place, but it was packed. She ordered shots of some pink drink, and we sat at a small table in the corner. Then she demanded, "Talk! Are you fucking him? Are you fucking your boss?"

"We haven't fucked, we went out to eat, and...well...we kissed...three times."

"Three times?" she repeated in the sardonic tone I knew all too well. "Easy there, tiger, you don't want him to think you're a whore."

"Shut up!" I said, tossing a peanut from the little dish they'd served with our drinks at her head.

She laughed, but she was still looking at me as if I were a mutant from another galaxy. "For real, Noah. I get that for you sex is something special and all, but fucking does have its advantages."

I laughed and shook my head. But Jenna wouldn't give up that easily, and she spent the next hour trying to get me to hook up with someone that night. By the time she was about to introduce me to the fifth guy of the evening, I looked at the clock and told her it was time for me to go.

"Sorry, Jenna, but I have to leave if I want to be able to keep my eyes open at work tomorrow. I don't want Mr. Stiff to call me into his office and shout at me again."

She chuckled.

"I didn't ask you how it was going," she remarked, a little warily. Nicholas had become an uncomfortable subject for both of us. No matter how close she and I were, she had known Nick since they were kids. She had always been there for me, but deep down, she'd never forgive me for breaking his heart.

"As long as we keep our distance, I think everything's fine," I said, lying like a dog. Nick's presence affected me more than I was willing to say.

Just then I saw Lion, tall and ravishing, walk through the door of the bar. He found us right away, as if he had a radar in his head. I smiled and said hi, and Jenna scooted over to let him sit.

"What's up, Noah?" he said, planting his big hand on her bare knee.

"Great. Tired, you know," I said, putting down my glass,

ready to go home. Now that I knew I wouldn't be leaving Jenna alone, it was time to make a break for it.

I said goodbye and walked off to where I'd left my car. It was later than I'd wanted, but I felt good knowing Lion was there now. Jenna's ability to stay up was legendary, and I just didn't have the energy for her anymore.

I got in and took off toward the freeway. It was Friday night, and the traffic was terrible, so instead of being one more car stuck at a standstill, I took an exit, even if it meant a longer route home.

I turned on the radio to distract myself. After ten minutes, I noticed something strange. The wheel started jerking to the right, and I was having trouble keeping it straight.

Shit!

I slowed down, realizing I was in the middle of nowhere, slipping and sliding through the light rain that had been falling almost all day. I pulled onto the shoulder of the road and turned on my blinkers.

I tried to remember what you were supposed to do in cases like this. I got out, surrounded by darkness, and looked in the trunk for a flashlight, a reflective vest, a safety triangle, anything...but I couldn't find them. I rooted around everywhere, throwing aside all the stupid things I'd left in there, using the flashlight on my phone, but...there was nothing.

A car zipped by so fast, I screamed and jumped back at least three feet.

"Dumbass!" I shouted.

Looking at the wheels of my Audi, I found a punctured tire, and I didn't have a spare, a jack, or anything else that could help me just then. How I wished I had my old Beetle back, with the spare tire right in the front. I cursed myself for trying to feel all fancy in my convertible.

I took out my phone and called the one person I knew would come help me as soon as I hit the green call button.

It rang once.

27

Nick

It was two in the morning, and I was asking myself what the hell I was doing there surrounded by all those shallow, stupid people I couldn't stand and who, to make matters worse, were sucking up to me like they thought they could become my best friend.

We were at a golf club, the kind of place my father would go to meet his friends, and I was there because it was a good place to seal deals. I understood the game: I'd gone with Dad a few times, and I liked playing. Not as much as surfing, but still, it was entertaining. The thing I didn't understand was why you would go to a place like that for a meeting. I found the whole thing irritating. Being surrounded by dudes in suits, sitting on leather sofas, smoking cigars, pretending to be the masters of the universe, having to watch people cross out clauses we'd spent six months putting together to their specifications.

I'd had to go there on the fly. That's why I was there in jeans when everyone else was dudded up. My shirt was nothing to brag about, and I'd had to borrow a tie from Steve, because otherwise, they wouldn't even have let me in.

I took out a cigarette, the sixth one I'd had that night, and watched Steve walk off to take a call. I had hoped he would give me an alibi to leave as soon as possible, so when he hung up, frowning and nodding, and came over to me, I gave him my full attention.

"I need to step away for a bit," he said with a grave expression.

Step away?

"What's up?" I asked, excusing myself from my colleagues, standing up, and walking with him to a corner where we could talk freely.

He smiled and shook his head. "Noah just called."

The sound of her name was like an electric shock.

"Apparently, she's popped a tire and doesn't have a spare. She's on the side of the road in the middle of nowhere. She asked me to come help her." He clicked his tongue.

Wait, what?

"I'll go," I said, surprising myself when I realized how badly I wanted to do it. "Tell me where to go."

"Nicholas, she asked me if I was with you and told me specifically not to tell you anything."

I grinned. "Looks to me like you didn't listen to her. I'm going, Steve. I'm not asking your opinion."

"Fine. I'll book a car home. I'm texting you her whereabouts now. There's a can of Fix-a-Flat in the trunk," he said patiently.

I gave him a friendly bump on the shoulder and walked back over to the men in suits. "Gentlemen, I'm sorry to inform you I have to leave for the evening. There's an emergency, and I'm needed immediately," I said, pleased with the indignant look on their faces. "We can meet back at my office at a more reasonable hour. Good night."

I didn't even give them a chance to respond before I left. Noah was always the perfect excuse.

I followed my GPS, but I got worried as I drove into an increasingly deserted area bordering a secondary road people often caught when traffic was bad. I'd always told Noah not to do that; it was dangerous, some of the places you passed through were really run-down, but she was always determined to do things her way.

I found her car not far from the exit. Visibility was bad, and it would be easy for a distracted driver to ram right into her. Except for her hazard lights, there was nothing to indicate she was in trouble. I flashed my brights to let her know I was there, then parked in front of her and got out. She got out, too, and we stared at each other, me wanting to stuff her into my car and speed off, and her acting like she'd just come face-to-face with Satan himself.

I looked her over as I approached. My headlights revealed every one of her curves against the darkness of the night and gleamed alluringly in her hair. She looked like an angel surrounded by blackness.

"What are you doing here?" she asked, crossing her arms. She wanted me to think she was angry, but I could tell she was terrified. Her miniskirt didn't leave much to the imagination. Without meaning to, I began stripping her naked in my mind... Were those lace garters I saw around the tops of her tender thighs?

I couldn't help but step a little closer to her than she might have liked. Normally I was very respectful of the distance between myself and others. Noah didn't make it easy, though.

"So that's how you greet the person who's come here to save you?" I asked, wanting to hug her, to warm her up and stop her shivering.

"I called Steve, not you," she said, looking away. The intensity of my stare must have made her uncomfortable.

"Too bad Steve works for me."

"Steve told me if I ever had a problem, I could call him."

"And who do you think told him to say that?"

I smiled as she gave me a stupefied look.

"Don't you have anything better to do? I know you're a very busy man these days. Plus, what about Sophia?" she asked with what seemed like mild disgust.

She wasn't trying to put me in a good mood if she mentioned Sophie. I could still remember the look on Noah's face when she'd run into her at the LRB offices. Even if she kept up appearances, I knew her well enough to see it had affected her just as it would have affected me if I had to think about her being with another man.

"She's with her parents in San Francisco... Now, come on." I grabbed her hand and walked with her around to my trunk. I dug around until I found the Fix-a-Flat and a reflective vest she could throw on—Steve always had everything ready for the worst-case scenario. I guessed it was his job, after all. "Here, put this on."

Noah jerked away but didn't refuse the yellow vest, which she donned without complaint.

"I don't need to tell you how irresponsible it is for you not to have a backup plan for emergencies like this," I said, grabbing the can of Fix-a-Flat.

Noah followed behind me at first but then ran forward, trying to grab the can, protesting, "I can do it myself."

As she crouched beside me, I told her, "I know you can. That's not the point. I'm here to help you. Stand back and let me do it."

"I don't want your help, Nicholas."

I turned, trying not to upbraid her, but I couldn't keep it all in. "Oh, so you don't want my help? Fine, I'll go. I'll take the Fix-a-Flat, and you can wait forever for a tow truck to come, and you can pay whatever it is they decide to charge you for putting a spare on in the middle of the night."

"This is why I didn't want Steve to say anything... You always wind up throwing everything in my face."

That wasn't what I was trying to do. As a matter of fact, I was happier being there in the middle of that busted road at two in the morning with Noah than I would have been anywhere else. That was the problem.

Angrier at myself than at her, I turned around and got to work. I knew she was watching my hands. The only sound was the cars passing by us and the wind that seemed to want to carry us away.

When I had finished and was about to take off, I found Noah leaning on the car and staring at me. A car passed, and I stepped toward her. She fell back against the door, and my hips were drawn magnetically to hers.

Our eyes met in the darkness, and I felt the painful need to touch her and see if her skin was as hot as mine was. I placed a hand on her thigh, and my fingers slid under her skirt.

"You're freezing," I said, pushing closer, wanting to feel her. She pressed a hand between us. I grabbed it and brought it to my chest, and she pushed me back slightly.

"Don't do this, Nick," she said, looking away.

"I just want to make sure you don't have hypothermia," I said, so softly that I didn't think she heard me. Everything seemed to vanish. All I wanted was to cup her cheeks and kiss those lips until the sun came up and we were both burning like fire... I hated not being able to just pull her close and hug her; I hated that she wasn't begging to curl up under my coat until the cold died away; I hated not seeing her smile from ear to ear knowing I was there.

I went to kiss her; I didn't even hesitate—what were those lips made for if not to be kissed by mine?—but Noah didn't let me: she crouched and slipped under my arm.

"I need to go," she said, barely wavering, opening the driver's side door and getting in.

Now I was the one who felt cold. I couldn't let her just leave like that. I'd been a dick, it was wrong, but I couldn't think clearly when we were alone.

"Hey, Noah," I said, kneeling till she could see me through the window. She rolled it down to see me better. "It won't happen again," I said. "I promise."

I don't know what went through her head just then, but I do know the look she gave me made me feel like a madman for days on end.

28

Noah

I DON'T KNOW WHAT HURT MORE ABOUT MY RUN-IN WITH NICK: him trying to kiss me, or him promising he wouldn't do it again.

I liked that I'd had the self-control to put a stop to things before they went anywhere, especially because of how hard it had been for me to get over sleeping with him during the holidays. Nicholas was just impulsive; he did what he wanted without thinking of the consequences. If he wanted sex, he should look for it with Sophia… Ugh. Just thinking about it made me want to pull all my hair out, but I wasn't going to be *that* girl, the one who left her boyfriend and then went to bed with him every time he felt like it. No, screw that.

And so I focused on the person who wanted more than just to get me in bed, the one who had invited me to the grand opening of LRB. I was nervous about the party, especially because Nicholas was taking Sophia and I wasn't sure I could deal with it.

When the day came, I donned a blue sequined dress, short and formfitting. I hadn't worn it in a year; it had sagged off me before, and I'd even had to wear a padded bra for the bust to look right. When I looked at myself in the mirror, I smiled: those were the boobs I was used to, the ones that had disappeared months ago. Now they were back in all their glory.

I wore a pair of heels Jenna had lent me the week before, cherry-colored Louboutins with rhinestones that matched my red bag. I grabbed my black coat, which was long and elegant, a Christmas gift from my mother, and walked outside when I heard Simon pull up.

Getting out to open the door for me, he said, "You look incredible," before grabbing my waist and bringing me in for a kiss.

Goddammit... Why did it always feel so uncomfortable when he did that...?

I pulled away to button my coat. It was getting windy out. Simon's car was a classic Porsche, gray, elegant, and it reminded me of the day I'd lost Nick's Ferrari... I still couldn't believe he'd forgiven me, but back then I guess we really had been in love.

What would Simon do if I wrecked or scratched *his* precious car?

He stood back from the open door like a gentleman, and soon we were off to the party.

The venue was huge, with high ceilings and murals. I was surprised to see so many people there, given the newness of the operation, but of course, it was just one subsidiary in a much larger group. I recognized one or two people there who asked me where my mother and Will were. But Nicholas was the boss now, and William had decided to step back and let him do his thing. He was busy enough being the father of a little girl at his age. I looked around distractedly while Simon grabbed two glasses of champagne and passed me one.

"You looking for someone?"

Shit.

I looked back at him and took a drink, then shook my head. "Just admiring the place... It's pretty," I said. Then I took another sip.

Since Simon's role at the company was important, he had to

greet almost everyone. At first, he dragged me along with him, but after an hour, I'd had enough, and I walked to the bar with the excuse that my feet hurt. As a waitress was changing my glass out for a new one of cold, bubbly rosé, I looked at the door as if magnetized.

There they were: the prom king and prom queen.

Sophia was out of sight in her long beige evening gown. Her hair was pulled to one side and fell over her shoulders in dark waves. The lights cast alluring shadows over her face.

And Nick...he was spectacular. That's the only word for it. Dark gray suit, white shirt, blue tie, a face that made you want to sin, to do bad, dangerous, forbidden things.

The lights went down just then, and dinner began. Simon walked over to accompany me to our table. He gave me all his attention: we chatted and laughed, and after dessert, we went out to the dance floor with the rest of the guests and our colleagues.

We had gone together, but we wanted to be discreet and not call too much attention to our relationship. So we decided to act like friends. But I'd be lying if I said I didn't enjoy seeing Nicholas's sour face.

At some point, I found myself alone having a drink, the fifth of the night, when Nick came over. I didn't see Sophia anywhere, but I could feel her presence, as though she were observing us. Simon was gone, I had no idea where he was, but at least there was a cool bartender there to keep me company.

"Did you get home okay last night?" Nick asked, sidling up next to me.

"Perfectly, thanks. In thirty minutes *flat*," I said, laughing at my own joke. "Maybe you should go into roadside repair." I took a drink.

"Fixing tires? Yeah. Good thing my future's not in your hands..."

I smiled for the sake of courtesy and brought my glass to my lips. Nick observed me uncomfortably.

"You came with Simon." It was an affirmation, not a question.

"Very observant... Did you figure that out because we entered together or because I haven't been apart from him all night?"

"I figured it out the first time I saw you with him at the office. I thought it was nothing... People can get fired over that."

I looked up. He was much more tense than he was trying to appear.

"Him or me? Who do you want to get rid of first?"

"I think you know the answer to that," he said, looking at my lips. I looked at his, too, and then at his eyes. I needed to focus.

"All I know is right now I'm starting a new chapter of my life. Just like you did a year ago. By the way, I'm super happy for you, Nick. It's so nice to see you in love again, happy, with that girl you fell for as soon as you laid eyes on her." My words came out with so much venom that I thanked the heavens Simon walked up just then. Who knew what I might have said next. My filter was gone, and that could be dangerous.

"Everything okay?" he asked.

Nicholas turned to him. "Just great," he replied with a strange grin. "Are you guys coming downtown after this?"

Simon looked at me, and I looked at Nick. What the hell was he getting at?

"You want to go, Noah?"

Go with him and Sophia? No thanks, I'd rather die.

But before I could respond, Sophia appeared out of nowhere and grabbed Nick's arm. He stiffened despite himself.

"Hey, guys," she said with an obviously false smile.

I returned the favor, enjoying the thought of getting a little revenge.

"I'd love to," I said, wrapping an arm around Simon's waist

and letting him wrap his around my shoulders. Nick didn't fail to notice.

"See you in a bit," he growled.

All that was left was to say goodbye to the guests. Not all of them, obviously. Nick took to the stage and thanked everyone for coming. In his suit, with his impeccable bearing and the triumph in his eyes, he was the personification of perfection. He had turned into what he'd always wanted to be. He'd exceeded everyone's expectations, and he had the whole world at his feet.

I felt proud, even if I wanted to chop him into little pieces and fry them one by one.

I followed Simon outside to the car, and we headed to the bar Nick had invited us to. It was modern, with a clubby feel, and just ten minutes away from the other venue. When I got there, I was happy to strip off my coat and order another drink.

Simon chuckled as I called the bartender over and ordered two shots of tequila. When he left to take care of our order, I leaned in. The music and the darkness readied me to take the next step, so I kissed Simon. He responded enthusiastically. I could taste the alcohol on his breath when he slipped his tongue in my mouth and it intertwined with mine.

"Two shots of tequila," the bartender said, forcing us to separate.

Simon was…a good kisser? Yeah, a good one.

I licked the back of my hand and poured salt on it, then stretched it out to Simon, who looked at me like I was out of my mind.

"What?" I asked, grabbing my shot glass and my lime and getting ready.

Simon laughed and did the same. "You have no idea what you provoke in men, do you?" he asked.

No, I didn't. The man I knew I'd ever made feel anything had confessed to me he was in love with someone else.

Speak of the devil...I looked over just as the two of them walked in the door. I glanced back at Simon and forced a smile, clinked glasses with him, and knocked mine back. The tequila burned my throat. Before I could start heaving, I bit down on my lime so hard, I almost swallowed it.

I could see Nick in my peripheral vision heading over with Sophia hot on his heels. I wanted to take off running in the opposite direction, but I decided against it, turning instead to the bar. Simon hadn't seen them, and he was about to start nibbling on my ear by the time Nick made it over.

I laughed as if he'd told me the funniest joke ever and grabbed his arm to turn toward Nick.

"I see you started without us," Nick said, signaling for the bartender to pour another round.

Jeez, another shot! My body wasn't going to be able to take it.

"Sorry, we haven't been introduced," Simon said to Sophia.

"Simon, Sophie, Sophie, Simon," Nick said gruffly. "Simon's one of LRB's investors."

Nicholas barely looked at his date. He was staring at me so hard, it made me angry, especially because I knew Simon was taking note of everything he did and said. I reached out to grab my shot, but Nick was faster and drank it without salt or lime—without *training wheels*, as he always called them.

I knew I should probably stop drinking, and I was happy when a familiar song boomed from the speakers. It was the perfect excuse to vanish.

"Shall we dance, Simon?" I asked, wrapping an arm around him and blinking, trying to look provocative.

"Sure," he responded, setting his glass on the bar and waving to Nick and Sophia. I could feel Nick's glacial stare on my neck almost boring a hole into me.

I turned my back to Simon and swayed to the rhythm of the

music while he gripped me around the waist. With his hand on my stomach, he made me tremble as his lips moved over my neck, exquisite, sensual, and not at all in good taste.

"You're trying to kill me, little girl," he said, and that made me remember how Nick had always called me *Freckles*... It had been too long since I'd heard that.

I tried to spot him at the bar, but he wasn't there. Where the hell had he gone off to? I was putting this whole show on for him, and when I realized he wasn't watching me, I got pissed, bad. I turned around, and before Simon could kiss me so lewdly again, I told him I needed to go to the bathroom. I stomped off the dance floor, smoke coming out of my ears, and drunk off my ass, as I might as well admit. The tequila had taken hold quickly. But before I could walk in, before I even made it to the long line of girls waiting to go, I felt a hand grab my wrist and force me into a hall packed with people and flashing green, red, and blue lights. For a moment, it sickened me, but then my back hit the wall, and a mouth I knew all too well struck mine just as a hard, wiry, hot body squeezed into me, sliding a knee between my legs and pressing in sensuously.

I tried to resist. I didn't want to be touched. Not in the least. I was angry, angry because he was with her, angry because he hadn't seen me dance when I was putting on a show for him, and furious because he hadn't stopped Simon from touching me. Where was the Nick I knew? What had happened to him?

He raised my wrists over my head and held them there. I could hardly move. My pelvis was imprisoned against the wall. Pinning my arms with one hand, he used the other to grab my chin and stroked my lower lip with his tongue. He said nothing, nothing at all; he just looked down and slipped his hot tongue in my mouth, all the way to the back of my throat. Our eyes met in the shadows, and what I saw made me shiver: he was suffering as much as I was at the immense space that had opened between us, the abyss between our lives that was almost impossible to cross. He had been with Sophia for a long time now, longer than our relationship had lasted, and I...I mean, I'd taken a giant step, since before I couldn't even talk to anyone of the opposite sex, and now I was going on dates with my boss and even kissing him.

What would do it? What would help us realize we had to be together? Was there anything left to salvage? To recover? Something to hold on to, however painful?

It seemed like the answer was no.

Nick must have heard my thoughts, as if that kiss had caused our two minds to meld. When he saw I was no longer struggling to get away, he let go of my hands, and I rested my head on his shoulder. Then I pulled him close, hugged him, squeezed him, imagining we were one. I needed to feel he wouldn't disappear. We'd kissed in desperation; it was a kiss we shouldn't have had, a forbidden kiss—at least it was now.

He pulled back a few seconds later and, with his lips brushing my ear, said, "Don't forget, he'll never make you feel the way I do."

I didn't know how to respond... What could I say? That he was wrong? We both knew he wasn't. He never would be.

"Noah," he said, since I hadn't replied. The reality of his words struck me so hard, I was too stunned to speak.

When he uttered my name, why did it sound like a question, an urgent one?

I wanted to say something, do something, but I felt a sharp, painful jab in my stomach, pushed him away weakly, turned aside, and threw up.

Nicholas needed just a second to react before grabbing my ponytail to keep my hair out of my face. He held me so I wouldn't fall over as I expelled all the alcohol I'd sucked down. I kept vomiting for a while longer and couldn't even worry about the giant mess I was making on the floor of that badly lit hallway. At least it was dark and the music was drowning out my retching.

When I thought it was finally over, I stood up, and Nick walked me out the back door.

"No, no," I said. I wanted to go back. Simon was still there. He'd be worried.

"I'm taking you home right now," he said in a tone that admitted no reply.

Nick called Steve, who soon pulled around the corner, then stuffed me in the back seat and got in.

"Feel better?" he asked in a strange tone of voice.

Honestly, I didn't. I felt awful. I wanted to get home and drink a giant glass of water, brush my teeth, cover up with a warm blanket. I was freezing. I started shaking, almost like I was spasming. Fuck...this was bad.

Nick pulled me close, took off his suit jacket, and draped it over me. Then he hugged me, and I rested my head on his shoulder, falling asleep or passing out almost instantaneously.

I opened my eyes and stumbled as Nick tried to get me out.

"Go pick up Sophia and take her to my place. Then come back for me," Nick said to Steve, not even looking at him as he lifted me in his arms.

"I can walk," I said weakly.

When we reached the door, he set me down, looked in my bag and fished out my keys, and took me into my apartment. Just as he was helping me into my double bed, I felt nauseated again.

"I need to go to the bathroom," I said, trying to hide how bad I felt. I didn't want him to know how irresponsible I'd been. Fucking tequila, fucking champagne. Only I would be dumb enough to mix those.

"Are you going to throw up?" he asked, sounding exasperated.

I looked up and saw the disgust in his eyes.

"You can go now, Nicholas," I said spitefully.

"Oh, I can go? Thanks for your permission."

"You're going to wake up my roommate," I groaned.

"I really don't fucking care," he said.

I clenched my teeth and stood up as straight as I could to keep him from looking down at me. It nearly killed me; I could feel the vomit rising in my esophagus, and still worse, when I straightened up, I felt something… Dammit, this had to be a joke.

I pushed him aside and went to the bathroom. As soon as I was in there, I saw my period had come.

That explained the fucking cramps.

Not even caring that Nicholas was out there, I took off my clothes, threw them in the basket, and got into the shower, turning on the cold water. That would help, surely. I wasn't in there long, just enough to clear my head. When I came out, I put in a tampon, wrapped up in a towel, and headed to my room, hoping he was finally gone. But no. He was sitting on the edge of my bed.

"You can go," I said, opening the closet and not looking at him.

"I'll go when I feel like it. Now drink this," he said, passing me a big glass of cold water.

I hadn't put on clothes yet, and my hair was dripping all over the rug.

"Turn around. I need to get dressed," I said.

He rolled his eyes. It's not like he hadn't seen it all before. But I didn't care about being reasonable just then.

I stood there staring until he turned. As quickly as I could in my intoxicated state, I put on some cotton panties, some shorts, and a pajama top.

"Done," I said and grabbed the water he had held out to me.

"Take an ibuprofen, too," he said. He must have opened my nightstand to find my bottle of it. And unless I was wrong, I had his letter in the nightstand—the same one he had given me so long ago and that I'd reread aloud more times than I'd like to admit.

I took the pill from him, shooting fire from my eyes, then got into bed, pulling the cover up under my chin and turning around to look at the wall.

I could feel him a few seconds later sitting on my side of the bed. He stroked my hair, brushing it carefully out of my face, and I closed my eyes at that contact, so warm, so profound.

"You should chuck it… Those words don't mean anything anymore."

After saying that, he left.

29

Nick

Steve dropped me at the apartment building I had left a long time ago with no intention of ever returning. Going back after more than a year had been hard: the memories, the fucking memories were there in every corner, every room.

Seeing Noah with Simon had been like having my heart cut open with a knife. Fucking Simon Roger! I'd have liked to split his face open! I could have kicked his teeth out of his head when I saw him kissing her neck, her skin…her lips.

Then came the moment when I pinned her against the wall, the moment when I forgot everything that had happened, when it seemed like we could erase it all and keep going with each other. Having her in my arms was always magnetic, pure attraction, and nothing could stop it. But then I was struck by a wrecking ball, and I felt an invisible veil I'd never perceived before fall between us.

What was it? Time? The way we'd remade our lives now, completely apart from each other? Love starting to freeze into a memory?

I was scared then, scared to admit that our separation was finally done, tangible, realer than I could ever have imagined.

I got in the elevator thinking about her face on the pillow, her hair spread over the white sheets, the letter I saw in her nightstand, always there, always close to her...

Had those words really lost all meaning?

Yes, of course they had... As much as I might lose control when she was there in front of me, as much as I might desire her, as much as I might wish to go back to where we'd left off, it was still true: she had cheated on me.

When I opened the door, I saw the lights were on. Sophia was on the couch, looking at the TV screen, even though it was off, with a glass of wine in her hands. I took off my jacket and dropped it on the loveseat across from her. When she looked at me, I saw something I didn't like.

"Were you with her?"

What was the point of lying? It was obvious I had been with her; it didn't take a genius to figure that out. "Yeah, I took her home; she wasn't feeling well," I said, turning around to pour myself a drink.

"She's with someone, Nicholas. He could have handled it."

Thinking of Simon irritated me. "Are you actually questioning me, Sophia? You know I don't like to answer to people." I slammed the bottle down.

She got up and came around to face me.

"What you and I have, it's not a game anymore, Nicholas. And if this keeps going on, you can't just not think about me. So yeah, I'm questioning you. I didn't care before what you did or didn't do. It was obvious what kind of relationship we had, but things are different now, and they have been for some time, and I'd appreciate it if you could keep your word to me."

I peered into her dark eyes and saw much more than she wanted me to see.

I stepped forward, grabbed her chin, and looked closer.

"I will keep my word," I said, stroking her softly with my fingers. "But you need to keep yours, too."

She closed her eyes. When she reopened them, I could tell she was lying. "I won't fall in love with you. You can stop worrying about that."

She turned around and walked to my room. I finished the rest of my drink and followed her. Now it was my turn to keep promises.

30

Noah

Even with Nick gone and a couple of hours of sleep under my belt, I woke with an upset stomach and a strong desire to puke. I almost fell out of bed running toward the bathroom.

I was so tired that I didn't even realize I had work that day. I had black goo in the corners of my eyes, huge bags under them, and streams of old makeup on my face. I did what I could with my base and blush, trying to work magic to hide my raggedness. I grabbed my bag, my coat, and my car keys and scampered out of the apartment. The last thing I wanted was to give Nick a reason to fire me. Nick: the mere thought of him brought back that kiss from the night before. As I was driving, I looked at my messages—I know, you're not supposed to—and found ten missed calls from Simon.

Shit!

I'd forgotten I wasn't technically single anymore. And what the hell was I going to tell him now? That my ex-boyfriend had taken me home after basically licking my tonsils?

I needed a coffee. That would help me think clearly, help me face the consequences of the night before. But just when I walked in and turned toward the elevator, I saw him. Nick, in a suit, staring down at his cell phone and waiting for the elevator, too. I took a deep breath, cursed my luck, and stopped beside him. I thought of taking the stairs, but fourteen floors while I was hungover wasn't really my idea of a good time. I tried to stand still as he looked away from his phone and toward me.

Fuck. If only I were one of those people who got amnesia after they drank. That would make the situation less uncomfortable.

"What are you doing here?"

"I work here," I said with a grimace.

Ignoring my impertinence, he said, "I figured you'd stay home; you were a wreck yesterday."

"Well, I didn't really want to give you a reason to fire me," I responded, ignoring his presence as best I could and walking into the empty elevator as soon as the doors opened.

He pocketed his phone and followed me. "How are you?" he asked. There was something odd in his voice.

"I'm fine," I said, surprised he was worrying about me.

Yesterday things had gotten out of hand again. I had provoked it, I knew, but I'd never thought he'd fall for it the way he did.

You should chuck it... Those words don't mean anything anymore.

His words returned to my mind as though drawn up from a dense fog. Why had he said that? To hurt me? If he really thought those words were meaningless now, why the hell had he kissed me again? Why had he taken me home to make sure I was okay? Why had he asked me how I was just now?

This had to end. I couldn't just keep stumbling blindly.

Without thinking about what I was doing, I stepped forward and hit the red Stop button. The elevator made an eerie clanging sound, beeped, and paused.

I turned to Nick. He was surprised and confused.

"Why?" I asked him, crossing my arms, wanting so much to protect myself in front of him, and feeling as if the only way to do so was to put a barrier between us.

"Why what?"

"Why did you kiss me?"

He stared, but he didn't speak.

"You shouldn't have done it," I continued.

His eyebrows arched. "I didn't hear you complaining."

I could feel myself turning red.

"Now I guess you'll try and pretend that little number you did on the dance floor wasn't for my benefit?"

I tried to feign indignation. "You're not the center of the universe, Nick. It had nothing to do with you," I lied. "Anyway, what does it matter? This is the second time you've come on to me… You're the one who's after me; you did it at your dad's house, you did it last night, and I don't like it. You're playing with my head, and—"

"And what?" he interrupted, coming forward. I stood my ground this time: I was going to deal with this situation. I was tired of the emotional ups and downs I felt every time we saw each other, every time I thought I could forget him and then he showed up and made me question my judgment.

"I'm tired of this, Nicholas. You and I are in the past, and I'm trying to move forward."

He didn't seem to care for that. "Move forward? With Simon?" There was poison in each of his words.

"With Simon or with whoever… I deserve to be happy, too," I affirmed. "I want you and me both to be happy, Nicholas, and if Simon—"

He didn't let me finish the phrase. He grabbed my wrist and pulled me so close, our toes touched. "Say it again. Tell me that Simon gives you the same things I do."

I felt my oxygen give out, being so close to him. His scent intoxicated me, and I tried to stand back to regain control, but he stopped me, putting a hand on my back and driving me into him.

"Someday, I'll be with someone else, Nicholas. You can't just keep anyone from ever touching me, forcing me to be there for you whenever you feel like it. I'm with Simon, just like you're with Sophia. You need to accept that." Even her stupid name tasted bitter in my mouth. "Remember her, Sophia? Your girlfriend?" I added with disgust.

His expression changed, and for a few seconds that seemed never to end, I watched the fury my words provoked seep into him. "You're playing with fire, Noah."

"I'm not playing anything; you're the one who's trying to play the field."

He laughed acidly. "Funny you should be the one to say that, don't you think?"

Always with the same shit. Dammit! Would he never stop reminding me?

I reached out and hit the button again, and the elevator returned to motion while we fought. Before the doors opened, I made one last comment:

"No matter how much this hurts...we both knew this moment was going to come."

For the first time since we'd broken up, I wanted him gone.

I turned right and headed for Simon's office. I owed him an explanation. When I walked in, he was leaning on his desk, his arms crossed, his face worried.

"What happened last night, Noah?" he asked when he saw me. "One minute you tell me you're going to the bathroom, and the next I'm worried sick and looking all over for you... I thought something had happened to you. For real, don't do anything like that again."

"Sorry, I know I left you hanging, it's just..."

"I was looking for you for an hour until some guy in a suit jacket came to tell me you'd gone home... Why'd you leave?"

Shit. I felt so guilty... I'd been a complete fucking idiot, and now I was risking my relationship with Simon even though it had only just started.

I stepped forward, uncertain, worried about losing something that actually seemed to be going right for me for once.

"I got super sick; I'm almost too embarrassed to tell you. I wish I could just say I had to leave because of an emergency or because one of my friends broke up with her boyfriend and called me to cry it out or, like, I twisted my ankle and had to go straight to the emergency room, but the truth is, I drank too much. I don't want you to think I'm a little girl who can't hold her liquor, but that's the deal: I was drunk...and I promise you my hangover right now is punishment enough. Please forgive me."

I took a deep breath to get over my monologue and saw that Simon's expression had returned to normal. He walked around his desk and stopped a foot away from me.

"Next time, tell me, and I'll be sure to get you home safe and sound... I know we've just known each other for a few weeks, but I like you, and I want you to trust me if you're ever in a bind."

Boys and girls, this was what a mature reaction looked like.

I smiled, not utterly sincere. He wrapped a hand around my waist and pulled me close.

"I had a good time last night. Sorry you can't say the same."

"I was fine until my third shot. That's where the wheels came off. The rest of it was great, though. Honestly, I can't believe what a wonderful time I had."

Simon's hand climbed the back of my ultramarine blouse,

and he pulled me close. After my argument with Nick, I wanted, needed, for this thing with Simon to work out. He kissed me tenderly. I grabbed him around the neck and made him do it hard. I needed to forget, one way or another, that other man who was just a few feet away.

We were breathing fast as we pulled back. Simon smiled.

"Am I forgiven?" I asked.

"If this is what happens afterward, you can get in trouble more often!"

I laughed just as the door opened. It was Nick's secretary.

"Mr. Leister has scheduled a meeting in an hour. He'd like everyone to be there."

The meeting was torture. I was in charge of the PowerPoint, which meant I had to stand at the front of the room while everyone else was gawking at me from their seats, Nick especially. If he didn't watch out, Simon and everyone else in the office would get suspicious, and that was the last thing I wanted. When we thought the meeting was over, Nick got up and asked us all to stay a bit longer.

"I want to bring up a touchy subject, but one that I think is important." We all looked at him attentively, uncertain why he'd turned so cold. "I don't know if some of you are unfamiliar with our company policy, and for that reason, I've made copies for everyone present, and I expect all of you to inform your respective staffs. The upshot of all this is, as I shouldn't need to remind you, fraternization between employees is strictly prohibited."

Nick looked professional and distant, and an uncomfortable silence overtook the room. I looked over at Simon, who was glaring at Nick.

"This is and has always been a rule in all the companies my

family has run, and I think it's a necessary one to keep everything running smoothly." Nick's eyes scanned the room, resting longer than necessary on Simon and me. "If that's clear to everyone, you can all get back to work. Thank you."

I could hear murmurs as everyone tried to rush out as quickly as possible.

How absurd!

Simon stood, but with no intention of leaving the room, while Nicholas packed his things in his suitcase. Seeing us there, he set his pencil down on the glass table and stood tall, ready to hear whatever Simon had to say.

"You know something, Nicholas?" Simon walked around the table, his chin held high.

I was nervous, unsure what to say or do. I shouldn't have made out with him the other night, not in front of Nick, at least, and I sure as hell shouldn't have brought it back up in the elevator. I had served him the opportunity to reprimand us on a goddamned platter!

"I think it's just peachy for you to order your employees to obey your stupid rules, but you're forgetting something: I'm a partner here, so anything you have to say about my private life, you can stick straight up your ass."

That verbal attack didn't faze Nicholas one bit. It even seemed to egg him on.

"I have a seventy percent share here, Baxwell, ten, so that leaves you with twenty. Our contract stipulates very clearly that the company is a subsidiary of Leister Enterprises. But hey, if you want to call a board meeting—excuse me, a meeting with me and my associates—go right ahead; you won't get any pushback from me."

Shit.

"Nicholas, you're being unfair," I said between clenched teeth. I couldn't believe what was happening.

"If either of you two ever manages to actually run a company, you can do with it what you please, but in the meanwhile, these are the rules. If I see either of you in a compromising situation again, or if I even suspect you are having some kind of romantic relationship, you'll both be out on your asses. Understood?"

I felt bad for Simon, I could see he wanted to bash Nicholas's face in but couldn't. Even if Nick deserved it, he couldn't hit his partner; he couldn't do anything, and he couldn't say anything. He'd pushed things as it was, and Nicholas was most likely angling for an excuse to push him out.

Simon took his things and walked out, slamming the door.

I was still standing there like a fool, my blood boiling, feeling angry and powerless. I hated Nick just then for being so selfish, for not wanting me for himself but not giving me to anyone else, for playing with me even though he knew my heart was constantly crying out to him.

"You want to stomp out that door like a teenager, too? Be my guest."

"What the hell is up with you?" I shouted.

"I'm trying to run a company," he said with a scowl. "And I'm not about to let you sleep with one of the partners."

"It's none of your business!" I screamed.

"You're amazing. Sometimes I have to struggle to remember why I ever fell in love with you. When I think about it, I remember the sex. Fine, it was good, but in no way does it compensate for all the shit you put me through."

Since when was this a conversation about us?!

"You say that like you're some kind of goddamned saint. Let me remind you that I slept with someone else because you intentionally made me believe you'd done it with two other girls behind my back. I made a mistake, but what's your excuse?! What do *you* have to say for yourself, Nicholas?! How many women have you banged since we broke up? Even me, for God's sake. I let you do whatever you wanted with me when you were with someone else! I've hit the bottom with you; I'm letting you treat me like your property or a fucking toy you can pick up and dick around with when you get bored. You won't let me get on with my life! Could you possibly be more selfish?!"

My hands were shaking as Nicholas walked around the table... It had been rash, but I'd needed to say that, and that was only the beginning of all I had buried inside.

"You know why? Because there's no way I'm going to let you move on until I have. That's how things are. I don't want to see you happy. I don't want to see you with anyone. I'm not fucking done with you!"

I shoved him as hard as I could and walked to the other end of the room.

"You *won't* touch me again," I said. My words provoked a predatory gleam in his eyes. "You think you can just do whatever you want with me, but you're wrong. As long as you're with another woman, yesterday's kiss is the last one."

He cornered me, resting his hands against the wall on either side of my head. "I can't stand seeing you with that jerkoff; it drives me crazy." His eyes were glowing with passion and determination.

I laughed. "You know, it's not like I love seeing you with Sophia."

He ignored me and brought his face close to mine. "I need to be inside you," he said, completely shameless.

"No."

He gave me one of those half smiles I used to like so much.

"You know perfectly well I can make you change your mind so fast, you won't know what happened." He ran his thumb along my cheek and across my lower lip. I grabbed his hand and pulled it away.

"I'm not going to play this game. Not this time. This is going nowhere, Nicholas. We're just going to hurt each other worse, and I've suffered as much as my body can take. I'm not dragging more people into this. You're with Sophia; I've got something with Simon. That's just how it is."

Nicholas shook his head. Great—he was angry again. "You don't have a goddamned thing with him, Noah. And you're not going to. At least not here."

I looked around. If that was the deal... "Fine. I quit."

He froze.

I walked out, shutting the door behind me.

That was that. I had no more reason to see him.

31

Noah

I'd made the decision in haste, but that night in bed, I realized it was the best thing I could have done. I had to get it over with , and there was no way I would ever do so working under Nick.

Simon called several times, hoping to get in touch with me and find out if I was okay. I'd ignored him. I was too focused on my anger at Nicholas. But I had to pick up eventually. I asked him if he minded if I went to see him at home, and when he got past the surprise, he happily gave me his address.

He lived in a complex only a block from Nick's place. By the time I reached the door, I knew what I had to do.

Simon looked worried as he opened up. He was dressed in gray sweatpants and a baggy dark red T-shirt. Red—the same color I saw everything in just then. I didn't even let him speak. I just threw myself into his arms.

Suck on that, Nicholas Leister.

Simon grabbed me around the waist with one arm and shut the door with the other. Soon he was lifting me off the ground in a gesture that reminded me too much of Nick. What the hell was it with dudes picking me up and carrying me?

Noah, focus.

He set me on the counter, and I leaned back, trying to gauge what his reaction had been. He was looking at me as if I were a stranger.

"When you called an hour ago to tell me you were coming, I promise you, this is the last thing I thought would happen."

I didn't want to talk. I didn't need that just then. I needed to get Nicholas out of my head, my body, my soul. Simon's green eyes with blond lashes stared at me as I took off my T-shirt and sat there before him in my bra.

"Jesus," Simon said, diving back in toward my mouth again.

I let him play with my tongue for as long as he wished, but when his hand descended my bare back, I stiffened involuntarily.

"Are you okay?" he asked, his hand pausing on the clasp of my bra.

"Yeah, just...can we go to your room?"

Darkness...that was what I needed. For the first time in a long time. Simon smiled and picked me up again, carrying me to a door in a shadowy hallway.

"I know how to walk," I couldn't help saying.

"I know you do, but I like feeling you the way I am right now."

And I could feel him, too—could feel his erection pressing into my body like a steel rod. Simon laid me on the bed, took off his T-shirt, and stretched out over me, careful not to crush me as he deposited soft kisses on my stomach. I closed my eyes. No, goddammit, why? Why did I want to cry so badly?

He unbuttoned the top button of my pants. It made me remember Michael, that night, his lips on my skin, his mouth on my mouth. I was reliving it all: the betrayal, the deceit, the worst error of my life. Was I doing the same thing again?

No! Dammit, I wasn't doing anything wrong. Simon wasn't just anyone, Simon wanted to be with me; I mattered to him, I mattered to him more than to Michael, to Nicholas...

Nicholas.

His face appeared in my mind, his blue eyes with their diabolical stare, his lips, the way they could kiss like there was no tomorrow, the way he'd drive me so hard into the bed, so desperately, I sometimes couldn't even breathe. The hands trying to undress me now weren't his, they never would be, and I didn't know if I would ever manage to forget what they had felt like, if I would ever be able to enjoy another man.

I felt a panic attack coming on. I pushed Simon away and stood up.

"I'm sorry… I can't do this," I apologized, buttoning my pants again and looking for the exit like an animal in a cage. That was me just then: a prisoner to my own emotions.

"Noah, wait, I'm sorry. If you're not ready…"

"I need to go," I said, ignoring him and walking out. I stepped past the living room, picked up my T-shirt off the kitchen floor, and threw it on quickly. By then, Simon had reached me and grabbed hold of me, forcing me to look at him.

"Can you tell me what's going on?" he asked, worried and exasperated. "Is it Leister? Because if it is, I can tell you right now, fuck him and his company policies, hear me?"

I shook my head and wiped away a tear with the back of my hand. "I just need to go home, okay?" I said, trying to control how lost I felt.

He watched me briefly, then nodded. "Fine," he said with a long sigh. "Whatever you need, you call me, okay?"

I nodded. I felt sorry for him. He didn't deserve this. He didn't deserve to have to deal with a person like me. I gave him a soft kiss on the cheek, grabbed my bag, and walked out without looking back.

Nicholas: 10. Noah: -5.

32

Nick

I didn't follow her after she slammed the door of the meeting room. It wasn't the right moment. I knew I'd thrown her for a loop. I'd been an asshole, but Noah just doing whatever she wanted with some other guy was something I couldn't take. It made me so mad, I started to question my judgment. I knew I had pushed her to get over me, and I knew that meant I needed to let her rebuild her life with someone else. But ever since I'd seen her with Simon, I wondered constantly if I'd been wrong.

I spent all night thinking it over, and the next day, I waited impatiently for the moment when I could talk to her. But to my surprise, she was the one who showed up in my office.

She didn't even knock, and that boldness made me want to kiss her more. I didn't bother to conceal my interest. Her pants hugged her in all the right places, and her T-shirt, even if it was nice, was a little revealing of those sexy curves I knew so well. Her cheeks were pink, her lips thick, a little swollen. With one look, I knew she'd been crying all night.

She had a piece of paper in her hand. She laid it on my desk.

"My letter of resignation. I'm not bothering with the two weeks. I'm just an intern; you can find someone right away. Simon will manage until you get someone in, if you even need anyone," she said without looking at me.

Shit!

I got up before she could run out, catching her wrist and pulling her around to face me.

"Wait, goddammit!" I ordered her. I leaned back, tried not to look her in the eyes, but noticed her lips pursing as she jerked away and crossed her arms. "Don't quit, Noah. That wasn't my intention."

"I want to quit, I need to quit..." she said, her eyes desperate.

"Why? Why would you leave a job that's paying you more than any other could? Do you honestly prefer losing that over a dipshit like Simon? I thought you were smarter than that."

"It's because of you, Nicholas. I don't want to see you anymore. That's why I'm leaving."

"Wait a second," I said, again trying to grab her hand to stop her.

As I looked into her honey-colored eyes, my mind started counting the freckles on her nose, but I already knew how many there were: twenty-eight, twenty-eight on her nose alone... I didn't want to not see them again. I didn't want to not see her.

"We haven't been dealing with this especially well, have we?"

Noah looked at the ground, and then back at me. "We only know how to hurt each other, and I..." Her eyes were moist, and she bit her lip. She didn't want to cry in front of me, but I knew her too well, and it would only be a matter of seconds before she lost control. "I need to get over this."

Her voice was soft as a whisper. I could barely even hear her.

Instinctively, I wrapped her in my arms, burying my face in her neck and breathing in the scent of strawberry on her skin...

"I miss you so much," she admitted, and those words cut straight through my soul.

I clutched her hair, pulled her head back, and stole a kiss, a kiss I needed just then, a kiss I had to give her before I told her what I had to say. It wasn't a deep kiss; I wasn't looking for anything but affection, love, longing. Our lips, pressing together, were sealing a sort of promise.

"There's nothing we can do to change what's happened," I said, admiring her face, pausing over every detail. "And I want to think that the rage I'm carrying inside *will* disappear someday, Noah. I hope it will, I really do, but right now, it just doesn't feel possible."

She listened attentively. "You're never going to forgive me for what I did, are you?" she asked, trembling.

"Of all the things you could have done...cheating on me was the one thing that could have ruined us."

Even that day, after so long, the mere thought of it was unbearably painful.

"I know..." she said, wiping her cheeks.

We stayed there in that strange silence, a silence that wasn't uncomfortable, but that felt like the prelude to an important decision. There was something I needed to say, something that had been stuck in my head for a while and that I couldn't forget.

"Noah, the thing that happened at Dad's—"

She cut me off. "You regret it, I know. You don't have to tell me."

"I don't regret it. To the contrary, I think it was the right ending for us, don't you think? I wanted to talk to you and ask if you were all right, but you vanished, and you wouldn't pick up when I called...and finally I realized it was better that way."

The light coming through the window shone in her eyes as she looked up at me. I wished I could see something besides that pain that looked just as powerful as mine. How could we suffer so much together when being apart made us agonize so?

"I'm leaving this afternoon...and I don't really know when I'll be back. Don't worry, Noah, I won't touch you again."

She took a deep breath, as though she could somehow steel herself and flee from her sadness.

"The worst thing of all is that even with all that's happened, I don't want you to go," she said, trying to control herself. On its own, my hand moved again and stroked her cheek. Her eyes closed, then opened again, glancing at it.

Before I could react, she grabbed it and turned it around, revealing the tattoo I'd gotten a year and a half ago. She looked at it for a second, and we were transported back to that special night...the night when Noah had sat atop me and scrawled messages of love on my skin.

You're mine, she had written, and I'd run off to get it tattooed there so her words would become reality in my flesh. Without warning, Noah pressed her lips onto my skin, and I quivered as if from an electric shock. I could feel it, I could feel the way the wall started to crumble, and worst of all, I was scared… I was scared to fall again, scared to make the same mistake, scared to be exposed again, to feel stripped of that sense of power I'd worked so hard to establish. *You're going to regret getting it. I know you are… You'll regret it, and you'll hate me because it will remind you of me even when you don't want it to…*

Noah's words after she saw I'd gotten the tattoo leaped into my mind as if she'd only just uttered them. And it seemed that even then, she'd known that what she was saying would turn out to be true.

"I need to go."

I tried to walk past her and go out; I was going out that door and wouldn't come back until I absolutely had to, but Noah panicked and grabbed me tight around the arm.

"No, no, no, no..." she repeated as the tears shrouded her

eyes, so swollen as their glassy brown irises begged to stop the inevitable. "Please...please... Let's try again. Let's try again, Nicholas..." she begged, her fingernails digging in.

I clenched my jaw. Dammit! Why did she have to make everything so hard? "It's not a question of trying, Noah. What we had is gone."

"I know you can love me again... I know you don't love Sophia. I know you love me, only me, remember? You said you'd always love me, no matter what happened. I never asked you to come back because I was waiting for time to heal us, but it hasn't, and that can only mean one thing. Now I'm doing it. I'm asking you to give us another chance."

"Don't ask me for something I can't give you," I growled, pushing her out of the way. But that touch made me freeze again. I looked at her to be sure she understood me. "I can't love anyone. That ship has sailed, okay...? I opened up to you once, despite all my instincts. I've tried, I swear I've tried, but I'm not made to love, I'm not a person who can be loved—that's a lesson I learned from you."

"I do love you," she declared softly. I hated to think of what a stranger would see in us: two people with bad pasts, bad relationships... We didn't know what love was, neither of us did. We'd suffered too much at an early age and had wound up making the people who tried to get close to us suffer, too.

"You don't love me, Noah. You grabbed the one weapon that could take me down and pulled the trigger."

"I'm here! I'm still here, and so are you! You can barely stay away from me, and that means something; it has to mean something! After a year, we can't stop coming after each other... Do you honestly want to end up with someone else? Think about it, Nicholas, because if you leave, if you leave and abandon me again, I might not be here when you come back!"

"Is that supposed to be a threat?" Just imagining that she might be with someone else horrified me.

"I've waited for you. I've been waiting for you ever since we broke up. A year and a half has passed, and I'm still waiting for you to come back to me, and you are doing it, but you can't commit. I can't bear it. It's now or never, Nicholas, because if you leave, if you leave me again, you and I are done forever."

Silence overtook the room, and her eyes were filled with disappointment and incredulity. I took a breath, preparing to talk again.

"Goodbye, Noah," I said with a terrible ache in my chest.

Noah stepped back as if the words had burned her. I knew what I was giving up if I walked out that door, but I couldn't give her what she needed from me. I watched as her sorrow became something else, something darker and harder to decipher.

"Goodbye, Nicholas."

She left without looking back. And soon, I was walking out as well.

Part Three

COUNTDOWN

33

The library was packed. Midterm exam and final paper season was upon us. I had no idea how long I'd been in there, since I'd picked a table without windows to keep from distracting myself or getting depressed when I saw everyone walking around, celebrating the last days of winter.

Jenna was there beside me, concentrating on anything except the biology book in front of her nose.

"Can we?" she asked for the eighth time.

I scowled at her. I'd had it.

"Come on, Noah. At this rate, I'll have the book memorized before you're done."

I giggled, then breathed out wearily. "One coffee, Jenna. A quick one. I'm serious."

She smiled, and we gathered our things and emerged from our self-imposed exile.

Outside, I saw it was nearly evening. I hugged myself to hold off the chilly wind blowing through the trees. I'd been in the library for so long that I'd lost all notion of time.

The two months I'd worked at LRB had taught me a lot about

the real world, but with exams coming, I was happy I could devote all my time to my studies. I'd saved some cash, and I could make it for a few months. Simon offered to find me a similar job at another company, and I was eternally grateful, but for now, it was better like this. As far as us...everything was on ice for the moment. I was honest with him and told him I still hadn't gotten over Nick. I needed some time alone. We still saw each other, but as friends. He'd pick me up, we'd grab a bite, sometimes we'd go out to dinner with friends—nothing major.

Jenna leaned into me as we exited the library, linked her arm through mine, and walked with me to the nearest coffee stand. I ordered a triple espresso and a pretzel; she got a hot chocolate. We sat on a bench and tried to enjoy our brief break.

"I was hoping to get a chance to invite you to Lion's birthday party. I'm throwing it at our place. It's gonna be great. He has no idea. I told him we should just try and grab a quick dinner because I have a big test the next day...obviously that's not true—my midterms are done the day after tomorrow. He's going to freak out."

I smiled, imagining the scene.

"When is it?" I asked, sipping my coffee.

"In a couple of weeks. I wanted to go ahead and tell you so you wouldn't have an excuse not to show!"

I tried to hem and haw—it amused me to watch her attempts at persuasion—and finally I said sure, I'd go, and she started to breathe easy again. I wasn't that into the idea: I was exhausted, worse than I'd ever been—my coffee didn't even help. But I also felt that going out and taking my mind off things could do me good. We talked for a while about nothing in particular. She told me Lion had gotten pissed at her a few days ago when he found her with a hammer in her hand, going to fix something. It seemed like nothing, but Jenna had already broken her finger with that same hammer not so long ago, and since then, Lion had forbidden her from touching his tools.

It was hilarious to me to think of Jenna trying and then failing to follow his rules.

"You should have seen him: *My tools, my rules!* he was shouting. And then all I had to do was stand back and watch him fix the bench for my makeup table without me even needing to ask. I'm a tactician, right? When I first asked him, he was like, *I'll do it when I can*, but when he sees me with a hammer in my hand, he rushes off to finish the job he thinks I've already started."

"You're evil," I said, standing up to go back in. We walked around the corner to the street the library was on, and I nearly ran into a guy on the sidewalk. A guy I swore I'd never see again. Michael.

"What the hell are you doing here?!" Jenna shouted.

He looked at me—eyed me up, rather—gawking at my body and face before looking over at her. "I'm back," he said and stared at me again.

It hadn't been easy to forget what had happened with Michael. Not only had he ruined my relationship with Nick, he'd also betrayed my trust, taking advantage of me in a moment when I was completely vulnerable.

"You said you were leaving forever," I said reproachfully, pulling close to Jenna. "That was the deal."

Michael shrugged, indifferent. "People change their minds."

I couldn't believe what I was hearing. Seeing him again was uncomfortable: I remembered things then that I'd buried deep inside and had sworn I'd never think about again.

Michael had thought he and I could have something after Nick and I broke up. For a while, he was obsessed with the idea that I *needed* to be with him, that I *had* to give him a chance. That was the only reason he'd done me the favor of not pressing charges against Nick. When he got out of the hospital, he came and saw me every single day—by then, Nick was in New York—and when I told him there was nothing between us, he cursed me, told me I'd played him, made up things I'd supposedly said, even tried to force himself on me. I had to threaten him with a restraining order.

His brother, Charlie, came to see me and told me Michael had already had problems like this before, that one girl almost got him kicked out of school. I learned that day that Charlie and Michael had suffered a lot after their mother had died. Michael had become unstable; Charlie had started drinking… It had been hard for them to get through it, especially since their father was totally absent—he had abandoned them when they were just boys. Michael took care of Charlie, but he had psychiatric problems of his own and became depressed. Eventually Charlie had convinced him to take a job in Arizona, and he'd sworn he'd never bother me again.

Jenna took out her phone, shouting, "I'm calling the cops." I'd never seen her so mad.

I glared at Michael: the whole reason my relationship had fallen apart and my life had gone to shit. After learning all his secrets, I realized he had taken advantage of me… Maybe I'd let him, but still, he used my vulnerability against me and twisted everything I'd said in therapy around so he could exploit me.

"What are you going to tell them?" Michael asked, unworried. "I haven't done anything; I've just come back after a year to see my brother and look for a job. Is that what you're going to tell the cops?"

Jenna stepped toward him. "What I'll tell them is how you harassed my friend and stalked her for weeks on end, you asshole!"

He barely looked at her. His eyes were frozen on me. "That might have worked if Noah had actually gotten a restraining order, but as things stand now, there's no evidence I've done anything."

I thought I'd done the right thing, not pressing charges, but now that I saw him there, looking smug, full of barely suppressed anger…I wasn't so sure. "Come on, Jenna," I said, hoping to get away as soon as possible.

"You keep away from Noah, you hear me?" Jenna warned him.

Michael smiled eerily, gave us a condescending look, and said, "You look precious, Noah."

"Fuck you!" I said, feeling the rage bubble up inside me.

I didn't wait for a response. I had to grab Jenna so she didn't attack him. She didn't care that he was twice her size and nearly a foot taller. We walked through the doors of the library. Knowing he couldn't see us anymore, I collapsed, sitting on the first bench I could find and hyperventilating.

Jenna sat down next to me, cursing, but also trying to calm me down.

Why had he come back? Why?

I'd convinced myself Michael was just a guy with problems, like so many others, one who would never actually hurt me. When he left, I thought he had done that for me, because I mattered to him and he didn't want me to be scared of him, but now, I had the sense that I needed to run away, that his being here could mean nothing good. I felt like I needed to do something, tell someone.

"I'm calling Lion."

"Don't even think about it!" I shouted, miraculously recovered and tearing her phone from her hands.

"We've got to do something!" Jenna protested in a rage.

"No. We're not going to do anything. He said he's here to see Charlie. Maybe he'll leave. A lot of time has passed. I don't think he's here because of me, Jenna."

Incredulous, she looked at me like I was crazy. "Did you not hear how he talked to you?"

I nodded. I felt a sudden urge to vomit. Stirring up those memories was bad—especially now. "I don't want trouble, Jenna. I don't want to think about what happened, and I certainly don't want you telling Lion about this. We're not going to do anything. End of story."

Before she could interrupt me, I continued:

"I'll be careful, all right? And if I see something I don't like, or he comes close to me again, I'll go to the cops, and you can tell whoever you like. In the meantime, let's keep studying."

Jenna was angry. "I've kept your secrets before, but I'm telling you, if I hear the least noise about that creep bothering you, I'm calling Nicholas. You hear me?"

I didn't talk back, despite my anxiety.

After running into Michael, I spent several days nervous and afraid. I tried to push my feelings down, though. I was busy anyway, trying to pack up my things and move to my new apartment. I'd finished my last midterm the day before, so I finally had time to deal with the move.

I'd found a loft off campus. It was an open space with a small kitchen, a living room, and a bedroom. The bathroom had a tub. It wasn't anything too special, but it was enough for me.

Unfortunately, there was a problem with the water, and I couldn't move till the end of the week. I asked Jenna if I could stay with her and Lion for a few days until the problem was fixed. She didn't hesitate and even said she'd help me take my boxes to the new place. What I didn't expect was that she would come with Lion in tow. I hadn't seen him in ages, but he was a sight for sore eyes.

"What's up, Noah?!" he said, bear-hugging me.

"Thanks for coming, Lion. You didn't need to."

"Oh, he did," Jenna replied, showing me her new nails, which were manicured with wild red gel.

I rolled my eyes and started picking up the boxes that were light enough for me and taking them to Lion's truck. He took care of the heavier ones, and soon Jenna and I were taking down everything fragile. There was more fragile stuff than heavy stuff, so we didn't get to relax.

At one point, I bent down to pick up a box of books, and I felt something like a dagger stabbing me in the back. I couldn't move.

"Are you okay?" Lion asked, coming over.

Jenna seemed not to worry until she saw my face, which I guess had gone blank. "Noah!"

I took a deep breath to see if the pain would go away, sitting back on the floor. "I think I just fucked up my back. I'm okay, though," I said, my voice trembling.

"Why were you picking up that box?! That's Lion's job, dummy."

I ignored her as the pain kept radiating, slowly becoming tolerable.

Lion bent down and looked me over with those green eyes that glowed so bright, it was no wonder Jenna had spent half her wedding speech talking about them. They were hypnotizing.

"Can you get up?" he asked.

"Uh..." I wanted a few seconds. "I'm not really sure."

Jenna shook her head while Lion wrapped his arm around my back. I tried to get up on my own, but the pain was now in my stomach, and I bent over, almost paralyzed.

"You've thrown your back out, doll," Jenna said, while Lion leaned over and picked me up.

"I'll take you to the car, and you can lie down and rest. It'll pass. You just pulled a muscle, that's all."

I nodded, unable to make a sound.

The pain...the pain was horrible.

Lion left me in the passenger seat and finished loading boxes in the back. When we finally left, I prayed for the trip to be short and to be able to lie down somewhere soft and warm.

"If you want, I'll call my massage therapist. She's the best—she'll know exactly what to do for you," Jenna said, sitting in the back and shoving M&M's between her lips, which were coated in purple gloss.

I couldn't say a word. I just wanted to lie down. When we got to Jenna's place, I still could hardly move. Lion was worried as he carried me back to the small guest room they had prepared for me. When he laid me on the bed, a jolt of agony shot through my body, and I had to close my eyes.

"Noah...are you sure you're okay?"

Jenna came in then with a glass of water and a muscle relaxer. I downed it immediately.

Lion seemed to doubt whether I was well, but he had to go to the airport in a couple of hours. He had a meeting in Philadelphia and wouldn't be back for four days.

"I'll take care of her," Jenna said, lying down next to me. Lion leaned down to kiss her softly on the lips.

"I'm going to head out, then. If you need help for the move, Luca's willing to lend a hand, like I said. Take care, Noah, and feel better," he said, rubbing the top of my head.

When he was gone, I fluffed up the pillows and started counting in my mind to distract myself.

"You sure you don't want to go to the hospital?" Jenna asked for the eighth time.

I had been saying I thought it was stupid just to go there for a pulled muscle, but the pain was getting worse again, after diminishing just a little, and I was about to faint. So her idea was starting to appeal to me.

"Let's just wait for the pill to do its thing," I said, aware that the mere thought of standing up and walking to the door would probably leave me seeing stars.

Two hours later, I knew something was wrong.

"Noah, you're scaring me," Jenna said, watching me writhe.

"Take me to the hospital," I said, terrified.

Just getting to the car was torture, and the trip to the emergency room was even worse. After we parked, I walked as best I could to the waiting room while Jenna filled out all the paperwork the nurse on duty had given her.

Then we waited. I got more and more nervous, especially once I felt something strange between my legs. I looked down and saw a red spot extending through my pajama bottoms. Jenna shrieked. The next thing I knew, I was in a wheelchair being taken to a room where someone hurried to attend to me. Jenna had to wait outside.

"Honey, can you hear me?" a nurse said, helping me out of my clothing and giving me a hospital gown to put on. "The doctor is on his way, but first I need you to answer some questions."

I looked at her. She had red hair and reminded me of Tweedledee or Tweedledum from *Alice in Wonderland*. Except she was a woman, and she wouldn't shut up.

"How many weeks along are you?" she asked.

"I mean, this just happened..."

Her brow wrinkled, and then the question...that fucking question brought me back to reality, like hitting the ground headfirst after jumping out of a tenth-story window.

"Wh-what are you talking about?"

She looked at me with surprise, then with pity. "Honey... I'm pretty sure you're having a miscarriage."

What the hell was she saying? Everything seemed to freeze, and the word *miscarriage* struck me like a giant hammer.

Miscarriage, miscarriage, miscarriage... It didn't matter how many times I thought it, it was impossible, impossible, because a miscarriage meant you had to be pregnant, and I wasn't.

"The doctor will be here soon… You just relax; I'm sure everything will be fine."

Everything will be fine? How could she say the word *miscarriage* and then tell me everything would be fine?

My mind started spinning. I tried to count on my fingers, remember numbers and dates, and the conclusion was always the same: it couldn't be. It was impossible. That eased my mind. The nurse had to be an idiot. I hadn't mentioned trying to pick up the box. I'd Probably torn something trying to pick up the box and I was having a hemorrhage and it was making it look like I was…

Because that was impossible, right? It had been way too long since the last time I…

The door opened, interrupting my tormented thoughts, and a middle-aged doctor greeted me stiffly.

"How are you feeling, Miss Morgan?" he asked as he came closer.

I didn't answer, and he motioned for me to lie back.

"I'm going to do an ultrasound, okay?" he told me, lifting my gown and touching my belly gently.

"I'm not pregnant," I said, repeating the phrase over and over in my head like a mantra.

I'm not pregnant, I'm not pregnant, I'm not pregnant.

The doctor observed me for a few moments with surprise.

"We'll find out in a few seconds," he said, sitting next to me and pulling over a rolling table. "This gel is going to feel a little cold, all right?"

I shivered as he rubbed it on my belly. Struggling to control my breathing, I watched what he was doing. He dragged some kind of machine over my belly, hit a button, and turned the screen to show me what he was seeing.

"I think this is proof you're mistaken, no?"

On the screen, in black and white, blinking a little, was the image of a baby... Not some tiny fetus, a real baby with a head, feet, and hands, taking up most of the screen.

"Oh my God!" I shouted, bringing my hand to my mouth in terror, pure, unadulterated terror.

"You're around sixteen weeks," the doctor said, turning toward the machine, unruffled after dropping that bomb on me, and sliding the handpiece around while he hit various buttons. He looked a bit worried at first. Then, after a few seconds that dragged on painfully, I heard a noise, constant, loud, echoing through the room. He sighed and turned to face me.

"We have a pulse, Miss Morgan."

So it wasn't a miscarriage. But this new reality made me feel like I was falling again. Only this time, I might never hit the ground.

"Am I going to lose it?" I asked, my voice quavering. The doctor turned the screen and showed me a black spot around the baby. I didn't need to be an expert to know it shouldn't have been there.

"This is an intrauterine hematoma. A big one. Since you told me you weren't aware you were pregnant, I'm assuming your period has been coming regularly. Or am I wrong?"

I tried to understand what he was getting at.

"I'm not especially regular, but yeah... I've had my period the past few months. I guess it was maybe shorter than usual, but..."

"Do you take birth control?"

"Yeah. To control my periods, actually."

"Do you ever miss a pill?"

Shit!

"I've forgotten one before; I usually just take it the next day..."

"That explains why you might have gotten pregnant, but that isn't what matters right now. The thing is, your body's been on the verge of miscarrying several times."

I looked back at the screen. Jesus. That was a baby... A baby

I didn't even know was growing inside me… I hadn't been careful at all. My God! I'd even drunk alcohol…

"Doctor…I didn't know. I literally had no idea… I mean, you can't even tell…"

The doctor remained calm. "Let's relax, okay? We're going to do all the tests we need to be sure you and the baby are both fine. You'd be surprised how frequent cases like yours are. Often you don't really notice the changes until the third or fourth month. For the first twelve weeks, the uterus remains entirely within the pelvis. You may not even see the pregnancy until it moves into the abdomen. Since you're bleeding, we're going to check you in and keep you here until everything goes back to normal. We don't want you experiencing any unneeded stress or strain. I know you just found out about this, and it must have come as quite a shock, but you need complete rest. When the bleeding stops, we'll do a cervical assessment. If everything looks all right, then I doubt we'll need to worry about premature birth."

Premature birth.

I felt like I was in a bubble, trying to understand what all these words meant: *baby*, *premature birth*, *intrauterine hematoma*, *miscarriage*… What the doctor had just said hadn't even registered yet. I was just trying to assimilate what I'd seen on the screen.

"The nurse is going to come ask you a few questions. We'll also do some blood work, just to rule out any additional complications. The most important thing for now, though, is for that hematoma to go away. I'm going to guess your progesterone is low. We'll take care of that till you reach the levels you need to hold on to that baby. Sound good?" His tone was weirdly buoyant—I guessed he was trying to calm me down?

But I was in a panic; I was having a legit panic attack. I wanted to take off running, disappear, go back to my life from just a few hours before.

"Doctor...I'm only nineteen. I'm not ready to be a mother."

He nodded gently. "You weren't planning on this...I understand," he said tactfully. "But the baby exists now, and so does the risk you'll lose it. You're young, and you've got some tough months ahead of you. You're going to need the support of the people around you. Do you know who the father is?"

The father.

Nicholas Leister was the father of that baby...and he was on the opposite side of the country, with another woman, and had made it utterly clear he didn't want to be a part of my life.

"I...I know who it is...but I can't tell you."

Just then, the nurse came in, and the doctor outlined all the tests that had to be done. Then he smiled and turned away. Once he was gone, the nurse sat close to me and patted the back of my hand.

"You need to relax, honey," she said as another nurse came in and the two of them went to work on me. "We're going to put an IV in to administer some vitamins and a sedative so you can rest. When you wake up, you'll have plenty of good news to look forward to."

"No, no, I don't want a sedative. You don't understand! This shouldn't have happened. I'm not ready to be a mother. I shouldn't be a mother, okay? They told me there was almost no way I could get pregnant, that it was basically impossible, and now..."

"And now you're four months pregnant, honey, and according to your medical history and the state you were in, it's a miracle."

A miracle.

I closed my eyes, trying to relax and take it all in. Four months... Fuck. *Damn you, Nicholas Leister!*

34

Noah

I DIDN'T KNOW WHEN I'D FINALLY FALLEN ASLEEP, BUT WHEN I opened my eyes, I found Jenna sitting in a chair next to me, looking pale and sick with worry. When she noticed that I was awake, she stood and leaned over me. I saw a blanket was covering me, and an IV was sticking out of my arm.

"Noah? How are you?" she said with fear in her voice.

Seeing her there, and remembering everything, I felt as if we were in a different dimension, as if my life weren't mine and what they had just told me had closed all the doors that had been open to me before. As if there were just one door left, and I would be forced to pass through it.

"Fine, I think..."

A baby... I mean, having a baby at all had only ever been a theoretical possibility for me. When I'd thought about having a child, I'd always imagined myself adopting one. Maybe. I'd been told the damage I'd suffered as a child could cause problems. That if I wanted to conceive, I'd need to go to a fertility clinic and be monitored the whole time. I never thought it was possible that I could get pregnant naturally...especially not if I was on the fucking pill! Nothing, absolutely nothing had ever suggested this could happen.

I sat up and uncovered myself, carefully lifted my gown, and looked at my belly.

"So it is true... I can't believe it." Jenna's words, not mine.

"What am I going to do?" I asked, resting my hands on my stomach to see if there was anything there that told me I was pregnant, and had been for four months.

Jenna shook her head and sat down again. "Noah, who's the father?"

I'd assumed that was obvious, but now that I thought about it, I'd told no one what had happened at Thanksgiving. No one knew except Nick and me.

"Nicholas," I whispered. Just saying his name made my heart ache.

Her eyes opened wide, and a huge smile appeared on her face. "Nicholas? Our Nicholas? But...when? How?"

What the hell was she so happy about?

"It happened during Thanksgiving, after Nick found out about his mom being sick. He was so sad, and things just..."

"Oh my God, Noah, this is fabulous! Wait, did you say Thanksgiving?"

She looked at my belly, then at me. Then she seemed to be counting backward.

"Four months, Jenna," I said without a trace of happiness in my voice. "Did the doctors not tell you?"

"Are you kidding? I didn't even know if my suspicions were right until five seconds ago when you lifted your gown and stared at your stomach like you had an alien in there."

"You really just found out?"

Jenna nodded. "I'm not family; they wouldn't tell me anything. I even had to fight the nurses to get them to let me in here."

I sighed. Never in my life had I felt so lost.

Jenna took my hand and placed it on my slightly bulging belly. No one would ever have guessed I was that far along.

"Noah, I was scared the baby could belong to some random dude you'd hooked up with in a bar. But it's Nick's! Your Nick! It's wonderful!"

I let go of her hand and scowled at her. "What's so wonderful, Jenna?" I replied, realizing just then that the constant beeping of the machines I was plugged into was driving me crazy. "Me being pregnant at nineteen years old by a guy who is with another girl? What the hell's so wonderful about that?!"

"Noah, relax, I just meant—"

"No!" I shouted. "Don't say anything, don't be happy for me, because this isn't good news—it's shit. I don't want a baby, I don't want to raise a baby alone, and certainly not Nicholas's." Tears started to roll down my cheeks. I wiped them away impatiently. "I didn't even know I was pregnant! What mother doesn't know she has a kid inside her? What kind of mother will I be? I don't have anything to offer."

She was lost. She didn't know what to say. She was scared to even open her mouth. "Noah, when Nick finds out—"

"Don't even think about it!" I cut her off in a panic. "Don't you dare tell him anything, Jenna. Not him and not anyone else!"

Not only was she surprised, it was clear she didn't agree at all. "Noah, you have to tell him."

Goddammit. I wanted to stand up and walk out, to be alone and think, but every time I imagined myself leaving, I remembered the image from that ultrasound. Before I could argue with Jenna, the door opened and the doctor came in.

"I've got good news, Miss Morgan," he said. He had a folder in his hand. He looked at it, took off his glasses, and focused on me. "You don't have any illnesses or complications, and the baby's heartbeat is normal, strong." I felt something warm in my stomach. "You're in the second trimester. This is when doctors usually recommend telling the family, but you're what we call a high-risk pregnancy. That sounds more alarming than it is. In two or three weeks, we can do another scan, and we'll be able to learn the baby's sex, if you'd like to know. You'll probably also start feeling some movement."

Jenna gawked at him like he was saying I had a Hello Kitty in my uterus. But I was feeling strange, too, something like vertigo... and I was utterly speechless.

Since we didn't respond to him, he went on talking, apparently unable to notice that we were both completely freaking out.

"It looks like we're out of the woods as far as the hemorrhage, but we'll still want to schedule another ultrasound to make sure the hematoma has fully healed. I'm going to put you on progesterone. The tests show your levels are really low. It's important for you to closely follow all the directions on the sheet I give you, okay?"

I nodded, overwhelmed by so much information.

"Complete rest, Miss Morgan. 'Complete' means getting up to go to the bathroom and nothing else, understand?"

I nodded again, wondering how in the hell I'd tell my professors I couldn't get out of bed without revealing I had a living person growing inside me.

"I'm scheduling you to come back in two weeks. If you have any more bleeding, you need to come straight to the hospital. Brown discharge is normal. You should expect some of that as the hematoma heals."

I nodded a third time, even though there must have been a million things I should have asked him.

"Have you spoken to the father?" he asked.

Jenna pursed her lips as I said no.

Why the hell was he asking that? It wasn't his business!

"It would be good if he could be there for you, especially these next few weeks, when you need to stay in bed."

I was about to speak, but Jenna interrupted me:

"My husband and I will take care of her, Doctor, no worries."

I felt infinitely grateful to her then and regretted being mean to her a few minutes before. She was the one person who could help me with this if I really planned to keep it secret.

And I did. This was going to be my secret...mine and mine alone.

When I got home, there was nothing to do but go straight to the guest bedroom. I was scared as I took each step. I didn't want to harm the baby. And when I got to the bed, I climbed in. Only then could I rest easy.

Lion would be gone for another three days, but Jenna and I would be fine on our own. Every time she came to see me and ask if I needed anything, I had the sense she was biting her tongue.

At first, we didn't even mention the baby; it was like I was bedbound with some mysterious illness, and Jenna respected my silence, even if I knew it was torture for her not to talk about it.

I was in total denial, but I followed all the doctor's orders, took my medicines, tried not to stress out, slept a lot, drank lots of liquids. Only when Jenna left me in peace did my mind go crazy seeking a solution. I'd be lying if I said I didn't consider an abortion: that would have been the easiest option, the one that would allow me to keep living as I had, the one that would keep me from having to see Nick again and admit what we'd done in the light of day. But just imagining that, just imagining hurting the baby...

I couldn't choose that road. Everything crumbled, everything I thought I knew, believed, or felt had stopped mattering the moment I'd seen the image of that baby on the screen. Not *my baby*—I still couldn't say that. I would get there, I guessed.

For a time, I kept thinking back to the moment of conception, the moment when I made the biggest mistake of my life. I blamed Nick for my sorrow, my anger, my rage…and now I blamed him for this. He hadn't forgiven me for what I'd done. Well, he'd sure as hell remember the moment he'd decided not to use a condom for the rest of his goddamned life. If I even decided to tell him. Which, for now, I wouldn't.

After this, I passed into a phase of thinking of all the things I wouldn't be able to do from that moment on. What would I do about school? How would I tell my mother? The same mother who'd gotten pregnant with me at eighteen and had given me endless talks about condoms and the pill; the same mother who thought getting pregnant so young had been the height of irresponsibility and idiocy… Sure, she always said she loved me like crazy and that one thing had nothing to do with the other. She had even gone so far as to *forbid* me from getting pregnant until I was twenty-five.

Then there was money. I didn't have a Swiss bank account or anything like it… My entire financial worth was twenty-five hundred bucks, if I was lucky.

I thought about where I was going to live. I'd rented the loft for a year, but it was no place to raise a kid. Shit—raising a kid? I was actually going to raise a living being? Me? I'd have to work like crazy just to pay for the baby's things. I surfed around on the Internet and saw strollers that cost a thousand bucks… I could afford approximately two fancy strollers, or maybe five to ten normal ones…it was pathetic! I was going to have to turn to my mother—me, who hated asking for money.

On the fourth day, Jenna came to my room. She'd told Lion I'd been diagnosed with sciatica, but she was looking at me pensively, and finally, she seemed to reach a conclusion.

"You have to tell him," she said dryly.

If I could have gotten up, I'd have walked away from her, but since I couldn't, I ignored her and went on reading the book in my hand.

"Noah, are we going to talk about this, or are we going to go on pretending you don't have a baby in your belly?"

I set the book down and glared at her. "There's nothing to talk about. I'll take care of it."

She laughed bitterly. "Oh yeah? How?" she asked, pointing at me. "You can't even get to the bathroom on your own."

I scowled. "This is just for a few days... In a week, I'll go to the doctor, and he'll tell me everything's fine. This craziness will be over, and I'll be able to get on with my life."

That plan didn't hold water for any number of reasons, but I tried not to think about that.

"Are you listening to yourself?" Jenna shouted. "This is only going to get worse, Noah! I mean, not worse, but people are going to realize! You're already showing a little bit."

We looked down at my belly. It was swollen. Not a lot, but still.

"I read about some moms who could conceal it till the eighth month almost. I'll have to buy some baggy clothes, but I can do it..."

She shook her head and looked at the ceiling, searching for the magic words that would make me listen to reason. "I don't get it. This is your child we're talking about! Why don't you want to tell Nick? Why?!"

I could feel myself heating up inside, and that was a bad sign. I was a walking time bomb, and I didn't want to take it out on Jenna. But I couldn't stop the following words from coming out:

"Because I begged him to come back to me, and he said no!" I screamed, trying to hold in my tears. "He said he couldn't forgive me, that what I had done had ended what we had forever. I gave him an ultimatum; he didn't care. He left!"

Jenna passed almost instantly from surprise to indignation.

"I told him I loved him, Jen, and he didn't care. I asked him to stay, and he didn't." I choked back a few sobs. "And now you want me to go tell him I'm expecting his child? Why? So I can tie him to me when he's made perfectly clear he never wants to see me again?"

"But I promise you, when he finds out about the baby..."

"He's going to want to take care of it? Take care of me, take me home with him, give me everything he has and more? You think I don't know that? But I don't want anyone to be with me because they feel obligated. I don't want to force him into forgiving me, and if I tell him I'm pregnant, that's exactly what I'll be doing."

Jenna shook her head, unsure of what to say.

"Nicholas loves you," she told me after a minute's silence. "I know he does. He's insanely in love with you, and when he finds out about the child, he'd going to be the happiest man on earth, Noah. What happened between you was awful, but have you considered that maybe this child is what you needed to put aside your differences and try again? I can't imagine a better reason to do it."

I saw the image she was trying to create in my mind: Nick and me, together again, with a precious little baby to take care of, both living the lives we had always wanted, even if I hadn't planned on being a parent for several more years. Yes, that was what I wanted: a life with Nick.

But I exhaled a long breath and shook my head.

"I don't want to keep talking about this, or about Nick, or about the baby. Just let me finish taking it all in before I have to face the rest of it, him, what we had..."

She leaned down and gave me a soft hug. "You're going to be a wonderful mother, Noah, and this baby is going to be the prettiest little thing in the world."

I blinked, trying as hard as I could not to cry again as the image of a little child with Nick's traits formed in my head.

Jenna put a hand on my belly. "I'll be your favorite aunt."

That made me crack up.

Jenna left to see what Lion was up to, and I covered myself with blankets and tried to rest, but I was so scared of having to tell Nicholas what had happened that I couldn't sleep a wink.

Those two weeks were the longest ones of my life, but they did allow me to think through a lot of things. I was finally able to call the child *my baby*. That was a big step. In my head, I started calling it *Mini-Me* because, boy or girl, it was mine and would resemble me. The name just clicked somehow. I had read enough on the Internet to know that it could already move its hands and feet, was sensitive to light, was receptive to stimuli. That meant it could hear me when I talked, which I did all the time when no one was around. It could move its neck, it was growing fingernails, it was supposedly the size of an avocado. And its sex could be determined.

We lied to Lion again when Jenna had to take me back to the doctor. He looked at us as if we were up to something. I got stressed out when I was dressing. I'd just been wearing pajamas the whole time and hadn't noticed how the baby and I were growing.

Forget pants. I put on a loose skirt and a Ramones T-shirt. Wow. Some mom I was.

We went to the maternity wing of the hospital, not the emergency room. I was freaking out, thinking someone would see us there. We looked like a couple of little girls who'd gotten lost and didn't know the way out. The women there were all adults, the kind it would be normal to call *Mom*. Whereas when I looked at myself in the mirror, I saw an overgrown high schooler reflected back at me.

They called my name, and I felt myself blushing and wishing

the earth would swallow me whole. Some of the women there were staring at me, many with their eyes on my belly.

We walked into Doctor Hubber's office, and a nurse asked me to lie back on the bed and wait. Jenna looked around, picking up a plastic model of a fetus in a uterus and showing it to me. She pointed at the vaginal cavity, said, "Here's where yours is going to come out," and started laughing.

I glared at her, getting more and more nervous. She replaced the plastic baby and sat next to the table. A few minutes later, the doctor came in and smiled.

"How are you, Miss Morgan?" he asked, walking over to me.

"Good, I think. You know...taking it all in. You can call me *Noah*, by the way."

Dr. Hubber seemed to find that amusing. It was the same routine as last time. He turned the screen of the ultrasound machine so I could see it, and he could reach the handpiece.

"Let's see how the baby is doing and if that hematoma is all better."

He spread the gel on my belly again and rubbed the device across it. Soon, we could see the baby on the screen and hear its heartbeat loudly.

"Oh, Noah, look!" Jenna said, leaning in to see better.

There, a little bigger than last time, was my Mini-Me, in a somewhat weird position, its hands squeezing what I thought was the umbilical cord.

"It's playing...that's a good sign," the doctor said with a grin. Then he took some measurements. Everything was perfect, including the head size. I could even see a little wisp of hair.

My eyes filled with tears... Seeing the child again, after finally coming to acceptance, and knowing it was healthy, made me happier than I'd been in years...and I wished I could share that happiness with a special someone.

"Would you like to know the baby's sex?" Dr. Hubber asked, showing the baby from different angles.

"Yes!" Jenna said.

"No!" I replied.

The doctor stopped and observed me. Jenna turned to me as well, just as the tears poured down my cheeks. I was crying because I didn't want to know Mini-Me's sex if Nick wasn't there. How could I refuse him that moment? Mini-Me belonged to him, too; maybe less to him than to me, but still, it was half Nick... That precious little baby playing with its umbilical cord had a father I was sure would adore it above all else. Was I going to let him miss out on that?

Jenna seemed to realize why I was crying and squeezed my hand tight.

"She'd rather wait, Doctor," she said for me.

Dr. Hubber nodded and looked back at the screen. "Unfortunately, the hematoma hasn't decreased much in size. I had hoped we'd see much better progress after two weeks' rest."

"So what does that mean?"

"It means you're still in the danger zone. And if you were to miscarry at eighteen weeks, that could be dangerous for you as well."

I looked at him, deeply afraid.

"We'll keep you on bed rest and prescribe you more vitamins. I know you're frightened, Noah, but this isn't out of the ordinary. It happens to lots of women, especially with their first pregnancy. Just be patient and stay in bed."

It all sounded so bad... Two more weeks of complete bed rest! What was I going to do?! Jenna couldn't just keep taking care of me, and Lion would eventually realize something was up. Plus, soon enough I'd no longer be able to hide what was happening under my Ramones shirt. Time was running out, dammit!

“We have to tell someone. Let me talk to Lion. I promise you he won’t tell anyone,” Jenna said on the way back home.

I’d made her stop at an ice cream shop. Suddenly, I was dying for a chocolate sundae with nuts. I guessed this was my first official craving, and I was licking my lips while she looked at me with worry.

“We can’t tell Lion,” I replied. “He won’t last long without needing to tell his best friend.”

“Your mother, then,” Jenna said, striking the steering wheel.

My mother… Dammit, I was more scared of telling her than I was of losing the baby.

“Look, just leave me a Tupperware full of food next to the bed, and I won’t have to move, and that way you can stop taking care of me.”

I could tell Jenna was getting pissed.

“I’m not leaving you alone. That’s out of the question.” She stared at the road for a moment in silence. “Noah, honey, it’s time. I’m sorry, but you’re four months along, you’re not going to be able to keep hiding it, you need to accept what’s happening… Do you want Nicholas to show up here and see you with a huge swollen belly? He also needs time to deal with this and figure out what to do; this will change his life, too.”

“Don’t talk to me about Nicholas. I don’t care what changes he has to deal with; I’m the one who’s dealing with the real changes here, not him.”

When we arrived home, we ran into Lion, who was parking near the front door. He walked over and smiled.

“How’s your back?” he said. I guessed he thought it was funny that I’d fucked it up badly enough just lifting a box of books that I had to spend weeks in bed. He’d tried to tell me before about the benefits of exercise…

If only he knew...

Jenna gave him a kiss and looked back at me doubtfully again. "Two more weeks of rest, they said." I could tell she hated lying to him.

Surprised, he replied, "Jesus, Noah, now I'm starting to get worried!"

I waved it off as I struggled to get out of the car. Jenna looked at me with worry. It was unnecessary; I could manage on my own.

"Lion, carry her upstairs," she said, with a little too much urgency in her voice.

"I'm fine, Jenna," I said.

But Lion was already on the case. "I don't mind," he said. "Come on, softy, grab me around the neck." He crouched, and soon I was in the air. I grabbed him tight, but instantly I was afraid. What if he tripped on a stair and dropped me on my belly? "I can tell you haven't been moving...you're heavy!" he said, laughing.

Jenna smacked him on the arm.

In a panic, thinking I'd been found out, I narrowed my eyes, feigning indignation. "Very funny," I said.

When we got to the bedroom, he laid me on the bed, and I got comfortable, taking a deep breath.

Lion stared at me for a moment. I wished I could read his mind. But at the same time, I thought it was probably best not to know what he was thinking.

"Anything you need, just shout," he said and walked out.

I didn't even turn on the TV. I just lay there trying to figure out what the best way to tell Nick everything was. My God, just the thought of his face, the surprise... He'd probably just get mad or blame me for it. He was going to fucking hate me! He'd hate me because I'd done exactly what the worst women did: try to pin him down. It was the oldest trick in the book, and it must look pathetic.

A few minutes later, I heard murmurs behind the door. And soon after that, Jenna came in.

"Lion wants to tell Nick."

"You told him?!" I shouted, sitting up.

She shook her head quickly. "He wants to tell him you hurt your back. I said he shouldn't say anything, but I don't know if he'll pay any attention to me."

Wait, what?

"Why would Lion want to tell Nicholas something so insignificant?"

Jenna bit her lip nervously, and I knew I'd caught her in something.

"Look..." she said, sitting down. "Shit, like...your two best friends being in love and breaking up, it's fucked up, okay?" she confessed. "And after it happened, Nick asked us to keep him informed... Like about how you were doing and all that."

"Nicholas asked you what?"

She had taken me totally by surprise.

"He wanted to know everything: how you were doing at work, at school, how you were dealing with the separation... I know I don't have any right to tell him stuff about you, but I thought that was a good sign... Technically, he's the one who broke up with you, so if he's interested in what's happening with you, maybe that means..."

I couldn't believe what I was hearing.

"What? That he'll forgive me? Jenna, Nicholas is just trying to control me. That's what he does, dammit. Even after he's left me, he's doing it through you two." I realized something just then. "I never told you anything about me falling off the motorbike, did I?" I asked, seeing then why he'd gotten so mad at his father's house. He thought someone should have told him. But I had hidden it from everyone because it was stupid, meaningless, and I didn't want anyone to chew me out over it.

"You fell off a motorbike?" she asked.

I exhaled and covered my face with my hands. "Jenna, tell Lion to keep his goddamned mouth shut. This is my life. You don't have a right to tell anyone about it."

She looked ashamed. I was just tired of the whole situation.

"Actually, tell him to come here."

"What?"

"Lion's party is next week, right?" I asked, looking out the bedroom window at the leaves piling up on the sill. "Invite Nick... When he comes, I'll be able to tell him."

35

Nick

Jenna wouldn't leave me in peace after I told her I couldn't go to Lion's party. I was up to my neck in work, and going would require me to cancel five meetings, plus another one with the real estate agent handling the apartment in Manhattan.

I was making all the necessary moves to go back to LA for good. It was the best thing for me, for family reasons, and for the company. I'd done all I could do in New York. Things were in order, and it was time to close that chapter of my life.

The whole reason I'd moved there in the first place was to get away from Noah, but I was tired of being in the shadows. My little sister was back in LA, my father, my friends... Sophia's family, too, even if that was what mattered least.

My phone rang again. I groaned and prepared myself for another onslaught. Traffic was horrible, and I kept having to look to both sides not to take out a pedestrian. That was another factor: New York was sucking the life out of me. I needed the beach. Urgently.

"Jenna, you're turning into a major pain in my ass," I said. I couldn't suppress my irritation any longer.

"You listen to me, Nicholas Leister," she replied. That almost-maternal tone made me laugh. "It's your best friend's birthday, the person who's always stood with you, who's been there for you every time you've screwed up. He gave you a place to stay when you ran away from home, did you forget that? You were the best man at our wedding. So move your ass unless you want me to come out there and drag you kicking and screaming."

I didn't have a chance to answer before I heard noises on the other line, and next thing I knew, Lion was there.

"Hey, brother," he said, and I pricked up my ears. "Jenna, beat it, I need to talk to him. Jesus, what is going on with you?!" Finally, I heard a door shut, and he continued, "Nick, you gotta come."

"Look, bro, I know it's your birthday, and I honestly do feel bad about missing it, but things are insane. I just can't make it. I'm sorry."

"It's about Noah," he said. I hit the brakes in the middle of the street, and it almost cost me my rear bumper, but it didn't matter. Judging by his tone, he needed my undivided attention.

"What about Noah?" I asked, turning onto a side street and parking.

"I don't know. I mean, she hurt her back like three weeks ago, and she's been at our place. She's supposed to be resting. She can't really move."

"Her back? What the hell kind of back injury requires three weeks' rest? Is she okay? Does it seem bad?" In my mind, I was already canceling all my upcoming appointments.

Lion paused for a few seconds. "Something about it doesn't add up, dude. Jenna's acting weird as shit. I've never seen her this stressed. And Noah... I don't know, she said her back hurts, but the other day I saw her moving around, and she was fine. I think they're up to something, and you need to be here."

It sounded ridiculous, but if Noah was sick...

"How did she hurt herself? What was she doing?"

"She was carrying boxes. She moved. I know I should have told you, but Jenna was on my ass about how we couldn't just keep telling you everything Noah did."

"Why the hell was she moving? Her lodging was covered!" I said, getting out and raising my hand to hail a taxi. I couldn't deal with driving and all this at the same time.

"I don't know, man. You know how stubborn Noah is. I guess she wanted to be independent..."

I got in the taxi and gave the driver my address.

"For God's sake..." I said between clenched teeth. "Where is she living now?"

"She's with us right now, but she rented a loft off campus."

I couldn't believe it! Before I knew what would happen with him and Raffaella, I'd put money aside for Dad and made him promise he'd use it to pay for her dorm. And now she was in a loft somewhere. She barely knew the city. I wouldn't be surprised if she'd found it in one of the roughest neighborhoods in town.

"Look, Nick, I already told you what I think you should do. I don't understand women, especially not those two. But something's not right, and it's got to do with you. When's the last time you ever saw Jenna so insistent about something that wasn't shopping?"

I would have laughed, normally, but now I was worried. It was weird that Jenna was pressing me so much, especially after the last time I'd seen Noah and everything had taken such a bad turn.

Maybe they were planning to chew me out together?

Ten minutes later, I reached my building and started making phone calls. I'd be leaving a lot of people high and dry that week. And I didn't really want to think too much about why.

I could only find one flight to LA that wasn't completely full, and after delays, I arrived on Lion's birthday. I didn't land in the best of moods. I wasn't ready to be back there, and I definitely didn't want to be at Lion's place, living it up. There was one thing that tempted me just then, and that was to lie down and sleep.

Steve had made sure my car was waiting for me at the airport. He'd texted me the location, so I was able to go straight there and get onto the interstate. I drove fast. I'd told Sophia I'd stop in and see her at the party, but I wasn't sure she'd show. She was almost as busy as I was.

Jenna and Lion lived on a residential street not far from UCLA. It was nice: not too many students, lots of young couples. The one downside was it wasn't close to the beach.

I got lucky and didn't have to look too hard for parking. I took off my tie, rolled it up and put it in my back pocket, undid a few buttons on my shirt, and ran my fingers through my hair. None of this worked: I still looked like an exhausted businessman who'd just stepped off a plane.

I knew Noah was going to be there, and that made me a little nervous. I had no idea how she'd act when she saw me come through the door. I just hoped it wouldn't turn ugly: I wasn't in the mood to fight with anyone.

I walked in and caught the elevator, getting out on the fourth floor. The door to the apartment was open; it was noisy, and I could see people drinking right by the entrance. I knew most of them, and they all raised their glasses, happy to see me. The first person I looked for was Jenna, who was wearing a slinky dress and heels. She had two drinks in her hands, but she put them down as soon as she saw me and hurried over.

"Oh my God, you're here!" she shrieked, almost hysterical.

"I'm here!" I said, imitating her high voice.

She didn't think that was funny. Plus she seemed on edge. That was not typical for her. "I mean, it's not like you confirmed..."

"I told Lion I'd try, but I didn't manage to find a flight till this morning... Anyway, now you've got me," I said, taking one of the cups she'd set down, drinking it, and grimacing with disgust.

"What the hell is that?" I asked, handing it back to her.

"Pineapple juice," she replied, arching her eyebrows.

I looked around, then back at her. "Pineapple juice... What are we, like twelve, and I just forgot...?"

Jenna murmured something I couldn't make out and handed me a different glass.

Whiskey...that was more like it.

"So, Jen...where's Lion?"

"In the kitchen. See you soon," she responded, vanishing in the direction of the living room.

I didn't know why, but I decided to follow her. The apartment was full of people, and I had to elbow my way through. When I managed to see past the heads of everyone there, I noticed Jenna was leaning down over someone on the sofa.

It was Noah. Jenna righted herself, and just then, Noah saw me. Even from across the room, I could tell she had gone pale.

Lion cut in front of me and hugged me so tightly, he almost broke all the bones in my back.

"Thanks for coming, dude!" he exclaimed, and I smiled back at him, but I kept looking over at Noah. She had turned her head and looked tense sitting there among the cushions.

Lion saw where my eyes were pointed and nodded. "Poor thing...she's been there since people started showing up. I told her there was no need to mingle, but she insisted."

"Sure," I said.

Only Noah would come down to a party in that condition.

I finished my drink and left my glass on the grand piano. After all, I was only there for one reason...right?

I knew something was wrong with her when I walked over

and she didn't take off running in the other direction. She looked funny there on the sofa in a black sweatshirt with a blanket over her legs. Her face was radiant; I even felt a pang in my heart as I came over and sat down in front of her on the coffee table. I smiled as I saw the twenty-eight freckles on her nose that I'd missed so badly. Then my eyes seemed to get snagged on her lips.

"Look at you… You look like a wounded little bird that can't fly anymore," I said, smiling.

I didn't want to relive the last moments we'd shared: her in my arms, destroyed, begging me not to leave her. That had tortured me every night since I'd gone back to New York.

"I didn't think you'd come," she said, gripping the blanket like a lifeline.

I turned my head to one side and nodded. "I made a few phone calls and got a seat on a plane. I feel terrible. I've only ever flown in business class!"

She nodded, but she didn't seem all there.

"Would you still be sitting there if you'd known I was coming?" I asked, since she hadn't bothered to respond.

Her cheeks turned a pink color too alluring for my mental health. But at least I was getting somewhere.

"Everything okay?" I asked, unable to keep my affection for her out of my voice. Something was weird, and I was starting to feel uncomfortable.

Noah looked all around, as if she needed someone or something to come to her aid. The music wasn't that loud, but I felt like I was deaf, and I had a feeling she did, too.

"I'm fine, just a little tired."

"Who are you looking for?" I asked, and that got her to look back at me. There was a fear in her eyes I'd never seen before… and that made every fiber in my body tense as I wanted to find out what had done that to her.

Then I realized it was me. Before I could ask her anything more, Jenna sat next to Noah on the sofa, took her hand, and squeezed it. Noah smiled.

"Everything good over here?" she asked.

Not letting me answer, Noah shouted, "Lion!" He rushed over. "Could you take me upstairs? I think this is enough for today."

Jenna frowned at Noah. When Lion leaned over, I instinctively rested a hand on his chest, stopping him.

I felt cornered. Everything was weird. Noah wanting Lion to help her instead of me had hurt like a kick to the stomach.

"I'll take her," I said, trying to look relaxed. I kneeled, catching her off guard, but she grabbed me tightly around the neck. She was trembling. I got out of there and upstairs as quickly as I could.

"I didn't ask you to take me," she hissed.

Great, now I'd pissed her off.

I went straight to the guest room. I knew which one it was: I'd stayed there a couple of nights after countless beers followed by one too many nightcaps.

I put one foot on the bed to pull back the sheets, a little too jerkily if her back really was hurt. Then I laid her down and covered her up. I looked at her all tucked in there and tried not to laugh.

She reached up and grabbed my hand, pulling me onto the mattress. She was leaning against the headboard and looking me straight in the eyes.

"I've got to tell you something," she said with a trembling voice, squeezing my hand until it almost hurt.

I narrowed my eyes, waiting for her to continue, and just as she opened her mouth, the door opened, and Sophia appeared on the threshold.

All the color drained from Noah's face.

"They told me they saw you come up here," Sophia said, observing me with feigned calm.

I stood up, looking back and forth between the two of them.

I could tell from Noah's reaction that nothing good could come of this, but the worst thing of all was, I had no desire to go downstairs with Sophia. To the contrary, I wanted to shut the door in her face and listen to what Noah had to say.

36

Noah

Say it, Noah, say it, say it, say it, say it.

I had been repeating that to myself ever since I'd seen him walk into Jenna's living room. With everything that had happened, with my anger at the whole situation, I'd just assumed my attraction to him would have vanished. I didn't know; I was going to be a mother now—didn't that mean my priorities would change? I guessed not because when I saw him crossing the room toward me, my entire body started trembling, and it wasn't just nerves.

He was nice to me. Too nice, given what I was used to, and that made it hard for me to speak. I was worried he'd notice something when he lifted me. I didn't know, maybe that I was a few pounds heavier, like Lion had said. But either he hadn't realized, or he'd decided to keep his mouth shut amid all that tension.

Despite everything, I gathered the courage to tell him we needed to talk. But it had all blown up in my face when the door to my room opened and Sophia appeared, just in time to interrupt one of the most important moments of our lives.

I didn't know if it was the rage inside me, my anger at Nicholas for bringing her, or the despair I felt when I realized they were still together, still a couple, that he still belonged to her...but jealousy started eating at me. Never in my life had I felt my heart beat so fast in the presence of someone else. Every instinct told me to walk out of that room and never come back. My mood must have affected Mini-Me because I felt something quivering in my stomach, a slight movement, almost imperceptible, but enough to bring out my maternal instincts and push aside any sense of decorum.

"Get out of my room!" I screamed.

Their eyes opened wide, and I grabbed the first thing I could find, a pillow, and threw it at Sophia. It barely touched her, so I tried again, but by that time, Jenna had appeared. She looked at Sophia with surprise and then at me.

By now I had grabbed something else—a lamp, I think. "Get her out of here!" I shouted as I lifted it.

A hand grabbed my wrist. It was Nick. He was livid. "What the hell is wrong with you?!" he shouted.

I wanted to hurt him. That fucking idiot... Couldn't he see? Couldn't he look into my eyes and see? With my other hand, I started hitting him until he finally immobilized me.

"Nicholas, let her go!" Jenna screeched, almost as hysterical as I was.

I tried to struggle, twisting, bumping against him, trying to get away. And just then, with that effort, I felt something damp between my legs.

I froze.

No.

No, no, no, no, no, no, no.

Panic took hold of me, an intense fear clutching at every cell in my body. I started crying, and Nicholas let me go and stood up, perplexed.

"Nicholas, get out of here," Jenna ordered him in a tone I'd never heard her use with anyone.

I didn't see him go, I didn't hear what he said—I just wrapped my arms around myself beneath the blankets.

"I'm sorry I brought him here, Noah. I didn't know..." Jenna apologized.

I shook my head, trying to calm down, trying to flush the adrenaline out of my body. I needed to relax for the baby, for *my* baby, my Mini-Me, who was stressed out because of me. I could tell.

Jenna stayed with me, smiling unenthusiastically and wiping away my tears.

"It'll all be okay," she said calmly. "I promise you, everything will turn out fine."

I nodded, wanting to believe her.

"A second ago," I whispered, "I felt something weird... I think the stress did something to the baby..."

Jenna opened her eyes wide, terrified, and I sat up warily. I got out of bed and walked to the bathroom. Jenna waited several minutes for me to come out.

"False alarm," I said in a trembling voice, relieved it was only a bit of discharge that might doctor said was normal.

She sighed and closed her eyes, and I felt peace again.

Being stuck in a room without much to do gives you lots of time to think. I'd need to go to the doctor soon. No matter what happened, I was going to have to make decisions and learn to deal with this on my own. And that meant, to start with, going to my apartment. I couldn't just stay at Jenna's place, driving my friends crazy.

What had happened the day before couldn't happen again. The pressure of needing to tell Nicholas was sapping my strength, and there was no more delaying. I had to get it over with; he was Mini-Me's father, and Mini-Me was going to be born in four months or so. That meant I'd have to start putting the baby's needs before mine. I didn't want to share this with him, I was furious at him, but there was just no choice.

I'd thought of trying the subtle approach, feeling him out, hoping he would react in a way I could remember and cherish forever, but seeing Sophia had put an end to any thought of tact or friendliness. So, the next day, in a bored and solitary moment, I made a decision, picking up my phone and looking for Nicholas Leister in my contacts. I'm pregnant, I wrote. *Send.* End of story.

If I said I regretted it as soon as I'd done it, would that sound cowardly?

I looked at the screen in silence, barely able to breathe.

After five minutes, the phone started ringing.

One time, two times, three.

I grabbed it between my thumb and forefinger, almost as if I didn't want to touch it, and threw it to the foot of the bed.

Shit... Why was I so terrified all of a sudden?

"Jenna!" I shouted, nearly breathless.

She hurried up to see how I was.

"Can we go somewhere?" I asked, getting up and opening the dresser.

"What are you doing?" she asked, alarmed. "Go back to bed!"

I grabbed some leggings and slid them on and threw on a sweatshirt. "I'm dying to go back to that ice cream shop from the other day."

I put on my sneakers before Jenna could stop me and looked her in the eyes. "I'm having the worst craving ever, the biggest one since I found out about the baby. Just take me, please. I'll stay in the car, I promise. I've just got to get out of here."

She hesitated, but after a few minutes of my whining, she

finally agreed. We got in her car, and once her building was out of sight, I could finally breathe easy.

I stroked my belly nervously, over and over.

Oh, Mini-Me…your dad's going to kill me.

Jenna's phone rang right as she got out to buy me an ice cream. I grabbed it with shaking hands and put it on silent, even though I knew I shouldn't.

I'd dropped a bomb, and now I was running scared.

When Jenna brought me the ice cream, I barely got down a few bites before the craving passed and I wanted to puke. It wasn't the baby; it was panic.

"I'm going to take you home," she said.

"No!" I shouted. "Why don't we go to the movies? That's something I can do, right? I'll be sitting down the whole time, I can rest…"

"If you want to see a movie, Noah, we'll stream something at home. But you can't be out and about. The answer's no."

"Jenna!" I shouted. "If I stay in that room anymore, I'm going to go crazy. Please just do me this favor!"

She snarled, "You've turned unbearable since you got pregnant. Has anyone told you that?"

"A couple of times, yeah, but come on, let's go!"

When we got to the theater, the next movie still didn't start for half an hour, so we waited in the car.

"I'm going to let Lion know we'll be late. He must be wondering where we are."

I grabbed the phone out of her hands before she could see the missed calls.

"What the hell is going on with you?" she shouted. "Give me my phone."

Shit.

"I'll do it, but promise not to get mad at me. I'm feeling really on edge right now, and I need you on my side."

She seemed to suddenly understand. "What have you done?" she asked, trying to stay calm. "What are we running from, Noah?"

"We're not running… We're just…hiding," I said, trying to convince her.

She snatched the phone and looked at the screen. "Fifteen missed calls from Nicholas!" she shrieked. "And ten from Lion! What the hell?"

I hid my head in my hands, and Jenna pulled them down to look at my face.

"Did you tell him?"

"Maybe…"

Instead of responding, she waited for me to explain myself.

"I might have sent a message."

"Telling him you had to talk to him?"

I looked at her in silence for a few seconds. "Telling him I was pregnant."

Her expression changed from angry to terrified. "Noah!" she shouted, unable to believe it. "Are you crazy? How could you?"

"It's what he deserves. I didn't want to tell him in person, Jenna. I was afraid of how he would react. Doing it over the phone meant giving myself some distance, some safety."

"He must be climbing the walls! Did you say anything else? What exactly did the message say?"

"I'm pregnant," I responded with a shrug. "That's it. Don't look at me like that—the way I found out wasn't exactly nice either!"

Jenna ignored me. "Did you tell him it was his?"

I stopped to think for a moment. "I mean, it's pretty obvious it's his," I said. But maybe it wasn't.

"This is Nicholas we're talking about!"

Dammit. Does he think Mini-Me is someone else's?

I'd been surprised to find out I was so far along because I wasn't showing. If Nicholas hadn't realized I was pregnant when he saw me, he would think it was someone else's!

"Give me your phone," I said to Jenna.

She passed it to me right away. "Yeah, talk to him," she said, taking a deep breath.

By the way, it's yours, I wrote. *Send.*

"Done," I said, leaning the seat back.

Jenna grabbed the phone and looked. "*By the way, it's yours*?! What in the hell is wrong with you?"

"Don't shout at me! It's the only way I can deal with him right now without losing it!"

"We're leaving," she said, starting her car.

"No, Jenna! Don't!" I begged. "Please, please give him time to let it soak in…for me to accept the situation. Please, God, stop!"

"You're crazy," she said. Her phone rang again. She saw it and picked up instantly.

"Jenna!" I shouted, but she ignored me.

"Yeah, she's with me," she said to whoever it was. "Tell him to calm down. No, Lion, you and I will talk about it, but I don't want her freaking out any more than she is; it's bad for the baby… Tell him!"

Shit, this was making me even more nervous.

"We're going home. You've got five minutes to think this over."

I looked outside. I felt like I was being taken to Guantanamo.

My whole body was throbbing when Jenna parked at her building. I was trembling. I had no idea what was about to happen. I didn't know what he was going to say. And worst of all: I was afraid it would all go to hell and he'd stay with Sophia and I'd lose my baby *and* the person I loved.

I opened the door to get out, and as soon as I was standing on the pavement, I saw Nicholas emerge from the building with his eyes boring into me in a way that made me wish I could disappear then and there. Lion was with him. I got back in the car without even thinking and hit the lock button. I was being such a coward! I felt like an idiot when Jenna crossed her arms and shook her head, looking at me through the window.

Nicholas came up next to her and glared. He looked beside himself, though he was trying to remain calm. I saw worry in his eyes. He pointed at the lock.

"Open up," he ordered.

I shook my head, looking at him like a deer in headlights.

He rested his hands on the roof of the car and leaned down, covering nearly my entire field of vision. "Can I at least get in?" he asked.

Jenna tossed him the key, and he came around to the driver's side. I looked at her hatefully. She grinned, took Lion's hand, and walked inside.

Nick opened the door, sat down, and started the car.

"Put on your seat belt," he said, driving off.

Why wasn't he blowing up at me? Talking? Saying something? This silence was killing me.

After a few minutes, he finally decided to speak.

"Only you would tell a person something like that in a text message." He took a deep breath as if he were trying not to explode.

"Yeah... I guess I wanted to do something original."

He turned to look at me. A vein was throbbing in his forehead. "You almost gave me a heart attack. I nearly crashed my car. What were you thinking?" He raised his voice a little.

Mini-Me started kicking, same as the night before. It was funny that it only ever did that when Nick was around... He had always given me a special tingling in my stomach, and now that had taken on a life of its own... I put a hand on my belly, and the human volcano next to me noticed. He stared at that part of my body for as long as he could before looking back at the road.

I didn't answer him. I felt it was probably best to keep my mouth shut. Nicholas kept driving. I thought he was still taking it all in. And maybe having something to do with his hands was helping him relax as much as he could.

I soon realized we were headed to the beach. When we arrived, I felt a sudden inner peace, the first inklings of relaxation. Nick seemed to feel the same thing. After contemplating the waves, he took a deep breath and turned to me.

"Am I really going to be a father?" I saw fear in his blue eyes.

I shook from head to toe. My God, that Adonis was the father of my child! "If everything happens the way it's supposed to...then we'll both be parents," I responded nervously.

"I still can't believe it... How is it possible?" He was still looking straight at me.

"Don't go there, Nick." I still hadn't forgiven him for this.

"Can I?" he asked. He reached out toward my belly but then stopped, waiting for a response.

I grabbed his hand and brought it toward my belly. It was incredible... In spite of all the bad things, all the things I still needed to let out, I knew I'd remember it forever. Nick pulled up my shirt and placed his hand on my bare skin. My whole body burned from his touch.

"How far along...?" he asked, rubbing me, stupefied before my warm skin. Have I mentioned how hot it made me, having his hands on my belly button?

"Five months," I said, then sighed. His hand was creeping a little low. I stopped him before I had a heart attack. I pulled my shirt down quickly.

"Enough touching," I said nervously.

Nick's gaze was at once intense and amused. "Have you felt it moving?"

"Sort of... I mean, not kicking, really—it's just this weird feeling kind of like...like popcorn popping inside me. I don't know if that's the right way to describe it."

He laughed, but I couldn't join in. The aftershocks of the tension in the car came back to haunt me.

"When did you find out?"

I realized it was time to be sincere. "Three weeks ago. A little more."

"Three weeks is a long time... Enough time to call and tell me, don't you think?" He was angry now and looked away.

"I was mad at you. To be honest, I still am."

"Mad? Why?"

"This is your fault," I said, pointing to my stomach. I remembered then the way he'd made love to me without protection... the idiot!

Nicholas laughed, incredulous. "I think it would be more correct to say it was *our fault*, Freckles."

"Don't split hairs."

He chuckled.

Before our eyes, the sun was setting as beautifully as I'd ever seen. I guessed it was a gift nature wanted to give me, laying the most beautiful colors over an image still too gray to look at for too long.

We both knew now what was going to happen. But I couldn't stop thinking about that last conversation I'd had with Nicholas before he moved to New York.

"I'm tired," I said. "You should take me home." I felt sad.

He wrapped an arm around me, tickling the nape of my neck softly before turning me to look at him. "Come with me," he said, catching me with my guard down. "Get your things and move into my apartment."

"No, Nicholas. I'm at Jenna's already, and in four days—"

"This isn't up for discussion," he interrupted me. He started the car.

"What are you doing?" I asked.

"I'm taking you with me."

Jesus. Here we go again!

"I don't want to go."

"You have my child inside you, and I'm going to make sure nothing goes wrong."

"I have *my* child inside me, and I'm already making sure nothing goes wrong, but thanks for your interest," I replied, indignant.

"Aren't you supposed to rest?" he asked, looking back and forth between me and the road.

"Yeah, but..."

"Until the doctor tells you otherwise, you're staying with me. End of subject."

I was about to reply, but I realized I didn't have a leg to stand on or to kick him with, which was what I felt like doing just then. So I crossed my arms and stared out the window.

He'd only found out about Mini-Me a few hours before, and he already thought he was the child's owner and master.

Yep, Mini-Me, that's how big of an idiot your father is.

37

Noah

It took forever to get to Nicholas's place. We didn't say a word on the drive back from the beach or at Jenna's, where we picked up my things. I hadn't wanted it that way, but he'd cranked up the music in the car and gone completely silent.

I tried to stay angry and look out at the cityscape, but of course, I glanced at Nick when I didn't think he'd notice. I didn't want him to catch me looking at him all desperately, as if I were dying for the father of my child to say something encouraging like *I'm so happy* or *everything will be fine*.

Not that I needed to worry about that. The magic moment had passed, we'd left all that tenderness back on the beach, and now the darkness of night seemed to seep into us. What the hell was with him? I mean, I got that no one could just accept the news of being a father like it was nothing, but damn, all I was asking for was a little small talk.

I didn't even wait for him to get out when he parked. I walked straight inside and to the elevator. I wasn't supposed to be walking, but I wasn't going to tell him that. I realized Nick had no clear idea of the problems that were plaguing my pregnancy, and I was kind of scared to tell him. Jenna was the one other person who could have informed him, but since Nick and I had left together, she seemed far more relaxed, even happy. What am I saying? She was over the moon. The poor dummy thought that just by me telling him, we were going to turn back into the same happy couple as before...

It was ridiculous, but I'd be lying if I said a part of me wasn't hoping for the same thing.

Nicholas hurried to catch up with me, and we got off on the fourth floor. He had my small suitcase in his hand.

As soon as I walked in, I realized this was no place for me...let alone for Mini-Me. The apartment was different: our photos, the pictures we'd chosen together, the colorful cushions...all that was gone. The old furniture had been replaced by expensive minimalist stuff totally lacking in personality, not to mention comfort.

Worst of all, I knew Nick hadn't chosen any of that... It had been someone else, and I only needed a second for her name to come into my mind.

Fuck: the reality was like a sledgehammer to the stomach. Sophia had been there. Nicholas had lived with her in that apartment, just as he was doing with me now... I walked to the bedroom without uttering a word, the same bedroom where we had shared the most intimate moments of our relationship. All I knew, all he had taught me, I had learned in that bed, in those sheets, in that home. I wiped away the tear rolling down my cheek. The room was different, too. Everything was.

I imagined Nick with her, kissing her, caressing her, touching her, doing the same things with her he'd done with me, as if it were a slideshow running in my mind.

Nicholas put my suitcase on a bench, turned to me, and said, "You should get in bed."

His words awakened me from the hell I was experiencing.

"Oh, so you're talking to me now?" I asked, trying to cover my sorrow with rage.

Warily, he responded, "I'm sorry I was so quiet before... I just need to think about all this... I wasn't expecting it, you know."

"Oh, and I was?"

"You've had a three-week head start, at least," he replied acidly.

"Well, I'm sorry I didn't come running to find you when I found out I had a baby inside me. A baby I wasn't looking to have and don't even want!"

As soon as I said that, I felt guilty and knew I was lying. Of course I wanted it, now more than ever, and anyway, there was no turning back. Mini-Me and I were connected: the maternal bond I'd heard about, which was supposedly there even before the baby was born—it was real.

"And you think I do?!" he shouted, wiping his face in an attack of nerves. He tried to breathe deeply and calm himself, but with little success, then told me more calmly, "We shouldn't be arguing about this, Noah. Please, just get into bed."

His words echoed in my head, impossible to ignore.

Nick didn't want the baby...

"In this bed? You want me to get in the bed where you've fucked God knows how many women?" I asked in an attack of rage and jealousy. No. No way Mini-Me and I were getting into those sheets. I'd rather die.

Nick didn't expect that response. That was obvious. He didn't know what to say, and his silence only confirmed the truth of what I'd said.

I grabbed a pillow and stomped all the way to the sofa, that horrible sofa that was every bit as uncomfortable as I'd imagined when I first saw it. I sat down, crossed my legs, and looked at the huge TV, the only thing Nick had probably chosen himself.

From the corner of my eye, I saw him walk toward the bar to serve himself a drink. He looked at the amber liquid in his glass for a moment, then put it down, walked over, and held out his hand.

"Let's go," he said calmly. "I'll get a hotel room."

That caught me unaware. When I realized he was serious, my irritation mellowed. "Are you serious?"

"I don't want you to be uncomfortable."

I nodded, getting up and standing to face him. I was dying for him to hold me. I was hurting inside. Everything was so strange... Since when had Nick given in to one of my fits? Normally we would have been screaming at each other, but there we were, cautious, trying to ignore all the things that still needed to be said.

Once we were in the car, Nick called the Mondrian in West Hollywood and booked the penthouse suite for the two of us. I guessed the surprises never ended with him.

"You don't have to spend all that money, Nicholas. We can go to my place, or you can drop me there. I'm worried this isn't a good idea."

Without looking over, he said, "I need somewhere I can work and have you close by. Price isn't a concern."

I sighed. My whole body was tired, and I was dying to climb into bed. Everything that had happened that day had exhausted me.

I fell asleep on the way, and Nick shook me awake softly when we arrived. When I opened my eyes, I saw a bellboy waiting patiently for us to get out.

Looking down at my leggings, my sweatshirt, my running shoes, and comparing them with Nicholas in his button-down, jeans, and boat shoes, I felt embarrassed.

I sat on a sofa in the lobby while he registered. I was a little worried I hadn't been resting enough. At Jenna's house, Lion had carried me around...and if I told Nick that, I'd also have to tell him in detail everything that might go wrong with my pregnancy, and that would mean revealing how fucked up my uterus was and all the things I'd been doing wrong those first few months... I'd been irresponsible. Just remembering all the alcohol I'd drunk made me sick to my stomach. I was incompetent, dammit; I wasn't made to be a mother. I still couldn't believe it had never crossed my mind...

Luckily for me and Mini-Me, the elevators weren't far away, and I was thankful when Nick took my hand to help me over. The bellboy came with us to drop off our bags, and Nick gave him a tip before he left. My jaw dropped. This wasn't a hotel room—it was as big as an apartment! I walked around, admiring the gleaming wooden floor, the huge white bed with the black headboard, the big square table with the Lucite chairs, the huge sofa, the desk, and the incredible views of the city.

I tried not to feel overwhelmed and not to think of the money all that must have cost. Instead I went to the bed. Nick had brought my suitcase over and opened it, and I took out some pajamas. Then I went to the bathroom. A shower would help me, would relax me... I didn't know what was going to happen between us. There was a strange tension in the room.

When I came out in my pajama bottoms and a baggy T-shirt, Nick was waiting for me, leaning on the table. I tried to ignore how nervous it made me to be alone with him after so long, and I sat on the bed, resting my back against the headboard, waiting for one of us to break the silence and mention the enormous elephant in the room.

I remembered the last time we had talked like this, alone, in a bed... I stroked my belly softly and held my breath. *Yes, Mini-Me...you were the result of that conversation.*

"What are you thinking about?" he asked, his stare so piercing, my heart sped up.

"Nothing... Just how the last time...you know, when you and I..."

Nick clenched his jaw. I guessed what was a good memory for me was one that enraged him. "I was an idiot. I was irresponsible."

Seeing his face so full of bitterness, I wished I'd never opened my mouth.

"What happened that night shouldn't have," I said, trying to hide my sorrow. "But it wasn't just your fault."

Nicholas scowled at me with his cold blue eyes. "What happened, Noah?" he asked. "Did you lie to me?"

"What?"

"I asked you if you were still on the pill, and you said yes. So tell me how the hell this happened."

Had he asked me about the pill? That night I was so absorbed in what we were doing that I could barely remember half of what we had talked about.

My heart broke again. "You think I did this on purpose?"

Nicholas rubbed his face, stood up straight, and walked to the other end of the room.

"I don't even know what to think... When you told me you were pregnant, it never even passed through my mind that it could be mine until you decided to let me know in that fucking message." He opened the minibar and took out a bottle. I stayed still, trying not to miss even one syllable of what he was saying. "We slept together one fucking time! One time in what, a year and a half, and then this happens?"

"Do you wish it were someone else's?" I didn't recognize my own voice anymore. I wanted to run away.

"You know perfectly well I don't."

"You're such an asshole for even thinking I could have tricked you. Like I wanted to just get pregnant at nineteen years old! You know what? There's no reason for you to even be part of this. I'm perfectly capable of doing this alone." That wasn't true, but I wasn't going to admit it to him.

Looking insulted, he asked me, "Is that what you want?" The vein in his neck was throbbing, his jaw was stiff, and his eyes could have burned holes in me. But I continued.

"You don't have to take responsibility for it. There are lots of mothers who raise children on their own. You've got way too much going on right now, and you made it very clear to me that you didn't want to see me again."

Nick shook his head and laughed sarcastically. I didn't like that at all. Obviously I didn't believe what I was saying, but it seemed evident that he didn't want the baby and regretted what had happened, and I wasn't going to be like all those other women who tried to trap a man with a child. No way—I'd be firm, even if the mere thought of it made me feel like I was choking. I didn't care; I wasn't going to put him on the spot.

"You've always gone through life trying to solve everything on your own. You never let anyone help you or tell you you're wrong. And you know what, babe? It's not a good look for you." *Babe*—that sounded like an insult. "But I'll tell you one thing: that baby you've got inside you is every bit as much mine as yours, so be very careful with what you say."

It took me a moment to respond. "Are you threatening me?"

"I will be a part of that child's life, and it will bear my last name."

Why was it that the thing I'd wanted to hear from the very first minute only made me feel backed into a corner? "The child will get what's best for it, and I'm the one who will make that decision."

"I doubt any judge will disagree that you aren't ready to take care of our child, don't you think? You have nothing, unless you decide to run to my father and beg."

Hearing the words *our child* stirred something inside me, but that vanished right away. I couldn't believe he was talking to me about judges and court.

“What do you mean?” I asked, a knot in my throat.

He was acting insane. With every second that passed, he was more and more like the Nick I’d been so scared to face.

“I’m telling you I have absolutely all the cards. You and I aren’t going to be together again, so we’d best work out every last detail before the child’s born. Shared custody, that’s what I’d recommend for starters… Now, if you’ll excuse me, I’ve got important things to do.”

He grabbed his coat and kcys and walked out.

After that came the fear and the tears and a terrible feeling of impotence. He was right, I had nothing, all I could do was beg, but that didn’t mean I wanted to hear it from him. If his intention was to lock horns with me, I was going to prepare myself.

38

Nick

I GOT IN MY CAR AND STOMPED ON THE GAS. I NEEDED TO BE alone and think. I saw that message—*I'm pregnant*—everywhere I looked. I tried not to let it get to me, I really did, but it all still felt like a sick joke to me, and now I was learning Noah didn't even want me to be a part of her and the baby's life. That was why she'd needed three fucking weeks to tell me, and I was sure she'd only done it because Jenna wouldn't let her hide it any longer.

I'm pregnant.

Never in my life had two words affected me so much. Two little words, and I'd nearly crashed into the car in front of me. Luckily, I stepped on the brake in time! My phone had slipped out of my hand, and I had to pull off the road to pick it up and read that message again.

The world was collapsing on top of me, as if suddenly I couldn't breathe, and the blood drained from my veins, and every rational thought vanished from my mind. I could only think one thing: *I'll kill him, whoever it is.* Fortunately, the next message had come before I did anything stupid… Only Noah would write messages like I'm pregnant and then It's yours and feel like she'd taken care of things.

I went into a typical student bar. I knew drinking wouldn't help me clear my head, but shit! Either I got some alcohol in my veins, or I'd be back in that room telling her that she and the baby were both mine and I would be calling the shots for both of them from now on.

The hatred I'd felt for Noah for so long had cooled when I put a hand on her belly and realized what was growing inside there was my child, our child. I never thought something like this could happen… I had tried not to think about it before, but knowing that Noah would probably struggle to get pregnant had hung over our heads as soon as we'd fallen in love.

I ordered a scotch, drank it quickly, and ordered another.

Had I said something about a judge?

I hid my face in my hands. The music there sucked, and there were too many people dancing and jostling me. The bar was right in the center of the room. I hated it. The scotch wasn't the highest quality either, and I grimaced as I felt it burn.

Noah was going to be a mother. At nineteen years old.

I hated myself just then. I hated making so many mistakes, forcing her to do something that we might both have wanted, but that she had made clear she also wanted to avoid.

Had I made her do it?

No, dammit, I hadn't. I'd made love to her, I'd treated her well, I'd held her all night, I'd wanted to wake up next to her. My very soul had ached when I'd opened my eyes that morning and seen she wasn't there. No matter what happened, she always ran away.

My mind began to dwell on the life we could have had if I had just gotten in my car and taken her to New York the night of my father's gala, the way I'd wanted to, the way I'd told her I would.

We wouldn't have made the mistakes we made, no guy would have put his hands on her, and I'd be with her and not in some dump trying to grapple with the idea of being a father. A father. Fuck. A father with a baby. My life was about to do a 180, and I only had four months to get ready for it.

What the hell would I do with the company? What would I do with Noah?

By the time I was on drink number five and my mind was getting cloudy, I noticed something, or someone, rather, sitting at the bar a few feet away. I knew who he was just by my body's reaction: every one of my muscles started flexing. I got up cautiously and walked to the corner, grabbing him by his T-shirt and picking him up off the ground. He had no idea what was happening.

"What the fuck are you doing here, you piece of shit?" I asked, pressing my forehead into his. I'd only ever felt like that once in my whole life, a year and a half ago—the worst night of my life.

Michael O' Neil pushed me backward, fire in his eyes.

"I paid you to stay the fuck out of my city!" I shouted and pounced on him.

We fell to the ground. Everyone scattered, and someone called security. Dammit! I was going to have to throw a lot of cash around if I didn't want to get in serious trouble. Whatever. I punched him in the ribs; he gave me one in the jaw. I could taste blood in my mouth. The only effect of it was to make me want to kill him and get the whole thing over with.

"You know what I decided? Fuck our deal," he said, rolling me over and punching me in the left cheek, opening a cut. "By the way, Noah looks better than ever."

The blood rushed to my head, I saw red all around, and the next thing I knew, three guys were pulling me off the asshole. They carried us both off in different directions. Since they knew who I was, they let me recover in a VIP room. They wouldn't let me go on my own, so I called Steve to come get me. He came in through the back door, and I could tell by his face that something was up.

"There are journalists outside," he said. "Someone must have tipped them off."

Shit. Just what I needed.

When we left, I tried to pretend nothing was going on, covering up the wounds on my face, but that didn't stop them from taking photos, lots of them, before I made it to the back seat of his car. Steve kept his mouth shut, but he was surprised when I told him to take me to the Mondrian. I didn't want to even think about how the press would respond when the news of Noah's pregnancy came out, let alone our family... It was going to be a scandal, especially because the media thought of Noah and me as brother and sister. Sophia was going to kill me, too—the scandal would be bad news for her family; it might even affect her father's political career.

I stumbled out of the car and told Steve to have my car brought back to the hotel. When I entered the penthouse, it was silent as a grave. That frightened me. The room was dark. That could only mean one thing... I turned on the light. It was empty. When I walked over to the bed, I found a note on the pillow.

Shit.

39

Noah

I ORDERED A CAR AS SOON AS NICK LEFT, AND AFTER A LONG WAIT and a longer drive, I was surrounded by unopened boxes and lying in bed with a bowl of dry cereal I'd had to look everywhere for. I didn't have milk—I didn't have anything in the fridge—but at least I was alone after all those weeks with Jenna.

I didn't know what I was thinking, going off with Nicholas, as if things could ever be the same as before. What had happened between us wasn't the kind of thing you just forgot, even if I was pregnant, even if he was the father. What he had insinuated in that hotel room was going to last in my memories for far longer than anything he had ever told me in the past.

How could he ever believe I could be vile enough, trashy enough, to try to trap him by having a baby? How dare he try to say he'd take it away from me when it was born!

I didn't even want to see him. If things had been bad before, now they'd reached a new level. I tried to relax; I didn't want to stress out Mini-Me, and even if it was hard, I finally managed to fall asleep, until five in the morning, when my phone started vibrating like crazy.

But there was no way I was going to talk to him. Had he really only just figured out that I'd left? What the hell had he been doing all night?

Better not to ask.

I sent him a message.

Leave me alone.

And he did. At least for a while.

The next morning, he showed up at the apartment. I guessed Jenna had waited to give him my address until a reasonable hour. I wished she had at least warned me first, though. I was tired of her and Lion getting mixed up in things that didn't concern them.

I opened the door and found him with two cardboard cups and a bag from Starbucks. He was wearing a suit. He had a black eye, a cut on his left cheek, and a split lip. He looked ridiculous, like a boxer pretending to be a businessman.

"Can I come in?"

I crossed my arms. I didn't want him to come in, but we did need to talk.

I turned around and walked to my bed. I hated having to do that, as though I were using my health issues to manipulate him; it looked almost like he was the adult and I was a little girl.

"If you start getting in fights again…that's going to be a point in my favor when we're trying to get custody of the child in court."

"That's enough, Noah," he said, putting the bag and the cups on the counter of my small kitchen. "You know I didn't mean that."

"You certainly seemed to have your mind made up when you said I wouldn't be capable of taking care of a child."

He rubbed his face and looked around. I felt ashamed of the lack of order there. My loft was the worst place imaginable for raising a child, and Nicholas must have been thinking the exact same thing just then.

"You could take care of a baby with both hands tied behind your back, Noah," he said, coming over. "Here, it's hot chocolate," he said.

I accepted it grudgingly. "Let's get one thing straight, though... I don't want to hear you say you'll take the baby away again, okay?" I said, more serious than I'd ever been.

"I would never do that. Jesus, who do you take me for?"

I shook my head. I couldn't stand to look at him or even have him in front of me. He'd hurt me again; he'd poured salt in the wound, had hit me where it hurt most, implying I couldn't give my child what it needed.

He sat next to me in bed. "Noah, look at me," he said firmly.

I refused. If I did, I worried I'd start crying like a schoolgirl, and I would not, could not feel weak at that moment. But he grabbed my chin and turned my face up, and I had no choice.

"I'm sorry for what I said yesterday," he said, caressing me. "I'll be here for you."

"This isn't what you want," I replied, my voice trembling.

With all my soul, I wanted to be with him again, start from scratch, have a family together, but he had told me that was impossible. Now I was pregnant, and yeah, things had changed. I had to think about Mini-Me, not just me, and that meant I had to be in Nicholas Leister's life somehow, even if he didn't want me there.

I would need to swallow my feelings, pretend we could go back to before...that was the only choice I had. It'd be like playing a role in a movie about loss and redemption. Nick knew that, too.

"Come back to the hotel with me," he said, wiping away one of my tears.

I'd have given anything not to have to rest then, to be independent and need no one, but that wasn't how things were. I needed him, at least until the doctor told me the baby was out of danger.

So I agreed, and I went back to the hotel. When we got there, Nicholas helped me get settled in and left again, saying he had things to take care of at LRB. He seemed strange, we both did, like different people, but I was grateful to be alone. I spent the rest of the day in bed reading *Wuthering Heights*. I'd never liked it that much—the characters were too tormented, the plot too dramatic for my taste—but something had told me to go back to it. Eventually I put it down and tried to sleep. I hadn't heard anything from Nicholas. I wished he'd call me at least once to see how I was. I realized I'd kept him in the dark about what was going on with Mini-Me. Everything had happened so fast, he hadn't thought to ask why I needed so much rest. He'd only found out I was pregnant a day and a half ago, but I knew it mattered to him, because we'd talked seriously or tried to. I closed my eyes and let sleep take me.

40

Nick

I had to go see Sophia. She'd been calling constantly since the night of Lion's party. She was furious. She knew I was in Los Angeles, but we hadn't even spent three hours together.

I had to get things straight with her. When I realized how little I cared about having to break the relationship off, it became clear to me that it would never have worked anyway. I would never be the guy she needed. Only Noah could make my whole world turn upside down. Of course she did—just the sound of her breath drove me utterly insane!

It was so strange, having her with me again without us shouting at each other, without me hating her. The past year and a half, I had spent all my energy on being resentful, wasting every ounce of my being on bitterness to hide the part of me that loved her, trying to ignore the terrible urge I had to run to her side and beg her to take me back. I'd needed all the self-control I could muster to leave her, to go, to convince myself that I could rebuild my life with someone else. To lie to myself, in other words. Now all those feelings were on hold. My former hatred seemed meaningless, and my love was crying to get out. A bigger and bigger part of me was dying to be with her, to hold her in my arms and stay that way until the end of time. I was relieved…as though at last, I was myself again. Hating the woman I loved had been the hardest thing I'd ever done. And now something told me to stop fighting, stop swimming against the current. My path was clear. My destiny was Noah.

Sophia was staying at a hotel. I'd told her my apartment was flooded. I'd had to make up something that would buy me time to get everything in order. I parked, preparing myself to face a person whom, despite everything, I didn't want to harm. She opened the door to her room dressed in a pretty plum-colored dress. I could tell by her face that she knew things weren't going to go well. I'd told her we needed to talk. That never means anything good.

I went in but kept my jacket on and didn't give her the usual kiss on the lips. She frowned as she invited me into her suite. I walked straight to the minibar and poured myself a drink. Sophia sat on the sofa and watched me as I tried not to look at her, taking a long slug of whiskey.

"You're leaving me, right?" she said, breaking the silence.

I looked her in the eye. "I don't think I was ever really with you, Sophia."

She shook her head and looked down at the table in front of her. "I thought…I thought we were getting somewhere, Nicholas. What did she say to you? What did she say to make you change your mind? Because a week ago, you were telling me you wanted to live with me."

Dammit. Yeah, I'd said that. I was tired of feeling so hurt over Noah, tired of waking up alone every night, thinking, asking myself if I'd been wrong to let her go… "I know…and I'm sorry. Shit. I really am. Sophia, I'm not doing this to hurt you, but I can't keep denying what I feel for Noah. If I'm not with her, I'd rather be with no one. I told you we were just hooking up, and you accepted that, but then things changed, and I'm not saying that was your fault. I got ahead of myself too, because it was—"

"Easy?" she interrupted me.

That stopped me in my tracks. She was right. Being with Sophia had been easy, pleasant; it had looked right from the outside. But there was no passion, no magic, none of that irrational longing to be with her, to possess her, to make her mine… I'd only ever felt that for one woman.

"I'd rather do this now than break your heart later."

She smiled mirthlessly. "What makes you think you're not breaking my heart right now?"

She didn't wait for me to answer. She stood, turned around, and walked off to the bedroom. I thought of going after her, saying I was sorry, giving her more reasons why what we had wouldn't work, but this was Sophia. There was no point in insisting, in telling her what to think. If she did love me, it wasn't the right way, and one day, she'd figure that out.

I wasn't the love of her life.

When I returned to my own suite, the scent of Noah's shampoo flooded my senses. It was dark; there was just one lamp lit in the corner. Noah was lying down with her head propped on a pillow and her hair flowing all over. I felt myself harden just by looking at her… Jesus, she was gorgeous!

I knew perfectly well that I'd be better off leaving, or at least letting the alcohol in my veins fade, but I could only think of one thing. I took off my shirt as I walked to the foot of the bed. My eyes stopped on the curve of her hips, her long legs with a pillow stuffed between them, her pink cheeks. I sat down and observed her. It had been a long time since my soul had known such inner peace. Seeing Noah sleep had always soothed me, and yet I was longing for her to open her eyes...for her to recognize that I really was the center of her world, dammit, and for her to look at me again the way she used to.

I looked at the book lying facedown on her nightstand. I opened it and started reading the page she had marked. My eyes landed on the following paragraph:

Because misery and degradation, and death, and nothing that God or Satan could inflict would have parted us, you, of your own will, did it. I have not broken your heart—you have broken it; and in breaking it, you have broken mine. So much the worse for me that I am strong. Do I want to live? What kind of living will it be when you—oh, God! would you like to live with your soul in the grave?

I ground my teeth. The next sentence, she had underlined with a pencil:

You left me too: but I won't upbraid you! I forgive you. Forgive me!

I closed the book and counted to ten.

41

Noah

I SLEPT ONLY FITFULLY, DREAMING I WAS GIVING BIRTH AND THE doctors were shouting that there were complications and the baby was in danger. I pushed and pushed. It was the only thing I knew how to do. Glancing around, I sought the one person who could make my worst fears disappear.

I can't do it alone… Nick… I need him, please…

Mr. Leister said he couldn't be here… He insisted that he didn't want the baby. Or you…

I was crying, not just from the pain, but because I was alone. Mini-Me was about to come out, but when he did, I didn't hear the loud cries of a newborn, just absolute silence. Some faceless presence approached me and handed me a bundle in a blanket.

I'm sorry… He was born dead.

It was a nightmare… I could feel the tears on my damp cheeks and my heart pounding at a thousand miles an hour. Then my eyes focused on the person in front of me. Nicholas had fallen asleep sitting on the sofa. I didn't hesitate to throw off the sheets, get out of bed, and walk over to him. I sat on his lap and lifted one of his arms, wrapping it around me. He jerked a bit when his eyes opened.

"Noah..." he said. He was disoriented, but then he hugged me tightly, almost instinctively.

I buried my face in his neck. I was shaking like a leaf.

"What happened? Are you okay? Is the...?"

I shook my head, feeling a knot in my throat, unable to talk.

"Why are you crying?" he asked, frightened.

I closed my eyes and just felt him touch me. "I had a nightmare..."

He seemed to relax, but his arms swelled as he squeezed me tightly. "Do you want to talk about it? Sometimes that helps..."

The whole situation was so strange. For virtually the whole time we'd been dating, I had tried to hide from him how hard it was for me to sleep when he wasn't there. Without even knowing it, he'd always protected me from my bad dreams. I'd always slept soundly at his side.

"I was having our child..." I said softly, "and you weren't there. I was pushing and pushing...but Mini-Me was born dead. And I...I..."

Nick squeezed me again; his big arms swallowed me, but the image of my dead baby just wouldn't vanish from my mind.

"That's not going to happen, Noah," he said, running his long fingers through my hair.

"How do you know?" I asked, leaning my head on his shoulders and opening my eyes.

He pushed me back so he could see me. "To start with, because there's no one and nothing in the world that could keep me away from you when the time comes."

"You promise?"

"I'll be holding your hand from the first contraction until you're through it. You have my word."

I hadn't expected him to say anything different, but still, an immense relief flowed through me. He reached down to touch my belly.

"Shouldn't I be able to feel something by now?" he asked, as if frustrated.

"You will soon..." I said, holding my breath as I felt his hand under my shirt. "Sometimes I think our child is hiding, waiting to be sure you're really here..."

"It's still hard for me to believe, you know?"

It was overwhelming...Mini-Me, him, us... I still couldn't grasp it all; there were just too many changes, and all of them were happening at once...

"I'm scared," I told him, hoping time would stop, wanting to go back to the beginning, to when it was just him and me, and all the new problems we were facing hadn't managed to hurt us.

"That's normal... I'm terrified. But everything will be fine, you'll see."

"But what if it isn't?" I whispered, scared to confess my fears aloud. "This wasn't supposed to happen. I wasn't supposed to be a mother, my body—"

"Your body's perfect," he said, leaving no room for doubt.

"Nick, the baby... I almost lost it," I admitted, too scared to look him straight in the eyes.

"What are you talking about?"

I tried to get a hold of myself before talking any further. "Remember the night of the LRB celebration...when you had to take me home...?"

Of course he did. He got instantly tense. I was close enough to see the vein in his neck throbbing menacingly. He couldn't have forgotten how drunk I was.

"I think that was the first time I could have miscarried... I thought my period had come...but it was something else."

"Don't feel guilty about what you couldn't have predicted," he said.

"I hurt our child...and I had to spend weeks in bed, and I

don't even know what the doctor's going to tell me the day after tomorrow when I go to his office."

"Is that why you had to rest...?"

"I've got a hematoma, and until it's gone, I can barely do anything. The doctor told me it's common with first pregnancies, but as time passes, it becomes more and more dangerous, not just for the baby but for me, too."

"Explain to me again what the danger is for you."

I saw so much fear in his pupils that I got scared myself. "Supposedly there could be complications if I lose it. But that won't happen," I said, determined to reassure us both.

Nick was speechless for a moment, as if suddenly the possibility of losing me and the baby terrified him. He stood, lifting me from the sofa, and laid me down on the bed. Then he paced through the room, his mind far away. When he came back over, he looked scared.

"I'm so sorry, Noah... This should never have happened. If I ever thought harm could come to you..."

I wanted to tell him that what mattered now was the baby, not me, that I was fine...but I couldn't because he closed my mouth with a kiss, his mouth seeking consolation in mine. I needed a few seconds to relax; it almost scared me to feel the passion in this kiss, a passion that seemed to have eluded me forever. His tongue licked my lips, and I opened up. His breath was intoxicating and made me shiver. I touched his hair, pulled him in, but he wouldn't kiss me any longer. Instead he looked me in the eye.

"Go back to sleep," he said, panting. "You need to rest, and I..."

He was about to go, but my hand clasped his, holding him beside me.

"Stay with me until I fall asleep, please."

A war seemed to be going on inside him. But he took off his shoes and lay down beside me. I let him pull me into his arms, and I rested my head on his chest. I didn't want to think too much about what had just happened; I didn't know where we were as a couple or how we would proceed. A kiss didn't mean anything, did it? Maybe? I fell asleep with him stroking my hair and his heartbeat accompanying me like a lullaby.

When I opened my eyes the next morning, all I heard was the clicking of computer keys. In front of the bed was a sheer curtain dividing the bedroom from the rest of the suite, and when I sat up, I could see Nick's blurry image on the sofa looking at his laptop screen, clearly displeased.

I remembered the moment we'd shared the night before. It had been a year and a half at least since I'd turned to Nicholas to feel better, a year and a half since I'd truly felt at ease in those arms... He had been good to me, but I had no idea what was coming next, and I was scared to ask.

Nick realized I was no longer asleep and looked up at me from his computer. I think we were both holding our breath—I know I was—until he finally closed the computer, laid it on the table, and walked over to the bed.

I didn't say anything, I just waited to see how I should react. I felt a tingle as he stood next to me and looked down at me from above.

"How are you?" he asked, stroking my cheek and brushing a strand of hair behind my ear.

"Great," I said almost automatically. My brain was too focused on his fingers touching me to pay attention to anything else.

He nodded and turned around.

"Are you leaving?" I couldn't help but ask.

"I've got lots to do, including finding you the best ob-gyn in

Los Angeles," he said, taking out his phone. "Get dressed. I'll have room service bring up breakfast."

I threw on a sweatshirt but didn't change out of my pajama bottoms. Ten minutes later, two huge trays appeared laden with enough food for an army. Nick was busy making calls, and by the time he hung up, I couldn't eat anymore. He looked at my half-empty plate.

"Eat," he said.

"I'm not in the mood for anything else," I said, pushing my eggs around with a fork.

We hadn't talked about us, and that was making me nervous. I couldn't stop thinking about what he'd said to me the last time we were together and how certain he'd seemed when he'd told me he'd never forgive me.

"Stop playing with your food. You've barely had a bite."

I frowned. "Is this the deal now?" I replied. "You're going to order me around all the time? If that's how it is, I'll go back to Jenna's."

He didn't like hearing that, but before he could say anything, someone knocked at the door. Steve came in looking preoccupied and holding a handful of magazines.

"It's everywhere, Nicholas," he said, not even seeming to notice me or the tray of eggs, fruit, cereal, and coffee.

"I know," Nick said, turning and walking over to the desk. Steve followed him. I got up and did the same.

"What's everywhere?" I asked and grabbed a copy of *People* from Steve before he could stop me. I saw the headline: *Nicholas Leister Up to His Old Tricks*. Underneath was a photo of him looking worse for the wear, with a cut on his face, emerging from a bar. I turned to the article page, but Nick snatched the magazine away and gave me an angry and menacing look.

"Go back to bed, Noah. Now."

Crossing my arms, I said, "Not till you tell me what's going on."

"I'll tell you whatever you want, but please, get back in bed."

He wasn't being bossy—he was worried for me; I could see that in the depths of those spectacular irises. I did as he said, feeling weird when I noticed Steve was watching my every move. Only once he saw me get under the sheets did Nick seem to breathe easier.

"Talk to Margot. She'll handle this," Nick said, throwing the magazine in the trash.

"You want to explain this?" Steve asked, looking over at me.

I'd never seen that expression, and it was obvious he was reprimanding Nick. This was the first time I'd ever seen a hint of anything threatening in Steve's eyes.

"I will when I can. For now, just do as I ask; talk to Margot and try to make sure nothing else gets out from now on. The last thing I need the press to know is that Noah's with me."

That hurt—why lie about it? But more important to me then was knowing what could have caused a reporter to write a headline like that, making Steve act disapproving to the young man he'd protected and cared for since he was just a little boy.

Steve walked past his supposed boss until he was beside me. I saw worry in his face as he asked me if everything was all right.

Behind him, I could see Nick crossing his arms and giving him a piercing look. He didn't like being ignored, and I was sure he didn't like another man standing that close to the bed where I was lying half naked.

"Don't worry about me, Steve," I said, trying to summon a relaxing tone.

I didn't think I convinced him, but at least he nodded, and without even looking at Nick, he walked out, not uttering another word.

"What was that about?" I asked.

Still staring at the place where Steve had been standing, Nicholas responded, "I guess his priorities have changed," but something in his voice told me he wasn't entirely upset about it.

"Are you going to tell me who you got in a fight with and why?"

He rubbed his thin growth of beard, which made him look like a bad boy, the very kind of boy I throbbed for.

"I ran into Michael at a bar close to campus," he said with a kind of defiance. He was looking me in the eye, and I even had the sense he was paying close attention to how I reacted. I tried not to let the news shake me, but I couldn't. Immediately I was tense, scared. "We got into a fight, they threw us both out, the press learned about it, and now they're trying to use it to discredit me as CEO."

Michael and Nick…fuck. Their last fight had turned out bad. But I hadn't worried about anything happening again once Michael was out of the city and Nick was in New York and focused on his company. The last thing I'd imagined was that they could run into each other again, let alone that they could come to blows.

"You shouldn't have gotten into it with him," I said. Maybe he thought I was upbraiding him, but I was scared because I knew he needed to stay out of trouble. If Michael pressed charges, I wasn't sure what would happen to Nick. But I knew we couldn't have a reprise of the first night they'd met.

His muscles flexed in his clothing as he stood at the foot of the bed. "Have you seen him again?"

Had Michael told him something about our run-in a month before?

"I saw him on campus; we barely exchanged three words. Nicholas, I don't want to see him any more than you do. I didn't think he'd come back, but I guess he has other plans."

"I don't want you seeing him, Noah." That sounded like a threat.

"I don't plan to."

He looked surprised. I supposed he hadn't expected that answer. Nicholas had no notion of the way Michael had harassed me in the weeks after he'd gone to New York. And I wasn't planning on telling him about it. I felt sure Michael's intentions went no further than an immature desire to fuck with Nick, whom he'd always talked badly about.

I blinked as I realized how important my response was to Nick. As important as it was to me that Michael really would stay away from me. "I promise."

"Good. Now I've got to go to the office."

That saddened me, but I couldn't just expect him to stay with me in that room while I was bedbound for what might be months on end.

"If you need anything, call me on my cell, and please, Noah, don't get out of bed."

I nodded, and he left. He promised he wouldn't be late, and he left me alone in that unfamiliar room waiting for his return.

42

Noah

The next two days were strange. Nicholas was burning the candle at both ends at the office, and when he returned in the wee hours of the morning, I was already sleeping deeply. I'd open my eyes and see the sheets on his side of the bed looking immaculate, with a note telling me to have a good day and not to do anything that could be bad for me or the baby.

The night before I was going to leave my prison for the hospital, I forced myself to stay awake on the sofa. I was irritable; I was stir-crazy. Everything still felt unresolved, and my anxiety and the fact that I hadn't had a normal conversation with anyone in almost forty-eight hours were getting to me. I was edgy, cranky, scared that things might turn out wrong, scared of what they might say to me at the doctor's, and that made the days, hours, and minutes pass in slow motion.

It was around two when the door to our room opened almost silently. From the sofa to the left, I had a perfect view of anyone entering. Nick stopped, surprised to find me there, and when I saw his face, I had the feeling of a person diving from the top of a roller coaster.

"What are you doing awake?" he said, trying to control himself, taking off his leather jacket and laying it on the sideboard. He was dressed nicely but informally, with no tie and certainly no suit, even though he'd had several sent over from his apartment. He definitely wasn't coming from work.

"Waiting for you," I said. He walked over, bent down to pick me up, and carried me to bed. I held on to his neck, surprised to be touched by him again after two days of virtually no contact.

My body quivered like never before, and I wanted to share that intimacy we always knew when we were together. Did he regret it? Did he hate me again, the same as he had before, and was he hiding it because of the baby?

He wouldn't even look me in the eye. He hadn't since I'd promised to stay away from Michael. I was scared that seeing him had awakened all those buried memories, reopened those wounds that now would never heal. I was scared that Nick still thought the best thing was for us to be apart and that nothing, not even his own child, could change his mind.

He tried to set me down, but I didn't let go of his neck. I pulled him in for a kiss. He paused just over my lips, so still that my heart almost stopped, and I saw all my fears were justified.

"I can't, Noah," he confessed in a whisper, pulling my arms open and standing. He didn't look at me again as he walked into the bathroom. I stayed in bed trying to absorb his rejection.

My heart felt like it was bleeding. So this meant we were back to where we'd started. I curled up in the sheets and tried not to notice the tears rolling down my cheeks. When he opened the bathroom door, I pretended to be asleep. I realized then that Nick hadn't been sleeping with me and then smoothing down the sheets. He'd been sleeping on the sofa, as far from me as possible.

The appointment with the doctor was at noon. Nick, to my surprise, was working in the hotel room. I got in the shower, ignoring him. In the mirror, I saw my eyes were red and swollen. I didn't want him to see how affected I'd been by his rejection of me the night before, so I spent a long time covering up the signs of it until I looked halfway presentable. It's amazing what good makeup can do.

What really set me off was when I went to pick an outfit and realized nothing fit me anymore. That was different for me: I'd never had problems with my weight; I'd never had to lie down on the bed and wriggle into my jeans. My baby bump was hardly visible, but I still felt like a whale. My bad mood was evident when I slammed the door on the way out of the bathroom. Nick looked up from his computer and looked at me with curiosity.

"I need the keys to your car," I said, salty and ready to escape that room ASAP.

"May I ask why?"

I looked at him incredulously. Had he seriously forgotten? "To go to the doctor who is looking after the health of your child."

He tried to conceal the beginnings of a smile and got up, closing his laptop and grabbing his keys, which he spun several times around his fingers.

"I'm well aware you have to go to the gynecologist. What I don't understand is why in the hell you'd think *you* were going to drive there."

I clenched my jaw. "I'm perfectly capable of driving. Actually, I'm better at it than you."

He wasn't bothering to hide his smile anymore or the interest in his eyes as they roved my body. I wished I could put on a parka. At that moment, I couldn't have felt less attractive, and him being so hot only made the whole thing that much worse.

"You can show me your driving talents another time, Freckles, but for now, the last thing I want to see is you behind a wheel," he said, grabbing his coat and opening the door. "Come on. I'm ready to meet my kid."

I stood still for a moment, then forced my legs to move. We took the elevator straight down to the parking deck, skipping the lobby. Once we got on the road, I felt I should tell him something, even if I wasn't in the mood.

"They might let us know the baby's sex today," I said, pretending it was no big deal, even if I was dying to know whether what I had inside me was a Mini-Noah or a Mini-Nick.

"Today?" he asked, looking over with surprise before focusing again on the road. The car swayed slightly from side to side as his hands slipped nervously on the wheel.

"I could have found out a few weeks ago, but...I decided to wait." I looked out the window.

I didn't want to admit that the idea of finding out without him had been unbearable to me. I didn't want him to know how much I needed him in those moments. More than ever, if I were being honest.

Nick took my hand and kissed it softly. I was surprised that the wall he'd seemed to be building up between us had crumbled so quickly. "Thanks for waiting for me," he said. I hadn't even needed to tell him my reasons. He knew me almost better than I did.

After a more or less tranquil moment of silence, the urge to know what he was thinking forced me to open my mouth again, despite my reservations. "What do you want it to be?"

Nick smiled. "What about you?"

"I asked first."

He chuckled. "I think I could handle a girl," he said after a few seconds' deliberation.

"You've got enough experience," I couldn't help answering.

He knew what I was getting at, but he decided against arguing.

"I seem to remember once or twice you called the baby Mini-Me. Unless I misheard?"

I blushed. Okay, yes, that was the name I used in my mind, but that didn't mean I assumed it would be a girl.

"I don't know if I could deal with a teeny-tiny Nicholas," I replied defensively. And yet warmth radiated through my body as I imagined a baby Nick in my arms.

"Freckles, are you implying that a little Noah would be any easier? I feel for your poor mother sometimes. God knows what she's had to put up with..."

I knew he was joking, but I still glared at him. "Don't worry, I'll take care of our little girl if she's as unbearable as I am...or as uptight as your dad."

By now, Nick was grinning from ear to ear. "Noah, if we have a daughter, she'll be the most loved little girl in the world. You can be certain no father will care for his daughter the way I will."

That remark put an end to any more sarcasm on my part, and I tried to turn away to conceal how much his words moved me.

I had never known what it meant to have a father who loved me above all else—that was something I'd never even been able to imagine, and the thought of Nick with our son or daughter made me realize I could be certain that, regardless of what happened between us, our baby would grow up surrounded by love.

We reached the hospital a few minutes later, and the fact that we were about to walk in there and see our baby on the ultrasound became suddenly so very real. Many women and their partners were sitting in the waiting room. Nick and I were the youngest ones. It was weird to find ourselves in that situation. When they called my name, I couldn't help grabbing Nick's hand before we went inside.

I was scared again. I had no idea what they were going to tell us, and today especially, it really struck me that there was no turning back. All I wanted was to bring a happy, healthy baby into the world, and the idea that my own body could prevent that dream from coming true made me hate myself.

Doctor Hubber greeted me affectionately as we walked into his office. He looked at Nick with curiosity, and Nick at him with feigned politeness, as they shook hands. I knew Nick was already trying to find things wrong with him.

"Doctor, this is Nicholas Leister, my…um, the father," I said, blushing and feeling like an idiot.

Nicholas said nothing. I'd have liked to see him mark his territory the way he usually did when we were together, but my thoughts were more with Mini-Me and my hope that everything would turn out all right.

Doctor Hubber told me to lie back on the exam table while he asked a few routine questions.

Nicholas concentrated on my responses, and I noticed the furrow between his eyes getting deeper and deeper. When the doctor asked me to lift my shirt so he could press the ultrasound probe into my belly, Nick stepped forward and closely observed each of the doctor's movements. The handpiece glided over my skin, still cold from the gel. A few seconds later, Mini-Me appeared on the screen. The baby was bigger than before and looked less like a tadpole; the arms and legs were thicker, stronger.

Seeing it had been amazing the first time, but now it was much more special. I looked at Nick's expression, which showed pure astonishment. I got it—it was one thing to hear about your baby; it was another to see it right in front of you.

The gynecologist kept moving the device around and making calculations and measurements.

"I've got good news," he said, looking at both of us. "The hematoma is basically gone. There's a little shadow there, but I feel confident in saying it'll be gone in no time."

"Does that mean the baby's out of danger?" I asked, excited and relieved, as though the weight I'd been bearing all those weeks without realizing it had finally been lifted.

"We'll keep checking every month, but yes, for now, everything is as it should be." He smiled. "You've done well, Noah."

I let my head fall back and sighed. "So that means I can live a normal life now, Doctor?"

Before he could respond, Nick interrupted him, an expression of distrust on his face. "You said the hematoma is *basically* gone. That means not entirely. Wouldn't it be better for her to keep resting for a few more weeks?"

What?! No!

I glowered at him, but he completely ignored me.

"She can do the usual things she does in her everyday life, Mr. Leister. But no stress, and no strenuous physical activity. As I told her the first time she was here, her medical history and subsequent factors make this pregnancy more risky than usual. That doesn't mean she should panic, but she should take it easy. She's well into the second trimester. Things will start moving a lot faster. The baby's grown a good deal since last time but a little less than I'd expected, and that tells me you're probably in for a spurt in the upcoming weeks."

"If you don't mind, I want to get a second opinion on all this," Nick said, still not accepting the doctor's words.

But the doctor didn't seem offended in the least. "I would be more than happy to recommend one of my colleagues to you, Mr. Leister."

"That won't be necessary."

There was a slight air of antagonism in the way they looked at each other. *Damn you, Nicholas.* I wasn't about to go to another doctor. This was typical Nick, always thinking he was smarter, always trying to get in the middle of things.

"Do you want to know the baby's sex?" the doctor asked. That was enough to clear the tension.

Nicholas smiled at me as if to say, *Relax*, and that only excited me more.

"We'd love to, Doctor," he said, gripping my hand.

The doctor slid the ultrasound device across my belly, and after what seemed like far too much time, he grinned and said, "It's a boy."

The world stopped. My heart, too.

A boy... My eyes filled with tears. Nicholas and I smiled at each other, remembering the conversation in the car. Nick's reaction is one of the memories I still treasure most. He gawked at the screen, motionless, for several seconds. Then he caught me by surprise, leaning over me and depositing a kiss on my lips, a kiss I received with pleasure and embarrassment because Doctor Hubber was just a foot and a half away. When Nick pulled away, he stared into my eyes, and I melted completely inside.

"Looks like Mini-You is now a Mini-Me," he remarked.

"Don't let it go to your head," I warned him.

Knowing now that the baby was fine and I could get up and move about, I started making plans in my head as we drove back to the hotel. Finally, I could grab the reins of my life. I needed to feel useful again. A person like me, accustomed to always being out and about, could think of no worse nightmare than spending almost a whole month in bed.

"I need to stretch my legs. Jesus. I want to go running. I want to go back to class, get a job..." I said, already dreaming of a busy future as I looked out the window.

"Did you not hear the doctor?" Nicholas complained. "The hematoma isn't gone; you can't just go back to doing whatever."

I turned. "Did *you* not hear the doctor? He said I can live a normal life. It's easy for you to tell me what to do—you haven't spent a month in bed."

Nicholas blew out a breath and gripped the wheel tight.

"We need to talk about my apartment… I know you don't want to go there, and I respect that, but we need to put things in order, somehow. The hotel's fine for now, but people know I'm there, and I can't be drawing attention right now."

What did that have to do with me?

"I've got my apartment, I paid the deposit, I'm ready to get settled in, Nick." I was actually excited to be there and relax while I prepared for what was to come. "You can go back to yours."

"Is that what you want? For us to live apart?" There was pain in his voice, pain and anger at being rejected.

"We can't *live* together if we *aren't* together." I hated to admit it, but that was a fact.

"Jesus, Noah, things have changed, don't you get that?"

I shook my head. He had said the very thing I didn't want to hear. "Yeah, things have changed. I'm going to have a baby. But that doesn't mean you and I have to get back together. I've accepted where we are, and—"

"And what?" he asked, cutting the wheel hard to the right and entering the hotel lot. "I fucked up. Now I need to take care of the two of you."

"You're going to take care of us?" I shouted, indignant. "I'm not your responsibility, and I refuse to be with a person who made it very evident to me that he was not going to love me again and that he certainly wouldn't trust me again, so let's start over. You can take care of the kid with me, but that's it: I won't live with you, I won't follow your orders, and I'm not going to change doctors. Until I give birth, all decisions are mine. When the baby's born, we'll figure out how to raise him together. But we'll each stay in our own home."

I got out and slammed the door. This was exactly what I'd been afraid of: Nicholas saw my pregnancy as a twisted way for me to get him to come back to me. But that wasn't how I did things. I didn't want Nicholas's sympathy, and I didn't want to be a burden for him… For God's sake! His rejection may have hurt me, but I would never try to manipulate him, I would never force him to do anything.

Nicholas waited until we had reached the room to resume his line of questioning.

"So your plan is for us to just go on with our lives, and then… what? We'll split custody? Is that what you want?" He sat on the edge of the bed and observed me as I took my clothing down from the hangers and folded it sloppily on a nearby table. I looked up at him for an instant. He appeared at ease, but I knew what those eyes were hiding. He didn't like what I'd said in the car at all, and hearing him repeat it back to me, I realized I didn't either. He continued: "Deciding on which days we get to keep him, which weekends, which holidays… Is that what you want? For our child to grow up with parents who live apart?"

My eyes grew damp at that horrible possibility. I knew what it meant to grow up that way. It was horrible. For half my life, I hadn't had a father; for the other half, I'd run scared from him, always thinking he'd hurt me. Nick had been through something similar: he'd seen his parents separate, his mother abandon him.

I imagined my sweet little baby, his big blue eyes, his blond hair, going through the same things Nick and I had been through, and my heart shrank in a way it hadn't before then. I bit my lip, trying to control the trembling, and Nicholas got up and came over to me.

"Let me take care of you," he asked, stroking my face and looking into the depths of my eyes with steely determination. "I know what I said, I know I said I'd never be able to forgive you, but ever since I left, I haven't been able to get it out of my head: your reaction, your sorrow...they've pursued me, Noah. But things have changed, the whole way I see everything is different; it's like I'm seeing things in color again after a long period of gray. When I saw our son on that screen, Noah... Fuck, I was the happiest guy in the world. Not just because I'm going to have a beautiful baby, but because I'm going to have him with the woman who makes my whole world better."

I closed my eyes and felt a tear escape. Nick leaned his forehead against mine, and his hot breath enveloped me.

"We hurt each other a lot, Freckles. Don't think I'm not aware of every hurtful word that's come out of my mouth. I wanted to see you suffer after I suffered because of the thing with Michael. But never, Noah, not even once, did I doubt that you were the one for me."

I opened my eyes.

"I left Sophia, Noah."

My heart sped up at the thought of them together, the nights I'd spent crying in bed because I'd seen them in a magazine or on TV. What Nick had said about her, that she was the right woman for him, smarter, more mature, more everything... I still remembered all that, and it stuck in my heart like a knife.

"You shouldn't have." I tried to look away from him, but he wouldn't let me. He didn't understand what I was saying, but I kept stumbling through my declaration. "Nicholas, you won't be able to forget that I cheated on you with another guy, and I won't be able to bear losing you again... I'm scared, I'm so scared, and I just can't put myself out there to see if what we have will or won't work this time."

"Let me show you that everything I'm saying is true, Noah."

I shook my head. He grabbed my face and kissed me the way I wished he would ever since we'd split up. His lips lighted on mine once, twice, then settled, forcing a sigh from me. His tongue pushed into my mouth, and I melted. He lifted me. My thighs wrapped around his. He bit my lip, sucked, kissed me, waiting for a response. He didn't have to wait long. His words had paralyzed me. For a moment, I could see the light at the end of the tunnel, small but bright. But to get there, I'd have to dodge all types of obstacles, obstacles I wasn't sure I could get past.

Nicholas let me down.

"You haven't even touched me for days. I thought..."

"I didn't touch you because I knew if I started, I wouldn't be able to stop..." he said, trying to justify himself. "I wanted to give you space. I didn't want to push you if you weren't ready."

I was speechless.

"I'm going to have a kid with you, Noah. *With you.* Maybe it'll take you time to believe it, but I'm not going anywhere."

Was he serious? Could his words really be true? I loved him with all my soul, and the one thing I wanted was for him to love me again the way I loved him.

"Let's take it slow, Nick," I said.

"Better: let's start from zero," he said.

43

Nick

I helped her pick up her things, and we packed our bags together. I didn't try to hide how in love with her I was as she walked through the room. I knew I couldn't just say my words and intentions were pure and expect her to just accept them, especially after I'd basically sworn to her we'd never be together again. But I didn't care; in the bottom of my heart I'd always wanted this to happen, for something to force me to go back to her and give me a justification so I wouldn't just feel I was deceiving myself.

My biggest fear had always been losing her. Losing her once and for all. When she'd cheated on me and I was apart from her for a year and a half, I thought I'd done the right thing. I didn't forgive people easily. Noah was right about that. My own mother was sick with cancer and still had to struggle for me to do so, and I wasn't even sure I was in the right.

Sorry, it was just a word...but it sure was an important one. Noah was the person who had opened my heart, and knowing now what it meant to lose that, knowing that I had a reason to join her for life, had given me the sense of security I had been lacking since the beginning of our relationship.

I had meant what I'd said when I told her goodbye for the last time. Or at least I'd thought I had. I'd really believed there was nothing Noah could do to change my mind, and now I realized there was, and everything had changed. I'd always felt I came second for lots of people. My father always put his business before me, and I knew now that he loved his current wife more than he'd ever love his firstborn child. My mother...she'd left me to run off with another guy, putting her vengeance against my father above any love she'd ever supposedly felt for me... And Noah...Noah was dealing with problems far graver than mine, and as hard as she'd tried to make me believe she loved me like crazy, I'd just found it easier to expect the worst, to not believe, to just pray for everything to turn out okay. I knew we had reached this point despite our problems and our insecurities, and after almost twenty-four years of living, I had finally found that something I had needed to relax and believe that love was possible and that there was someone out there who would put me before anything else.

That child on the way was my hope for unconditional love, and the person giving him to me was the very one I loved with all my heart. How could I not forgive her? How could I not let the past go when she had given me everything I'd needed since I first saw her, even if I couldn't grasp that for so long?

Finally, I felt peace, in my soul and in my mind. It was as if the storm that had raged in my world suddenly dissipated, and the bright sun was now blinding me. I guessed that was what it felt like to truly forgive someone. Infinite calm...unconditional love.

At her apartment, I noticed her looking all around, taking things out of boxes, insisting on putting them on shelves. It made me nervous. I almost had a heart attack when she got up on a chair to reach a shelf. I walked over and picked her up before I freaked out.

"Shit, Noah!" I shouted, setting her down and taking the object out of her hands. "This is your first day up and about after weeks in bed. Maybe relax a little?"

"I'm just nervous, and I can't stay still. I'm sorry," she said and walked off, as if being close to me burned her. She crossed the room and stood as far from me as possible.

"Are you sure you don't want me to spend the night here?" I asked, hating having to leave her.

It was going to be a struggle to separate. I wanted to take her to live with me, dammit; I wanted to care for her, give her all the things she needed.

Before she could answer, the door opened, and Lion and Jenna came in, smiling radiantly and holding a bundle of blue balloons.

"It's a boy!"

I looked over at Noah, surprised, and she shrugged, smiling. A second later, Jenna was leaping at her to give her a hug, letting the balloons fly off toward the ceiling. Lion came over with a little blue teddy bear in hand and smiled like a true dickhead.

"So you're a daddy, huh?" he said.

Despite myself, I felt a knot in my throat. I really was going to be a father. I needed to start getting used to the idea.

"We've got to celebrate!" Jenna proposed, clapping and jumping into my arms. "You know, if you don't choose me as the godmother, I'm going to tell all your dirty secrets." I reached out to yank her hair in response. "Where should we go?" she continued. "Dinner, a bar? We could even have a weekend away. This is a special occasion—we need to do it up!"

All I needed was one look to know none of that appealed to Noah just then. We hadn't expected a baby, and even if I was happy, I knew Noah needed reassurance that it wouldn't change anything. She was finally able to live normally again, and the first thing she had said was she wanted to go back to class, work, go out. She didn't want the kid to become her sole focus.

I didn't want to keep bringing it up. I knew her well enough to know that sooner or later, she'd get used to it, but I didn't want her to break down in the meantime. And if she did, I wanted to be there.

"Let's go dancing," I said, suppressing my desire to stick her back in bed and force her to stay there. She looked over with surprise. "I mean, don't jump into a mosh pit or anything, but a little dancing could be fun, right?"

She smiled, and I felt my heart stop.

"Yeah, it could be fun," she said. It was the first time I'd seen her happy since we'd left the doctor's office.

Jenna agreed, and Lion and I went outside while Noah changed clothes. I took out a cigarette and smoked for the first time since I'd found out I was going to have a kid.

"How are you handling it?" Lion asked, trying not to stare. He lit a cigarette of his own.

"Just trying to accept the fact that in four months, my life is going to change, and it will never be the same again."

"What about Noah? Are you guys back together?" he asked tactfully.

I looked at the door to her building.

"I'm working on it," I responded as the girls reappeared. Noah had changed from her jeans into a T-shirt dress, transparent tights, and high boots. She'd let her hair down, too, and had put on lipstick and eyeliner. I swear to God, I'd never seen her look more beautiful.

Now I wanted more than ever to take her back home and stick her in bed—almost as much as I wanted her to enjoy the night and feel free. She came over with doubt written all over her face.

"You okay?" I asked her, wanting so badly to pull her in and kiss her until she was breathless.

She nodded, but she didn't look me in the eye. I knew it would take us a long time to return to what we'd once been, but I needed to reclaim her as mine, now more than ever.

I started my car, Noah got into the passenger seat, and immediately I noticed her squirming and fidgeting.

"What's up?" I asked her.

Noah shook her head, but I wouldn't give up that easily.

"Noah, you can tell me."

"Just... What are we going to tell our parents?"

That's what she's so worried about?

"Noah, don't worry about what people will say, okay? Our parents know our story; we'll just tell them we're back together. And as far as the baby... They won't find out till you're ready to tell them."

"My mother's gonna have a stroke." She rolled down the window to get some fresh air. "Plus, we can't just tell them we're back together. We need to see how things go. It would be best not to say anything. You can barely tell now anyway, right?"

We looked at her stomach. True, it was hardly noticeable, but that would change soon: she was five months pregnant. Our parents would find out before long, and so would everyone else. I felt anxious to protect her from any rumors that might come up. Everyone thought I was still with Sophia Aiken, and when the news about Noah came out, it would be a scandal. I was going to have to get ready to face it.

"I don't think we have too much longer to draw it out, but we won't say a word till you're ready, okay?"

She nodded. Soon we arrived at the club. It was deafening, and I asked for a VIP room. Jenna couldn't stop talking about the baby, what we'd name him, where we were going to live, what color we'd paint his room... It started to get on my nerves. Noah tried to share her friend's enthusiasm, but even Lion could tell Jenna was overdoing it.

Lion and Jenna went out to dance while Noah watched from her seat. Jenna came over at one point and pulled her out onto the dance floor, and they enjoyed themselves for a while. I observed each of Noah's movements, holding my breath, but ten minutes later, she was back there sitting down beside me.

She wasn't having fun.

"You want to go? Are you tired?" I asked, alarms sounding in my head.

She forced a smile and shook her head.

We held out for another hour, and finally I insisted we leave. I knew something was up, and even if she was trying to hide it from our friends, I could tell what mood she was in. We said goodbye to Jenna and Lion and walked to the car before driving home in silence. But once we were inside, I couldn't hold back anymore. I pulled her close and squeezed her in my arms.

"Tell me what's worrying you."

She hugged me and rested her head on my shoulder. "I don't think it was a good idea, going out tonight," she said. "I don't belong in places like that anymore, you know? Parties, staying out late, college… I'm changing, the old me is gone. I'll have to get used to being…"

"You don't have to get used to being anything, Noah. Becoming a mother doesn't mean you have to change."

She shook her head. She seemed unable to emerge from her mental turmoil. "No, that's not true. You heard Jenna—she couldn't stop talking about the baby… That's what people are going to see me as now: a mother. I'm not going to be the same girl as before, and I'm so scared because I don't even know who I am…"

I didn't want her to go down that road. There was no need for her to think she'd given up anything.

"I swear to you, you will go on being the same person I met

three years ago, Noah...the same person who drove me crazy when she walked into my kitchen and gave me a dirty look, the same one who lost my Ferrari, the same one who played twenty questions with me, who wanted to be a writer and travel and open an animal shelter, the one who wanted to learn how to surf, the one who swore she'd kiss me every day for the rest of my life, the one who thought she could never have kids... You will be all that and more, Noah."

She shook her head and pulled away. "I know it's horrible to say this. I want this baby, I really do," she confessed with her eyes full of tears. "But I don't want it now, you know? I don't even know what I'm going to do tomorrow, what I'm going to do for a living... I'm dependent on you now, Nick, and even if you keep saying you want to come back to me, I can't just act like the past year didn't happen..."

"Noah," I said, but she interrupted me.

"This isn't what I planned for my life; this isn't what I wanted. I know it sounds all traditional, but I wanted to be married, I wanted a home, economic security, a job, a life. I wanted to start my family after that. I haven't got a thing except uncertainty, and I'm scared to bring this baby into the world and not be able to give him the best."

"He will have the best, Noah, and you will, too. I'm here. Look at me. I'm not going anywhere."

How could I make her understand that my entire goal in life was to make her happy?

"But you did...you left," she said, pulling away when I tried to touch her. I wanted her to calm down, to see how good things really were.

"I had to," I said, turning suddenly serious. "This year and a half of separation has changed both of us, Noah. We can't pick back up where we left off. We weren't good for each other then. I didn't make you happy, and you hurt me more than anyone ever has."

She held her breath for a moment.

"I'm not trying to throw that in your face. I just want you to see things from a different perspective. Fate has decided to bring you and me back together. The baby brought you back to me. And I'm happy. And you will be, too, Noah. I'll make sure of it."

"But what if I can't make you happy?"

I shook my head. "That won't happen..."

I kissed her on the lips. I needed her more than ever. I wanted to make love to her slowly, feel her skin against mine, listen to the moans coming from her lips, hear her repeating my name... But I'd promised her I'd go slow.

"I should leave," I said. Her cheeks were flushed, and she was so adorable that pulling away took all my might. "I'll call you tomorrow, okay?"

The feelings I saw in her eyes made me kiss her again. I whispered in her ear, "If you want me to stay, just say the word."

We stood up, and she took a step back.

"I'm okay."

That stung, but I forced a smile. "Bye, Freckles."

44

Noah

Despite the intensity of our discussion and all the emotions I was feeling, I slept better than I had in months. I slept like a log, or maybe I should say like a baby, but waking up wasn't as pleasant as those hours I had spent in dreams.

A cramp shot through my whole body, and cold sweat covered my neck and back. I opened my eyes just as nausea made me start retching, and I had to hurry to the bathroom to throw up what little I still had in my stomach from the night before.

God.

I stayed there kneeling for a long time in front of the toilet, my forehead sticky, my legs trembling. When nothing more came up, I felt strong enough to get in the shower and try to look past that first bout of morning sickness.

Wasn't that supposed to happen when you first got pregnant?

Everything with my baby was so different from what I'd read or thought. I get it, every woman is her own world, but still… I thought I'd managed to avoid it.

I had to go to class that day; I no longer had a doctor's note, and I needed to get back to work, too. Now that midterms were over, I could focus on making some money. When I left LRB, Simon had offered to help me get a job at his former company, and I told him I'd think it over. Now that I didn't have to be on bed rest and I could move around again, I'd called him and told him I could start Monday—a.k.a., the same day. I was terrified to admit to him that I was pregnant, but I also wasn't going to hide it.

I threw on a skirt and a black sweater. I didn't want to have to admit my jeans no longer fit. I went outside, ferociously hungry. My nausea was gone, and all I wanted was to stuff myself with every food that began with the letter *t*: tacos, tortilla chips, tamales, and tiramisu to finish… These thoughts put me in such a trance that I hardly noticed who was waiting for me leaned back against a black Mercedes.

"Good morning, Freckles," Nick said, walking toward me. Before I had quite grasped that he was there, he gave me a peck on the lips. "You want to do breakfast?"

I nodded passively, and ten minutes later, we were sitting in a fancy brunch spot.

"How are you?" he asked as I tore through a plate of pancakes with maple syrup and a glass of freshly squeezed orange juice.

"After vomiting up an organ? Great, I guess."

"You were throwing up? Noah, why didn't you call me?" I couldn't tell if it was anger or worry speaking.

"Trust me…you didn't want to be there. Anyway, I'd be willing to bet it'll happen often from now on, and I can't call you every time something as common as morning sickness happens, Nick. Just relax."

He didn't seem especially convinced by my response, but he did enjoy watching me stuff myself. "Are you going to work after class?"

I nodded as I finished my meal. Then I looked up at him. God, he was handsome today! How had I not noticed before? Another type of hunger suddenly scaled my list of priorities. First pancakes, then Nick… I should be ashamed of myself!

"There's nothing I could do to convince you to come work for me again, is there?"

I dropped my guard and looked him in the eye. "I swore to myself I wouldn't mix you and work, Nicholas."

He nodded, thinking, and I was surprised to see he didn't get mad; he just calmly accepted what I was saying. "How would you feel about me picking you up?"

I hesitated for a second. "You don't have to be my babysitter, Nick. I can take the car and stuff like that."

He seemed to ignored that. "I want to."

I wasn't going to argue with him, so I said, "Sure, pick me up at seven."

When he dropped me off at school, he tried to kiss me on the lips, but reflexively, I turned and let his lips land on my cheek. I got out before he could say anything. It was still hard for me to get over what had happened between us, and I wanted to take it slow. If there was one thing I knew, it was that Nicholas's kisses could be addictive…and I needed to spend some time in rehab.

It was weird, going back to my routine. Nobody really treated me differently, and soon I was back to doing things as if nothing had changed. I was living a white lie. I chatted with my classmates, told my professors I'd been sick, and when I was at work, I hardly even remembered I was pregnant. The office was small, and my job there was basically the same as at LRB. Plus, the people there were great.

I was happy to feel like myself again: just plain Noah, not a chocolate egg with a little toy inside.

When I walked out, I was tired; I often was now that I wasn't spending all day in bed. I had about half as much energy as before, and when I saw Nick standing there waiting for me, I was grateful not to have to do the driving myself.

"How was your first day back?" he asked once we'd gotten inside.

"Very stimulating. No one noticed anything." I was probably a little too happy about that. I ignored Nick's nonplussed reaction.

It got quiet, and a few minutes later, Nick said something that made me instantly tense.

"I'm leaving New York. My apartment's on the market. I'm going to move back here full-time and live with you."

"What?" I asked, incredulous. Nick's whole life was in New York: his job, his future...

"Aren't you happy about it?" he asked, wounded, reaching out to touch me.

But I twisted away and told him, "You shouldn't make a decision like that so fast. You think everything between us is resolved, but you and I destroyed each other before. What makes you think we're ready to start from zero now?"

"We're going to have a child, Noah."

"That's not a reason to abandon your old life. You're forcing things, and that's not the resolution I want."

He shook his head and cursed. "I'm ready to start over. I know it's going to work... I don't know what the hell you want from me. I thought you'd be happy. I'm doing all the things I'm supposed to do."

"Exactly, that's exactly it: you're doing what you're supposed to do, not what you want to do."

"I want to be with you," he replied, furious.

I shook my head. We had arrived at my apartment. "Well, I'm not sure that's true. What I think is you're doing what you believe is right."

I got out and walked toward the door, but Nicholas shouted at me to stop.

"Why do you have to make things complicated? We're having a child, we have a reason to be together, and instead of accepting it, you—"

I cut him off. "I begged you to come back to me, and you said no. I'm glad to know our baby is going to have both of us, and I'm sure you'll be the best father in the world, but for now, that's all you're going to be, Nicholas."

"You know perfectly well that I can't accept that."

Looking him in the eyes, I knew what he was saying was true. But he had never been fully happy with me. We had hurt each other—a lot. I didn't want to start a toxic relationship again based around the sole fact that we were going to be parents.

"I asked you for time, I told you I wanted to go slowly, I want to focus on the child… Our thing can wait; I don't want you rushing into decisions you might regret for the rest of your life."

"Goddammit, Noah, why won't you believe me when I tell you I want to be with you again?"

"Because you still haven't told me you love me!" I shouted.

A pause followed. Nick stared at me, full of sorrow and rage. He hadn't forgiven me. Not yet. And he knew it.

"The last time I told you I loved you, you broke my heart. I swore I'd never say those words again, but that doesn't mean I don't want to spend the rest of my life with you and the baby."

I held back my tears as best I could. "That's not how it works, Nick. Go back to your job, go back to New York, because the bubble we've been living in these past few days just popped."

I didn't wait for a response. I walked inside. He didn't follow me.

It hurt, pushing Nick away from me like that, but I knew I'd been right to do so. He needed to figure out what he really felt for me, and I needed to think about whether getting back with him was the best for both of us.

I didn't want it to end, I really didn't; I didn't want to cause problems, but for Nicholas, it was all or nothing, and I couldn't just wipe the slate clean and start over. I didn't feel secure, especially if he wasn't ready to love me. Attraction was one thing, and so was sex, but we'd never had problems with either of those. The hard thing was we didn't know how to love each other, we didn't know how to respect each other, and we couldn't start over if Nicholas remained afraid of opening his heart to me.

Despite our argument, the next day he was there in front of my apartment building, waiting for me. He had two cardboard cups in his hands and a stern look on his face. I walked down the steps and over to him.

"Hey," he said.

"Hey," I replied, grabbing the cup he handed to me.

Hot chocolate… My child was going to be a sugar junkie.

"I'm leaving in three hours. I came to say goodbye."

I knew I'd told him to go, but his words pierced me like bullets. I looked down to hide the sadness in my eyes, but he immediately grabbed my chin and forced me to look at him.

"I'm doing this for you," he said, his thumb stroking my cheek. "If there's one thing I learned during our separation and all the pain we went through, it's that I can't make you do anything you don't want to or aren't ready for."

I bit my lip.

"So I'm going. I'll call you every day. We can start off talking, we'll make plans, you can tell me your worries and I'll tell you mine, we'll talk about how we'll raise the kid, we'll think about names, we'll talk about the future. Because I love you, Noah. I love you, and I'm going to love you for the rest of my life."

My heart stopped. I couldn't believe what he was saying.

"If I didn't say it before, it's because I don't think you can express love with words. I thought I had to show you with my actions, with everything I was willing to do, and deep in your heart, you do know I love you, but you're deathly afraid of letting me in. And I get that. That's why I'm going. I'll be here for your doctor's appointments and anything else you need. We'll take it easy the next few months, but Noah, I am going to be a part of that baby's life. I'm headed back to New York to put things in order, but my next step will be moving back to Los Angeles."

I was speechless.

Nick grabbed my cup and put it next to his on the hood. Then he embraced me and pulled me in tightly. I could feel his lips on the crown of my head and the beating of his heart.

"But I'm going to need something before I go… Two things, actually."

I waited for him to tell me. He turned and looked for something in his briefcase. When he turned back, he had a credit card in his right hand. He passed it to me. It was an AmEx Black Card.

"Use it," he said.

I didn't even touch it. "No."

"It's on my account—just use it for anything you need. It's not a suggestion, Noah. I'm not going to give in on this."

I crossed my arms, almost wanting to vomit. "I told you I don't want to be a kept woman, Nick."

"Why are you so damned hardheaded? What if the tables were turned? What if you were the one with all the money and I had to give birth to our child? Wouldn't you want to give me everything, Noah?"

"Yes, of course I would."

"Let's do this," he said. "If you don't want to use the card for you, fine, but use it for the baby, okay? Anything you need for him, put it on the card. And if you want to take care of your own things, fine."

I could do that, right…? After all, Nick was the father. I wasn't going to deprive my child of the benefits of being born to a dad who could get an AmEx Black at just twenty-four years old, was I? I accepted, if reluctantly, and he seemed to relax.

"What's the other thing?"

"I want Steve to stay here with you while I'm gone."

"What?! No! I don't need a babysitter, Nicholas! I don't want Steve following me around all day. It's ridiculous!"

"He's a bodyguard, babe. His job is to follow people around."

That was just insulting. "Why? Why the hell do you want me to have a bodyguard?"

With a stern expression, Nick explained, "First, because it will keep me from going insane while I'm in New York. Second, because you're pregnant and alone, and if anything happened to you, I could never forgive myself."

I shook my head, but I also knew there was nothing I could say to change his mind. "Fine," I said, giving in.

I couldn't decipher the expression on his face.

"Noah, leaving you here is the hardest thing I've ever done in my life."

I didn't want him to go either, but we needed to do this right; we couldn't screw things up again, not with everything that was at stake.

That week, everything seemed to go back to normal. I went to class; I kept hiding my pregnancy. Every day, Nick sent me a bouquet of flowers and had my breakfast delivered. I ended up making friends with the delivery guy. There was always enough food for a horse: coffee, tea, muffins, croissants, pancakes, chocolate donuts, eggs, toast...everything hot and ready to eat.

"You're crazy, you know that, right?" I told him the seventh day after he'd left. We talked every day, twice a day, sometimes more. Anytime he had a free moment, he'd call me, and I did the same during my breaks, or at least tried to. It was almost better just to wait because he obviously had a harder time getting away than I did.

During one call, I had to hold my phone between my shoulder and ear while I filled one of my last empty vases to put the enormous bouquet of blue roses he'd sent me inside.

He was justifying the daily deliveries. "It's a good way to be sure you're eating," he said. I could hear him typing on the other line.

I rolled my eyes. My eating enough wasn't going to be a problem. I was hungry all the time, and not just regular hungry: I was craving weird things, like buttered bread and bananas or spaghetti and peanut butter. Either I was losing my mind or my sense of taste or both... I don't know, but the weirdest things suddenly felt like delicacies to me.

"How were your spicy oranges?" he asked, amused.

"Interesting. I'll make you the recipe one day," I replied, sitting down and kicking my legs up on the table. I sighed wearily and stroked my belly distractedly.

He told me he was wrapping everything up to make the move to LA as soon as he could but that it was taking longer than he'd imagined. He needed to hire someone to replace him, a new set of eyes and ears up there, and he hadn't found anyone he trusted.

I told him how classes were going. Summer break was coming up fast, and we were all focusing on our papers and getting ready for our finals in a couple of weeks. I was due in August, so I'd have at least a few weeks to deal with Mini-Me's arrival before figuring out what to do about work and school.

It made me sad to think I might need to drop out, but after thinking it over, it seemed like the best thing.

"You don't have to, Noah," Nick replied when I told him. "There are tons of women who study and have kids, there are day cares, and I'll be there to help you..."

"I don't want my son being raised by babysitters. I don't want to screw this up. I'm afraid if I stay in school and try to raise our child, I'll end up not doing a good job at either. And you barely have time to call me; you're not going to be able to stay home and take care of a baby."

"*My* baby," he said, and I grinned. "And you're forgetting one small detail: I'm the boss. I can do whatever I want."

"Yeah?" I answered sarcastically. "Then tell me something: Can you be here for my next gyno visit?"

It was silent on the other line.

"I'm not judging you. I get it, you're going to have to work and I'm going to have to take care of the kid... We'll see what I do about school. Maybe I can do online classes..."

I didn't love that idea—I liked going to class—but you can't have everything, and I just couldn't see myself leaving my child with someone else.

"Noah, this is temporary," he said, stopping my head from spinning. "Things are crazy right now, but I'm putting steps in place so I can be there for you one hundred percent."

We hadn't talked about us as a couple, but in all our conversations, we always included the other person in our plans. I liked that, but I was scared that what we were building could fall apart. That was why I didn't press him when he told me he couldn't come back just yet.

What I didn't expect was to see him earlier, on the news at

four. When I heard his name on the TV, I turned the volume up and listened with worry.

"Former employees of Leister Enterprises are picketing in front of the new LRB headquarters and asking for their jobs back."

The reporter was someone I'd seen before on the BBC. Behind her was the entrance to the building where I'd once worked, surrounded by workers carrying signs. The police had cordoned the area off, but no one looked like they were going anywhere.

"Just over a year ago, the son of prominent lawyer William Leister inherited the empire Andrew James Leister had built through many years of struggle, making Leister Enterprises one of the most prosperous and highly regarded companies in the United States. There were many who thought it rash to cede all that responsibility to a young man who had never run a business before."

I turned the volume up, staring indignantly at the screen.

"Leister's first action as CEO was to shut down two large companies his grandfather had begun, letting more than five hundred employees go as a part of an ambitious restructuring plan that would see him opening a new subsidiary. It remains to be seen whether this gamble will prove successful or will be the first major failure in the Leister saga. Today, his former employees have gathered at the doors to LRB demanding their old jobs back..."

This was ridiculous. I knew Nicholas was working just then, but I needed to talk to him. He picked up on the third ring.

"Are you okay?" he said, immediately worried.

"Yeah, I'm great, but I'm guessing you're not... You're on the news... What happened? Were you planning on ever telling me, Nicholas?" I couldn't believe he was having problems and hadn't even bothered mentioning it.

"You don't need to worry about it."

I laughed sourly. "I don't have to worry? They're raking you over the coals!"

"That's what the press does. They take a few rumors and lies and make it a breaking story."

"But...what about the employees you let go and what they're saying about LRB?"

I felt personally wounded. I didn't like hearing bad things about Nick; it was no different than if they were saying the same things about me.

Nick sighed. "I had to let those people go. Both those companies were headed for bankruptcy within the next four years. They were basically unprofitable, and they were being run into the ground. Closing them now meant making enough out of the liquidation to start a new company and hire everyone back. But things like that take time!"

"You don't have to explain yourself to me. I know you didn't do it for fun."

"In this business you have to make tough decisions sometimes. Decisions you might even fucking hate."

"Nicholas, you're a pro. These people have no fucking idea."

He paused for a moment, then said, "Leister Enterprises is making record profits. My idea is to open another branch of LRB in a year. That will allow us to hire back something like seventy percent of the people we let go."

I knew Nicholas would never let people go without having a backup plan. Those people were criticizing him at the very moment when he was working to take care of them.

"So what's going to happen now?" I asked, worried he'd have to stay in New York longer than we'd imagined.

"Nothing. Let my lawyers do their job. I told you, you don't need to worry about this."

"Okay..."

We had more conversations like this one over the next three weeks as things got more and more complicated. It turned out that being separated and talking every day was even harder than it had been to go a year without talking to each other. I needed him with me, and as the baby grew, so did my urge to beg him to come back.

"I need to touch you, Noah," he confessed to me one night. "So much time has passed that I don't remember what it feels like to be inside you."

"Nicholas..."

"I shouldn't have left, I should have been more selfish, I should have selfishly made love to you every goddamned morning in that tiny apartment you're so proud of."

I smiled at that small loss of control and felt the heat provoked by his words spreading through me. "I hope nobody heard you say that."

"I'm at my apartment, in my bed, in the same bed where you drove me crazy taking off all your clothes, remember?"

I closed my eyes. Of course I remembered. Nicholas between my legs, kissing me, licking me, making me his. That hadn't been right. We'd caused each other so much pain then, and yet I wouldn't trade that moment for anything...

"Come back, Nick," I said, provoking a longer-than-comfortable silence.

"What?"

I smiled at the ceiling, nervous, the phone starting to make my ear hot. "Come back to me."

"Are you serious?"

"I want to try. For real. I want you with me every day. I want to kiss you, I want you to hold me, Nicholas. I want you back here, and so does Mini-Me."

He laughed. "I'll catch the first flight I can, and I'll do all the things to you that are passing through your head right now."

I covered my mouth with one hand, as though my instincts told me to hide my joy and embarrassment even when nobody was there. It was true: I had naughty thoughts passing through my head...

"Speaking of Mini-Me...I've been thinking about a name."

"What? For real?" That caught me totally by surprise. He'd already thought of a name? *Mini-Me, I mean Mini-Nick, is going to have a first and last name?*

I touched my belly without thinking.

"Yeah. I'll tell you when I see you. But if you don't like it, we can always pick another. You've probably already got others in mind..."

My cheeks felt hot. The truth was it hadn't even crossed my mind.

We said goodbye and *I love you* and promised we'd see each other again soon. Meeting again would be special, because at last, we were on the same level... I was dying to kiss him, to let him do everything he wanted to me, give me all he wanted to give. I could see the future, and it was so beautiful.

I was finally ready to start from zero.

45

Nick

Work was giving me endless headaches. People who'd been let go were trying to take us to court, there were protests—it was the worst time imaginable for me to just up and leave. I hadn't wanted to tell Noah what was going on because I didn't want her to worry, but I was afraid it would take me longer to get back to Los Angeles than either of us wanted.

It was harder than ever for me to be away from her. I was driving Steve crazy. I called him constantly to find out if Noah was eating, how she looked, if he thought she was healthy… I was obsessed with the thought that something might happen: the press finding out she was pregnant, or that nightmare that woke me up every damned night about Noah losing the baby and dying while giving birth.

Noah was six months pregnant now. She hadn't sent me photos, but Steve told me she was showing. He said she seemed edgy and was scared of how other people would react, especially our parents. When we told them, it was going to be World War III, but I couldn't care less. I was finally happy after a long, long time. I loved that girl more than anything in the world, and I wanted the baby with all my heart.

46

Noah

I NEEDED NICK TO COME BACK. THE BABY WAS GETTING BIGGER and bigger, and there was no more hiding it. I didn't press him because I knew that if he wasn't here yet, it was because he really couldn't travel. I was certain Nick wanted to be with me, maybe even more than I wanted to be with him. Everything was weighing on me. My mother had called me twice asking me to come see her or saying she could drop by and take me out to lunch. I told her I was busy with exams and that I'd go see her when I could. But I knew my voice sounded weird to her.

"You're hiding something, Noah, but it's fine. We'll talk when we see each other," she told me one Wednesday.

Apart from Jenna and Lion, Steve was the only one who knew what was going on. I never told him, but just the way he treated me made it evident. I supposed Nick must have kept him informed.

Three weeks after Nick left, there was a big problem: I opened my closet, and there was almost nothing in it that fit me anymore. I called Nick without thinking about whether he was busy or in a meeting. He picked up on the first ring.

"You need to come back, Nicholas," I said, trying not to cry. "I can't hide it anymore… I'm huge! My clothes don't fit, people are looking at me weirdly… Please come back! We have to figure out what to say to our parents!"

I was having an anxiety attack, the kind I sometimes couldn't avoid.

"Excuse me a second," he said to someone, then to me: "Calm down, now, Freckles."

"I can't calm down!" I shouted. My room was a wreck, my clothes all over the floor. Even my underwear didn't fit right. I looked horrible, and I was so scared Nicholas would see me and think my body had turned gross after just a couple of weeks… "I can't do this, I need to see you, I need you to hug me and tell me everything's going to be okay, I need—"

"I just sent a ticket to your email," he said in a voice as serene as mine was panicked.

"What?"

"I need to see you, too. I can't travel this weekend, so I've sent you a ticket to come see me. I was going to call you tonight and tell you, but since you're freaking out, it's better to surprise you now, right?"

I exhaled in relief and fell back on the sofa.

"I really get to see you this weekend?" I asked, suddenly excited. The last traces of my anxiety vanished like a wave hitting the shore.

"Yes, my love. Do you think you can hold on for two more days without going crazy?"

I grunted. "If you were fat enough to have your own gravitational pull, you'd be in a bad mood, too, smart-ass," I said, trying to sound mad. It clearly didn't work.

At last, I was going to feel his arms around me and his lips against mine.

You hear that, little guy? I thought, rubbing my belly. *We're going to see Daddy!*

Since I couldn't travel to New York with only a baggy Ramones sweatshirt, I gave in and let Jenna take me out to buy maternity clothes.

I hated that word: *maternity*. It sounded so weird and abstract, like something a robot would say.

"Relax," she told me, "we'll find something that will look good on you. You're lucky—you're one of those girls who stays the same except for her belly. If I saw you from behind, I wouldn't even think you were pregnant."

"Great, Jenna. From now on that's what I'll tell people: please just address me from behind."

I was in a pissy mood, but Jenna handled it fine; she even seemed to be amused. Somehow, that only made the stress worse.

For some reason, maternity clothes cost three times as much as normal ones, and that made me freak out again because I could only afford them with Nick's card. I still hadn't used it yet, and it seemed stupid to pull it out just for some stupid rags.

I walked to where the athletic gear was and bought a couple of pairs of leggings and three hoodies. Meanwhile, Jenna was busy mixing and matching shirts and pants until she found three combos that worked, plus a close-fitting gray dress.

"What the hell is that?" I asked, horrified. "The idea is to hide it, not show it to the whole world."

Scowling, Jenna said, "Stop hiding my godson, okay!"

For some reason I couldn't quite pin down, her words bothered me. I felt the baby kicking. I knew when he was asleep now and when he was awake. I could also tell if I'd had sugar because his little legs would start dancing around, as if he loved it... I hated not having Nick there to feel those first few kicks; it had been amazing, and that was another reason I needed him back. He was missing so much.

No, I didn't want to hide it…at least, not anymore.

On Friday, I caught my flight from LA to New York. Nick had gotten me a first-class ticket. I had no idea how thankful I'd be. If I had to puke, it was better to do it in a bathroom only a few passengers had access to. Because I didn't have morning sickness anymore: I had morning, noon, and night sickness. Add that to the list of surprises a high-risk pregnancy had in store for me. Steve sat beside me on the way. A man of few words, he spent the whole time reading a biography of Pablo Escobar. I didn't comment on it, but it did make me chuckle.

It took five and a half hours to get to New York, and I slept almost the entire time. We got in around nine p.m. I'd listened to Jenna and dressed better than usual, in the dress she'd picked out, plus a black coat and my favorite Adidas. I was comfortable, and my belly was sticking out for all the world to see, like, *Here I am!*

People looked at me differently. There's a strange energy that surrounds you when you're pregnant; people are at once excited, nervous, and admiring. This was my first time strolling around like a real, live pregnant person, and honestly, I enjoyed it.

Nick would be waiting for me at the airport, and we would go straight to his apartment for dinner.

I was so nervous, so excited to see him… We had told each other so much since he left, including all the things I'd been too scared to say in person, and I was dying to feel myself a part of him, a part of his life, again.

I hadn't checked a bag, so as soon as we got off the plane, we went straight to arrivals. Steve carried my little suitcase. I could have done it myself, but he'd insisted, and finally I'd given in. I kept walking faster and faster... I wanted to see Nick, wanted to just get there, wanted to feel whole again.

It seemed to take forever. Then, at last, we walked through the doors, and I saw him: there he was, a bouquet of red roses in hand, waiting for me. He was wearing jeans and a sea-blue V-neck sweater. It wasn't just the roses that made him easy to pick out: it was his mussed hair and his blue eyes shining like two lamps on a beautiful summer's evening.

We smiled as if someone had just injected liquid happiness into our veins. My heart swelled until I thought it wouldn't fit in my chest anymore.

And then...as if in a horror movie...it happened.

I don't know if you've ever had a traumatic experience yourself, something that marks you forever. Something that happens in slow motion right before your eyes with your brain registering all those tiny details you'd pay to forget.

I saw everything...and I still remember every godforsaken detail of the fifteen seconds that passed, fifteen seconds when I was certain I would die.

I remember the scream getting caught in my throat. I remember my legs were paralyzed, and I couldn't even take off running.

The first shot exploded and burst the bubble of our happiness. I stopped. Nick fell to the ground. The bullet had struck him in the back.

I can still see the look of surprise on his face as he looked down and saw the blood spreading on his clothes and pooling at his feet. There was pain on his face, and I thought my heart would give out.

Then it all happened quickly. Someone hit me from behind, and I fell. For a moment, the airport racket, the people walking past, all that seemed to stop, leaving a void in which the sound of that pistol reverberated—but then it started again.

"Don't move, Noah!" Steve shouted, waking me from my lethargy, my state of shock.

I saw four police officers tackle a man as people ran back and forth, horrified. My eyes were glued to the man I loved, who was on the floor like me, his eyes open, life draining out of him.

"Nicholas!"

47

Nick

I GUESS IT'S TRUE WHAT THEY SAY ABOUT YOUR LIFE FLASHING before your eyes when you're about to die. Or not really. Because I only saw one thing: Noah.

I didn't need to think, that was just how it was—*Noah is my life*. The images that flashed before my eyes weren't the best moments of *my* life; they were the best moments of *our* life, and not the life we had shared up to then, no. I didn't see those moments, with their ups and downs, or the breakup, or the cheating. I saw something else: I saw my life with her to come.

I saw us walking on the beach, celebrating our son's birthday; I saw her, beautiful and radiant, waiting for me in bed every night to cover me with kisses and caresses. I saw her getting pregnant again, but this time we were ready—there were no surprises, no fears, no insecurities. I saw her with me in the kitchen, arguing but then stopping so we could kiss each other all over, right there, leaning against the countertop. I saw her crying, laughing, suffering, growing. I saw her life before my eyes, her life with me…and I loved it.

Then I asked myself, *Why am I seeing this? Why do I feel like*

I'm being permitted to see something I'll never have? I felt a hole in my chest, an emptiness consuming me...

No.

No fucking way.

It wasn't my time. Not yet.

48

Noah

I DON'T KNOW HOW TO DESCRIBE THE MOMENTS AFTER THE SHOTS were fired, but I can easily say they were the worst ones of my life. They're blurry in my mind, but at the same time as clear as if they were projected in HD.

From what I heard later, the ambulance didn't take long to arrive. But to me it seemed like hours, days, while I was keeping pressure on a wound in Nick's ribs. Steve was doing the same where a bullet had struck his arm. There was a pool of blood around him. I kept thinking about how fast the body makes blood and whether it could do so fast enough to replace all the blood he was losing.

I didn't faint. I think God helped me hold it together, at least until the paramedics arrived to deal with the situation. I stood there staring at the ambulance after its arrival, my hands hanging at my sides, my mind blank. I didn't even have the wherewithal to ask them if I could go along. Nick left on his own, on the verge of death, and all I could do was watch.

I remember that when I could no longer hear the ambulance, I looked down, saw the bloodstains on my hands, and buckled. I sobbed until I could hardly breathe, hiccupped, felt a pair of hands grab me as I started to plunge to the floor.

"Take a deep breath, Noah, please," Steve said, holding me up. He carried me away from all the horrified onlookers who were examining the scene as if it were something out of a terrible episode of *CSI*.

We grabbed a taxi and took off for the hospital. The more time passed, the worse I felt.

"Why did he go alone? How come you didn't go with him? How come we both didn't?"

"They wouldn't let us, Noah," Steve said, pulling his phone out and writing rapid-fire messages.

The nearest hospital from the airport was just a few miles away, but it took forever to get out of the airport. We managed to make it in twenty minutes, and when we arrived, I took off running. All I could think about was finding someone who could tell me Nicholas was okay. I wanted to see him, I needed to see him, I was dying inside remembering him lying there bleeding; it was all too much for me. But with each step, I started seeing more and more black spots, and eventually Steve took my hand and sat me down. Someone brought me water.

A doctor came a few moments later and took my pulse.

"Miss, I'd like you to calm down," she said, looking at her watch. "Ross, call emergency and check on that guy."

I looked at this Ross imploringly.

I heard him talking to someone about Nick, and a horrible pain clawed at my stomach. "What's happening?"

The doctor turned to me, worried. "You're having contractions. You need to calm down; the stress is making it worse."

Before I could say anything, Ross came back over.

"Nicholas Leister is in surgery. He has two bullet wounds. He's in critical but stable condition. They're going to operate on his lung and his left arm."

"Oh my God!" I shouted, covering my mouth. "What are they going to do to him? What does *critical but stable* mean? Call back and get more details!"

The doctor looked up to ask me if Nick and I were married.

"What? No. What does it matter?"

Ross answered for her: "We can't give you any more information then, Miss Morgan. Only immediate family can—"

"He's the father of my son!" I shouted desperately.

It didn't matter; they wouldn't tell me anything else. Steve called William and my mother, and they told him they were headed straight to the airport to catch the first flight out.

I had to stay where I was, without news, able to do nothing but pray.

An hour later—the longest hour of my life—the contractions went away, and everything in my body seemed to go back to normal.

My mother called me. She and William were both hysterical. Nick's father had talked to one of the doctors. I found out thanks to them that Nick had a collapsed lung and major soft tissue damage in his left arm. His condition was dicey, and he'd needed transfusions to avoid going into shock.

I listened to what they had to say, hung up, and sat there motionless.

Nick wouldn't die… He couldn't. We had a life to live together; we needed to finish what we'd started. After all we'd gotten through together, he couldn't just leave me like that.

The event was soon all over the news. Steve tried to turn off the TV, but I told him to leave it. The would-be assassin's name was Dawson J. Lincoln, he was forty-five years old, and he was a former employee of Leister Enterprises. He'd lost his job, hadn't found another one, and had decided to take his frustrations out on his former boss.

"Nicholas Leister is undergoing emergency surgery for two gunshot wounds. His attacker is in custody in New York. Initial reports indicate the attack was premeditated, as the aggressor knew the exact time and place he could find Leister before making an attempt on his life. In recent months, the young lawyer and heir to one of the most renowned firms in the country had received severe criticism in the press for laying off hundreds of workers in the past year. The two companies he closed were on the verge of bankruptcy..."

I stopped listening when they started covering the attacker. Once again, they were making Nicholas look like trash. Well, I wasn't going to listen. Someone had tried to kill him! Nick! I rubbed my face. I needed him to be okay. I needed to talk to the doctor.

I remained in the waiting room for three hours, only getting up for water or to go to the bathroom. I hated that place; there were people crying all around, waiting, like us, to hear something about their loved ones. The stink of hospitals had always made me sick, and now it was worse than ever.

The only thing noteworthy about those three hours was the appearance of two men, tall and strong like Steve. They conferred with Steve for a few minutes, looking stern as they stood by the door to the waiting room. I didn't pay them much attention, but when two surgeons passed by them and came over to me, I shot out of my chair.

"Are you a family member of Nicholas Leister?" one of them asked.

"I'm his girlfriend," I said, controlling the quivers in my voice as best I could.

The second surgeon, the one with the short curly hair, decided to speak, apparently not caring about hospital regulations. "He's stable. I can tell you that much. The next few hours are critical. He lost a lot of blood, and there was significant internal damage where the bullet pierced his lung."

I nodded, biting my lip and trying to hold it together. "Will he be okay?" I asked.

"He's young and strong, and we'll be keeping a close eye on him."

That wasn't an answer.

"Can I see him?" I pleaded.

They both shook their heads regretfully.

"Only close family members. I'm sorry."

Steve put an arm around my shoulders. "He's going to get better, Noah," he whispered as I held on to his shirt, unable to keep myself from crying any longer.

My phone rang. I wiped away my tears and picked up. It was my mother. One of William's friends had lent them his private jet. They'd be in New York in about five hours. I felt so relieved to know my family would soon be with me, and William would move mountains to make sure Nick was okay. But then it occurred to me... If they came, if they saw me...

It was time to spill everything...and, just as I'd feared, I would have to do it on my own.

Since I refused to leave the hospital, Steve had someone bring me my suitcase and something to eat. I wasn't hungry, but I forced down a bowl of soup to keep from having to listen to him. Then I went to the bathroom and changed clothes, picking the baggiest outfit possible to spare my mother a heart attack as soon as she saw me. Of course, I was going to tell her, but I needed to wait till the time was right. I didn't want to distract anyone from the thing that was really important just then: Nick.

So, six hours later, six hours of trying and failing to sleep while my neck, stomach, and back ached as if I'd been beaten, I saw my mother and William walk through the doors of the waiting room.

I ran into my mother's arms. I needed her more than I had ever needed her before. She pulled me in close and stroked my hair with her long fingers. As far as I could tell, she didn't notice my belly. She must have been too afraid to pay attention to anything but what was most urgent.

I told them what had happened, and Will went to see the doctors. They wouldn't let him through, but they did tell him there would be visiting hours in the morning. Nick's condition hadn't changed. Stable—not better, not worse—but the doctors seemed to think that was reason for hope.

We didn't have much time to talk before two cops came in and took a statement from me and Steve. I told them everything I'd seen. Reciting it made the terror return. I would never forget the echo of those two shots. Never.

When visiting hours came, they would only let one person go in, and we decided it should be Will. It was hard to resist the urge to kick down the doors to the ICU and race in, shouting about the injustice of being kept away from him, but I stuffed all that down. I needed to be calm if I wanted to make it through all this, calm if I didn't want my baby to get hurt... My baby...

I looked at my mother, who was sitting next to me, worried, her fingers interlaced with mine.

My mother... We'd been through tough times; things between us had gotten too mixed up. What had happened to how close we'd been in Canada? When had I stopped trusting her, stopped telling her things?

I took a deep breath and turned to her.

"Mom," I said, swallowing, "there's something I need to tell you..."

My mother looked at me with simultaneous worry and indulgence. "I know what you're going to tell me, Noah," she said, squeezing my fingers. "And I think it's good, honey. It's good that you're back with Nicholas. I'm even happy about it, okay?"

Her words surprised me. I was also relieved to see she had no idea about the pregnancy.

"I should never have opposed your relationship... Seeing you two apart, seeing what a wreck you've both been this last year, has been killing me inside. If Nick's the one who makes you happy, I'm not going to get in the middle of it. That's all I want, Noah, to see you happy."

I nodded in silence with moist eyes and tried to come up with the words to confess to her I was six months pregnant. Pregnant by a boy she had never wanted for me until just then—a boy who was her stepson.

How did I tell her? How do you tell a mother that in three months she's going to be a grandmother? I could feel Steve's stare on me, and he seemed to be telling me to be brave and spit it out.

Shit...

"Mom," I said, taking advantage of Will's absence, "I need to tell you something else. Something no one planned for, but that just happened..."

I mean...it didn't *just* happen, but I wasn't about to go into details.

My mother looked at me with worry. She didn't seem to know where I was going. My mouth seemed to freeze, and I put her hand on my belly. Her eyes opened like saucers, and she pulled her hand away, scared.

"Noah...no. Tell me you're not..."

It was time for the truth.

"Pregnant?" I finished the phrase for her in a near whisper.

She shook her head, then looked me over, her eyes finally resting on my belly, well hidden in a gigantic sweatshirt.

"How far…?"

I cleared my throat and swallowed. "Six months. But I only found out two and a half months ago… I didn't want to hide it from you, Mom, but I was shocked, just like you. I needed time to admit it to myself, time to tell Nick, time to think about what I was going to do with my life…"

"Nicholas knows?"

The tone was a new one, one I'd never heard her use before, the tone, I guess, all mothers use when their daughters waylay them with such an unexpected secret.

"Yeah, he knows."

Mom shook her head. Scared as I had been to tell her, I felt ready to deal with her reaction. Nicholas was fighting for his life, and the baby was the only thing keeping me from falling apart. It was all I had of him right now, a part of him, a part of us, and for now and forevermore, that baby would be the most important thing for both of us, our port in the storm, our unbreakable connection.

I took my mother's hand and placed it on my belly again.

Her eyes filled with tears, but I knew her well enough to know everything that was passing through her head: how young I was, how hard it would all be, how many times she'd told me it was better to wait, prepare myself, grow, get an education…

But life was like that sometimes, unpredictable. You couldn't control what came, what would be there when you rounded the corner. You couldn't know whether you were on the right path. Fate had brought me here, and all I could do was give it my best… And my mother would have to do the same.

"It's a boy," I finally said.

The image of the baby in my arms appeared in my head, with

his chubby little cheeks and his precious eyes… My baby, who might not even meet his father.

My mother shook her head, unable to believe it.

"If Nick doesn't make it through this, I don't know what I'm going to do," I confessed, deathly afraid. My mother hugged me; we cried, we cried for ages, I don't know for how long, and we talked, and the things we said were beautiful. She did chew me out for being irresponsible and for not telling her sooner. Then, eventually, William came, and we told him. The shock almost killed him. Never before had I seen him so worried, so scared, so utterly helpless.

Everyone loves their children in a different way, and for Will, Nick would always be a little black-haired boy with blue eyes stuffing frogs into his pockets.

Nick had to get better…not just for me and the baby, but for all of us. No one would get over it if he left us. No one.

49

Noah

Thank God, Nick responded to treatment, and two days later, he was out of the ICU. They relaxed about the visits, and I was finally able to see him. He was sedated and had bandages all over his torso. His left arm was in a cast and immobilized. He had a shadow of stubble on his face, which gave him a disheveled look I'd never seen before.

I was able to go in alone. It was for the best because seeing him lying there so weak and fragile broke my heart. I felt the deepest hate for the man who had done this to Nick. I ran a hand through his dark hair, hoping to get a response. But the response didn't come.

I didn't cry, though; I don't know why. I just stayed there looking, memorizing his traits, wanting to hug him and knowing I couldn't because it would hurt.

Now I would be the one to hug him too tightly…it was ironic how things changed.

I sat next to him and took his hand.

"Nick…" I said with a knot in my throat. "I need you to get better, okay? I had so much to tell you already, and now…"

I bit my lip and tried to see if he reacted somehow, if a miracle would happen the way it always did in the movies. His eyes remained closed, and I kept talking; I didn't want to go crazy in that funereal silence interrupted only by the beeping of machines.

"Our parents know about Mini-Me... My mother nearly freaked, but I guess you lying here helped her decide not to kill me for getting pregnant."

I told him about his father's reaction, about how the phone wouldn't stop ringing with people asking how Nick was. I told him the police had caught the guy who did it and said he could relax because Steve had brought in two security guards to make sure nothing like that would happen again. I talked about myself, about how surprised he'd be when he opened his eyes and saw me, about our baby and how he was kicking like a soccer player... It didn't matter how much I said, Nick just stayed there with his eyes closed while I faded and faded into a shadow of what I once was, so far gone that I wondered if anyone would even recognize me.

"Noah, honey, you need to rest," my mother warned me, patting me on the head. I was lying in a loveseat in Nick's room and had my head in her lap. "Everyone's left the hospital to shower and get some rest. You need to sleep in a bed, honey; this isn't good for you or the baby."

"I don't want to leave him alone," I said, looking over at him.

The doctors were afraid the loss of blood and oxygen after the shooting might have caused neurological damage. Everything was in limbo, and all we could do was wait.

Wake up, please, I need to see those blue eyes, I need to hear your voice again.

"He won't be alone, Noah: Will and I won't leave his side. Lion said he'd be back in half an hour, and Jenna said she'd take you to Nick's place and stay with you. Please, just go rest for a few hours..."

Lion and Jenna had come as soon as they could and hadn't left our side except to get some sleep themselves.

My mother was right, I was exhausted; I'd barely slept in four days. I was terrified of closing my eyes, then waking up and finding out Nick was no longer there.

"What if he wakes up and I'm not here...?"

"Noah, if he opens his eyes, you'll be the first person I call. Please. If Nick could talk right now, he'd be furious to know what terrible care you're taking of yourself..."

I finally agreed, despite myself. I gave Nick a kiss on the cheek to say goodbye and left his room, looking for Jenna.

Steve drove us both to the apartment. I hadn't been there since right after Jenna's wedding. Walking back in, I couldn't forget what we'd done there, the things we'd said... Those walls didn't house good memories, and I struggled to remember the days when Nick and I couldn't keep our hands off each other and Nick gave me everything I needed and more. I didn't want to be there anymore. Let alone without him.

"Take a shower, and I'll make us some dinner," Jenna said with an unconvincing smile.

Nick was like a big brother to her. I'd seen her crying and hugging Lion when they got to the hospital, and I knew they were doing no better than I was. I nodded and went upstairs. In the bathroom, I stripped naked slowly. My eyes were focused on the mirror in front of me. It was obvious I was pregnant. I got in the shower, washed my hair, brushed my teeth. When I got out, I put on black leggings and grabbed one of Nick's sweaters from the closet. It smelled like him. That calmed me down, gave me hope.

Jenna and I had dinner in silence on the sofa, with the TV on in the background. I wasn't really hungry, but I forced myself to eat everything on my plate. Then I went to Nick's room, hugged the pillow, smelled his traces there, and closed my eyes, trying to sleep.

A few hours later, Jenna woke me up with a smile. "Noah, he's awake!"

I jumped out of bed so fast, I almost fell.

Oh my God! Oh my God! Nick's awake!

50

Nick

I didn't even realize I was opening my eyes. I'd been in the dark, in a deep night full of muffled sounds and random words that I struggled to put in order and comprehend. Then, all at once, I could see the hospital. It was bright, and the machines were beeping; I'd heard them for days, I realized, along with the soft voice of a girl whose words had soothed me like a lullaby urging me to sleep.

I opened my eyes. I needed that voice. But instead, I found something totally different.

"Oh my God, Nick!" Sophia shouted next to me.

I groaned in pain. My head felt like it was about to explode.

"I'll call a doctor," she said and ran out.

I blinked, trying to get used to the light and the blue of the evening sky outside. The room was small, with only enough space for my bed, a two-seater sofa, and a TV. I tried to get up, but my arm throbbed, and I realized moving around was a bad idea.

Sophia reappeared with the doctor. I let him examine me and give me some information about my condition, but while I listened, all I could manage to do was formulate one question, a question that made me tense, nervous, upset...

"Where's Noah?" I asked, trying to get up and instantly regretting it. An unbearable pain shot through my ribs, as though I were being burned alive from the inside.

Fuck.

Sophia helped me lie back over the pillows.

What was Sophia doing there?

"Noah's at your apartment, resting, I think."

I took a deep breath and tried to calm my nerves. Looking down, I saw the bandages on my ribs and my arm immobilized against my chest, making it impossible to move.

Son of a bitch, I thought, wondering who had done this to me. "Where's Steve? I need to get up, I need—"

"You can't, Nicholas," Sophia said, and this time, I looked closer at her and saw her eyes were red and swollen. Her hair was pulled back on her head, and she was wearing jeans and a plain white shirt. "You need to rest. Please, stay still."

I lay back, trying to remain calm. If Noah was resting, that meant she was okay, right? Steve had to be with her...

I looked back at the girl who was gazing at me with a mixture of relief, joy, and longing. I remembered when I'd told her we were done. Of all the girls I'd been with, Sophia was the only one I really never wanted to hurt. In her own way, she had helped me that past year. What we had shared was far more than a friendship, and yet, in the end, that was all we could be: friends.

No one and nothing could do to my body and soul the things Noah was capable of with a single glance, and Sophia had always known that.

"What are you doing here, Soph?" I asked.

She shrugged and wiped a tear from her left cheek.

"I needed to see you and be sure you were okay. When I heard on the news what happened..." She grabbed my hand, carefully.

"You know how you can tell the relationship you had with someone wasn't even a relationship?"

I didn't react as I observed her.

"When no one from their family even picks up the phone to tell you something's happened to them."

"Sophia, you and I..."

"I know. We broke up a month ago. I didn't forget. I just thought..."

I needed to end it with Sophia, for real. In her eyes I saw a glimmer of hope. It was time to be direct with her. Sophia had hoped Noah's mistake meant I could never really take her back, but that was over, we had passed that point, we'd moved ahead, matured...

"Sophia, Noah's going to have my child," I told her as tactfully as I could.

I felt her hand go cold, and instantly, she let me go. She seemed to need a couple of seconds to assimilate my words, seconds to let any glimmer of hope she had disappear. "Is that why you got back with her?"

"I got back with her because I love her," I said calmly. Not only did I love her, I loved her more than anyone else. But I didn't say that because I didn't want to hurt Sophia.

She nodded and looked lost, as if that were the last thing in the world she'd expected to hear. "You know, for a moment, I thought...that you'd opened your eyes because you heard my voice. I thought I saw..."

I'd opened my eyes because the very voice I needed to hear was the one that wasn't there. I'd opened them because I was desperate to find Noah. "I never wanted to hurt you, Sophia. This past year with you... You were the flame that lit up my nights."

Sophia nodded and took a breath, and from her face, I could tell my message was clear. Sophia wasn't a little girl you had to explain everything to step by step; she was a grown woman, the only woman I might ever have fallen in love with if Noah hadn't come into my life and made everything else pale in comparison.

I was relaxed as she bent over and gave me a subdued kiss on the corner of the lips.

"I'm happy you're okay."

I nodded and watched her gather her things and leave the room. Another door had closed, but it was one too small for me to ever fit through, and just then, I saw the open portal of the life I was ready to start with Noah awaiting me.

51

Noah

DOZENS OF JOURNALISTS WERE GATHERED OUTSIDE THE HOSPITAL, and Steve refused to let me get out where they could see me. No one had any idea what information the press had about me, but exposing myself to them in my current state was the last thing any of us wanted to do just then.

Steve called the director of the hospital to get him to let us in through the back door, which was reserved for ambulances. When I finally reached Nick's room, an hour had passed since he supposedly woke up.

I entered with my heart in my throat, and when I saw him open his eyes for me, smiling at me from the bed, wounded but with happiness in his sky-blue eyes, only then did I feel I could finally breathe.

"Where'd you run off to, Freckles?" he asked, opening the one arm he could move, and I wanted to get under it, squeeze him tight, and never let him go.

And that's pretty much what I did.

I buried my face in his neck and let him hold me as much as he could. When I felt him pulling back, I climbed up into the bed and stayed there silently, listening to the beating of his heart.

I couldn't speak: the words were caught in my throat.

Nick didn't say anything either. We knew the terror we'd both felt. I had learned firsthand what it would mean to lose him, to really lose him, while he had lost his mobility, his strength, and very nearly his life.

I was scared to open my mouth, scared to put into words what could have happened.

They didn't give me much time with him, and strange as it sounds, I felt better when I left. The pressure in my chest when I saw him vanished. I knew it was crazy, I knew Nick was suffering more than I was, more than anyone, however much he tried to pretend he was able to deal with the pain like it was nothing.

The next three days, I spent as little time with him as I could. I kept finding excuses to be busy. I started organizing his return to LA on the same private plane that had brought our parents out there. I found a nurse who could travel with us once the doctors said Nick would be discharged soon, and I cleaned his apartment so it would be ready for him to sell or go back to.

I would go in to see him when I knew he was asleep, and when he opened his eyes and pulled me into him without saying anything, I knew he was doing it for me. He didn't understand, but since this was what I needed, he gave it to me without asking questions.

I... Once again, I became that girl whose head operated contrary to everyone else in the world. It was well known that traumatic experiences threw me into a mental fog it was difficult to emerge from, but why the hell couldn't I just let it go? Just be myself, the person Nick needed in those moments?

But I just wasn't, and Nick didn't complain. We didn't even talk about the baby. The subject only came up once.

"Steve told me you had contractions on the day of the accident..." he said on one of the few occasions when I got close enough to let him kiss me on the neck while his hand caressed my belly tenderly. I got a knot in my throat.

I didn't respond because I couldn't stop thinking about that word, *accident*. It hadn't just been an *accident*, had it? The idea of this being an *accident* made it sound like an act of fate, a bad throw of the dice that had led to an outcome nobody wanted. Why would he say this had been an *accident* when the truth was that someone had tried to kill him?

"Noah, where are you?" he whispered in my ear. "Come back from wherever you've gone off to, because I'm dying to see you."

I didn't understand his question, and I was happy when the nurses interrupted us and told me I needed to leave.

I didn't want to be with him, I couldn't do it, and I didn't understand why. As soon as I walked into that room, I wanted to break down. I felt cornered, trapped, and that feeling only went away when I left.

I had everything perfectly organized on the day we flew out. Our parents were already back in LA, and Nick was getting better, too. He'd have to see a physiotherapist who could help him recover the movement in his wounded arm. They'd said it would be a long process, but he should be thankful even to be alive. Not everyone in similar situations was so lucky.

I'd never been on a private plane. Nor was I really excited to do so. Flying in general was unpleasant for me. Doing it on a tiny plane made matters worse.

They rolled Nick on in a wheelchair and settled him into the beige leather seat in front of me and next to a huge window of a kind I'd never seen on a regular plane. The only passenger besides us was Judith, the nurse.

During the flight, Nick seemed less energetic than usual. The stress of traveling and getting discharged from the hospital had probably worn him out.

He fell asleep, and I was glad because it meant I didn't have to talk to him or explain whatever the hell was going on with me, but when I went to the restroom, I found him with his eyes open, staring at me on my return.

I stopped, realizing Judith was gone.

"I told her she could go sleep for a few hours in the cabin in the back," Nick said, knowing what was going through my head.

He was finally clean-shaven again, his hair was washed, his old hairstyle back. He was wearing a dark T-shirt and faded jeans. He had bags under his eyes, and each of his handsome features reflected tiredness.

This trip could have been so different... We could have been taking off with a coffin instead of Nick, organizing a funeral instead of a move...

I bit my lip until it hurt.

"Noah, come here," Nick asked, holding out a hand with a look of combined worry, uncertainty, and anguish.

"I almost lost you, Nick."

"I know...but I'm here, Noah," he said, leaning forward, wanting to reach me, but unable to stand.

I started crying where I stood. I'd been holding back the tears for two weeks now, trying to be strong for him, for me, for the baby...but I wasn't strong anymore; I was the very opposite: weak, or something worse than weak...

"Noah..." Grief stifled his voice, and he reached toward me while I cried, feeling paralyzed.

"You can't die," I said, wiping away my tears clumsily. "Do you hear me?!" I was suddenly furious with myself, with the world... What was happening?

Nick took a breath and nodded. But I still had more to say.

"You promised me you wouldn't leave my side, you swore that nothing would separate us! And you almost left me again!"

Nick didn't respond. But his eyes were moist now.

"We were going to fix things! We were going to raise this child together!" The sobs began choking me.

"Noah..."

"What would I have done if you'd died, Nicholas?!" I shrieked, disconsolate. I covered my face with my hands. I couldn't take it...

I imagined getting up in the morning knowing Nicholas wasn't there...not being able to kiss him, hug him, feel his skin against mine, get lost in his eyes—not knowing ever again what it was to feel safe... I opened my eyes a moment later, wiping the tears from my face and looking up at him.

A tear rolled down his cheek, and I felt as if I were having a spasm, an electric shock that passed through my whole body. I came close to him and let him wrap his arms around me. I sat on his lap, but carefully, and cried and cried, not knowing if or when or how I would ever stop.

"I've never been so scared in my life," I confessed as my tears left dark blotches on his T-shirt, and I trembled all over.

"I know," he said, stroking my hair and squeezing me. "I know because I was just as scared as you were... But I'm not going anywhere, Noah. I'm staying right here..."

I let him go on talking and inhaled the scent of him, his heat, his nearness, the sound of his heart beating hard against mine.

"I'm sorry for telling you to go... If I hadn't done that, this never would have happened; it was all my fault, Nick. Once again, I almost lost you and it was my fault..."

"You're not to blame for anything, okay?" he said, almost angry.

"If I'd just known how to accept what you wanted to give me...if I hadn't been so scared of us getting back together..."

"Noah... Stop it, okay?" he said and gave me a kiss meant to replace my terror with desire. He kissed me the way only he knew how, the way I had been longing for him to do ever since he'd left for New York... That was the kiss I'd wanted when we broke up, when he'd told me he could never love me again...

"I love you, Nick," I said, pulling away to catch my breath. His eyes traveled over my face, trying to memorize my every feature. I put a hand on his smooth cheek and stroked it. I never wanted to be apart from him again.

He kissed every inch of my face, lifted my shirt, put his hand on my belly. "Nothing will ever separate us again, Noah, I swear that on our child."

I hugged him again. I didn't want to move, didn't want to feel any distance from him. And I remained like that until, eventually, we fell asleep.

I don't know how long it was until I opened my eyes again, but it must not have been long, because we were still in the air. Outside, it was night, and it was completely dark apart from the faint lights lining the cabin.

Nick was awake and looking at me, toying with a few strands of my hair.

"I don't think I ever told you how much I like your freckles," he said, tracing out circles with his long fingers on my cheek, my ear, and my neck.

"You have," I said, looking him in the eye.

"I've given you that impression, maybe, but I don't think I ever put it in words. I know where each and every one of them is, and I know when new ones have appeared... They drive me crazy."

I smiled. He was so intense when he talked. I had always hated my freckles before I met him.

"You think our baby will have freckles like yours?" he asked, amused.

"I don't think babies have freckles, Nick," I replied with a smile.

Now he rubbed my belly. "You're so much bigger than the last time I saw you," he said, his thumb rubbing the edge of my belly button, making me shiver.

"That's a very subtle way of telling me I'm fat," I said, frowning.

"You're perfect. I've never seen you looking more beautiful, my love."

I felt a sudden vertigo and got lost in his blue eyes.

But then I remembered something.

"You told me you were thinking of a name…" I was curious to know what it was.

"I was…" he said. I think he was actually nervous!

"I promise not to laugh at you if it's terrible."

"I'd like to call him *Andrew*." He was excited but tense, awaiting my reaction.

"Andrew? After your grandfather?"

Hearing my reaction seemed to relax him somewhat.

"Yeah. After my grandfather. He was a person I could always count on. He loved me, and he gave me the most important opportunity in my life. He trusted me blindly, he left me everything he had, and if he were alive, there's nothing that could make him happier."

"Andrew Leister," I said. "I like it."

Nick kissed my lips and smiled meekly. He was happy.

"Andrew Morgan Leister," he corrected me. "He deserves to have his other grandfather's name, too, right?"

The memory of my father came into my mind, and my eyes filled with tears. Nick had never understood exactly how I felt about him or how, despite all that had happened, I could still love him. I didn't understand it either, but that's how it was. You can't control or manage how you feel sometimes. I loved my father despite everything he'd done, and the little girl inside me was still sad he was gone.

"We don't have to," I replied.

Nick kissed me on the neck. "He was your father. Without him, you wouldn't be here, in front of me, with my first child inside you. We do need to do it."

"I'd have figured you'd prefer *Nicholas*," I said.

"There's only room for one Nick in your life, Noah, and that's me."

I laughed at his possessiveness. Nick was just like that, but it was also true: there would only ever be one Nick in my life.

"Andrew," I said, looking at my belly. Just then, I felt a powerful kick, then another, and it was almost as if I'd received a seal of approval.

"Give me your hand!" I shouted. The baby seemed to have caught my enthusiasm. He kicked a third time, right as Nick placed his hand where mine had been.

"Can you feel it?" I asked, happy that he finally had the chance to experience the thing I'd first noticed weeks before. He nodded, looking enchanted.

"Fuck..." he said when another one came, even more powerful. It was one of the most beautiful things I'd ever felt, my baby alive and kicking, literally.

Nick looked into my eyes. "Thank you, Noah... Thanks for this."

There was nothing more to say. I let him hold me while an amazing sensation suffused me: the sensation of happiness.

52

Nick

I WAS FUCKED. I WAS SO ANGRY ABOUT WHAT HAD HAPPENED TO me that I struggled to keep it in and put on a good face in front of Noah. I didn't want her to worry, I didn't even want her to think about it, but my mind was on it twenty-four hours a day.

Someone had tried to kill me.

I was obsessed with the idea that it could happen again, but that this time, instead of targeting me, they'd go for that beautiful woman who kept coming and going as though nothing had happened. Noah was back to her old routine, going to class, working, and coming to see me after. We still weren't living together, and it was driving me insane.

Steve took her to school and picked her up, and he kept tabs on her so nothing would happen, but if I'd had my choice, she'd have stayed with me, and I'd never have let her out of my sight. I could hardly get out of bed, my recovery was slow, and the only reason I ever left the apartment was to go to the hospital. The nurse Noah had hired helped me out around the house, but I hated feeling like an invalid. I needed to be with Noah and know she was always okay.

It was torture whenever she came to see me. With a smile on her face, she'd tell me how her day had gone, filling the room with joy and making me yearn to grab her, strip off her clothes, and possess her again.

We hadn't made love since Andrew was conceived. Six months without feeling her the way I loved most, six months without sinking inside her and making her moan. Worst of all, though my body was destroyed, in my mind, I was still capable of climbing Everest.

One or two days after moving back to Los Angeles, she showed up in a tight gray dress that left nothing to the imagination. It clung to her belly, too, which was getting rounder and prettier. Her hair was down, her eyes gleaming more than ever.

It was warm out now, and her skin was again taking on that brown tone that looked so good on her. I could feel myself getting hard, and I had to control myself not to say to hell with the doctor's orders and make love to her on the spot, going deep inside her and reminding us both of all we were missing.

"Nick, are you listening to me?"

I silenced my lusty thoughts and paid attention to her as she rolled her eyes. "Sorry, what were you asking me?"

"I didn't ask you anything; I was telling you that I'll be finished with classes soon and you're getting better, and I'd like us to go shopping for things for the baby. We don't even know what we're missing or how much space a baby needs. I've been thinking we could move my bed against the wall, and that would make more room for the baby and the changing table..."

Diapers...and to think I was imagining tearing her clothes off and bringing her to orgasm.

"You're including me in this equation?" I asked incredulously. Did she really think I was going to live with our newborn baby in that loft?

"Of course..." she responded, blushing for some reason I couldn't quite grasp. "I know we haven't talked about it again, but...you are going to live with me, right?"

Was she asking me?

I couldn't help but laugh.

"I doubt there are many forces in the world that could keep me from getting in bed with you every night, Freckles. Of course, I'm going to live with you, but sorry, it's not going to be in this so-called apartment." I wasn't about to give ground there.

"But—"

"No buts, Noah," I cut her off, pulling her close and giving her a peck on the lips. "I'm not going to raise our child in a matchbox."

She blinked at me, startled by my response.

"We'll figure something out," I said.

I started feeling better as the days passed, and after a month, I was able to go back to work. Noah was in her last trimester, and there was no more hiding it. Standing in the kitchen, taking sips from a cup of coffee, I heard it the first time we hit the news.

I cursed between clenched teeth as I saw a photo of Noah walking down the street, her belly sticking out, making it impossible to say the story wasn't true.

For the first two weeks after I was shot, the news had spent at least ten minutes a day talking about me, Leister Enterprises, and the downsizing measures. But the heat had died down, and I'd relaxed as it all became old hat. But then the scandal about Noah being pregnant with my child broke, and once again we were the center of attention.

I was shocked when I saw Noah trying to get through the door of her building while the journalists crowded around her and she kept repeating, "No comment." Steve was there, furious, trying to help her enter her own home. Rage flooded through my veins.

Dammit.

53

Noah

I guess I'd known it was going to happen, but I'd never thought it would affect me. Nick was the one they wanted to talk about, but as soon as they found out I was expecting, the journalists wouldn't leave me alone.

Nicholas was furious and kept insisting we leave my apartment and go to his, where it was more secure. Eventually we had no choice. It had been less traumatic than I'd expected telling everyone about my pregnancy, my friends and professors all knew, but that wasn't the same as being on the news.

At first, it was just Nick, Nick, Nick, and how we were stepbrother and stepsister, and all the stuff about our parents… We were like circus freaks being gawked at by the masses, and once they had said everything they could about him, they turned to me, my appearance, my clothes… It was just crazy. I almost fainted when I saw us on the cover of a gossip rag. The headline said, *The golden bachelor, Nicholas Leister, has finally settled down and will be a father at twenty-four years old. Are those wedding bells we hear?*

I couldn't believe it.

The day I saw that, I arrived home angrier than ever. I didn't want to be in the public eye, and I sure as hell didn't want my life being sold for people's morbid curiosity like I was a star in a soap opera.

I walked out of the elevator and found Nick in his workout area, and all my anger disappeared when I saw him there shirtless, sweating, and lifting a weight with his left arm, following the rehab routine his physical therapist had given him.

How could we not be in the news with him looking like a Hollywood star?

I watched him, entranced, until he noticed my presence. He smiled and dropped his dumbbell on the ground between his legs.

"Hey, Freckles," he said, grabbing a towel next to him and wiping off his face and arms.

I could just as well have told him not to bother, that I loved the sight of the sweat dripping down his abs, but instead I just stood there and let him get up and come to me.

"Everything okay?" he asked, giving me a peck on the cheek.

That was something that had been bothering me, more than I liked to let on: neither of us was touching the other apart from a few tender little kisses. I was scared he wouldn't want to because his wounds still hurt, but if he was able to lift weights, what was stopping him from doing all the things that passed through my head every night as I lay by his side?

Maybe he didn't like me as much as he used to; my belly kept us apart... Just the thought of him finding me unattractive horrified me.

Nick pushed a strand of hair behind my ear and grimaced. "What's eating at you?" he asked, looking at me with those eyes that drove me wild.

I wanted to kiss him all over, touch that hard, defined stomach, wanted him to ram me against the wall and fuck me for once.

But I decided to keep my mouth shut. I wasn't going to ask for something he clearly didn't want to give.

"Nothing. I'm tired. I'm going to shower." I turned around to walk out, but Nick stopped me, scanning my face for a sign, a clue that would tell him what was going on.

"Is it the journalists?" he asked, planting a soft kiss behind my ear.

"No… I just want to shower and go to bed."

He put his hands on my shoulders and held me there, a reassuring expression on his face. "Noah, they'll get tired of us… It's just a matter of time till they start stalking some other couple. This is Hollywood."

He tried to calm me down by stroking my arm, but I was pissed now, and I stopped him.

"Don't touch me like I'm a fucking doll, Nicholas."

His eyes opened wide with surprise as I pulled away from his grasp and walked off down the hall.

I looked at the bed…that fucking bed where he must have done it all with Sophia Aiken. That only made me madder. Maybe he wasn't attracted to me anymore. But he could at least try to fake it.

As I took my pajamas out of the drawer, he appeared in the doorway and stared at me, leaning against the frame.

"What did you mean by that?"

"Nothing," I said, wanting to take off my clothes but embarrassed to have him watch me. I could feel tears stinging my eyes, but I used all my self-control to keep them from falling. Still, I gave myself away, and that made me feel more pathetic than ever.

"Noah…" he said, walking closer.

"Look, I get that you don't find me attractive, okay? But if you don't want to touch me, at least don't treat me like I'm your fucking little sister, Nicholas."

I tried to go to the bathroom, but he stopped me and pushed

me against the wall, putting a hand on either side of my head and staring me in the eyes.

"What the hell are you getting at?" Those words had hurt him as much as uttering them had hurt me.

I took a deep breath, trying to keep my hormones in check when he was so close, so handsome, and not even fully dressed.

"I'm talking about the fact that you haven't touched me in months. I know I'm huge now and probably that doesn't do it for you, but I'm not made of stone, you know? You're over there lifting weights, waiting for me half naked like I don't have eyes, like I'm just some dumb pregnant woman who can only think about crying babies, diapers, and cradles. But I have my needs, too! Did you ever think about that? My hormones are out of control, and you won't—"

He hushed me with a deep kiss. I closed my eyes, and everything I was saying suddenly evaporated from my mind. He pressed me into the wall with his body, and our tongues intertwined. He was hard. I almost melted in his arms. Breath labored, he stood back, glaring.

"I still can't grasp what the hell goes on in that head of yours, Freckles, but if you ever insinuate that you don't turn me on, I'll get mad; it's an insult, and I won't stand for it. If I haven't touched you since we've been back, it's because I thought you didn't want it. It had nothing to do with me not wanting you."

My heart sped up.

"Why wouldn't I want you?" I asked. "I was waiting for you to get better, but you never once showed me that you were interested, and Nicholas, that's never happened before."

"Jesus, Noah...you just don't get it."

He reached under my dress and pulled it over my head. I was trembling with anticipation, and with fear that he wouldn't like the changes my body had undergone.

He looked me up and down, examining my new curves. "So... what is it you want me to do?"

"What?!" I shouted.

"Apparently, I haven't been taking care of my girlfriend's needs... So tell me what you want, and I'll do it."

If he hadn't been devouring me with his eyes, and I hadn't seen the clear outline of an erection in his pants, I'd have thought he was saying it because he felt obligated to...but no. I knew that look better than anyone.

"Touch me," I said, quivering as I awaited his caress.

"Where, Freckles? There are a lot of places I could touch you, and I sure don't want to treat you like a little sister."

He stroked my cheek. But I didn't want some cheesy petting, so I grabbed his hand and brought it down inside my underwear, where he fingered that part of me that had needed him so badly.

He smiled. "Here? You like that?" He was enjoying his effect on me, and so was I. He bit my ear, hard.

I closed my eyes. "Yes," I said, throwing my head back.

His tongue reentered my mouth, tasting me, exploring me, his teeth almost gnawing, as if he'd never needed contact with me more than in that instant.

I licked him all over, from his chin to his jawline, feeling his pulse racing in that vein on his neck—racing for me. He grunted as I descended to his shoulder. His fingers were deep inside me now... He lifted me up with his free arm and, with fire in his eyes, said, "Noah, I want to make love to you... Can I? Tell me if I can. I don't want to do anything that might—"

I shook my head. "The baby will be fine," I responded, panting and emitting a moan when his fingers slid out. "Don't stop..." I reached down and touched him over his pants.

He hissed as he laid me on the bed. He tore off his pants. Okay, I admit it, I'd been wrong about him not wanting me... "No one else could ever turn me on like this, Noah."

He bent over me, grabbed the elastic of my panties, and pulled them off frantically.

"Turn over," he said. "I don't want to crush you; I want to make sure you're comfortable."

I did as he said, and he got behind me. He unbuttoned my bra and kissed every inch of my back. Now my belly didn't come between us. He slid inside me gently, and I thought I'd lose my mind. I closed my eyes, trying not to scream.

Nick grabbed a pillow and put it under me so I'd be more comfortable, and then he started moving…

I couldn't hold it in anymore. I shouted as our bodies ground together in unison, faster and faster until I let all that suppressed longing explode in a roar of pleasure. Months of tension seeped out of me, and I wished we could just keep doing it until I no longer had the strength to move. And Nick obliged me; he didn't stop—he kept thrusting and kissing my back.

Finally we both came, me groaning into the pillow, him biting my left shoulder.

I fell asleep almost instantly.

I don't know how much time passed until I opened my eyes, but when I did, I was under the covers and curled up beside him, while he ran his hand up and down my bare back.

When he noticed I was awake, he smiled. "I lost you for a while, Freckles."

I laughed. "I think I fainted from pleasure."

"Oh yeah?" he asked, turning me onto my back and positioning himself over me, careful not to make me bear his weight.

"I missed you, Nick," I said, tugging on a lock of his hair.

"I could tell," he said, kissing me on the lips. "But not as much as I missed you, Freckles."

Andrew kicked just then, as if to remind me he was there. I frowned, and Nick looked at me with worry.

"It's nothing, the baby's just moving," I said.

He rolled over, leaning his head on his palm, and observed me, totally in love.

"What's it feel like?" he asked, reaching over and touching my stomach.

I watched his hand and thought it over. "It's strange... especially when he does it really suddenly."

Nick listened closely, then kissed my belly, and I felt all warm inside.

"I can't wait to meet him," he said, hugging me close.

Same, I thought to myself.

One day I wrapped up an exam and found Nick parked outside waiting for me. He looked excited, but I didn't know why. I was happy, too—that was one more class I wouldn't have to deal with.

Fifteen minutes later, we were in a part of town I'd never been to before. There were lots of tall buildings, but not exactly what you'd call high-rises. It was a nice area, with palm trees on the streets and well-tended yards. Nick parked in front of a discreet white house. It had a wraparound porch and wood steps leading to the door. It was two stories. It looked like something from a fairy tale.

"You like?"

I looked around, a little confused.

"It's not really your style," I responded. Nick was a guy who liked big downtown apartments with floor-to-ceiling windows or mansions overlooking the beach.

"No, it isn't. I bought it with you in mind."

I couldn't believe what he was saying. "You did what?"

He got out of the car and came around to help me out. Then he took some keys from his back pocket and dangled them in front of my face.

"You've got two more years of school, Noah. I don't want you to have to give up anything, and if I have to leave New York, move in with you, and wait while you figure out what you want to do with your life, I will. I know what I want, my future is settled, and in part, that's because I had the time to think and do things the conventional way. You're the one thing I was missing in life, and I'm going to adapt to you until you're ready to make changes. I don't want to drag you off to something that's my taste because that's not who you are. I always thought I'd want to live the way I grew up, but I don't want thousands of square feet dividing us, my love. I want to look up and see you whenever I want. This house is yours. It's my gift to you."

I shook my head. I didn't know what to say. The house was precious, cozy, perfect—the very house I would have chosen to start a family in.

Nick continued. "You're going to have Andrew soon, and I know you don't want to live in my apartment. So, Noah, please, accept this gift."

He didn't give me time to respond before tugging my hand and taking me up to the door. He opened it, and we stepped into what would be our new home.

The afternoon sun left a trail of orange light across the floor of the living room. It was furnished with white sofas on a gleaming wood floor. The spaces were diaphanous, with big windows giving a view of the mountains. The more Nick showed me, the more I loved it. We walked upstairs to our future bedroom. It was big, with a giant bed in the middle. The white curtains let in the sunlight. The roof had exposed wooden beams. The bathroom was black marble with a big tub and a separate shower. Maybe it wasn't a mansion, but every single detail was taken care of.

We crossed a small hallway. At the end of it was a kind of sitting room with a window looking out on to the backyard. There were doors on either side. He opened the one on the right and invited me in.

"This will be our baby's room… I thought you'd like it."

It was precious. Everything was painted white, with the same wood floors as downstairs. He hadn't furnished it yet, apart from a little bench under the window, the kind you can open to store toys inside.

I smiled. I could see Andrew. I could see us. I could see our baby in that room sleeping placidly, playing, crying, laughing. I could see the three of us sharing our finest moments. This would be our house, our home, our little corner of the world.

"I love it!" I shouted and turned around.

Nick kissed me. In his eyes, I could see feelings he was trying to keep from overwhelming him. "I want to give you everything, Noah… I want you to be happy with me and for us to raise that little boy the way our parents didn't manage to raise us."

"This was a nice way for you to escape my loft," I said, laughing.

"The house is in your name," he added. "I don't want you to worry about anything except for the baby and all the things you wanted to do before you got pregnant. I'm going to do everything I can to make sure that your life remains your life…"

I shut him up with a kiss.

"Thanks, Nick," I said. "You've really made me happy. I love you."

After another round of hugs and kisses, we spent the afternoon planning how we wanted to arrange the place and when we would actually move.

My new life had started, and I was loving it.

The first week of month eight I spent at school, more or less. I no longer cared if people were looking at me every time I entered or left the library, and I learned that the best thing to do when you knew people were talking about you was just to ignore all of it.

Everyone got used to it, and people helped me out whenever they could: carrying my backpack or my laptop, even buying my lunch. My belly was the star attraction in my department. Everyone wanted to touch it, everyone wanted to know when the baby was coming… Meanwhile, I was starting to notice the challenges. Andrew had almost tripled in size, and I felt like a walking barn.

Nick didn't like me spending so much time outside the house, but I only had a week left until summer vacation. I needed to get through this final push. Soon, I'd have a newborn at home, and I wanted to make sure I didn't have to add to that burden by retaking any of my classes.

At the library one day, something happened that had already happened months before—I ran into Michael.

We stared at each other for a few seconds, and I went on walking, intending to go past him on my way out. But he blocked my path and looked at me with something I hadn't seen in him before: disgust.

"So you let him knock you up… That's a pretty pathetic way to lock him down, don't you think?"

That stung.

"Leave me alone," I demanded.

He caught my arm as I tried to go around him. I struggled to get away but couldn't.

"Did your boyfriend tell you he and I ran into each other?"

I froze.

"Maybe I shouldn't have done what I did, though…"

I was about to take out my phone and call Steve to come get me when Charlie, Michael's brother, came over.

"Noah!" he said, completely ignoring the tension between Michael and me.

I forced a smile as he hugged me tight.

"Jeez, you're huge!" he said, laughing.

I wanted to run away, I couldn't stand Michael's stare, and even if I was happy to see Charlie, I'd sworn something to Nick, and I wasn't about to break my word.

"Charlie, it's great to see you, but I've got to go..." I said.

He looked at his brother, who was now standing a few steps away, and nodded, sighing.

"Call me when you can. This is my new number," Charlie said, scribbling his number on a scrap of paper and handing it to me. Then he leaned in and whispered in my ear, "We've got a lot to talk about."

Trying to remain calm, I nodded and left.

Something told me this wasn't going to be the last time Michael gave me trouble.

54

Nick

Noah was huge. The poor thing had always been thin and small in stature, and I sometimes worried her belly would weigh her down and she'd end up stumbling forward.

There was still another month left, and I was scared of what would happen as the baby kept growing. Noah's mood was a roller coaster too. She could be happy and relaxed one minute and crying over nothing the next.

When her birthday came, we had a combination birthday party/baby shower at Dad's house. Jenna invited everyone and their mother. Noah was sitting in the garden on a plush chair someone had brought out for her and opening presents with a smile.

My sister kept shouting at the sight of all those gifts. She was like Noah's little helper. From the moment we arrived, Maddie couldn't leave her alone.

Jenna had organized things to a T, with blue balloons everywhere, a big cake with a baby in the middle of it, and all sorts of toys and gifts.

A lot of my friends were there, too, and I was happy for the opportunity to escape to play Xbox with them for a while. All those women gathering to talk about babies was cramping my style.

A few hours later, I went to the kitchen to ask if Noah's chocolate cake was ready. I was grateful to Jenna for handling the baby shower part, but this was about Noah, too, and she deserved a big cake with a twenty in the middle. When I took it out to the yard, everyone was surprised and sang "Happy Birthday." Noah blew out the candles.

A while later, when everyone was distracted, I walked with her toward the pool. She smiled, remembering old times.

"Did you bring me here to do something dirty, Nick?"

I laughed. "It wouldn't be your birthday if I didn't do something dirty, Freckles," I said, kissing her full lips and feeling her warmth in my arms. Eventually we stopped, and I took a small box out of my pocket.

"Your present," I said.

When she opened it, her eyes grew wide with surprise. I thought she might cry.

"You've got it… I thought… I thought you'd thrown it away. I thought…"

I silenced her with a kiss and wiped away her tears. "I could never have thrown away that pendant, Noah. I gave you my heart two years ago. Now I'm giving it to you again…"

She stroked the silver heart that I'd given her when she turned eighteen.

"I sent it to a jeweler so they could embed a little blue diamond in it. Because, you know… Andrew's going to be a part of this too now, right?"

"It's the best gift you could ever have given me. I've missed this pendant. I've missed all it meant for you and me."

"I know… It should never have come off, Noah. It was wrong of me to take it."

She shook her head. "You did what you felt in the moment, Nick… I hurt you. I didn't deserve to wear it."

I took it out of the box.

"Now nothing and no one will ever move it from where it belongs," I said, carefully putting it around her neck and kissing her bare shoulder.

"If you're tired and you want to go back home, just tell me and we'll leave."

She shook her head. She looked happy. "I want to enjoy this day. It's perfect in every sense of the word."

55

Noah

After the party, we got a move on finishing Andrew's room. Nick and I went to buy all the things we needed: a changing table, a stroller that looked more like a mutant robot than a regular stroller...and hundreds of other things I hadn't even known existed until then. My mother helped us out.

At the party, everyone had given us tons of stuff, lots of it very expensive. That's the advantage of being friends with millionaires... We still had time before the baby was born, but I felt like I needed everything taken care of beforehand if I wanted to relax as much as everyone told me I needed to.

I no longer recognized myself. I was going through emotional swings that drove Nick insane. But he dealt with everything with patience.

I ended up calling Charlie. I needed to tell him that we couldn't be friends anymore, even though that hurt. My relationship with Nick was too important, and I wasn't going to risk it. I realized that wasn't the kind of conversation you had over the phone, so when I called him, I said we could meet up one afternoon and have a cup of tea, and he told me to come over. He swore Michael wouldn't be there.

When Charlie opened the door, I felt happy, and we hugged each other as tightly as my body would allow.

"You look hotter than ever," he joked.

I rolled my eyes and went inside. My memories of *that night* overwhelmed me, and I had to take several breaths to calm down and get through what I'd gone there to do.

Charlie hadn't deserved me giving him the cold shoulder for so long. I shouldn't have done it, but I didn't know if there had been another option. After breaking up with Nicholas, I had changed for the worse, closing myself off. I wouldn't have been a good friend anyway.

He told me he had quit school and spent five months in rehab. I felt bad that I hadn't even known he'd relapsed. He told me he was better than ever now, though, that he'd actually become a new person in the past few months.

We had a great time until a certain inevitable subject came up.

"I know you don't even want to hear my brother's name, but I promise you, he regrets everything he did to you, Noah," he said with a pleading expression. He seemed more worried about me forgiving and forgetting than Michael himself had. "He was rehired on campus, and he's working with students with mental health problems… He really helps them, you know?"

"I know he's your brother, Charlie, but I just want to leave him and what happened behind, okay? I'm really sorry that means I need to leave you behind, too, but I can't risk being around him. I hope you understand."

Charlie nodded. He was sad, though. "I'm glad you're back with Nicholas. You look happy."

"Thanks," I said, hugging him. "And thanks for being a good friend."

I left feeling ambivalent. I hated goodbyes, but I was about to start a new life, and if Nick had managed to start over from zero, so could I.

When I got home, I was a little woozy, and I went straight to bed. Nick arrived a few hours later and was quieter than usual.

"Do you mind cutting off the AC?" I asked him as I lay back and watched him take off his jacket and tie.

He grimaced, but he did what I asked. Then he turned to me but seemed to hesitate for a moment.

"I know you went to see him, Noah," he said, throwing me off completely.

Cold sweat dripped down my back. "How...?"

"Steve."

Of course... Fucking Steve. "I went to see Charlie, that's all."

"You go to see Charlie, and then you come home and you're all exhausted... It wouldn't happen to be that a certain person had anything to do with that?"

"What? No!" I sat up, shaking my head. Then a sharp pain jolted through my back, and I felt like I could barely breathe.

"Noah?" Nick said, hurrying over.

I inhaled slowly and deeply, and the pain passed as quickly as it had arrived. "It's okay, don't worry, I'm fine," I said, lying back on a pile of cushions.

"You don't look okay. You're fucking pale."

He pushed a sweat-soaked strand of hair out of my face.

"Noah, you've got a fever." He looked alarmed.

"No... I'm fine, really. I'm just a little tired."

He seemed to be wavering between his anger at the fact that I'd gone to see Charlie and his apprehension at my condition. I didn't want to see him that way. I didn't want him to think I'd broken my word.

"Nick... I didn't see Michael. I promise."

"What pisses me off isn't you seeing him or not, it's you going there without even telling me. I could have gone with you. Your friend isn't the one whose face I want to break, you know?"

I forced a smile so he'd relax. "That's done with... That's why I went to see him. If I was going to cut him off, he deserved an explanation at least."

Nicholas looked me in the eye, then bent over and kissed my forehead. The kiss lasted a few seconds—he was also trying to see how hot I was.

"I'm fiiiiiine."

But then, as if my body wanted to prove him right, I felt another sharp pain and had to shut my eyes.

"Nick..." I said, frightened, and grabbed his hand.

"I'm here," he said. I'd never heard him use that tone before.

It passed, and I fell back again, and Nick said, "We're going to the hospital."

"No! We don't need to. They're just Braxton-Hicks contractions, really, it's norm—" I couldn't finish the phrase before curling up once more in pain. I clenched my teeth and tried to hold back my tears. Not very effectively.

"I don't know what's happening..."

"I think you're going into labor, Noah," he said, getting up from the bed. I reached out desperately for his hand.

"No, it's impossible. I've still got time left..."

And then, like a bad joke, I felt my thighs and the sheets beneath them go damp.

I opened my eyes with fear.

"Goddammit, Noah, what's happening?! You're scaring me."

"I think my water just broke."

When I sat up and saw the sheets were soaked, I nearly hyperventilated.

I wasn't ready for this...not yet.

Nick lifted me and carried me to the bathroom. I was so scared, but he was so calm, or at least he was able to keep a grip on himself and do what had to be done, and I was grateful for that. He sat me on the edge of the sink and grabbed my face in his hands.

"Breathe, Noah," he told me, stripping off my ruined dress.

"I'm disgusting," I said, trembling.

Nick seemed not to notice, or not to understand. "Do you want a shower?"

I nodded, and he turned on the water, making sure it wasn't too hot.

"Stay here," he said, walking out and returning right afterward with clean clothes.

After helping me out of my underwear, he stood me under the warm shower. I stayed there for just a few minutes. When I got out, Nick wrapped me in a towel and dried me attentively from head to toe. No sooner had I dressed again than another contraction made me buckle over. The pain was so bad, I wanted to disappear.

"Let's go to the hospital, Freckles," he said, kissing my forehead once I was able to breathe normally again.

I nodded, scared.

The baby wasn't quite ready yet…

56

Noah

THE NEXT FEW HOURS WERE THE MOST PAINFUL AND FRIGHTENING of my life.

I had been right that it was too early, but when my water broke, Andrew got stuck in the birth canal, and that meant there was no turning back. I dilated quickly, and by the time I arrived at the hospital, they took me straight to the maternity ward. Idiot that I was, I assumed that since it had come on so fast, I'd need just a few pushes and I'd be done, but nothing could be further from the truth: I was pushing for eight hours. Eight hours of strenuous effort, until my strength gave out and I thought I'd be incapable of continuing.

"Noah...you can't stop now, you need to push. Come on, Freckles, just one more," Nick said softly in my ear. He was holding both my hands, and I was gripping him so tightly, I thought I'd break his fingers.

"I'm so tired," I said in a moment of respite after a contraction. My whole body hurt, the epidural seemed to have worn off hours ago, and I was just praying for the whole thing to end.

I could hear the doctors talking quietly, saying something about my pelvis and how the baby didn't have enough room to get out. I'd always known it: I wasn't made to bear children.

"Nick... Get me out of here...take me somewhere, I don't care where, far away. I can't take the pain anymore," I begged, watching the tears stream from his eyes.

"When all this is over, we can go, my love. I'll take you wherever you want to go. But for now, you have to push."

Another contraction made every muscle in my abdomen tense. I clenched my teeth and pushed. The nurses were encouraging me, the doctors, too. Someone put a damp cloth on my forehead, the contractions paused, and I wanted to die when I realized the baby still wasn't out.

"This isn't working..." I moaned.

"Doctor, she's exhausted. Do something, dammit!"

"We can't risk a Caesarian right now. It could endanger the mother," the obstetrician remarked.

Nick went pale.

"Noah...when this next contraction comes, I need you to push as hard as you can, okay? I'm going to use the forceps; we need to get this little guy out—he's going into fetal distress."

My baby was suffering, and it was my fault. He was suffering because I wasn't able to get him out.

"Sit up," the doctor told me, and I did even though I was barely strong enough to raise my head. "Mr. Leister, get behind her and help her hold that position."

Nicholas supported me with his chest. Feeling his arms around me gave me the strength to continue.

"You can do it, babe... Come on, just one more."

Right then, the next contraction came. I don't know where I found the strength, but I did. Squeezing Nick's hands, I pushed and pushed until I nearly fainted.

"He's out!" the doctor said, and just afterward, we heard the hysterical screaming of a very angry baby.

I collapsed into Nick, unable even to keep my eyes open.

"Noah, look, he's beautiful."

I opened my eyes, and the nurse brought over a tiny little thing wrapped in a blue blanket.

"It's a boy. He's a handsome one, too," the nurse said, passing him to me.

My arms were quivering, and Nick helped me hold him to my chest.

"Oh my God!" I exclaimed.

Andy stopped crying when he heard my voice. I was sobbing like crazy. I bent over and kissed the top of his head with its mop of black hair.

"He's perfect," Nick whispered in my ear. "Thank you, Noah. Thank you for this. I love you so much. You were great."

But they took him from my hands then, and I couldn't go on looking at him.

"He needs to be in the incubator until we know everything's in working order. This little boy was ready to get out of there!"

I bit my lip when I heard him cry again. I was angry that he had to suffer. He had been so happy with me...

Andrew Morgan Leister was born on a Saturday in July weighing exactly 5 pounds, 5 ounces. He spent two nights in an incubator, and then they gave him back to me. I was discharged a few hours later, and Nick drove us home so we could rest. I still felt weak, exhausted. I had only slept for a few hours. All I could think about was my precious baby, the baby that was now placidly sleeping in the car seat in the back.

Nick had stayed by my side the whole time and was as tired as I was, but he looked happier than I'd ever seen him.

Our parents had come to the hospital. They were crazy about Andrew, as everyone was; they wanted to hold him and bundle him up and rock him to sleep, but he only found peace in my arms.

Journalists had mobbed us on our way out, and the scene had been so frantic, I hadn't stopped to think about the normal people who would just be happy for us. But when we got home, I found tons of balloons and gift baskets and cards congratulating us.

Nick took Andy inside in the car seat. I was so happy to be home. The past few days had been tough.

Once we were inside, I picked up my baby and went upstairs to the bedroom. Nick was right behind me. I should have taken the baby to his crib, that cute little crib we'd set up in his nursery, but the mere thought of leaving him there stung. So we went to sleep with Andy tucked in a co-sleeper between the two of us.

"I can't believe he's with us now," Nick confessed, rubbing Andy's pink cheek with one finger.

"He's the prettiest baby I've ever seen," I said, leaning over to sniff his head. He smelled wonderful…

I wasn't just saying that because I was his mother; he really was special, with his blue eyes and his chubby cheeks. We'd dressed him in the onesie Jenna had given him, turquoise blue with the words *I'm number one* printed on it.

I smiled, happy to be home, happy to be with Nick, happy the worst was over… Or so I thought.

Strange as it may seem, we didn't have any trouble adapting to Andy. He wasn't the type of baby who cried all day long. We even had to wake him up ourselves sometimes to get him to eat.

For some reason, I could only breastfeed for the first two weeks after he was born. He struggled to get enough milk out on his own, and we had to look for other solutions. It pained me to lose that special bond. It had felt magical to feed my baby, to feel him against me like that. But there was nothing we could do.

"Look at it from the positive side," Jenna said, cradling Andy in her arms. "Your tits won't sag."

I rolled my eyes. If she ever had her own baby, she'd understand why this depressed me so much.

"I want one," Jenna said right afterward, catching me off guard.

I laughed. I was busy folding Andy's clothes and putting them away in his little dresser. There was so much of it, and he'd probably never even get to wear half of it. He was growing fast—he looked nothing like the tiny thing he'd been when he was born. Now he weighed almost ten pounds.

"Tell Lion," I said, sitting down in front of her and watching Andy chew the pacifier with his thick little lips. Some parents said pacifiers were bad, but when he stopped nursing, we decided to give him one, and he couldn't stand to have it taken away.

"I told him…but he says he wants to wait." She grimaced. "I might have to have a little '*accident*.'" She put this last word in air quotes.

"Jenna!" I exclaimed and slapped her on the shoulder.

She laughed so loudly, the baby woke up. I took him from her and laid him in the crib.

"I was kidding!" she said.

She and Lion left a little later, and Nick came upstairs. By then, I was sitting on one of the sofas, holding Andy in my arms. He wouldn't stop staring at me. It was almost as if he wanted to tell me something.

Nick kissed the top of my head and sat in front of me on the ottoman.

"You look good," he commented with a smile, bending over and looking back and forth between us.

"I can't believe it was just three weeks ago that I nearly pushed my guts out trying to bring this little guy into the world," I said, rubbing Andrew's soft, fuzzy hair. His skin was so smooth, I could touch him and hold him for hours.

"I wanted to tell you something, Noah," Nick said, suddenly serious.

I looked up at him. "Did something happen?"

I knew he was nervous about the trial against his shooter, which would start in two weeks. Miraculously, he was out on bail, and neither of us could wait until he was locked up for good.

"No, nothing...or actually everything," he said, grabbing my hand and kissing my knuckles. "What I wanted to tell you, Freckles, is that you've made me the happiest man in the world." He bent over and kissed Andy's head, but he had closed his eyes again and was back to sleep, oblivious to the world. "All the stuff we've been through, all the situations we've had to face together, just think... It's been a long time now since that first kiss in the car on a summer night just like this one, under the stars. I remember I was dying to find an excuse to taste your lips, touch you, caress you. You've made me a better person, Noah; you saved me from a lonely, empty life, a life with no love, a life governed by hate. You're always able to find a way to forgive others for their errors. You always want to see the positive side of all the people in your life... And if there's one error I've made, it's not doing this earlier..."

My heart was fluttering as I saw him bring a little box covered in black velvet out of his pocket. When he opened it, my breathing stopped as I saw a beautiful, dazzling ring.

"Marry me, Noah... Share your life with me. Let's do it. Be mine, and I'll be yours forever."

I covered my mouth with my hand. For a moment, I was speechless.

"I..." I paused. Then I looked at Andrew there, asleep between the two of us, and my hands shook. Nick picked up the baby and laid him carefully in his crib.

Coming back, he kneeled before me and looked me in the eye. "What do you say, Freckles?"

I smiled. I couldn't help it. Then I pulled on his collar and kissed him feverishly.

"Is that a yes?" he asked.

"Hell yes, it is," I replied, tears of joy in my eyes.

He grabbed my hand and slid the ring onto the third finger of my left hand.

"I love you so much," he said, kissing me again.

He picked me up and took me to our bedroom. We made love as if possessed, touched and kissed each other, promised each other the moon and the sun. I wanted him to kiss me all over, and he did. I wanted to feel him close to me, and he fulfilled my every wish...

When Andrew was a month old, Nick had to go back to work. In reality, he'd been working the whole time, but from home, sitting on the sofa with his computer on his lap. I loved going to the living room and seeing Andy asleep on Nick's chest while he typed away, his eyes focused on the screen. It made my heart melt. Two heads of black hair, two pairs of sky-blue eyes...they looked so much alike, it sometimes bothered me.

"You must be happy," I accused him once while we were playing with the baby in bed. "He doesn't look a damned bit like me..."

Nick smiled proudly but shook his head. "He'll have your freckles... I know he will."

"And he'll hate me for it."

Nicholas laughed. "Our baby's going to be a heartbreaker, Noah. I don't have the least doubt about that."

Andy laughed for the first time, and we both looked down at him, enraptured. We'd fallen in love with that little boy, and now we were completely at his mercy.

One Monday not long afterward, Jenna picked us up for a drive around the city. I was nervous, I'd barely left the house since I'd had him, but she pushed and pushed, and eventually I brought out the robot carriage—which I still wasn't very skilled at using—so we could take a stroll through a nearby mall. It was hot, and I didn't want Andy to get too much sun, so we stopped at a café to talk about the wedding and all the preparations—Jenna, of course, was already making plans.

"I already told you, Jen," I warned her wearily. "We're engaged, but we won't actually get married until the kid's a little older."

"That's ridiculous."

"It's not. I can't organize a wedding and deal with a newborn!"

"I'm going to organize it for you, stupid!"

I shook my head, exasperated, and went on listening to her tirade. Our parents had been happy when we told them we were getting married. Doing things backward—having the baby first—hadn't sat well with them, and they were glad we were fixing that little oversight. They had raised us to follow conventions: love first, then marriage, then cohabitation, *then* children—but I guess it was evident by now that Nick and I were far from conventional.

Honestly, I hadn't even thought about getting married; I was too focused on the baby and Nick, and the proposal had taken me completely by surprise. We were really young to be making a lifelong commitment, but we were young to be having a kid, too; then again, we'd been young when we'd gone through things most people never had to experience.

I was happy, Nick was happy—that was the important thing.

A few hours later, it was time to go home. By then, Steve wasn't constantly following me around anymore. I'd kept telling Nick it was too much, having someone trailing me all the time. Steve was the best in his profession, and honestly, the poor bastard was bored to tears following me to the park or to the store to buy diapers.

Nick was a different case: he ran around with important people, his trial was all over the news, and someone actually had tried to end his life. I was scared for him.

Nick finally agreed, and that same day, he and Steve took off for San Francisco. He'd told me he'd try to come back that night, but I knew his meetings there usually stretched on for a long time. This was the first night I'd spent without Nick since I'd had Andrew, and he was nervous. I wasn't worried; I knew perfectly how to handle the baby, and I declined his offer to go along. I didn't want to get on a plane with a tiny baby, and I also didn't want to interrupt Nick's work.

I explained all this, and Nick stopped pressing me.

"Are you sure you don't want me to stay with you?" Jenna asked when I told her to drop me off at the pharmacy. Andrew had a diaper rash, and it was really making him ornery.

"Don't worry about it," I said, telling her I'd walk home once I was done there; it wasn't far, and it had started to cool off now that the sun was setting. I hugged her and said goodbye, and she crouched to kiss Andy on the head.

"All the outfits I bought him are the best ones," she said, and I couldn't help but roll my eyes. That day, he was wearing little white shorts and a tiny T-shirt that read: *Party tonight at my crib*.

"Take care of my godchild!" she shouted as she went back to her car.

I went inside and bought ointment. On the way home, pushing the carriage along the same street where I took a walk almost every day, I felt something strange. A chill went up my spine. I turned my head to look, but there was no one there. Suddenly, I missed Steve being by my side. I'd nearly forgotten what it was to be alone. I kept walking, hoping to get home as soon as possible and shake off that sense of foreboding.

Andy hadn't stopped crying since we'd gotten out of Jenna's car. His rash was bad, and anytime he rustled, it stung, and he shrieked hysterically. The only thing that calmed him down was being held, and it had to be belly down along my forearm, with his head tucked into my elbow. I picked him up like that once we got home, leaning back a little, and it reminded me of how Nick would hold him on his chest. At last, he fell asleep again, and I wrapped him up and laid him in his crib. I stood there for a moment, gawking at him.

How could you love a person so much and so instinctively? My little man with his pacifier in his mouth and his chubby cheeks was the most beautiful thing I'd ever seen. It hurt me viscerally when he cried, and I was over the moon when he smiled. I couldn't believe I'd lived a whole life without him... Now just thinking about being apart from him was agony.

By then, Nick was back at his hotel—no surprise, he'd had to stay the night. I called him from bed, and we talked for a while. When I hung up, I fell straight to sleep. I was exhausted.

When I opened my eyes, every hair on my body was standing on end. Don't ask me why; they just were. Nothing seemed out of the ordinary, but I had a feeling that made me sit up. I was breathing fast, and I got up, trying not to make any noise.

Calm down, I told myself. I'd probably just had a nightmare.

They weren't as frequent as before, but with Nick gone, it was normal for them to come back.

I couldn't remember what it was about, if I'd even had one, but I tried to readjust to reality and relax before I went to see the baby. Andy was attuned to my mood, and if I was upset or nervous, he would instantly get angry and start crying.

Once I felt normal, I walked out of my room and down the hall to Andrew's.

My heart stopped.

Someone was there.

My baby wasn't alone.

57

Noah

My entire body stiffened, petrified, on the threshold of my child's room. I froze in fear. The woman with her back to me heard me and turned around automatically. I couldn't believe it. I knew her, and that only terrified me more.

"Briar."

The red-haired girl standing before me looked nothing like the gorgeous one I'd lived with for months. Her hair was cut to her shoulders, she had bags under her green eyes, and there wasn't a drop of makeup to hide her imperfections. She was wearing plain black pants and a gray sweatshirt. I repeat: she in no way resembled the girl I'd known.

"Don't you dare walk through that door, Morgan."

What a stupid way to talk to me, not using my first name, like we weren't close once. I clenched my teeth in fury.

"What the fuck do you think you're doing here?" I shouted. Andy was asleep, and Briar was too close to him for my comfort. She had been standing by the crib watching him until I interrupted her.

She reached into her purse and pulled out a knife with a gleaming blade… My heart was racing. But I didn't step back.

"I just wanted to meet Nick's child," she said, turning back to the crib with a sick expression of delight.

I didn't fail to notice that she'd said Andy was Nicholas's kid, not mine. I tried to remain calm when all I wanted was to shove her away, grab my baby, and take off running.

"He's gorgeous...looks just like him." She bent over and stroked his head.

When I stepped forward, she held out the hand holding the knife, and I stopped, my eyes fixed on its sharp tip.

"I told you not to come in here," she hissed in a rage.

"Briar, please..." I begged when she reached in and picked Andy up. He woke immediately.

I saw him blink several times, confused. I knew what would happen by the way she was holding him. Andrew started crying, breaking the tense silence. I wanted to take him from her, soothe him, tell him it would be okay. Hatred flooded my body. Nothing mattered then. I'd kill her. I'd kill her if she hurt my baby.

Briar rocked him so he'd stop crying, and I felt as though time were stopping when the blade in her hand got dangerously close to him.

"You're doing it wrong," I said, desperate for her to get the hell away from my newborn baby.

Briar looked up.

"Put him on his belly," I said, trying to control my tone. "Like that..." I nodded when she did as I said. At least now she could hold him with one arm and let the knife hang at her side.

Andy complained but eventually calmed down, and Briar seemed pleased with herself as she rocked him, humming a song I had never heard before.

"You know what?" she said, staring at me. "My baby had blue eyes, too..."

I didn't understand.

She seemed to recognize that and continued: “I didn’t get an abortion. Nicholas’s father gave me money to…but I didn’t.”

But that meant…

“I lost him.” Her eyes welled with tears, and now I saw it again, their beautiful emerald color. “My entire family turned their backs on me when I told them I was six months pregnant. I tried to hide it, but I wasn’t you. I couldn’t help showing. You could tell when I was just eight weeks along.”

Jesus…

“He was a redhead like me, but he had Nicholas’s eyes.”

Hearing her was breaking my heart. Not just because her baby had died, but because Nicholas’s had, too. Seeing my child draped over her arm, I understood the horror she must have felt.

“I only ever held him once.”

“Briar… I’m so sorry…”

She brought Andy close to her face to smell his little head.

“I warned you about Nicholas…but you wouldn’t listen to me.”

Now the sorrow in her eyes had changed to hatred. Andy was wriggling again.

“Briar, please… Please, give me my baby,” I begged her, crying. But she shook her head.

“I was first, Noah. You don’t deserve to be a mother… And Nicholas doesn’t deserve this baby.”

I didn’t know what to do. I looked around desperately, trying to find something I could use as a weapon. Briar was crazy. I’d always known she had problems; she had lied to me about Nicholas sleeping with her when we were together, had lied to me when she said he’d forced her to get an abortion…

“I’m a better mother than you,” she said, grabbing my bag off the changing table. I hadn’t left it there—she must have found it and packed it while I was asleep. I felt like the worst mother imaginable. How could I have not heard her?

My eyes paused on the baby monitor by the crib. It was off.

"Briar, you can't take him!" I shouted when she threatened me, waving the knife and telling me to get away from the door.

Andrew woke up again and started screaming.

"Look what you've done!" she said, furious.

"Briar, please, give him to me; I'm his mother!"

She stopped caring how she held him, and he twisted and turned in her arms; he was terrified, and she was touching him right where the rash itched most.

"Give him to me, dammit; you're hurting him!"

His cries filled the entire room. Briar dropped the bag on the ground, struggling to control him, still gripping the knife all the while. I saw her look up past my shoulder and heard a noise. Before I could turn, someone grabbed me from behind. I felt a man's hard chest against my back and a hand over my mouth, trapping my scream in my throat.

"I've been dying to hold you like this," a familiar voice whispered in my ear.

I felt my heart skip a beat.

Michael.

I tried to break free of him, but I couldn't. His whole body stank disgustingly of alcohol.

Briar's eyes lit up when she saw him, and I asked myself what connection there could be between the two of them. How the hell could the two people who had hurt me most be in the same room threatening me and my baby?

"You've got everything you need, right, babe?" Michael asked Briar, and she nodded as she picked up the bag again.

I was terrified—terrified and enraged. "Let me go!"

"I'm taking him, and there's nothing you can do about it," she told me, not even bothering to look up.

Michael pulled me back to let her through.

"Wait for me downstairs," he said. I'd never heard him sound so gruff.

As she stepped past me, I shouted, "No, Briar, no... Please... give him back, please..." I cried and tried to struggle out of Michael's grasp. She stopped for a moment, looked at me, looked at Michael, and then looked at Andy.

"Sorry, Noah," she said, walking downstairs.

"No!" I cried as loudly as I could. Andrew was shrieking hysterically as Michael turned me around and slammed my back against the wall.

"Did you really think you were just going to go on with your life as if nothing had happened? Did you think I was going to let that piece of shit just have you?"

I started sobbing. I couldn't believe this was happening.

Nicholas was gone, Steve, too...

Then I remembered a conversation I'd had with Nick a few weeks ago. I hadn't paid much attention; it was hard for me to take his obsession with security seriously; he was always worried about someone hurting us again...but now I recalled why he had agreed to take Steve with him...

"I installed an alarm, Noah," Nick told me while I was giving Andrew his bottle, staring at him in a trance and not really listening. "I know your history with alarms, and I don't want you to have to punch in a code every time you come and go, so it's just a panic button; you hit it and it alerts the police. Are you listening?"

I looked up from the baby and smiled. "Yeah, panic alarm, of course I'm listening."

Nicholas sighed and walked over. "Panic button, Noah. It's under the kitchen counter."

Just then, Andy gurgled adorably, and I stopped paying attention again.

Nicholas took him from me and looked at me angrily. "Goddammit, Noah, this is important!"

I scowled at him and raised my hands in the air. "I heard you. You need to stop freaking out. I got it, now give Andrew back."

Nick sighed, shook his head, and did as I asked. "Remind me to tell you exactly where it is..."

But I wasn't listening to him anymore...and I definitely never reminded him.

"The ten thousand he gave me to go away was enough for a while...but your little boyfriend has way more money than that, isn't that right?" Michael asked, pulling me out of my trance.

Money... Why wasn't I surprised?

"You're a son of a bitch," I said, hating him as I'd never hated anyone.

Michael clenched his jaw, and before I could duck, he slapped me across the face. "Don't ever talk bad about my mother, you hear me?"

I was trembling, but I tried to stay strong. Had he really hit me?!

"Now, tell me where the fuck the safe is."

I knew there was one in our room. Nick had chosen the combination—it was the date the two of us had met.

I told him where it was, and he pushed me into the bedroom. He looked at the unmade bed, the costly furniture, and the photo of Nick, Andy, and me that Jenna had taken and we'd framed and hung over the bed.

"What would your boyfriend say if I were to fuck you again right now on your pretty little bed? You think he'd forgive you again? Or would he leave you hanging like he did two years ago?"

"You're sick," I said.

Michael laughed and moved the picture. Behind it was the safe, gleaming silver.

"Enter the code."

He hurled me around in front of him. I did what he said, and his eyes lit up when the door opened.

"Damn...you hit the jackpot with this guy," he said, grabbing the stacks of money piled up there along with a few documents. "If this is what he's got at home, I don't even want to think about what's in the bank."

I clenched my fists. "Take the fucking money and get out of here."

Michael smiled, stuffed the stacks of hundreds into his backpack, and nudged me down the stairs. Briar was waiting on the sofa, with Andy sleeping in her arms.

"Can we go now?" she asked nervously.

"In a second, dear," Michael responded, looking around.

He pulled me toward the kitchen, and I felt adrenaline seeping through my every pore.

Where is that fucking alarm, Nicholas?

Briar got up with Andy and followed us. I hated seeing her holding him as if he were hers, as if *my* baby belonged to her. Michael dropped the bag of money on the counter and forced me into a chair. Briar looked back and forth between us. She was like a child waiting to be told what to do.

"What's your plan, Michael?" I asked, trying to hold him there for longer. If he left before I could hit that alarm, I'd probably never see my baby again. "Take the money and my child to get vengeance on Nicholas?"

"That's exactly what I'm going to do," he said, smiling and opening the fridge. He took out a beer and stared at me. "I love seeing you so scared... Walking through his house, drinking his beer, knowing I have his family at my mercy."

I trembled, asking myself how I'd been so stupid as to ignore who Michael O'Neil really was.

You're always able to find a way to forgive others for their errors.

Nicholas's words hit me harder than Michael had just a few minutes before. I had wanted to see the good in him, it was true. I wanted to find some reason why he had taken advantage of my vulnerability, and now I had to admit that not everyone in the world is good. There are people who are just plain evil; it's a fact.

Andy groaned yet again, and Michael glared at him.

"I was quite excited to meet little Mr. Leister here..." he confessed, walking over and reaching for him.

I jumped up. "Don't you touch him!" I shouted. Andrew started crying—that was what I'd hoped would happen.

Ignoring my warning, Michael stroked his head.

"He's hungry," I said, looking Michael straight in the eye. "Let me make him a bottle."

Michael smiled, walking close enough that I could smell the liquor on his breath. I wanted to puke.

"You can ask nicer," he said.

"Please," I begged, trying to control the disgust and hatred I felt toward him.

He grabbed me around the waist and planted a revolting kiss on my neck. Stiff as a board, I tried not to cry.

"Shut him up," he whispered in my ear, pushing me away.

I walked around the island to grab a bottle, formula, and milk. As I readied everything, I felt along the underside of the counter for the fucking alarm.

Meanwhile, Michael handed the baby off to Briar and finished his beer with that stupid smile on his face. I couldn't understand why he was still there. If I were him, I'd have left as soon as I had the money, but his amusement hinted that he was more interested in making me suffer than in lining his pockets. He felt like he was in Nicholas's shoes, and that was what he really enjoyed.

Finally, my fingers found something, and I inhaled quickly:

it was the panic button! I pushed it, hoping the police would get there soon.

I heated up the milk in warm water, and when the bottle was ready, I walked over to Briar.

"Let me feed him," I begged.

"No," she said, tearing the bottle from my hands.

"You know what, Noah?" Michael said, his voice taking on a darker tone. "I could have given you all this, too. We could have been happy if you hadn't gone for Leister... What is it? You like someone treating you like shit? Tell me... If that's what you want, I could do that to you, too."

"Leave me alone!" I shrieked. "You're a fucking idiot, and you're going to spend the rest of your life in jail! Same for you, Briar! Don't you see he's manipulating you? He did the exact same thing to me!"

"Shut up!" Briar said. "Michael helped me more than anyone ever has...and we're leaving here together... Isn't that right?" Her eyes glimmered with emotion as she looked at him.

I shook my head in disbelief. "What the hell have you done to her?" I asked him.

Michael tried to answer, but the sound of sirens howling in the distance stopped him. I would have been relieved if I'd managed to get Andy out of Briar's hands. But if the police came in and that psycho still had him, I didn't want to imagine what might happen.

Michael turned around, set his beer on the counter noisily, and grabbed my arm. "What the fuck have you done?" he said, shaking me.

My teeth were chattering, but I smiled. "Silent alarm. You've got about half a second to get out of here."

Briar looked at Michael and then at me, terrified. Andy started whining and wriggling, maybe because the sirens were already piercing his eardrums.

Michael let me go, grabbed the backpack from the table, and shouted, "Come on!" to Briar, opening the door to the backyard.

Briar was scared to death. I could see it in her eyes. Andy was crying, and all she wanted was for him to calm down, I thought. So I tried begging.

"Briar, please give him to me."

Michael didn't wait for her. He ran out without looking back.

I hoped, I wished with all my strength that the police would catch him, but I couldn't look away from the woman standing before me, the one who had my child in her arms. She started walking backward as I approached her, trying to guide her toward the front door.

She stopped, frightened.

"I'm sorry, Noah."

I thought I would die when she opened the door. Andrew's screams were tearing at my soul. My baby was suffering, and there was nothing I could do; he was being taken from me; my worst fears were coming true.

Two cop cars parked on the corner. Briar saw them and paused, her pupils dilated.

"I'm the one who should have him," she said, squeezing Andy tightly and staring at me, full of hate.

His screams got louder and louder. She took off running just as a police car screeched to a halt in front of the house.

"Drop the weapon!" an officer with a pistol ordered her.

I covered my mouth with my hand and prayed for them not to let her keep my baby.

Briar looked away, but another car was there. All possible avenues of escape were cut off.

"Drop it!" the cop shouted again. Briar's eyes filled with tears. A second later, her knife hit the pavement.

"Now, carefully set the baby down, take two steps back, and get on your knees!"

I held my breath and stared at Briar, who seemed to be in a state of utter shock. She lifted Andy, gave him a kiss on the head, and kneeled slowly, leaving him on the ground. The little thing cried and jerked like never before.

A sob escaped my throat as she backed up and did as the police said. I ran toward my little boy, picked him up, and held him tight. Never had I been so afraid. Never in my life had I wanted to kill someone. My legs trembled and I kneeled, scared I might fall over. Andy cried against my chest, and I did all I could to calm him down.

I didn't even know what was happening around me. All I cared about was knowing my child was safe with me.

"Miss, let us help you," an officer said, lifting me to my feet. I was trembling from head to toe and could hardly control my hysteria.

"Michael…he escaped through the back door…" I said. They asked for a description and sent a backup squad after him.

I went inside, and the officers on the scene asked me questions. They wanted a doctor to examine Andrew and me, but I refused, saying I just needed to calm down, and I went into Andy's room with him and locked the door.

The white onesie with a pattern of bees I'd put on him to sleep was dirty from the asphalt. I took it off and changed him, still crying. I sat with him on the sofa and cuddled him until he finally stopped crying. He had his eyes on me the whole time.

"It's over," I whispered, cradling him to my chest. "It's over, baby…"

Only when he was deep asleep did I go back down to the living room with him.

"Mrs. Leister, we need to ask you a few questions," an officer told me. "Your husband's on his way. We've already informed him of what happened."

Nicholas. I hadn't thought of him once. I hadn't had room in my mind for him: my baby, that was the only thing in the world just then.

"Miss, we've captured Michael O'Neil," one of the men on the scene told me. "He was on the run, but he wasn't hard to find. He was unarmed, thankfully."

I nodded, but I didn't feel any type of relief. I still couldn't believe what had happened. I was in a panic; I wanted to lock myself away with my baby and never see anyone else again.

"Apparently, Mr. O'Neil was treating Miss Palvin in a program for people with psychological disorders."

What?

"Briar...?" I asked, unable to believe what I was hearing.

"She was committed four and a half months ago. She had tried to commit suicide, and her parents took her there. I guess O'Neil broke her out without anyone knowing it."

I couldn't believe it... But then, taking advantage of his patients seemed to be his specialty. Michael must have been overjoyed when he'd found out he was treating someone connected to my past as well as Nick's. I could almost imagine them talking: Briar, so hurt after all that had happened with Nick, and Michael reveling in her pain and encouraging her to use it to hurt us.

I stopped crying and spent the next few hours making my statement. I did everything at home. I told them there was no way I'd go to the station.

I called Jenna after the police left. I didn't want to be alone. She and Lion hurried over, both of them terrified for me.

"I'm tired," I said after we had tea together in the kitchen. Andy was still sleeping in my arms, and I couldn't let him go. "I'm going to lie down a bit."

Jenna nodded and told me not to worry. They hadn't been able to talk to Nick once he caught his plane—I guessed it didn't have Wi-Fi.

I got in bed with Andy and tried to rest. My body was still suffused with terror. I didn't know how long I'd need to get over what had happened.

I opened my eyes a few hours later. My heart almost stopped when I saw Andy wasn't with me in bed. Terrified, I sat up, only to find Nick sitting across from me with Andrew sleeping against his chest, rubbing his nose softly into the top of the baby's head. He noticed I had woken up and glanced over.

I took a deep breath and cried again.

Nicholas sat up with the boy in his arms and walked over. Not only was I sad, not only was I scared, I felt so guilty, I could hardly speak. Everything had been my fault... Nicholas had warned me about Michael; I hadn't wanted to listen. Charlie had probably given Michael my address... My child could've been dead right now because of my negligence...

"Nick..." I sobbed uncontrollably. "I'm so sorry..."

He squeezed me as tightly as he could with our baby sleeping between the two of us. I buried my face in his neck and let myself go.

"Shhhh..." he said, clutching the back of my head. "There's nothing to be sorry for. Even I didn't think that bastard would take it that far."

When I'd gotten a hold of myself, I looked into his beautiful blue eyes, now bloodshot, which were looking at me in a way I'd never seen before.

"Andy's okay," I said, trying to console him, and me, too.

"I don't know what I would have done if something had happened to you both, Noah."

I hugged him and kissed his cheek. "At least you're back," I said, kissing him, holding him close for what could have been whole minutes.

"Did he do anything to you?" he asked, touching what I supposed was a small bruise where Michael had slapped me. He looked scared, almost holding his breath.

"I'm fine... He threatened me, but he didn't do anything," I responded, trying to stay calm and convince him it hadn't been so bad, even if I felt like I had been through hell.

He stroked my cheek and confessed, "I want to kill him," and I saw hatred invade his features.

"He'll be in jail for a long time... That's punishment enough."

Nick pulled me in, and we kissed, desperate and tense. As we separated, I heard Andrew make a soft noise while he turned his head. He was awake and looking at us. I smiled and rubbed his little mop of hair.

"I don't even know how to tell you how much I love you both," Nick said.

We got into bed, the three of us. Nick was holding me from behind; Andy was close by my belly.

No one was ever going to hurt our family again.

58

Nick

FINDING OUT ABOUT WHAT MICHAEL AND BRIAR HAD DONE while I was in another city, unable to do anything but catch a plane, had been torture. I couldn't relax until I was finally home a few hours later.

Jenna and Lion were awake, drinking coffee and talking softly, when I opened the door. Everything had settled down: there were no police officers, no blood…none of what I'd imagined as I was on my way over.

"Where's Noah?" I asked instead of saying hi. I couldn't beat around the bush; I needed to see with my own eyes that the two people I loved most in the world were all right.

I went upstairs and looked into the baby's room. When he wasn't there, I went to our room. My nerves were raw. But when I walked inside, I breathed a sigh of relief. Noah was asleep, and next to her, our precious baby was awake and moving his little arms and legs.

I was nervous as I walked over. Andy looked up, sucking on his pacifier, his eyes swollen from crying. I grabbed him and squeezed him carefully.

They'd tried to take him from us.

Andy moaned a little, and I took him over to the sofa in front of the bed.

"Hey there, champ," I said as he took one of my fingers in his tiny hand. "You were a brave little boy, Son." I kissed his cheeks and sniffed that wonderful baby smell coming off him.

Andy smiled as if he'd understood me. As I held him, I couldn't keep the tears from streaming down my cheeks.

How could they have done this to us?

Briar... Michael... That bastard was going to rot in jail. I'd make sure of that.

It must have been horrible for Noah. That never should have happened. Steve should have been there. I should have been there.

I thanked heaven I'd put the alarm in and Noah had known how to use it. Otherwise...

The next day, when things were calmer, Noah told me everything that had happened in detail. My heart pounded as she went through each moment.

It hurt, too, to learn that Briar had lost the baby when she was six months pregnant. I never found out. If I had... It must have been so hard for her to go through that alone. Her son had been mine, too, and I regretted not being able to be there for her when she miscarried.

I felt like I should visit her. Michael could go to hell, but Briar... She was sick. Two weeks after the break-in, I went to the hospital where she was locked up. She was being treated for bipolar disorder. I'd always known she'd been struggling, but I didn't really understand.

Her life had been like mine. She'd grown up alone, surrounded by caretakers who didn't love her. Her parents had ignored her until she showed up pregnant, and even then, they'd given her none of what she needed. I wanted her to get over everything that had happened, I really did. But I'd never forgive her for trying to steal my child.

At the hospital, I learned she was doing better. She was taking her meds and seemed calmer. I found her sitting on her bed reading a book. Noah had told me she'd looked ragged and unwell. The Briar I saw before me now was anything but.

She was wearing jeans and a blue cotton T-shirt. Her short hair was pulled back, and her beautiful eyes had an expectant expression when she saw me come in.

She was waiting for me. They'd told her I was coming.

"Hey, Nicholas," she said, closing the book and putting it on her nightstand.

I asked her if I could sit down. "I don't want to take up too much of your time," I said, not knowing how to express my mixed feelings just then. "I just wanted to say I'm sorry about what happened with our child. I never knew; if I had, I would have supported you no matter what."

She looked relaxed as she listened.

"Fate didn't want that baby to be part of our lives," she said. Her eyes misted over. "He was beautiful, though..."

I grabbed her hand. Her words hurt.

"I'm so sorry," I said, and it was true. I adored my son and was counting the seconds to be back home with him and Noah. But that didn't mean my heart didn't crack when I learned my other son never had the chance to live.

"I'm sorry for what I did, too," she said. "I don't know what happened... I... Michael... I thought he loved me, you know? He said things...about Noah...about you... I thought..."

"Just focus on getting better, Briar," I said as I stood up.

Her eyes widened. "Do you think one day I could be like you

two? That I could find someone who would love me the way you love Noah...?"

I chose my words very carefully. "I think there's someone for all of us. I never thought I'd love someone as much as I love Noah. You know better than anyone how damaged I was inside. So yeah, I think you've got a bright future ahead of you, Briar. One day you'll get up, and someone will turn your world upside down.... You've just got to wait for it."

I turned around but stopped in the doorway, keeping my back to her.

"I gave him your name," she said. "I just needed to tell you that."

I took a deep breath and walked out.

59

Noah

TWO YEARS LATER...

I'd just graduated. Happiness was flowing through my veins, and I was all smiles. It wasn't easy—why lie? Going back to school after having Andrew had been no picnic. I hated being away from him, but slowly all three of us learned to adapt. After Briar tried to kidnap him, I was obsessive, but with time, that died down, and Nick helped me feel safe again until I could finally let other people care for him while I worked on my degree.

Nicholas was everything he'd promised he would be and more. He swore he would prioritize my dreams and ambitions and make sure I didn't have to give up anything, and he did. Nick...my beautiful boyfriend. The beautiful boyfriend who became my husband.

We put off the wedding several times until we finally felt we could plan it without stressing out. By then, Andrew was a little man, two years old! He drove us all crazy, but he was old enough to stay with his grandparents for two weeks while we were away enjoying our honeymoon.

So there I was, accepting my diploma from the department head and glancing around trying to find my two favorite boys.

I did a turn on the stage, and right then, Nick stood up. He had Andy on his shoulders, who was clapping for me, his hair messy just like his father's, his eyes showing joy over something he couldn't even understand. Mom and Will were there, too. They clapped, and Anabel and Maddie grinned.

Anabel had beaten her cancer, and she'd repaired her relationship with Nick. Maddie was still living with Will, but she spent the weekends with her mother. They came over a lot. Nick's mother and Maddie were both crazy about Andy. Maddie was a little beauty now, with her blond hair and angel face. Even at ten, she'd become a head-turner.

After graduation, we had a little celebration at home. The whole family and all our friends were there. At one point, Nicholas caught me by myself when I'd gone to the kitchen, and he grabbed my hand to drag me off to the bedroom.

My back struck the door softly as his lips touched mine passionately.

"Tomorrow you'll finally be mine. There's no escaping, Freckles," he said. As his mouth explored my neck, he seemed almost to be worshipping me.

"I've still got time to jilt you at the altar," I warned him, laughing. He bit my shoulder playfully, but hard enough to produce pain and pleasure at the same time.

"Explain to me again this dumb idea about not sleeping together until we're married."

Jenna had come up with that. She'd challenged us to avoid sex for two weeks so our honeymoon would be more passionate and romantic.

"I don't know what you're talking about," I responded, pulling him close and yielding to him. Our tongues wrapped around each other, and I moaned as he touched me down below, torturing me pitilessly.

"Does this count as breaking the rules?" he asked. I threw my head back, sighing and closing my eyes to better soak in his caresses.

"You've always loved being a rule breaker, so I don't know why you'd worry about it now..." I said, pressing down into his hand, seeking the pleasure my body desired.

Nick kissed my breasts, and his fingers went on playing with my body. "Come on, babe... Give me what I want," he whispered in my ear.

But just then, someone knocked.

Nicholas stopped.

I opened my eyes, panting, trembling.

"What the hell are you two up to?" Jenna said on the other side of the door.

Shit.

"Jenna, go away," Nick ordered her, giving me a peck on the cheek.

"If you don't come out right now...!"

I cursed. I hated her with all my might just then.

"Should we go back to the party?" Nick asked. He clearly found all this very funny.

"You're an idiot. I'll get you back for this, though."

He pinned me against the door again and stared into my eyes.

"What makes you think I'm not suffering as much as you right now, or more?"

I looked down between his legs. That was enough to show me he was telling the truth. "No sex before marriage..."

"Our parents would be proud."

I laughed, and we opened the door to see our pain-in-the-ass friend.

"Mommy!" Andy said, reaching out his little arms for me to pick him up. Jenna was holding him on her hip. She was six months along now, and her belly was visible under her yellow dress.

I grabbed my little treasure, and we went down to the backyard. Lion was overseeing the grill with William next to him. Both had on aprons that said *Kiss the cook*. Presents from Jenna, obvs.

Andy started squirming, and I set him down. He took off running toward the swings, where Maddie was ready to embrace him. She loved playing with her little nephew.

Nicholas went over, too. He loved those two kids more than anything in the world… I looked around. My whole family was there. All smiling faces.

The next day was going to be brilliant.

60

Nick

I STARED AT THAT BEAUTIFUL WOMAN IN FRONT OF ME. SHE TOOK my breath, my words away... Seeing her enter the church had almost literally floored me.

Our family and friends were there. Any and everyone we cared about had come to see us united in matrimony.

Noah was excited, and her eyes gleamed as she tried to hold back tears.

"I do," I said, being sure my pronunciation was clear and loud.

"Noah, do you take this man to be your lawfully wedded husband, to have and to hold, in sickness and in health, until death do you part?"

She smiled and looked me in the eyes.

"I do."

"Then in the name of God and by the power vested in me by this church, I now pronounce you husband and wife. You may kiss the bride."

Nobody had to tell me that twice. I cradled her face in my hands, and we kissed until we could hardly breathe. Our families applauded, and finally I forced myself away from her.

"You're all mine now, Mrs. Leister," I said, happier than I'd ever been.

Noah smiled, and I kissed away a tear that fell from her eye.

We had decided to get married in front of the sea. It was a warm day, a perfect day, and Noah was a knockout. She looked so good in her dress, I wasn't sure I wanted to take it off. The white lace hugged her body and gave way to a cloud of tulle below her waist. Her shoulders were bare apart from two satin straps that crossed in the back, revealing her stunning figure. Her freckles were brighter than ever...and she had a spectacular tan, which she'd been working on in the days before the ceremony. Long story short: she was driving me wild.

"Ready to go?" I asked her, hours later, while we were out on the dance floor. I'd asked them to put on "Young at Heart," and Noah had cried, remembering that wonderful night years ago when I'd shown her what a good dancer I was. That was the last night we'd spent together before splitting up, and I'd wanted to remind her of it to say that interruption never should have happened. Now, four years later, we were redeeming that moment and, at the same time, swearing we'd love each other forever.

Noah looked around for her mother, who had our boy in her arms. He'd hung on longer than anyone could have hoped, running, playing, and dancing before finally crashing and falling asleep.

"He's fine, Noah," I told her, kissing her on the forehead.

"He's never spent so long away from us..."

"He'll have a blast playing with Maddie and eating your mom's cookies."

Noah grinned.

"I love you so much," she said, touching the nape of my neck.

I kissed her again. I needed to be alone with her. Now.

We said goodbye to the guests and our family and Andrew.

With him, we got a little weepy. Noah grabbed him and he woke up. In his teeny tuxedo, he was just to die for.

"My prince," Noah said, kissing his cheeks. "You behave, okay?"

I took him from her to stop her from going into hysterics. If he started crying and she did, too, who knew where it would all end?

I tossed him in the air, making him laugh, then hugged him and rested his head on my shoulder.

"Nick, don't you think...?"

There was a warning in my expression. It was time for me and my wife to be by ourselves. We weren't taking the baby. That issue had been decided.

My mother came over and held her arms out for him. "You guys go... This little thing is in good hands."

She kissed me on the cheek and walked off with him.

Any tears soon disappeared amid the noise, the crowd, the music. But Noah stayed there looking at the place where my mother had stood with Andrew.

"Come on," I said, lifting her in my arms. "It's time to go, Freckles."

She tried to smile. "Yeah, I guess we should get a move on."

Everyone crowded around the door, waiting to see us off. We ran toward the white limousine that would take us to the hotel where we'd reserved the honeymoon suite. We were staying near the airport, and the next day, we'd be flying to Mykonos in Greece. I'd rented a beach house just for the two of us. We'd be there for one week and would spend the next week at a five-star hotel in Croatia.

I didn't want Noah to have to think about anything. She'd spent two whole years completely devoted to her studies and our child. She needed this vacation as much as anyone, and I was going to make sure she lived it up.

When we got to the hotel, they had all the usual stuff for newlyweds. Our room was huge and had a spread of champagne, desserts, and fresh strawberries.

Noah's jaw dropped when she walked in. "Did you do all this?"

"Amazing what a phone call will do, right?"

I ran my fingers through her hair and pulled her close, asking, "Are you ready to make love until it's time to go to the airport?"

Her eyes burned with desire. "Didn't you say our flight doesn't leave till noon?"

I smiled lustily. "I sure did."

We spent the night making tireless love. I had finally made her mine, with everything that implies. We stripped bare and kissed and touched each other as if in a fever. We threw her dress aside and immediately forgot it. We did it carefully, passionately, tenderly, and hard. We gave ourselves to pleasure the way you only can with a person you're insanely in love with.

Because if loving like crazy was a crime...then we pleaded guilty.

EPILOGUE

Noah

EIGHT YEARS LATER

I closed the door to the garage and smiled.

"Daddy's not going to believe it, Julie," I told my two-year-old daughter as we walked around the yard to enter our amazing home.

It hadn't been long since we'd moved: that day marked two years exactly. When we found out we were going to be parents again, we realized our house in the city was too small, and we decided it was time for a bigger one near the beach so the kids could enjoy the sea and all it offered.

Nick had been the one to really push for it. He'd given me the little house near downtown to allow me to keep studying after I had Andrew. Then, for one reason or another, we found ourselves not wanting to leave until it was inevitable. Nick was overjoyed to be by the beach again, and I was happy for him. Andrew was now an ace surfer: at ten, he was already competing and had earned countless trophies. So we didn't have to sell him on the move either.

Andrew was a carbon copy of Nick. There was no denying they were father and son, but I'd known it would be that way as soon as he was born. Since I couldn't spot a single trait of mine in him, I was happy to have a little girl who was just like me: a blond daughter with a freckly face so cute, you wanted to kiss her all over. The only thing she'd inherited from Nick were her eyes, the same sky blue as those of Andrew.

Julie hadn't come as a surprise: actually, we'd been trying for another baby for six years. I had been right to think my first pregnancy was a miracle. Looking back, I think God gave us Andy because it was the only way to be sure we'd get back together.

We were overjoyed when we found out she was a girl. Nicholas was mad about her. She was just like her mother, though: she couldn't care less about swimming in the ocean, let alone getting on a board and riding waves. She was happy in my arms, and I loved giving her all my time.

One day Andy came in soaking wet, with sand all over his feet.

"Can we eat the cake yet?" he asked, sitting at the table and pinching his sister's cheeks. Julie screamed like a banshee, and Andrew laughed with that same mischievous expression his father had dozens of times a day, especially when we were alone.

"When Daddy gets here," I said.

Nick was turning thirty-five that day. I still couldn't believe how quickly time had passed. It seemed like just yesterday that we were walking together on the beach in Mykonos completely absorbed in each other, kissing all night and falling asleep and kissing all morning as soon as we awoke. I had turned thirty in June. It was hard for me to believe that, too.

Nick had asked me not to go all out for his birthday. He wanted a relaxing night with the family, and I respected that wish…more or less.

I smiled as I put the last bit of icing on the cake I had baked for him. The kids had gone to the living room to watch cartoons, but from Julie's shouting, I assumed they were fighting about something.

I jumped when a pair of hands gripped me around the waist and a muscular body pressed into my back.

"Did you cook me something, Freckles?" Nick whispered, biting my earlobe sensually.

"Don't get used to it," I said, setting the spatula down on the table to greet him as he deserved. "Happy birthday." I wrapped my arms around his shoulders and pulled him in for a kiss on the lips.

Nick smiled. "No surprise party?" he asked, rubbing my lower back tenderly but hungrily.

I shook my head. "Just us," I replied. He smiled with satisfaction and gave me a squeeze.

A small person came in to interrupt us, distracting us from our flirting.

"Daddy!" Julia said, reaching up for him to pick her up. Nick reluctantly pulled away from me and obeyed his other favorite girl.

Unlike Andy, who'd always loved for Nicholas to throw him in the air and spin him around, Julia hated it. She was fussy in that way. Nick kissed her blond hair and rested her on his hip, opening the fridge and taking out a bottle of wine. In the background I could hear video games on the TV.

"How is the most beautiful little girl in the world?" Nick asked as he gave her a tickle. She laughed, showing her only two teeth and kicking her legs back and forth so Nick would put her down. She took off to find her brother.

Nick came back for another kiss.

"This is going to be a long night..." he said sensually.

I felt a tingle of anticipation in my stomach and hurried to finish the cake.

We had a pleasant night together as a family, with dinner and the obligatory "Happy Birthday" song. Julie applauded like crazy; it was one of the only songs she could make it through without messing up. Andrew, in the meantime, tore through the cake he'd been staring at for the whole meal.

When we put the kids to bed, I grabbed Nick's hand and took him back downstairs.

"I've got a surprise for you," I said, nervous, unable to stop myself from smiling like an idiot.

He looked at me with suspicion. "What have you done, Freckles? You don't have clowns ready to pop out from behind the sofa or anything like that, do you?"

I rolled my eyes. I'd only done that *once*!

"Come on…you'll love it," I said, opening the front door and walking to the garage. Nick had his hands in his pockets, watching me, curious and amused.

"Ready?" I asked, biting my lip.

"Am I?!" he answered.

I ignored him and hit the button on the garage door opener. When the door was all the way retracted, Nicholas gawked at what he saw.

"Happy birthday!" I shouted.

"Fuck…" was all he could say at first. "Are you crazy?" he asked, stepping forward.

"I always told you I owed you a Ferrari. And I don't forget my promises."

He couldn't believe it. When he laughed, my chest swelled with pride. He turned around, picked me up, and spun me in circles.

"I can't believe it," he said, then looked at me with a furrowed brow.

When he set me down, I knew the storm was coming.

"You didn't…" he started to say as I stepped back. "Tell me you didn't spend the money I put in your account on a present for me."

I shrugged. "I told you I didn't want it."

"You're my wife!"

"And you're my husband!" I said, grinning.

"I don't know whether to kill you or kiss you all over… Tell me, smarty-pants, what do you think I should do?"

I smiled. "I think we should go racing."

Acknowledgements

I've been writing this trilogy for five years. When I started with *My Fault*, it was one of those stories where I had to drop everything and get to work, no matter what else was going on. Noah and Nick came to me at the perfect moment, and now, after all this time, I can finally finish their tale.

It's scary to leave behind characters you know more than you know yourself. They become so real that saying goodbye to them hurts just as badly as saying goodbye to someone you know.

I still can't believe their story has been published and that people from all over the world have connected with something that came straight out of my head.

Thanks to everyone who has done their part to get this book on the shelves today. To my editors Aina and Rosa, without you, this book wouldn't be what it is today. Thank you for making me give it my all and for teaching me what it means to work professionally in the publishing world.

Thank you to Wattpad for giving me the ideal forum to showcase my work and for helping me connect directly with my readers. To everyone who writes there and dreams like me, keep at it. You never know who might be reading you.

Thanks to my agent, Nuria, for reassuring me when there are things I don't understand and for supporting me from the beginning.

A giant thank-you to my parents for teaching me that you have to fight for what you want even when everything seems to be against you. From them, I learned it doesn't matter how many times you fall: you have to get up and keep going.

Bar, I'll never tire of thanking you for the enthusiasm you put into this book and for reading it even more times than I have. You are my first reader, and I hope you will be there with me for all my projects in the future. Your advice is golden!

Eva, thank you for becoming one of my best friends almost without realizing it. Thanks for putting up with all my insecurities, calming me down better than anyone else, and making me laugh like I never have. I hope to see you live your dreams the same way you've seen me live mine. You'll achieve anything you set your mind to.

And finally, to all the people who have been waiting months for this ending, I hope with all my heart that I've lived up to your expectations and given Nick and Noah the grand finale they deserve. There's nothing like writing for yourself, but when you know that so many people are anxiously expecting something you're creating, it's truly marvelous.

I hope you'll all be with me for a long time, and I look forward to sharing with you all the stories still to come.

This book is for all of you—this book is all *your fault*!

About the Author

Mercedes Ron always dreamed of writing. She began by publishing her first stories on Wattpad, where more than 50 million readers were hooked on her books, and made the leap to bookstores in 2017 with Montena's imprint, launching the Culpables saga, a publishing phenomenon that has been translated into more than ten languages and has its own movie adaptation by Prime Video. Her success was followed by the sagas Enfrentados (*Ivory* and *Ebony*) and Dímelo (*Tell Me Softly*, *Tell Me Secretly*, *Tell Me with Kisses*), which consolidated the author as a benchmark in youth romantic literature with more than a million copies sold.